ABSOLVED!

A sound of chanting rose into the evening air of the seemingly deserted village. Then Athaya saw a stream of oil lamps, carried by the villagers as they approached the church. A white-clad, glassy-eyed woman knelt at the altar steps.

Before her, the priest lifted his hands. "Almighty God, this child comes before you to renounce the gift of foul magic given at her birth by Satan. Who brings this woman for the sacrifice of absolution?"

"I, her husband, do," a man said, his voice breaking with tears.

The priest raised a silver chalice to the woman's lips, but she jerked back and let out a high-pitched wail of terror. Two men stepped forward and held the woman down, while the priest lifted the chalice to her lips and forced her to swallow the poisoned wine.

After a few minutes of agony, the poison did its work; she gasped once, and her body went limp.

"Behold, O Lord," the priest called out, "we have saved this woman's soul from hell and delivered it unto you."

The congregation broke into song in joyful celebration.

CALL
OF
MADNESS

Julie Dean Smith

A Del Rey Book
BALLANTINE BOOKS • NEW YORK

To Chris

Non Tam Pares Quam Superiores

"For the Devil shall call them with madness,
and thus are his children made known unto him,
and bidden to do his evil works upon the earth."

—Adriel of Delfarham
Essays on the Nature of Magic

CHAPTER 1

✳

"**Y**OU'RE CHEATING AGAIN, DAMN YOU," THE drunken man said to the black-haired young woman sitting across from him at the gaming table. He glared at her with bloodshot brown eyes and pounded his fist on the pockmarked wood. "Ain't nobody has that kind of luck against ol' Rafe."

Athaya shrugged her shoulders, and the silver studs embedded in her leather doublet winked in the torchlight. "It isn't luck. I'm just better at this than you are."

"HA!" he belted out, punctuating his comment with a gurgled belch. "The day a damned woman half my age beats me at cards is the day I'll hang myself." He peeked at the downturned card in front of him and flipped it over with a triumphant flourish.

"There. A ten and a queen. Beat that if you can."

His opponent took a look at her own card and tried to hold back a smile. "Get a noose ready," she said, laying the ace next to the king already faceup on the table. She leaned back in the rickety wooden chair, and her expression was undeniably smug. "That's another two crowns you owe me. I believe that makes it an even ten."

The man's eyes bulged. He got to his feet, wavering slightly, and reached over to snatch the woman's wrist with a thick-

1

fingered hand as she scooped up the pile of silver coins in the center of the table.

"Not so fast!" he said. "I don't pay up to anybody who wins by hexing the cards! You hear that?" he shouted to the other patrons in the dingy little tavern. "She's cheating me!" One or two grizzled heads looked up in mild annoyance from their games at the other tables crowding the cramped, smoke-filled room, but none of them seemed overly interested in the drunken man's accusations against his young opponent.

"Get your filthy hands off me," Athaya said through clenched teeth, glaring intensely at the grimy fingers curled around her wrist, "or this will be the last game of cards you ever play."

For a moment, she thought the threat might work. Rafe stared at her incredulously, blinking several times as if attempting to make his eyes focus clearly. But then a gap-ridden smile slowly formed about his stubbly, unshaved chin. His laughter began as a series of wheezy giggles, soon expanding into loud, hearty guffaws. Gleefully, he slapped his thigh with his free hand.

"Feisty little devil, ain't you?" he said, twisting the skin of her arm until she winced from the burn. "I like that in a woman."

He yanked her roughly out of her chair, sending it toppling sideways onto the soiled rushes scattered across the floor. Moving quicker than Athaya thought a man of his bulk could, he reached for the dagger on her belt and snatched it away before she could grab it. He pulled her close to him, the blade poised near her slender white throat, and she felt her muscles tense beneath his grip. With one quick motion, he scanned her body from head to toe, openly admiring the firm curves hidden inside the snug-fitting wool breeches and steel-studded doublet.

"I don't like it when people cheat me," he said, drawing his face closer to hers. The smell of stale beer on his breath made Athaya grimace. "But you're much too pretty to punish. What's say we make a bargain? I'll forget about the game if you apologize to me real nice."

He cocked his head in the direction of the narrow flight of stairs which huddled against the back wall of the tavern and slunk upward through the shadows toward the upper floor. "Understand?"

Athaya's eyes flickered nervously toward the back of the inn. There could be little doubt as to his intentions. The only thing upstairs was a row of tiny rooms sparsely furnished with bug-infested cots and thin, moth-eaten curtains for doors—the working place of the tavern's whores.

She held her jaw firm, trying to appear far less worried than she was. When she had decided to go out into the city tonight, she hadn't exactly pictured the evening ending like this. Just a few drinks, that's all she'd wanted. A few drinks, and the chance to spend some time away from home.

"Uh, look—if you're mad about the money, then just keep it, all right?" she offered, earnestly hoping that the little pile of silver would be enough to satisfy him. "Keep all of it."

"I'm goin' to," he said, leering. "But you're still gonna make it up to me." He tightened his grip on her arm, forcing her to bite her lip to keep from wincing. "So what do you say, love? It's a sight better than me slicing your throat, which is what usually happens to people who cheat me."

"But I swear to you I wasn't—"

"Shut up and come on," he growled impatiently as he yanked her away. He pushed her toward the staircase, following directly behind her as she mounted the well-worn steps. Athaya felt the tip of her own blade digging into her back.

With increasing desperation, she glanced back at the other patrons in the tavern, calmly guzzling their ale and continuing with their games. Somehow she had expected that a few enthusiastic volunteers would have come to her rescue by now, but even the serving girl, weaving between the tables and refilling goblets from a wooden pitcher, did not seem unduly alarmed by Athaya's situation. Athaya doubted if more than a handful of the dozens of people crowded into the tavern were even aware of what was going on, and not one of that handful looked the least inclined to do anything about it.

"Hurry along, now," Rafe said, giving her a rough shove. She stumbled against the wooden railing and bit back a curse as she recovered her balance and continued.

When they reached the top of the stairs, Rafe gestured toward one of the small rooms just across the hallway. The tattered door curtains were pulled back, showing the room to be unoccupied. Athaya was sickened by the sight of the soiled cot lying near a puddle on the bare wood floor, certain that there were far more lice than straw inside the thin mattress. The floor was spotted with dried mud, tracked in by the last visitors to this room, and a squat, yellow candle sat in a tin cup on the floor, shedding a sickly glow on the scarred, soot-smeared walls.

"Inside," came Rafe's voice in her ear. Athaya could not tell whether his slurred words came from the beer he'd consumed or from eagerly contemplating the events to come.

Athaya turned around slowly, favoring him with a sultry, seductive look. She couldn't fight past him, but maybe there was another way out of this. Dropping her chin, she tossed her head and allowed her elbow-length hair to fall gracefully around her shoulders. Rafe held the dagger loosely now, lowering the blade slightly as if no longer convinced he'd need to use it. She took a step forward, glancing only momentarily behind him toward the common room below, and rested her hand on his shoulder. Running her tongue slowly over her lips, Athaya pressed her chest brazenly against his, immediately conscious of the firm bulge which strained against his breeches.

I think I'm going to be ill, she thought sullenly, still careful to sustain the look of pleasure on her face. *How do I get myself into these things, anyway?*

"Kiss me," she said, in a low, hushed voice. Tensing her muscles, she steeled herself as he bent over her, trying not to turn away from the stench of rancid ale on his breath. He reached out slowly and dug a greedy, jagged-nailed hand into her hair.

With an ear-piercing cry, Rafe suddenly doubled over, clutching his groin in furious agony. Athaya grabbed him by the shoulders and shoved him backward, sending him tumbling noisily down the staircase toward the common room.The dagger flew from his hand and clattered to the ground at her feet. Seconds later, Rafe was curled into a pitiful little ball at the foot of the staircase, moaning and rocking from side to side with his face twisted in pain.

The success of the blow took her off guard—she hadn't expected it to work quite that well. Rafe was easily twice her weight, and she hadn't hit him very hard. Still, she was infinitely grateful that her brother Nicolas had taught her such an effective technique for fending off unwanted advances, even though she had never expected to use that particular bit of knowledge. She would have to remember to tell him how well his lessons paid off.

Quickly collecting her wits, Athaya snatched up the dagger and bounded down the steps two at a time. She straddled Rafe and crouched down to pin him to the floor with the weight of her body. The silver blade of her dagger flashed in the dim torchlight as it found a resting place on the sticky flesh of his neck.

"I'd rather sleep with a mind-plagued wizard." Her voice was low and fluid and gently threatening. She stood up cautiously, keeping the dagger close to his throat, and watched as he tried, without success, to hide the pain inflicted by her well-placed knee.

If you weren't so drunk, you'd feel twice as bad, Athaya thought, looking down at him in disgust. His face had a sickly green cast to it, and he looked as if he were just about to retch. He rose gingerly to his feet, his hands clutched between his legs. Still pale and shaken, he slowly staggered across the room. Roughly shoving aside a startled young man who had been watching the proceedings from the doorway, Rafe stumbled out into the street, muttering curses under his breath.

Athaya walked back to the gaming table they had so recently deserted and counted out the silver coins. Replacing the dagger in its sheath, she rummaged impatiently through the tattered deerskin pouch tied to her belt and drew out a long, slender looca-pipe made of polished cherrywood. She lit the bluish tobacco from the candle on the table and stuffed the tip of the pipe between her lips, drawing a deep breath of the soothing, sweet-smelling smoke.

Realizing that her cup was almost empty, Athaya signaled for the tavern owner's young daughter and ordered another bottle of wine. The round-faced serving girl, her apron streaked with grime and soot, bobbed a clumsy curtsy and scurried away through the rotted oak door that led to the tavern's kitchens. She returned in an instant with a flagon of rich red wine. In exchange for the flagon, Athaya fished a coin out of her pocket and handed it to her.

"Keep the rest," Athaya said softly.

"Oh! Thanks kindly, ma'am!" the girl squealed, her eyes wide. She caressed the coin as if it were made of silk, curtsied again, this time more gracefully, and hurried away to show the prize to her father.

Athaya filled her goblet and sank back in her chair, lazily shuffling the cards with half-closed eyes and flipping them onto the table in a halfhearted game of solitaire. She sighed despondently, glancing around the smoky room at the drunken sots hunched over their tables, and contemplated whether or not to go home.

Ugh, that's worse than this place, she thought with a shudder and resumed her game of solitaire.

She took another puff from her looca-pipe, filling her lungs with the calming smoke and trying to erase all memories of Rafe from her mind. Although her experience was not that wide, Rafe's attack only increased her suspicions that the majority of men did most of their thinking with an organ located a good distance from the brain. She had met precious few men in her life who were sincerely good, without being obsessed by their prowess either on the battlefield or in their beds. Offhand, Athaya could think of only two truly good men—her brother Nicolas, and Tyler.

Tyler. Athaya smiled at the very thought of him. With a twinge of shame, she realized she ought to have told him she was going out tonight. But what difference would that have made? He would have told her not to go, she would have gone anyway, and in that event, she would now be feeling even more guilty than she already did. And besides, after this game she would head for home, and he would see for himself that there was nothing to worry about.

Athaya held back a yawn. It was late, the smoke from the pipe stung her eyes and numbed her thoughts, and she had drunk enough wine to make her sleepy.

Then a shadow fell across the cards, and in the corner of her eye, she saw a flash of white linen as someone settled into the chair that her earlier opponent had vacated. Athaya looked up, recognizing the young man whom Rafe had shoved aside during his humiliating exit.

"Every time Rafe loses a game, he thinks somebody's hexing the cards," he said lightly. His voice was tinged with a faint, unfamiliar accent.

The man looked a few years older than she—twenty-five, perhaps—and was by far the best-dressed man in the tavern. His deep blue doublet and crisp white shirt stood out from the sea of brown and black wool covering the backs of the other tavern patrons, most of them local farmers, miners, and tradesmen. A soft-crowned felt cap was cocked to one side on a head of straw-like blond hair, giving him a carefree, innocent air like that of a traveling minstrel, and his hands were smooth and soft, as if more accustomed to a harp than a plough. But despite his friendly brown eyes and engaging smile, Athaya offered no greeting. If this man claimed friendship with someone like Rafe, then she wanted nothing to do with him.

"Were you?" he asked, leaning forward on his elbows.

Athaya frowned. "Was I what?"

"Hexing the cards."

Her eyes flashed, and she flung her cards down angrily. *"Please!* I've been insulted enough for one night."

She took a deep drink of her wine and puffed on her pipe a few times. Somewhat mollified by the numbing effect of both, she added, "Besides, there's only one plague-ridden wizard in Caithe that I know of, and he's up at Delfar Castle."

The young man balked for a moment, then looked at her with surprised confusion. "Sorry, I didn't mean any offense." Then, assuming it would explain everything, he added, "I'm not from around here."

"Congratulations," Athaya said dryly. She'd intended the remark to be sarcastic, but the moment the word was uttered, she was surprised at how much truth it contained. Given the choice, she would have left Delfarham long ago. There were better places on the Continent than the congested and squalid capital city of Caithe. *There had to be,* she added inwardly.

Her new companion scooped up the cards from the table and began shuffling them, gazing at them intently as he turned them over in his fingers. "Well, they're not marked," he said, setting them back down again. "I guess Rafe was just the victim of a run of good luck." He chuckled to himself. "But don't bother trying to convince him that you were playing an honest game. He's an awfully sore loser."

Athaya furrowed her brows. "If you're not from around here, how come you know all about this fellow Rafe?"

She gave him an icy stare, tapping her fingernails on the tabletop and watching his composure begin to melt under her gaze. The young man squirmed in his seat. His eyes flickered toward the staircase, and Athaya knew, with queer satisfaction, that he was thinking of what she'd done to the last man who'd crossed her.

"I've only been in Caithe for a few days," he explained quickly. "I'm a messenger—from Reyka," he added, with a touch of pride. "I came in here for a drink this afternoon after

I delivered my letters and won a few crowns dicing with Rafe. That's how I know he's a sore loser. Swore I was cheating, and when he heard I was from Reyka, he accused me of putting spells on the dice and called me a mind-plagued wizard.''

Athaya laughed softly, regarding her naive companion with a smile. "I hope you realize how much of an insult that is around here," she commented.

He stared at her blankly, and Athaya laughed again. Obviously the young messenger had never been to Caithe before. "Well, never mind that now," she said, picking up the bottle of wine and swirling the contents around. "Care for some?"

He leaned over and plucked an empty goblet from the next table. "Thanks. And by the way, the name's Jaren. Jaren McLaud."

"Cheers, Jaren," she said, and they clicked the rims of the pewter goblets together and drank.

They sat together for close to an hour, and Jaren watched Athaya begin another game of solitaire, being unwilling, as he said, to challenge such an obviously superior cardplayer and surely lose whatever money he had. Instead, he chatted away on a variety of topics, balancing her relatively pensive and sullen mood. He told her about his journey from Reyka, how terrible the roads were and how repulsive the inns, and filled her in on the latest court gossip from the Reykan capital of Ath Luaine.

"Osfonin was fairly upset, of course," he said, speaking of the Reykan king. "He never expected his son to return home so dead set against marrying the Caithan princess. Apparently she wasn't quite what he'd been led to believe. Surprising, since Prince Felgin isn't known for being all that particular about his women." Jaren laughed to himself as if aware of some private joke and drained the last of his wine.

"I mean no insult to your noble king or his fair daughter," he added hastily. "I only repeat what I've heard in my travels. But it is well known that Kelwyn has been seeking a husband for his youngest child for quite some time and is . . . er, having difficulties selecting the right one."

"That's a diplomatic way of putting it," Athaya observed, suppressing a smile. Everyone in Caithe knew about Kelwyn's plight. His futile efforts to find a match for his only daughter had been a source of jokes throughout the kingdom for nearly five years.

"Unfortunately, there are those less kind," Jaren replied with a sigh. "Some of the other people I've spoken to here in Caithe say that whoever the lucky bridegroom turns out to be, he'll want twice the dowry just to take the princess off Kelwyn's hands."

"And has your Prince Felgin found himself another bride?" Athaya asked distractedly. Conversations that consisted mainly of court gossip tended to bore her rapidly.

"No. But now there is talk of a southern alliance with Cruachi, so Osfonin may send his son to that godforsaken desert to meet the emir's daughters. Lord, I think he's got over twelve."

Jaren rattled on for another few minutes about the Cruachis, making lighthearted fun of their ornate manner of dress and complimenting their widely known talent for breeding swift, strong horses. But soon his lively chattering trailed off. As he sat across from her, now strangely silent, Athaya sensed that he was engaged in some sort of internal monologue, as if trying to decide on a subject of conversation that was likely to interest her more than the dealings of the Reykans or the Cruachis. Twice he looked as if he were about to say something and twice he thought better of it and merely smiled at her like a tongue-tied suitor. Athaya found such unexpected speechlessness odd in one who had approached her so boldly, but she thought nothing more of it. In fact, she found it somewhat refreshing.

"I take it from what you said earlier that you don't like it around here very much," Jaren said finally. His tone was casual, but Athaya detected a hint of purpose behind his words. "When I said I was only a visitor here, you seemed to think I was fortunate."

"Oh, I don't know," she replied with a shrug. "Delfarham's probably the same as everyplace else."

"If you're bored here, why don't you leave? Travel somewhere. See the world."

Athaya shook her head resolutely. "Impossible."

"What—no money? You'd be surprised how far you can go on just a few crowns. And if you're really that good at the gaming tables, you could hustle your way to the far side of the Continent and back with your winnings."

"It's not the money," she said, laughing softly at Jaren's unrepressed exuberance. "And it's not that I wouldn't like to get away from home for a while. But my family would never allow it.''

''Why not? For heaven's sake, you're what—nineteen? Twenty? High time for you to see a bit of the world. Reyka, for instance,'' he added. It was barely noticeable, but Athaya thought she detected an increasing lack of nonchalance in his voice. ''Not many Caithans come to Reyka anymore. Oh, I've met one or two, but no more. And that surprises me. It's beautiful country. To the west are glorious sand dunes bordering the sea—and the forests! The white pines are as tall as the highest cathedral spire in Reyka. The land's a bit wilder than yours here—the crags make it seem so, anyway, and there's always a touch of silver in the sky, whether it be blue or gray.''

''Sounds very nice,'' she said, feeling obliged to say something. But Jaren had obviously not heard the flatness in her voice, and thinking she was more interested than she was, jumped at her words as a hint to go on. He spoke with enthusiasm, and Athaya was beginning to think he possessed a bit too much of it for a relatively mundane topic.

''The capital is farther north than Delfarham, and autumn comes early there,'' he went on. ''In fact, the leaves are probably starting to turn even though it's not September yet. Yes, I'll be glad to get back in time to see the color.''

He paused for an instant, and Athaya sensed that he was about to give her some sort of explanation for this florid description of his homeland.

''Listen,'' he said, dropping his voice down low. ''I'm going back home in a few days . . .''

He paused again, choosing his next words carefully, but Athaya didn't need to hear them. She should have seen through his motives before, but the looca-smoke and wine must have dulled her senses too much. With a slow dawn of realization, she leaned back in her chair and scowled at him. *So that's what he's been getting at . . .*

Jaren smiled innocently. ''Why don't you—''

Suddenly filled with rage, Athaya swept her hand across the table, sending the cards fluttering to the floor like dead leaves. ''Look, Jaren,'' she said, pointing a finger in his face, ''I've had just about enough lewd propositions from men for one night. You'll have to find some other woman willing to be your bedmate on your way back home.''

"B-but that's not what I meant!" he stammered, both surprised and hurt by her accusation. "Not at all!"

Athaya wasn't listening. Gathering up her looca-pipe, she stalked away from the table, thoroughly disgusted. She had been insulted once too often and decided to head for home. There, at least, the insults were not quite so degrading.

"Wait! Please come back," Jaren was saying, hurrying up behind her. "I didn't mean what you think. Let me explain—"

Athaya was just about to step over the threshold when she collided with two large men blocking the doorway, one of whom promptly plucked the dagger from her belt. The men were dressed in drab wool tunics and hose, liberally stained with mud, and had lightweight black cloaks flung carelessly over their shoulders. Athaya's nose wrinkled at the stench of the dried manure that clung to the sides of their leather boots. The taller of the two admired the fine workmanship of her dagger with dark, greedy eyes that looked smaller than they were next to the huge, sharply curved nose that jutted from his face like a beak. The other man was more muscular, with two scraggly mops of gray hair on each side of his balding head, and looked as if he would snap the laces of his tunic, so tightly did it cling to his frame.

"Do you mind?" Athaya asked sourly, resting one hand on her hip. She held out her hand, silently requesting the return of her blade.

The taller man smiled and handed the dagger to his burly companion, who slid it securely inside his boot.

"Are you the young lady who was playing cards with Rafe earlier?" he said, clasping a pair of callused hands together behind his back.

Athaya could feel her face grow hot. *Oh, not again,* she groaned inwardly. "So what if I am?" she replied, trying to inject some confidence into her voice.

The larger man moved to one side and leaned against one of the pockmarked tables, while his tall, beak-nosed companion took a step forward and set a hand on Jaren's shoulder. He gave the slightly built messenger a condescending look.

"I think you'd better leave," he suggested. "My friend and I have some business to discuss with this young woman."

"Now look, er—gentlemen," Jaren began. The corner of his mouth twitched slightly as he glanced at the burly man at his side, easily half again his weight. "Why don't we sit down and discuss this calmly, and I'm sure we—"

The tall man snapped his wrist to one side, and a thin stiletto suddenly appeared in his palm. "Are you going, or do I have to help you to the door?"

Jaren stood motionless for several heartbeats and exchanged a worried glance with Athaya. Then, with lightning speed, he grabbed the man's wrist and pushed him back, trying to wrest the blade from his hand. In the corner of her eye, Athaya saw the other man snatch up a heavy wooden pitcher from the table, but before she knew what was happening, he swung it full force at the back of Jaren's head. The blow was well aimed, and Jaren had not seen it coming in time to duck out of the way. Reeling, he let out a low moan and crumpled to the floor. A thin stream of blood seeped from the wound and trickled down his neck, staining the collar of his shirt bright red.

You'll have one hell of a bump on your head when you wake up, Athaya thought. But in light of Jaren's recent proposition, she couldn't offer any more sympathy than that. At the moment, she was busy enough worrying about herself.

Suddenly she felt a thick arm snap around her throat like a vise, lifting her feet off the floor and dragging her back. The heavyset man threw her against the wall, and her head struck the hard oak with a sickly crack. She was dizzy; her eyes refused to focus, and the peasants in the tavern, now showing more interest in her predicament than they had earlier in the evening, were nothing but blurred images swimming in midair. Her attacker struck her across the face and his cheap bronze ring bit deeply into her cheek.

"That's for my friend, Rafe," he growled. "Nobody goes around makin' a fool of him. You hear that?"

He shook her roughly by the shoulder, banging her throbbing head into the wall again. Already unsteady from the wine, Athaya was limp in his arms, unable to see or think clearly enough to put up a decent fight. The burly man dug his fingers deep into the flesh of her arms, and she bit her lip, trying not to give him the satisfaction of hearing her cry out. Through her hazy vision, Athaya saw his accomplice poke Jaren with the toe of his boot a few times to satisfy himself that the Reykan courier would cause no further trouble, and then he came toward her with cool resolve, ready to inflict a few of his own punishments.

He stepped in front of her, motioning his friend to stand aside. "You really should be more careful who you cheat at cards," he told her, narrowing his eyes menacingly. "You could get hurt . . . or worse."

He reached around and grabbed a handful of hair, slick with blood from where her skull had struck the wall, and Athaya bit back a cry of pain as he flung her to one side, sending her careening toward an empty table. She stumbled into it, knocking it on its side, and sending empty cups flying. The edge of the table jutted into her ribs, and she gasped desperately for breath as she hit the floor. The stink of soiled rushes tortured her nostrils, and she rolled to one side, wishing that she could simply pass out and save herself any more agony. Her head throbbed worse than ever, she felt as if she would be sick, her eyes watered from the smoky air, and she cursed herself inwardly over and over again for ever being so stupid as to drink enough to make her lose her quick reflexes and become so vulnerable to attack.

"Hey, I don't want no fights in my place!" boomed a low, baritone voice. The owner of the tavern ran out from the kitchens, throwing his greasy apron aside and snatching up a heavy earthenware pitcher from one of the tables. He raised it over his head, prepared to throw it at the next person who moved.

"Get the hell out of here," he yelled to Rafe's friends. He pointed toward the door. "You ain't welcome here. Get out!"

A drunken old woman let out a witchlike cackle of laughter from the back of the room. "You tell 'em, Oren! Throw them bastards out!"

A low buzz of conversation rippled throughout the room. Fingers pointed toward the commotion, and one robust-looking man—a blacksmith, judging from the tiny iron shavings clinging to his soot-smeared smock—got to his feet.

"You heard him," he said. "Get out." The three other men at his table stood up at his side, and they made an intimidating quartet.

Rafe's friends were merely amused by this display. "I'm afraid we haven't finished our discussion here yet," the tall man said. He glanced down at Athaya, who lay in a crumpled heap on the floor, clutching her head. "This is none of your concern."

"Oh, it ain't? Oren's my friend and he just told you to get out. And you're still here." He pushed his thin woolen sleeves up to reveal the firm muscles of one long-accustomed to using a blacksmith's hammer. "It looks as if me and my friends here are going to have to show you the way out."

In an instant, the common room erupted into a wild brawl. The blacksmith and his friends pounced on Athaya's attackers, and soon every man who'd had just enough to drink to be eager to fight joined in the fray. Athaya briefly caught a glimpse of Oren, the tavern owner, rolling his eyes in resignation as he headed back toward the kitchens. He was obviously used to this sort of thing.

The noise was deafening. Men shouted as they threw their punches, women screamed in high-pitched voices for whichever side they favored, and every so often Athaya heard the crack of wood as chairs were hurled across the room and broken to bits. Athaya crawled behind an upturned table for shelter, protected from the flying bits of wood but unshielded from the pitcher that toppled off another table nearby and spattered her clothes with cheap wine. Dazed, Athaya shook her head, trying to clear her vision despite the dull pounding between her ears. She didn't know which felt worse, the noise that made her head split open with pain or the increasingly nauseous feeling in her stomach.

Poking her head around the edge of the table, she noticed that the room was more crowded than it had been a moment ago. Near the tavern's doorway she saw a handful of men—all dressed identically—trying to break up the fight. The newcomers wore the uniforms of the King's Guard. Over their shirts of chain mail they wore deep crimson surcoats adorned with King Kelwyn's coat of arms, and heavy brass clasps held thick black cloaks around their necks. The guardsmen whipped out their swords, and the gleaming steel made a convincing argument for putting a stop to the fight. One of the guards bent over Jaren—still lying in an unconscious heap near the door—and nudged him with the tip of his blade, but once he saw that the young man wasn't posing much of a threat, the guard walked away to subdue the more lively troublemakers.

Four of the guardsmen hauled away the two men who had attacked Athaya—no doubt directing them to the town gaol—and two other uniformed men calmed the tempers of the blacksmith and his friends and saw that they went back to the more harmless pursuits of drinking and gambling away their meager earnings.

Standing in the center of the room, the captain of the guardsmen surveyed the place with a clearly agitated expression. Pulling off his gloves, he ran his fingers through a crop of golden hair, paying little mind to the rest of his men as they went about their duty. His sword hung casually from his belt as his eyes darted around the room, and a worried frown creased his forehead, forming dark lines on the deeply tanned skin. He exchanged a brief word with the tavern owner, who had recently emerged from his hiding place in the kitchens to survey the damage to his shop, and the owner promptly pointed an accusing finger in Athaya's direction.

The captain looked down at her, huddled on the floor near the upturned table. Closing his eyes, he slapped a hand over them in a gesture of futility. He handed the tavern owner a few coins for his troubles and then crossed the room in five swift strides. He bent over her, stretching out his hand, and Athaya accepted it with a scowl and grudgingly let him pull her to her feet.

"Thanks, Tyler," she mumbled, allowing herself to be led to a three-legged stool in the corner. She walked unsteadily, reeling with dizziness. She sank down onto the stool, rubbing the lump on the back of her head where it had struck the wall. Coughing, she wiped the sticky blood on the front of her breeches and began picking thin slivers of wood from her hair.

The captain hooked his thumbs in his belt and shook his head in resignation. He was openly displeased, but Athaya could tell by the tilt of his brow that his anger was offset by sincere concern and profound relief that she was safe.

"What have I told you about this place, Athaya?" he scolded, but his voice had little anger in it. Letting out a thin sigh, he picked up a rag from the floor, soaked the edge of it in wine, then knelt down in front of her and began wiping off a thin trickle of blood from her forehead.

"Ouch! Stop it, Tyler!" Athaya snapped, wincing from the sting. She swatted his hand away. "Leave it alone."

"Stop being such a baby and hold still." Cupping her chin in his palm, he held the rag against her forehead until the bleeding stopped. Satisfied that it was only a minor cut, he tossed the rag aside and turned his attention to the bump on her head. It was bound to look worse than it was—head wounds usually did—but he seemed reasonably convinced that she was all right. His touch was gentle; even though her cuts still stung, she couldn't help but smile at the contrast between his careful ministrations and the imposing figure he cut clad in his soldier's uniform bedecked with chains of rank, and carrying a deadly weapon on his belt. She alone knew the inner man behind the array of intimidating adornments, and that secret knowledge made her eyes shine.

Tyler glanced disparagingly at the jagged tear in the sleeve of her shirt and the streaks of blood on both knees of her borrowed breeches. Conscious of his gaze, Athaya absently tried to wipe the smudges from her face, but her hands were just as dirty, so it did little good.

Getting to his feet, Tyler held out his arm and gestured toward the door. "Come on, let's get you home and cleaned up."

Athaya glared at him, her blue eyes narrow and threatening under the thick, black lashes. "What for?" she asked warily.

The captain looked away, checking to see if all of his men had returned, and obviously trying to delay giving her the bad news as long as he could. Athaya cleared her throat noisily, and when Tyler turned back and saw her commanding glare, he gave her the message he'd been ordered to deliver.

"Your father wants to see you right away."

Athaya groaned and cradled her aching head in her palms. "Damn it all," she said, "that's *just* what I need to cap off an absolutely hellish day." She squeezed her eyes shut tightly, desperately wishing that when she opened them again, she would be a different person in a different place—and definitely one who did not feel so queasy.

Tyler helped her up and gently laid his thick, woolen cloak around her shoulders, seeing that once again she'd neglected to bring her own. She wished he would keep his arm around her, knowing how much safer she felt when he held her, but knew he did not dare do so in such a public place. But he must have been thinking the same thing, for Athaya felt his hand linger on her shoulder just a moment longer than it should have, and caught a glimpse of sadness in his eyes—a sadness that was often there of late.

"I think you ought to know . . ." he ventured, dropping his voice down to a whisper. "Your father is really angry this time."

Athaya let out a sharp, humorless laugh. "So what else is new?"

"Don't push him too far, Athaya," he cautioned her, knowing full well that she would do just that unless specifically warned not to. "I mean it. Not tonight."

She nodded slightly. She wasn't too drunk to realize he was serious and she didn't want to disappoint him. He was only trying to protect her, and that was something—for whatever inexplicable reason—that she was becoming increasingly unable to do herself.

"I'll be careful."

Athaya followed him out of the tavern and into the warm summer night. The air was still and heavy and not much cooler than it had been earlier in the day. A waxing moon shone like a large, bright pearl among the tiny, glittering stars; in the distance, at the end of the main road, was the silhouette of Delfar Castle, quietly overlooking the calm sea waters. The moonlight gleamed on the lime-washed fortress, making the stones look like molten silver. Only a handful of lights still burned in the towers at this late hour, the faint glow winking in the night like the stars above them. On any other evening, Athaya would have found the sight quite beautiful, but tonight she walked steadily forward, her hands clasped over her stomach, and her eyes focused on the ground as if she were afraid it would drop out from under her the moment she stopped looking. The cobblestones seemed to float beneath her feet, and the shops on either side of the street pitched and swayed as she passed by.

After they had gone only a few yards, Athaya's footsteps halted abruptly.

"Tyler?" she said, her voice barely audible.

"Yes?"

She laid a hand on his shoulder. "Wait here."

In a few quick strides, Athaya hurried into a dark, litter-filled alley, clasping one hand over her mouth. Tyler started to go after her, but soon he heard the dry, heaving sound of her retching and decided that the princess would much rather be left alone.

CHAPTER 2

✥✥

CAPTAIN TYLER GRAYLEN ESCORTED KING KELWYN'S only daughter, her Highness, the Princess Athaya Chandice Theia Trelane, from her private apartments to the royal audience chamber at Delfar Castle, keeping a firm grasp on her arm to keep her from stumbling on the uneven stone staircase. Although Athaya's head was somewhat clearer now, she still felt woozy and tired and, if not for her father's summons, would have gladly stayed in her rooms and hidden under a mound of bedcovers for the next twelve hours. Her stomach felt as if it had been turned inside out—and it had, she supposed, since she had been sick again just outside the main gates. The mere thought of food made the color drain from her face. This was not the first time she had ventured out into the town's taverns—she could occasionally be found there of late—but never did she remember having returned from her nocturnal adventures feeling so completely and utterly awful.

Although the cathedral was on the opposite side of town, Athaya could faintly hear the church bells somberly tolling the second hour of the morning as she and Tyler crept through the dark and empty halls. They entered the anteroom to the king's audience chamber through a carved oak door, embellished at its peak by an ornately gilded plaque proudly displaying the Trelane coat of arms. The crest was a simple one. *Per pale gules and or, two lions passant guardant sable.* But Athaya thought the pair of black lions seemed more ominous tonight and once she imagined that the lower lion turned to her, baring its sharp teeth as if ready to devour her alive.

Athaya expected that the rest of her family, with the exception of her father and herself, would have long since retired for the night. She was unpleasantly surprised to see that this was not so. *Out of all the people I'd choose to avoid at this moment,* Athaya thought miserably, *it would be her.* She cursed under her breath, halting her footsteps momentarily until Tyler gave her a gentle nudge of encouragement.

In addition to the usual pair of guards standing at their posts on either side of the double doors that led to the inner chamber was a plump woman in an overly snug gown of deep green silk. Her shrill voice threatened to splinter the timber ceiling beams above her as she spoke in an unnecessarily loud, imperious tone to a bored-looking young man, roughly a year older than Athaya, who was clearly trying not to listen to a word she said. A lightweight satin robe was flung casually over his dressing gown, and he leaned against the mantel over the fireplace, tapping his fingers restlessly on the smooth sandstone. When the young man saw the captain and Athaya enter the room he strolled away from the woman with pointed indifference, making her cheeks flush crimson with anger. She wheeled around, ready to scold him bitterly, but when she saw Athaya resting listlessly on Tyler's arm, her expression quickly shifted from petulant fury to malicious satisfaction.

"Ah! So *there* you are." Queen Dagara, Kelwyn's third wife, set her thick hands on her hips and regarded her stepdaughter with unbridled disgust. "Look at you! You look like you've been sleeping in those clothes." Dagara clicked her tongue noisily. "If I didn't know better, I'd think you were a common chambermaid parading around in her mistress's cast-off gown. I can only imagine what a sight you made *before* you cleaned yourself up."

Athaya stared down at a patch of frayed carpet on the floor and absently smoothed out another wrinkle from her blue velvet skirts. Considering the amount of damage that needed to be repaired, Athaya thought she looked passable enough, but she was too exhausted and drained to bother arguing.

The man in the dressing gown sighed deeply and ran his slender fingers through a fluffy crop of sandy-brown hair. "Can't you leave her alone just this once—"

"Stay out of this, young man," Dagara said, flapping her hand at him as if he were an annoying insect buzzing around her ears. "This is none of your affair."

"I was only trying to say that if you're going to yell at her, you can at least do it tomorrow when she feels better. You can see for yourself that Athaya's not well."

"Not well," Dagara mimicked. "I'll say she's not well. But it's no fever she's got, Nicolas, it's a damned hangover and you know it. Hmph! You think she feels bad now, just wait until her father gets ahold of her."

Nicolas opened his mouth to say something else, but the queen cut him off abruptly.

"That'll be enough out of you. Now either stay here and be quiet or get out altogether. Honestly, Nicolas, you have to stop acting as a champion for your sister when she does nothing but act in a reprehensible fashion. It reflects poorly on you and tempts me to think you're as much of a wastrel as *she* is."

Nicolas waited until Dagara turned away before he rolled his eyes and sauntered back toward the fireplace. He picked up a brass rod and began poking at the burning logs, glancing back only once to see the look of bitter understanding on his sister's face. Of her two older brothers, Nicolas was the only one she was close to, and if they had one thing in common above all the others, it was that neither one of them could possibly understand why their father had taken this graceless, shrewish woman as his wife. She was certainly nothing like Chandice, the mother of Kelwyn's three children, or Eviene, the soft-spoken, indulgent, but not overly intelligent stepmother Athaya remembered from her childhood. No, Dagara was hard and rough as an old oak tree and had been ever since she had married Kelwyn Trelane fourteen years ago.

Satisfied that Nicolas would cause no further trouble, Dagara turned her attentions back to Athaya and flashed a jeweled finger in the princess's downcast face. "These humiliating incidents have to stop. You're making a laughingstock out of your father, your brothers, and of me. I will not *have* it!"

Tyler stepped in front of Athaya, as if shielding her from the queen's biting words. "Your Majesty—"

"Silence, Captain," Dagara snapped. "You aren't entirely

without fault in this matter, you know. If the men under your command were half as observant as they're supposed to be, they wouldn't have let Athaya sneak out of the castle unescorted.'' The queen shook her head in disbelief, waving her arms in front of her as if shooing away a flock of pigeons. ''It is totally beyond my capacity to understand how an entire squadron of reasonably well-trained soldiers could allow her to walk right through the gates under their noses without noticing a *thing*!''

Tyler flinched at the insult. Reasonably well trained! He knew, as did anyone at Delfar Castle, that the men in the King's Guard were among the best soldiers in all of Caithe. Athaya had known Tyler long enough to be able to recognize the simmering anger and resentment under his seemingly nonplussed exterior. It was subtle, but it was there—the slight thrusting out of his chin, and the tiny lines around his mouth growing more pronounced. Athaya admired the way he could restrain his temper. That was something she just couldn't manage to accomplish, especially where her father and stepmother were concerned.

''Your Majesty, I questioned the men myself, and they all swore upon their honor that the princess did not pass through the gates.''

''Oh, for heaven's sake, Captain, of course that's what they'd tell *you*. They're simply covering up for each other, that's all. Upon their honor! Honor among thieves, more like it.''

Tyler held back a sigh of frustration. ''Your Majesty,'' he said, his voice smooth and even, ''I deeply regret this inexcusable incident and promise you that steps will be taken to ensure that it will not happen again.''

He bowed low to her, and Dagara seemed slightly mollified, perhaps more by Tyler's eloquent deference to her than by his actual apology. She paced the floor in a tight little circle, casting an occasional glare at Athaya, who kept her eyes focused on the floor and looked as if she were trying to burn a hole in the carpet by concentration alone. Athaya was still quite pale, but her cheeks showed two red streaks of color. The captain fidgeted nervously, wondering how long it would take Kelwyn to call for his daughter, and hoping he would do it quickly, before Athaya broke down and said something unspeakably offensive to the queen in a fit of temper.

''Is his Majesty ready to see the princess now?'' he asked.

The queen cast an exasperated glance toward the door to the

audience chamber. "He's inside with Durek at the moment. Once again, Durek is trying to make him see reason about this absurd proposal he's making to the Curia. Honestly, I'll never understand why your father persists in badgering his bishops about the Lorngeld. They're not going to change their minds. But don't worry, Athaya," she said, careful not to stray off the subject for long, "he will deal with you shortly. He's absolutely livid, you know. He received a message from Osfonin of Reyka earlier today, and it did not please him in the least."

The queen circled her with slow, deliberate steps. She shook her head from side to side, paying no mind to the way Athaya gripped her hands into white fists, trying to keep a tight rein on her emotions. "You *had* to do it, didn't you? You had to openly insult Osfonin's son Felgin and send him back home completely determined never to marry you. Hmph! Or any other Caithan for that matter. I'm ashamed that Kelwyn must call you 'daughter,' " Dagara added with dark calm. "You are an insult to the Trelane name."

Athaya looked up from the floor for the first time, and her eyes glittered menacingly in the dim firelight. She could see Tyler turning away, his eyes closed tight in hopeless resignation, but she did not care. Dagara had finally pushed her too far.

"At least that name is mine by birth," Athaya said slowly, calculating each word to inflict as much pain as possible. "*I* did not sell myself in marriage to the king of Caithe, purchasing influence at court with my dowry and insinuating my way into the ranks of the nobility through petty intrigues instead of honorable merit. I was born of royal blood, Dagara. Unlike *you*."

"*Athaya!*" The deep baritone voice split the air with its harshness, and even Dagara, utterly paralyzed with anger at Athaya's bitter words, was startled. Durek, the eldest of Kelwyn's three children and heir to the crown of Caithe, left the doorway to the audience chamber and stormed across the anteroom, his crimson cloak billowing out behind him. He gave his young sister a withering glare—one she was sure he'd learned from Kelwyn, but didn't do half so well—and then embraced Dagara's trembling hands and kissed her lightly on her powdered cheek. He avoided looking at Nicolas completely, as if unaware his younger brother was in the room at all.

"Did you hear what she said to me, Durek?" Dagara said, clinging to him with despair, her lower lip trembling in an unconvincing display of injured pride. Athaya almost laughed aloud. The queen had no pride to injure.

Durek released his stepmother's hands, patted her gently on the shoulder, and faced his sister with complete disgust. He was neither as handsome nor as slender as Nicolas, and his dark brown hair was already growing sparse despite his having just turned twenty-eight. He habitually dressed more plainly than his younger brother as well, and his solemn ash-gray doublet— a silver girdle its only adornment—made him look well past thirty. Athaya was self-conscious of his condemning gaze, but would have been more so had it not been for his eyelids, which drooped down on either end, giving the constant impression that he had been awake too late the night before. He and Athaya had never been close, and in her darker moods, Athaya would openly claim that the only things she liked about her oldest brother were his young wife, Cecile, and their two-year-old son, Mailen.

"How dare you speak to the queen like that," Durek said to her in a cool, level voice—the voice that would issue royal commands one day, when he eventually inherited Kelwyn's crown. Athaya sighed inwardly. He would be even more intolerable then.

Athaya folded her arms across her chest in defiance. "Just because you profess undying devotion to her doesn't mean *I* have to," she said petulantly.

Dagara turned away, dabbing at her eye with the corner of her sleeve. "What did I tell you, Durek? She hates me!"

"There's no time to go into that now, Dagara," Durek explained softly, his eyes filled with sympathy. Then, with a violent change in expression, he turned back toward Athaya and gestured sharply toward the double doors behind him.

"Go on in, Father's waiting for you. And be careful, little sister," he added with a spiteful gleam in his eye. "Rhodri's in there with him. Badger him the way you do Dagara and perhaps that plague-ridden wizard will turn you into a toad."

Athaya scowled as she pushed past him and headed toward the audience chamber, trying to ignore the flutter of apprehension that always came over her when Rhodri's name was mentioned. While Durek flatly despised the wizard and all the rest of his kind, Athaya feared him. She did not know exactly why, since he had never done anything to harm her. In fact, it was more logical to expect that she, like the king himself, would be grateful to him for his past service to Caithe, even though he was one of the cursed Lorngeld—the Devil's Children—those born with the powers of magic, and thus, the plague of madness. But in spite of his heritage, Rhodri had served Caithe well. If the wizard had not bestowed magic on the young Kelwyn when he inherited his throne and instructed him in its use, then Caithe would not be the growing power that it was today and its provinces would have remained disjointed and at war, as they had been since the Time of Madness.

Athaya opened the door to Kelwyn's audience chamber, bracing herself for the onslaught to come. Despite the late hour, a fire burned brightly in the spacious, wood-paneled room. The king was hunched over a large mahogany table, scribbling notes with a quill on a piece of parchment, while the wizard Rhodri, elegantly intimidating in his deep blue robe lined with silver, lingered by the window and gazed through the latticed glass at the moon glowing brightly over the Sea of Wedane. He had a look of cool pride in his eyes, as if he had just conjured the beautiful sight before him into existence and was now quietly admiring his handiwork.

The wizard pulled the window open to catch a whiff of the salty sea air, and a gust of wind whisked through the chamber, snuffing out the candle by whose light the king was writing.

"Damn it all, Rhodri," he growled. Kelwyn absently traced a design in the air, whispering a word that Athaya did not know, and suddenly the candle flared up again with a soft crackle.

Athaya felt a shudder ripple through her. It always discomfited her when she witnessed her father using the magic that Rhodri had given to him. Kelwyn was not of the Lorngeld—none of the Trelanes had ever been. Logically, then, he should not be able to work magic. And why would he want to, knowing that the powers came from the Devil? Did not the priests say that all magicians were either doomed to madness or doomed to hell? But it was not only her father's magic that disturbed her. She felt ill at ease whenever Rhodri worked his spells, also. Athaya had always been taught to be wary of the Lorngeld, and it was difficult to put her prejudices aside, even though Rhodri was a close advisor of the king.

Kelwyn set down his quill, sprinkled fine sand on the parchment, and gently shook it off as the black ink dried. Out of the corner of his eye, he noticed his daughter standing in the shadows near the door.

"Athaya," he said, expelling the word from his mouth like a rotten piece of meat. "Come here." He folded the document twice and dripped hot, yellow wax over the fold. Then, taking off his signet ring, he pressed it into the wax, setting his royal seal on the message.

"Good evening, your Highness," Rhodri said, inclining his head toward her as she approached the king. She returned the wizard's greeting with a hesitant nod.

Kelwyn rose from his chair and clasped his hands behind his back, stepping around the table to face his reckless daughter. He moved without haste, carefully planning every motion before he made it. He rarely spoke in haste, either, knowing that such a habit was dangerous in kings. Thus, Athaya always knew that when he was angry with her, it was not like a quick, petulant storm that would soon blow over, but a thoughtful, more decisive anger that would linger for quite some time. Much as she hated to admit it, Athaya was intimidated by him. Kelwyn was not just her father, but also a powerful ruler, and he looked every inch the monarch he was. A jewel-encrusted gold collar was set on his strong, broad shoulders—Kelwyn had always prided himself on his ability to retain the firm, muscular build of a much younger man—and only the slightest trace of silver could be found in his well-trimmed brown hair, brushed into a crisp curl beneath his chin. His gold coronet glittered in the candlelight as he fixed his disapproving royal gaze on her.

He's acting awfully calm, Athaya thought anxiously. *Tyler was right. I'm really in for it.*

"I sent for you nearly four hours ago. Apparently the captain and his men had a rather difficult time finding you, as you had decided to sample the vintages for sale at a few of Delfarham's more disreputable taverns without telling anyone. Is that correct?"

"Yes, my Lord," she answered quietly.

"I also understand that you were located in a highly questionable tavern, engaged in a brawl with two known criminals who claimed you cheated their friend at cards. Is that correct?"

Known criminals? She certainly hadn't been aware of that. It was a good thing Tyler found her when he had, or there was no telling where she would be right now. Dead in a ditch somewhere, most likely. *A fitting end,* she thought with bitter amusement. *I never lived the way I was expected to, why should I die conventionally?*

"Yes, my Lord."

"I also understand that upon leaving this tavern, you suffered from the aftereffects of too much wine and looca-smoke."

Athaya's stomach churned at the mere memory. "Yes, my Lord."

"I see," he said, drumming the tips of his fingers on the polished mahogany. "Well, I suppose I should be glad that you have not decided to add lying to your list of accomplishments for the evening."

Athaya averted her eyes from her father's condemning glare and caught sight of Rhodri calmly viewing the proceedings from the windowseat, his face wrapped in aloofness. Athaya almost wished the wizard would look smug or maliciously happy as he watched Kelwyn scold her. At least then she could have a reason for being irritated by his presence. But he remained passive, his slender hands folded in his lap and his shoulders slouched down, looking like a bored priest listening to the last confessions of a dying man out of duty and not out of any genuine sympathy.

"I will not waste my time by berating you for your deplorable behavior tonight," Kelwyn continued. "Even through these thick walls, I could clearly hear Dagara taking care of that task quite well. Suffice it to say that you are never to leave this fortress without an armed escort under any circumstances."

Why not? Athaya cried inwardly. *What does it possibly matter to you what I do? If anything happened to me, you'd only be losing a daughter you never cared about in the first place. Why can't you just admit that?* Rationally, she knew that she had no right to bemoan the fact that Kelwyn displayed little feeling for her. Heaven only knew how much of his disapproval she brought upon herself by continuing to be spiteful and argumentative. The only thing he had ever expected of her was to grow up to be a delicate peach of a princess, fragile as a glass goblet, who could be admired for her beauty and grace, and who had few other thoughts in her head beyond how to please a husband.

The king had been miserably disappointed.

Kelwyn's soft leather boots made no sound on the carpeted floor as he returned to his seat. He shuffled through the scrolls piled up on the table and drew out a document, holding it up for

Athaya to see. The parchment was rumpled and torn, as if it had been angrily crushed into a ball and smoothed out again.

"Do you know what this is?"

"No, my Lord."

"Ah. Then I will tell you." He unfurled the paper, and Athaya could see the regal green ribbons streaming from the bottom. "It is a letter from Osfonin of Reyka. Would you like me to read it?"

Athaya shifted her weight to her other foot. Kelwyn didn't have to read the letter; she already knew what it was going to say. And she also knew he was going to read it to her whether she wanted him to or not.

"I'll skip over the polite platitudes and get right to the heart of it." He ran his finger down the page until he found the part he sought. "Here it is. 'And offering my regrets that both our hopes cannot be realized, my son Felgin professes his inability to discuss marriage with your noble daughter at this or any time, due to differences between them which he feels could not be reconciled.' There's more, but I think you get the general idea. It's all worded very graciously, but I have no doubt that Osfonin is furious." Kelwyn carelessly tossed the paper aside. "Well? What do you have to say for yourself?"

Athaya knew that nothing she could say was going to help matters. She struggled to find words which would simply not make the situation any worse, but none would come. Kelwyn stared at her, tight-lipped, as he shook his head from side to side.

"You *knew* how important this marriage could have been to reestablishing relations with the Reykan government and yet you deliberately set out to ruin everything by being outwardly rude and antagonistic toward the prince. You countered his every word with an argument—more than once shaming him into revealing that he isn't quite the scholar he professes to be—and then had the gall to challenge him to a chess match when you knew full well that he wasn't as good at it as you are. And I thought it had to be a joke when I heard you'd actually suggested playing the match for money!" Kelwyn let out an exasperated sigh. "I won't even bother mentioning the rest of it. I'm just lucky Osfonin is merely offended, and not on the verge of invading us for the insult you've dealt to him."

Athaya dropped her eyes. *Can I help it if Felgin was a puffed-*

up, egotistical snob? No wonder he's almost twenty-seven and still hasn't gotten a wife.

She took a deep, steadying breath. "I spoke the truth to you about the, uh—events of this evening, so I will not lie to you now. Candidly, Father, I think that a marriage between myself and Felgin would have been a terrible mistake and I cannot profess to be unhappy that the arrangements did not work out."

"I see," he said, narrowing his eyes slightly. "And why, in your infinite wisdom—which apparently your king does not have—would this match have been such an error?"

Athaya nervously picked at a piece of embroidery on her skirts. Her cheeks grew hot under her father's gaze, and she felt like a child of four. "I . . . we just didn't like each other," she said, cursing the weak-sounding words the moment they left her lips.

Kelwyn's eyebrows shot up. "You didn't *like* each other? Good Lord, girl, that was more than obvious. But since when has *liking* someone ever had anything to do with a proper marriage?"

I'm told it mattered to you. At least the first time. She choked back the cruel words, knowing that to voice them would be an unforgivable impertinence.

"There is something more," she continued, trying desperately to dig herself out of the hole in which she found herself. "Father, I agree that it is only right that Caithe and Reyka be allies. But the differences between Felgin and I on certain subjects . . ." She looked uncomfortably at Rhodri before going on. ". . . might cause more problems between our respective countries than it would solve."

"What do you mean?" he asked curtly. "Explain yourself."

Athaya swallowed hard. She could tell from the cold look in his eye that he already knew what she was about to say, and rightly so, in light of the number of long-winded speeches he had endured from Durek on this subject. Athaya hadn't wanted to bring it up, especially in Rhodri's presence, but now she had little choice.

"Prince Felgin is of the Lorngeld, Father. You knew that before you ever invited him here. Putting it plainly, I do not wish to marry a man of his race, nor do I want to risk having my children—your grandchildren—doomed to either insanity or damnation."

She glanced aside at Rhodri, still sitting in the windowseat with his hands folded in his lap, motionless as a marble statue. She would have expected him to show at least a shade of annoyance at her words, but if he was offended by her remarks he did not show it. In fact, he looked slightly bored, as if he'd heard this argument so often that it had ceased to surprise him.

Kelwyn, on the other hand, was visibly angry. "Must you assume that what the priests say is right, simply because they are priests?" he cried, banging his fist on the table. "You're starting to sound just like Durek!"

Then, like a horse checked by its reins, he paused to collect his thoughts and continued in a much calmer tone. "I do not mean to insult the men of the Church. Right or wrong, their teachings have helped Caithe through some very dark times and prevented a great deal of misery and destruction. But I disagree with their views on the damnation of the Lorngeld, and I know they are wary of me because I am the first king in a great while to stand up and say so. I may not be a natural-born Lorngeld, but I understand them and their ways and I think the priests will listen to me because of that."

Although Kelwyn had already begun work on this latest project, Athaya knew as well as anyone that it was not getting off to an auspicious beginning. Her father had summoned the highest-ranking members of the clergy to Delfarham for the purpose of presenting his arguments, and while none had been so bold as to refuse it, they had come reluctantly, knowing they would only be forced to argue against their king and risk incurring his wrath. It was becoming clear that his battle on behalf of the Lorngeld would not be an easy one, especially since Kelwyn had vastly underestimated the clergy's violent reaction to what they called his unspeakable plan to marry his own daughter to the Devil himself.

"They have to change their minds," Kelwyn went on, full of passion. "I simply refuse to believe that what they say about the Lorngeld is true. Just look at Rhodri! Why, without the power he gave me, and his own efforts in teaching me how to use it, I never would have been able to put an end to the civil war as quickly as I did. Rhodri may be a fully trained wizard, but in light of what he's done for Caithe, I certainly don't think he's damned to hell for it, do you?"

Athaya focused her eyes on Osfonin's letter, unwilling to look

either at her father or at Rhodri. She certainly hoped the wizard
was not destined for hell. She supposed herself already headed
in that direction and could think of any number of people with
whom she would rather spend eternity.

"Might I say something, your Majesty?" came the rich, tenor
voice from across the room. Rhodri rose fluidly, the silvery
threads in his robe glittering like ice in the moonlight. Though
several years Kelwyn's junior, the wizard looked much older
due to his unusually pale skin and snowy white hair, and the
moonlight only served to make his features more colorless. He
stepped soundlessly across the carpet to join the king and his
daughter.

"Princess Athaya, I understand your feelings about me, and
those like me. I cannot take offense. You have the right to believe
what you will, whether I agree with you or not." Rhodri smiled
thinly, but the look in his eye—which Kelwyn could not see—
plainly told her that the reason he was not offended by her beliefs
was simply because he found them too ignorant and contempt-
ible to bother with.

"But as for Prince Felgin, I do not think your marriage to
him would bring about the calamities you anticipate. Not that
such a marriage is likely to come about now," he added regretfully, glancing at the green-ribboned letter.

"Are you trying to tell me that if I had married him, our
children wouldn't be born with the curse?"

"No. That is a possibility, of course, but one never knows
who will be given the gift. But I lived in Reyka for many years
and know that in that land, the Lorngeld are honored and respected. And to be a royal Lorngeld is an even greater distinc-
tion. As Felgin's wife, you would have been the most revered
woman in the land. I think you knew all of this, and even though
I disagree with your reasons, I find it admirable that you would
refuse such a match on the strength of your principles."

"That'll do, Rhodri," Kelwyn interjected, unexpectedly annoyed that the wizard seemed to be taking Athaya's side in this.
Rhodri bowed and returned to his seat, reclining in the luxurious
cushions with catlike grace. Athaya gazed at him in mild surprise. Apparently the wizard didn't think a marital alliance with
Reyka was as crucial to Caithe's future as Kelwyn did. *Or maybe,
despite all his pretty words, he simply doesn't care*, Athaya
thought.

"Whether you acted out of spiteful or 'noble' reasons," Kelwyn said, with a cursory glance at the wizard, "the situation has not changed. I must still send a reply to Osfonin. I finished writing that reply earlier this evening." He reached for the sealed letter on his desk—the one Athaya had seen him writing when she entered the room.

"What does it say?" she asked, more from courtesy than from any desire to know the answer.

"I have simply informed Osfonin that because his son has no further intentions of pressing his suit with you, I can only assume that this unwillingness is a sign of hostility toward the Caithan people. I admit that your behavior was far from ideal, but if that alone can destroy such an important alliance, then obviously Osfonin wasn't as serious as he claimed when he suggested that his son might be a good husband for you. He has insulted Caithe—an insult which we are prepared to answer if need be."

Athaya's eyes grew wide. "But you can't say that!" she sputtered. "You're practically declaring war on them!"

"Not quite. I merely want Osfonin to reconsider his situation. I was most serious when I approached him about a possible alliance between our two countries. Caithe has grown powerful over the last few years, and the Reykans would be well advised to realize that. We are no longer their poor, inferior western neighbor, but a powerful peer, which could be an enemy to them just as easily as an ally. I think it would be in Osfonin's best interests for his son to take another look at you and reconsider his feelings about this marriage."

Athaya felt her stomach tighten. "You mean Felgin's coming back?"

"Not exactly," Kelwyn said, tapping the end of the letter on the table. "You see, Athaya, I didn't just summon you to scold you for your behavior tonight, which, I'm sure you're aware by now, was inexcusable. Your solitary jaunts through the countryside are not only unseemly, but they are extremely dangerous. The civil war is over, yes, but that does not mean that everyone in my realm is unswervingly loyal to me, or has your own personal welfare at heart."

Kelwyn stood up slowly and laid his hands flat on the table. "But since you seem to have an uncontrollable desire to leave the confines of this castle, I've called you here tonight to give you a commission." A smile lingered on his lips as he motioned toward the sealed letter. "You, Athaya, are to deliver this message to Osfonin personally."

Athaya reeled as if she'd been struck.

"What?" she cried. Her jaw hung open stupidly. There had to be some mistake . . .

"You heard me. I'll have Captain Graylen and a dozen of his men escort you there. You will depart for Reyka at dawn, the day after tomorrow."

Athaya couldn't believe what she was hearing. "But, Father, you have no idea . . . how could you do this to me? Osfonin will toss me out of his court before I can open my mouth to say a single word!"

"Perhaps that is just what you need to quell your desire for midnight ramblings through the streets of Delfarham," Kelwyn said mirthlessly. "It is your own fault that this letter had to be written at all. You humiliated me, as well as all of Caithe. Your punishment is fitting."

Athaya hung her head in complete misery. She could see it now. Osfonin would furiously order her out of his presence while Felgin sat by laughing himself into convulsions. But what could she say? Deep down, she knew Kelwyn was right. It was a fitting punishment. Suddenly her head began to pound, and the queasy feeling in her stomach began to return. Would this wretched night never end?

Kelwyn gathered up his letters from the table. "It's very late, and I, for one, am going to bed. And I urge you to do likewise, Athaya. You look as if you're in dire need of some rest." With one last glare at his daughter, he turned on his heel and stalked out of the chamber.

Athaya heard a soft rustle from the windowseat and jumped—she had completely forgotten that Rhodri was there. He closed the wooden shutters and drifted across the room toward her, blowing out the candle on the mahogany table with one gentle breath.

"Don't worry overmuch, your Highness," he said to her. "Osfonin is not a temperamental man. I think you will find him most genial, in spite of the unfortunate circumstances of your visit."

"You've met him?"

Rhodri shrugged with undeceiving modesty. "Only once, a long time ago. But I was quite impressed."

As if the king of Reyka has to worry about impressing you, she thought, quietly amused.

"I was introduced to him many years ago by an old teacher of mine." Rhodri paused. For a moment, Athaya saw a shadow pass over his face, but it was quickly gone. "I don't think your audience with Osfonin will be as unpleasant as you expect."

Athaya nodded imperceptibly. "I hope you're right."

"I bid you good night, then," he said. Rhodri bowed to her and left the room, closing the heavy door noiselessly behind him.

Now alone in the chamber, Athaya slumped down on a woven straw mat in front of the fireplace and gazed at the hypnotic flickering of the flames.

Why do I keep doing this? she thought glumly. *Why do I always back myself into corners and then complain when I can't get out?* She thought back to Durek's warning and cupped her chin dejectedly in her palms, wondering if it wouldn't be best for everyone if she simply asked Rhodri to turn her into a toad after all.

CHAPTER 3

✳✳

THE FIRE IN THE AUDIENCE CHAMBER HAD NEARLY DIED away when Athaya heard the faint slip of an iron latch. She turned around warily—half expecting that her father had returned with another admonition that he'd forgotten to deliver earlier—and saw the carved oak door swing slowly open, admitting a stream of mellow torchlight from the anteroom beyond. Athaya let out a quick sigh when she saw the familiar visage poking around the edge of the chamber door.

"Tyler," she said, relieved. "Come on in."

He closed the door, the latch slipping into place with a soft click, and sat down beside her on the mat in front of the fireplace. Red embers glimmered weakly in the darkness, and the captain's smoothly chiseled features were only faintly illuminated by the crimson glow.

"Are you all right?" he asked.

Athaya shrugged her shoulders weakly. "I've been better." She leaned against him, thoroughly drained of energy. Tyler wrapped his arms around her and gently pulled her close to him, brushing the back of his fingers against her cheek. She closed her eyes and drank in the sweet smell of leather that clung to his skin.

"I'm so tired," she moaned, curling up closer to him. The warmth of his body was soothing, and more than anything, she wished she could simply drift through the rest of the night right here, in his arms.

"Do you want me to take you up to bed?" he asked. Then, seeing the questioning arch of her eyebrows, he added, "*Your* bed?"

"Oh, you're no fun," she replied teasingly. She sighed, burrowing her head into the curve of his shoulder. "But even if we really could, *I* couldn't. Not tonight." She stifled a yawn. "It's funny, though. I'm so exhausted I think I could sleep for a week, and yet I don't feel like going to bed." Athaya paused. "I don't like the dreams I've been having lately."

"Bad ones?"

Athaya nodded. "Nightmares. Heart-pounding, cold-sweat-running-down-your-back-type nightmares. I don't know why. Probably because I've felt so frustrated lately. Kind of restless."

Tyler frowned. "Why?"

"That's the thing—I have no idea. All I know is that I want to get away from . . . something, I don't know what. I feel as if all the walls are closing in on me, and there's nothing I can do to stop them."

"Does this have anything to do with why you went to that tavern tonight?"

"I suppose so," she told him with a sigh. "I thought that blowing off some steam and having a few drinks would get this . . . this *thing* out of my system, whatever it is. I was feeling depressed this afternoon and figured maybe I could cheer myself up by winning a few crowns at the gaming tables."

"And so you did," he pointed out. "From a ruffian who probably wouldn't have paid you anyway, and who sent two friends of his to knock you around."

Athaya made a sour face. "Please, Tyler, I've been sufficiently scolded for that already. But I'm glad you showed up when you did."

"So am I," he said, suddenly more serious. "I was awfully worried about you. It wasn't just foolhardy, your going off like that alone, it was damned dangerous. Didn't that ever occur to you?"

She pulled away slightly, with a look of vague confusion on her face.

"Yes, but it didn't seem to matter. It seems odd to say it now, but at the time, I really didn't care what happened to me—if I ended up alive or dead. Oh, Tyler, please don't look at me like that," she said, seeing his expression of hurt and shock. "I wasn't thinking clearly at the time. I know it doesn't make a lot of sense. It's just that lately I feel as if there's something terribly important I'm supposed to be doing, but I haven't the foggiest idea what it is. I feel . . . lost most of the time. Confused. It sounds silly, but it's been bothering me for quite a while now. Months, in fact." Then, with a resigned half smile, she said, "I'll wager it's because of this whole disaster with Prince Felgin. This all started about the same time he showed up here last June. I guess I feel guilty about the way I acted, and my mind has decided to torture me about it until I make amends. Speaking of which," she added reluctantly, "did Father tell you about our upcoming journey?"

"I'm afraid so. He mentioned it in passing on his way out. I'm supposed to go see him tomorrow morning to get the details. Or rather, later *this* morning. I think it's after three o'clock."

"Forget the time. I'm more than willing to stay up until all hours of the night if it means I can be alone with you for a while." She began to caress the inside of his thigh with her hand, listening with intense delight as his breathing began to quicken.

Tyler swallowed and laid his hand atop of hers. "Unless you want to end up doing something we'll both regret later, you'd better stop that."

"I wouldn't regret it," she whispered, her eyes filled with suppressed emotion. Then, as a blanket of sadness settled over her face, she added, "It's not being with you that I'd regret. It's the consequences."

"I know," he said, sighing deeply. He tucked a thin tendril of hair back behind her veil. "But it's just too risky. You're the one who admitted that first, not me."

Athaya nodded in reluctant agreement. "I can just see it now. I'd end up being one of those lucky young ladies who can conceive children just by thinking about it, and then where would we be? I'd be ruined for life and would have to be married off to someone deplorable like Felgin to hide my shameful condition, and you—you'd get drummed out of the King's Guard in the blink of an eye. Assuming, of course, that my father didn't have you tossed into the dungeons for a few decades first."

Tyler said nothing, knowing he couldn't refute a word of what she'd said. But Athaya knew that there were times, increasingly frequent times during the last year or so, when both of them wondered if the risk might be worth taking despite the inevitably disastrous results.

Athaya stared into the dying embers in the fireplace, their red glow almost gone. "Sometimes I wish we could just run away," she said quietly. "I don't care where. Just someplace where we could forget everything we ever were and everyone we ever knew and start fresh. A brand new beginning."

"That would be one alternative," he said, lacing his fingers between hers. "But it's not exactly the most responsible one."

Athaya rolled her eyes in frustration. "Please don't start telling me again about how I have a duty to live a certain way and marry certain people just because of my position in life. I've been hearing that since the day I was born and I can take it from almost everyone except you." She brushed an angry tear from the corner of her eye. "It hurts too much when you say it."

"That's because you know deep down that it's true," he said, looking directly into her eyes. "I'm not happy about it either. But you were born to a unique destiny, Athaya. Neither one of us can change that."

"Good Lord, Tyler, you make it sound so damned philosophical."

"I'm just telling you the truth, Athaya," he said, giving her hand a gentle squeeze. "You wouldn't want me to do otherwise, would you?"

She smiled wanly. "No, I guess not. Archbishop Ventan makes a career out of telling Father only what he wants to hear, and I certainly don't want you being like that."

Athaya gazed into his eyes and wondered how she had ever gotten through the days before Tyler had joined her father's service three years ago. "You're too good to me," she said warmly.

He smiled and took her hand, touching it lightly to his lips. "I know." Then, knowing that they were alone, he bent down and kissed her gently.

She turned to the side, accepting his kisses with eagerness. A tingling surge of happiness flowed through her, and she quickly forgot all about her troublesome family, her upcoming trip to Reyka, and her disastrous evening at the tavern. The only thought in her mind was the sensation of Tyler's hand as it swept up and down the curve of her back and the tender touch of his lips on hers. Nothing else seemed more important at this moment than to feel the full weight of his body pressing down upon her. She rolled onto her back and gently pulled him toward her.

Just then, she was struck by a piercing rifle of pain through her head and neck as the rough surface of the mat dug into the tender wound on the back of her head. She arched her back and cried out a curse, sitting bolt upright. On her way up, her forehead struck Tyler's with a heavy clunk.

"Oh, I'm sorry!" she said, with a tearful giggle, unsure whether to laugh at her clumsiness or cry out from the pain. Then, after a moment's hesitation, she burst out laughing, a kind of relieved, tension-banishing laughter, and watched as Tyler looked at her with a curious expression of both frustrated desire and amusement.

"That wasn't very romantic, was it?" she observed.

Tyler massaged his forehead, trying to determine whether or not he was going to develop a lump. "I've had smoother encounters."

Athaya arched an eyebrow. "Have you, now?"

"What did you expect, my love? That I passed my thirty-fourth birthday without ever having been with a woman?"

"No." She slumped back onto her side, resting her head on her forearm. "Maybe you should have stayed with one of them. You have every right to try and find someone else. A good wife to take care of you. You deserve your own happiness, Tyler, especially since you can't have it with me."

"But I *do* have that with you! Don't you know that by now?" He lifted up a lock of her hair and smoothed it between his fingers. "You know how much I love you, Athaya."

"You do?"

"Come now," he chided her softly. "I've certainly told you often enough."

"Just keep on telling me. I'm afraid I need to be reassured of that all too often. And I love you, Tyler," she added, "even though you're *much* too old for me."

Tyler tweaked her lightly on the nose and then reached over and plucked a cushion from a footstool next to the fireplace. He set the soft pillow underneath Athaya's head.

"Better?" he asked.

Athaya nodded, and then clasped him by the shoulders, drawing him down to her. "Now . . . where were we?"

Their lips met, and soon the pain in her head was forgotten as she concentrated on living this rare, precious moment to its fullest. The room seemed much warmer now, despite the dying fire, and she could sense Tyler growing more desperate, more eager, with every fervent kiss and caress. As his lips brushed down her neck and toward her breast, Athaya knew she should stop him and push him away before it became impossible to do so. She promised herself that she would do just that . . . after one more minute. Just a few more minutes . . .

"Well, well. What have we here?"

In sheer panic, Athaya pulled away from Tyler with fearful violence and scrambled to her feet, wheeling around to face the direction from whence the disembodied voice had come. In the far corner of the room, lingering in the doorway, she saw a robed figure in the shadows of an oil lamp, and her first, terrifying thought was that Rhodri would waste no time in informing her father of the guard captain's indiscretions with the princess. But then she noticed that it was not a blue-and-silver robe he wore, but a satin dressing gown, and her eyes burned at the mischievous, young face that grinned back at her with unabashed delight.

"*Nicolas!*" she cried out, shaking visibly with relief. "Don't you ever, *ever* do that again! Do you hear me?"

Nicolas set down the lamp on Kelwyn's mahogany table. In the darkened room, even the soft light of the oil lamp seemed harsh and unwelcome.

"Sorry, little sister," he said. "But you two had better be more careful. What if I had been Father, or Durek—or even worse, Dagara-the-Dragon-Queen?" He put two fingers to the sides of his temples and wiggled them impishly.

Tyler got to his feet and brushed the patches of soot from his rumpled doublet. He reached over and straightened Athaya's headdress for her, putting the blue veils back in their proper place, while she shook out the wrinkles in her skirts and rearranged the folds of her scalloped sleeves.

"That's better," Nicolas said, nodding with amused satisfaction. "Much less incriminating."

Athaya shuffled across the carpet and sank down into her father's oak chair. "This is so embarrassing."

"Not half as embarrassing as it might have been if I'd walked in a few minutes later." He leaned over and pecked his sister on one of her crimson cheeks. "It's too bad, you know," he continued with sincere regret, shifting his gaze from his sister to Tyler. "I can't think of anything I'd like more than to sit up in the front row of Saint Adriel's Cathedral and watch you two say your wedding vows."

Tyler's eyes took on a wistful expression as he gazed at the young prince. "Believe me, your Highness, there's nothing we'd like better ourselves."

Nicolas grimaced. "Come on, Tyler—it's just the three of us. You can cut all the 'your Highness' stuff. I don't go around calling you 'Captain Graylen' every waking minute of the day, do I?"

"No, but—"

"Well then, there you have it," he said resolutely. "Consider that an order."

Athaya propped her head up with her fists. "I'll ignore the fact that only Kelwyn has the authority to give orders to the guard captain and go on to ask you what you're doing here."

"I just wanted to make sure you were all right. Which, apparently you are, given the healthy activity which I found the two of you engaged in."

"Would you please—"

"Yes, Athaya, I'll be serious," he said, appeasing her with a solemn, Dureklike expression. "I heard Father telling Tyler about sending you to Reyka and I followed him all the way back to his chambers trying to talk to him out of it. Unfortunately, all he did was glare at me as if he was convinced that I had something to do with your little excursion in town tonight. I have a sneaking feeling I should consider myself lucky that I'm not getting punished, too." Nicolas threw his hands up in a gesture of futility. "After that, Dagara and Durek accosted me in the hallway outside of Father's chambers and yelled at me for annoying him. Dagara ordered me to go to my rooms, and so, dutiful as always, I came straight here to see you."

Athaya shook her head, bemused. "Careful, Nicolas. One of these days you're going to get in as much trouble as I do around here."

"Impossible," he said, waving his hand in a gesture of dismissal. "You've already set an all-time Trelane family record."

"Well, Father always wanted me to excel at *something*," Athaya said dryly, unable to hold back a smile. Ever since they were small children, Nicolas had possessed a knack for cheering her up, no matter how despondent she felt. He lived within the same walls and dealt with the same people. Why was it that he always seemed to be in such high spirits, while she consistently looked for clouds on the horizon?

"I think it's time we all got some sleep," Tyler said. He couldn't help yawning. "I have to be on duty again in just over three hours."

The captain offered his hand to Athaya and pulled her up, while Nicolas picked up the oil lamp and trailed after them. When they had reached the anteroom, Nicolas unlaced his sister's arm from the captain's and wrapped it around his own. "Come on, Athaya, *I'll* walk you to your rooms." He glanced playfully at Tyler. "Just to make sure you get there with your virtue still intact."

It was definitely the smell of smoke, thick and pungent. Athaya wandered through the deserted corridors of the castle thinking, *Where is everyone? Why am I alone?* The stones beneath her feet were hot, the walls black with greasy soot, and the faint odor of charred flesh lingered in the air. She followed the rancid scent, knowing she should flee and save herself, but compelled by some unseen force to see what lay ahead.

Then she heard the voices—wild, hysterical voices drowning in a sea of screams. Athaya began to run, stumbling over the hot, rough stones, but with every step she took she seemed to lose ground, pushed away from that which she knew she had to reach. But she struggled on, knowing that giving up and turning back would be a worse fate than whatever mystery lay ahead. Her breath was ragged and deep when she reached the heavy double doors to the Great Hall, and she flung them open effortlessly, as if they were made of driftwood.

A burst of boiling air seared her flesh. The Hall was completely enveloped in flames. Orange tongues of fire licked upward from the floor to the timber-beamed roof, making the spacious room look like the depths of hell itself. She could feel the heat, but her skin remained uncharred. She stepped into the room, brushing the strands of fire aside as if they were thin reeds. She ran ahead, stumbling over sharp bits of bone and limbs that were blackened and dried by the heat. The echoing screams were louder now, assailing her ears like a thousand angry church bells. *"Athaya!"* the voices wailed, half-mad with pain. *"Athaya, help us!"*

The center of the hall was not burning, as if surrounded by a protective circle of wards. Inside the circle was a crowd of people she did not recognize—strange, desperate faces crying out to her to save them. In the midst of them stood Tyler, calm and resigned, silently waiting for what he knew would come, what he knew she could not stop. Suddenly the wards dissolved, and the fire closed in, and Athaya saw the countless faces burst into flames and explode in a shower of boiling blood and flesh. And Tyler still remained, looking upon her with quiet courage, his face unchanging as the flames burned his flesh to black and turned his eyes to running, liquid streams. Athaya, spattered with gore, began to scream and scream, until she had no more voice left; then the flames came after her and viciously began to burn her, too.

Athaya awoke with a start, jolted back into consciousness by the vision. Her hands were shaking violently, and her gown was damp with sweat. It took several minutes for her breathing to relax into its normal rhythm, but after a few minutes she gradually realized that, despite her tortured dreams, there was no real danger here. No servants had come running to her bedside, so she must not have screamed aloud after all.

Still weary, Athaya slid out of bed and hobbled to the washbasin in the corner. She splashed the cool water on her face, but felt only more wet and not much better. Her mouth felt pasty and dry from the wine she had drunk the night before, and her skin felt sticky and in need of a decent bath.

But why Tyler? she asked herself. *And why was he just standing there? Why wasn't he in pain like the others? Why didn't he scream?*

She pushed that thought away, cursing her own mind for tormenting her so, and pulled the bell-rope for a maid to come help her dress.

"Ah!" Cecile cried out, plucking a black bishop from the chessboard. "You have lost one of your churchmen. Take care not to lose the other, Athaya, or you will have no one left to pray for the rest of your men when I snatch them, too."

Cecile tucked a golden curl back inside her veiled cap and laughed musically as she placed the captured prize on her side of the board. As she waited for Athaya to make her next move, she touched the edge of a lace handkerchief to her forehead. Even in the shade of the courtyard's crab apple trees, the August afternoon was growing hot.

Athaya studied her remaining chessmen, conscious that her opponent could best her if she didn't begin playing more cautiously. Cecile was surprisingly good at the strategic game and showed much foresight and thought when making her moves. Athaya could not play carelessly with her as she could with most of the other court ladies and she found the game challenging enough to keep her mind off her other worries. She was grateful that Cecile had made no mention of the previous evening, even though Durek would not have failed to inform her of every detail in yet another attempt to persuade his wife to avoid friendship with the troublesome princess. But Cecile was much stronger than she looked beneath all her silk and lace and stood firm in her resolve to choose her own friends and not let her husband choose them for her.

Athaya was weighing the risks of attacking Cecile's knight with her remaining bishop when she caught sight of a familiar, portly figure padding across the courtyard toward them wearing a black skullcap and cassock. "I see yet a third black bishop in this game," Athaya murmured, watching the prelate approach. Because of his large frame, the hem of the robe rode a few inches above the ground, revealing two meaty feet encased in leather sandals. His hands were folded dutifully in front of him, hidden by billowing sleeves adorned with strips of black velvet. This stout figure was Archbishop Daniel Ventan, the highest-ranking clergyman in Caithe. All the souls in Delfarham were under his divine protection, and he strutted with an air of pride at knowing that he was charged with such a vital responsibility. Athaya had never understood what he had accomplished to merit such an honor—outside of doing virtually everything that Kelwyn asked him to—but the upper echelons of the Church were crowded with such men, so Ventan was hardly an exception.

"Good day, ladies," he said, bowing his silvery head to them. "A fine summer day, is it not?"

"It surely is, your Excellency," Cecile replied. "For all except Athaya's chessmen, I fear, who are losing their battle quite badly. Will you join us?"

"No, actually I've come on somewhat more official business.'' He turned to Athaya. ''I will not take you away from your game for long, my Lady, but I would like to speak with you privately.''

Lord, what have I done now? she thought worriedly, rising to her feet. After lightheartedly cautioning Cecile not to move the chessmen around in her absence, she followed the archbishop to a secluded corner of the yard. His eyes were overly small for such an abundant body, and Athaya fidgeted nervously as the tiny gray orbs darted around the courtyard to ensure that no one else was nearby. She knew of only one topic which Ventan was inclined to be surreptitious about, and considering her precarious position with Kelwyn at the moment, she fervently hoped that her father would hear nothing of this conversation. She didn't want to do anything that would cause her father to add to her already overflowing pot of troubles.

''Is something wrong, Archbishop?''

He smiled, showing a vast expanse of slightly yellowed teeth. ''No, not at all. I did not mean to worry you, but I thought it best that we keep this between ourselves. I wanted to give you something.''

Ventan reached into his voluminous robes, pulled out a small leather pouch, and handed it to her. Puzzled, she unloosed the strings and shook out a slender purple jewel suspended on a silver chain. The jewel was about the length of Athaya's little finger and slightly curved like the tooth of a wild boar.

''What's this?'' she asked, admiring the way the sunlight sparkled on the strange gem. The light seemed to give it life and filled it with an odd, pulsating kind of energy. ''I've never seen anything like it before.''

''It's a corbal crystal,'' he told her proudly. ''They're quite rare in Caithe. This particular crystal was given to me by a fellow bishop who had journeyed to Cruachi, where the gem is more common.''

''But why are you giving it to me?''

Ventan leaned close to her, as if he were somehow in fear of being overheard, even though there was no one within earshot. ''The corbal is used to guard against the evil of wizards,'' he said in a hushed tone. ''As you know, the Lorngeld are abundant in Reyka, and when I heard you were to venture there, I thought you should have the crystal for protection. I . . . did not think it wise to give it to you in his Majesty's presence, knowing his sympathy for their kind. He might have objections to your carrying the gem, and—"

"And what he doesn't know won't hurt him," Athaya concluded, surprised by the archbishop's rare display of intrigue. Ventan shrugged, but did not offer any argument.

"I only seek his Majesty's peace of mind," he said simply, drawing his fingertips together to form a steeple.

"Something he certainly never gets from me," she murmured, turning the gem over in her hands. It looked like an indigo icicle, slightly transparent in the bright sun.

"I can understand Kelwyn's sympathy for the Lorngeld, however," Ventan went on, shaking his head from side to side. "They are, after all, his subjects, and their plight is extremely unfortunate. Just yesterday one of them came to me—a young man who works in the salt mines near Feckham. He was suffering from delusions and sporadic outbursts of violence. He almost struck off his wife's head with an ax three days ago because he thought she was trying to kill him."

"What was she doing?"

"Nothing. His wife swears she was merely cooking supper at the time." Ventan clicked his tongue with futility. "Needless to say, she's gone now. Took their baby girl and disappeared. Apparently she had no idea she was married to one of the Lorngeld. Not that there's any way she could have known, mind you. The madness is often the only sign. But in any event, to make my story a short one, the young man's father brought him in to me yesterday." Ventan emitted a heavy sigh. "We've scheduled him for absolution tomorrow morning."

Absolution. That term always grated on Athaya's nerves. To her it was merely a less repugnant way of saying "murder." But it had to be done. Athaya knew that as well as anyone. When the madness came upon them, the Lorngeld became extremely dangerous and had to be destroyed for the protection of everyone around them. Two centuries ago, not long after the Time of Madness, a bishop named Adriel had written a treatise on the Lorngeld espousing his views that absolution was their only route to eternal life. For his efforts in saving their souls and winning the Devil's Children back to God, he had been sainted shortly after his death, and Delfarham's massive cathedral bore his name to this day.

"Does this man understand what's going to happen to him?"

Athaya asked quietly. Despite the heat of the afternoon, a cold shudder rippled down her spine as she thought of the unfortunate salt miner from Feckham.

"Yes, I explained it during his more lucid moments. He's willing. It's always better when they're willing."

Athaya looked away. *Of course it is,* she thought wryly. *It certainly reflects poorly on the Church when the priests have to pin down their victims on the altar and shove the poison down their throats.*

"And they have nothing to fear," Ventan went on. "The *kahnil* works quickly and causes little pain. The next thing they know, they're home with the Heavenly Father."

If such a one exists, Athaya added inwardly. Her own feelings about God were mixed. She couldn't honestly say she did not believe in Him, but she couldn't honestly say that she did, either. But she was careful never to voice these doubts to anyone, with the possible exception of Tyler or Nicolas. Such a lack of faith would have only served to add fuel to the fire that Dagara and Durek, and sometimes Kelwyn himself, seemed all too eager to build under her.

"It is sad," Athaya murmured, not knowing what else to say.

Ventan obliged her with a nod. "Indeed. But that does not alter the fact that they are a doomed race, scorned by God. That is why I simply could not condone your marriage to Prince Felgin, much as Kelwyn urged me to do so. Had such a marriage actually come about, I fear that it would have led to disastrous consequences."

I'll say, she thought to herself. But she was not thinking of Felgin the wizard, but of Felgin the self-righteous boor who succeeded in doing nothing but bringing out the worst in her—something she was sure he'd regretted doing ever since. And now that she thought about it, she did recall that Ventan tried to persuade Kelwyn that the marriage wasn't a good idea. Curiously, it was the only time she could think of when the archbishop had not acquiesced to the king's wishes, and that alone was proof of how strong his convictions were on the subject of the Lorngeld.

"Caithe simply cannot make alliances with kingdoms where wizardry is allowed to run rampant," he continued, suddenly filled with resolve. "Courting such a danger would be unnecessarily foolish. And soon Kelwyn will have to realize that many others besides myself and Prince Durek disagree with him. I don't expect him to have much success with the Curia. I have already spoken to several of the other bishops who have arrived for this council, and they are all quite adamant about retaining the sacrament of absolution. I sincerely doubt that Kelwyn will be able to abolish it, as he hopes."

"Strange that Rhodri doesn't seem overly enthusiastic about helping him, either," Athaya mused aloud. She had always found it quite odd that as one of the Lorngeld, Rhodri was aloof, and at times even hostile, toward his own people, as if their fate was somehow their own fault. But then, Athaya reasoned, how could he possibly do anything on their behalf when current canon law forbade the teaching of magic to the Lorngeld and made it heresy to shelter any wizard from absolution?

Any wizard but Rhodri himself, Athaya reminded herself. Being the king's advisor certainly had its privileges.

At the mention of the wizard's name, Ventan's fleshy lips turned down in distaste. "I'd be surprised to hear that Rhodri cared about anything except himself," he said snidely. "Oh, Kelwyn's told me often enough that without Rhodri we'd still be enmeshed in a civil war, but I just can't believe that he gave magic to the king for such a noble reason. He's rich enough now, so perhaps that was the reward he really wanted." Ventan furrowed his graying brows. "But I have the feeling he still wants something more."

Athaya held up the glittering purple gem and grinned mischievously. "Does he know you have one of these?"

"I never actually mentioned it," Ventan said. Then, with a sly arch of his brow, he added, "But have you ever noticed how irritable he gets whenever we're in the same room together? Frankly, I'm sure most of it is because he despises me, but some of it's because of this." He pointed to the ring on his left hand. "The diamond is surrounded by tiny corbals. Rhodri knows it, but he's too proud to ask me to take the thing off."

Athaya laughed, strangely pleased at the image of the powerful Rhodri being at the mercy of a simple piece of crystal. She briefly fantasized about someday finding enough corbals to make an entire necklace—something she could wear whenever she wanted the ever-watchful wizard to keep his distance.

She slipped the gem around her neck. "I feel safer already."

"The crystal is most effective in bright light," Ventan told her. "It seems to function poorly in darkness, although it does not totally lose its power." He handed her the leather pouch. "Keep this. The pouch is lined with velvet so you won't scratch the crystal's surface. They are somewhat delicate and do not work well if scratched or damaged."

"Thank you," she said. "It was kind of you to think of my welfare."

"I shall leave you to your game of chess, then. No doubt Lady Cecile is anxiously waiting to continue, and if I may be so bold as to observe, my Lady, I think it best that you get out of this direct sunlight. You look somewhat pale."

Too much drinking the night before does that to a person, Athaya thought, surprised that she didn't look worse than she did. But she thought it best to keep her depravities from the archbishop and, after thanking Ventan again for his crystal, returned to the welcome shade of the crab apple tree.

CHAPTER 4

✖◉✖

THE NEXT MORNING DAWNED HOT AND HUMID, A FITTING preamble to what Athaya expected to be an unpleasant day of riding. As she watched Tyler's men strapping the saddlebags to the horses outside of the stables, she thought that the uncomfortable heat was most suitable to the task at hand and knew that it would only grow warmer as they rode away from the breezy seacoast and headed inland toward Reyka.

Tyler was weaving among his men, giving last-minute orders and making sure they had enough water, provisions, and money to get them through their journey. Athaya leaned against the stone wall of the stables, tearing apart a piece of straw as she observed him going about his task. She loved to watch him work; Tyler was a natural leader, and the men under his command liked him a great deal. He wasn't an easy taskmaster, but he was always fair and just and was highly respected for his abilities, especially by Kelwyn himself.

"Anxious to leave?" he said as he came toward her, flicking a speck of dirt from the front of his crimson surcoat.

"Not funny, Tyler." Athaya tossed the shredded piece of straw aside. "I'm looking forward to getting away from here for a while, but I absolutely dread meeting up with Felgin again."

"Now, Athaya, I've told you before that you were a little hard on him while he was here. Frankly, I didn't think he was all that bad.''

"You're only saying that because he told you how good of a swordsman you were," Athaya replied, smiling wryly. "But I hope you're right. Maybe Felgin will keep his father from humiliating me more than I deserve.''

"Don't worry so much," he said, offering her his most reassuring smile. "I'm sure Osfonin is a reasonable man. He'll be fair with you.''

Athaya looked away, still somewhat doubtful. "That's what Rhodri tried to tell me.''

Her observation did not seem to give any added weight to Tyler's argument, so he thought it best to change the subject. "Nicolas stopped by earlier—he tells me that the whole family's coming out to see you off.''

Athaya rolled her eyes. "I can hardly wait.''

"Cheer up. We'll be on our way in less than an hour." He tossed a half-filled saddlebag next to her feet. "Keep an eye on this for me, will you? I still have a few more things to pack and I don't want Lieutenant Parr running off with it. He's probably the most efficient man in my squadron, but he's got a nasty habit of trying to organize everything for me before I'm ready.''

"Maybe you've trained him too well," Athaya remarked, casting a glance at the slender, brown-haired young man who was strapping his bags to the side of a piebald gelding. "Either that or he has visions of being a captain himself one day.''

"All of my men have high ambitions," Tyler said lightly, "or they wouldn't be in my squadron." He slipped inside the stables and headed toward his rooms in the barracks on the upper floor.

All around her, the courtyard was bustling with activity. The guards on morning duty slowly patrolled up and down the battlements, kitchen servants and chambermaids ran to and from the well, fetching water for the day's cooking and laundry, and the stableboys were feeding and brushing down the horses not being taken to Reyka by Athaya, Tyler, and their party. In the far corner of the yard, across from the stacked bales of hay, a cluster of young recruits to the King's Guard practiced their archery, and even at this distance Athaya could hear the drillmaster scolding them soundly whenever they failed to hit their mark. But despite the activity surrounding her, Athaya felt detached from it all, as if an invisible observer. The day-to-day life at Delfar had grown dull and routine, and she wondered, somewhat glumly, when she had lost her interest in it. As she scanned the courtyard, she fancied that even if she were to let out a high-pitched, hysterical scream of anguish, no one would hear her, or notice that she was there at all.

"Your Highness?"

Athaya wheeled around sharply. She had not heard the wizard approach.

"I'm sorry I startled you," Rhodri said with a smile that told her he was not sorry at all. His sapphire gaze reflected subtle amusement.

"It's all right. I'm just a little edgy this morning." *And your sneaking up on me like that won't help matters.*

"I wanted to ask if you would be so kind as to do me a small favor," he said. He reached into his deep blue robes, drew out a scroll tied with a red ribbon, and handed it to her. "I have an old friend living in the Reykan capital—his name is Hedric. Would you deliver this letter to him when you arrive?"

Athaya took the scroll with a somewhat puzzled expression on her face. She had never known Rhodri to send a letter to anyone, and certainly not to anyone outside of Caithe. The fact that he knew someone in a distant place like Reyka surprised her. She did not expect that people like Rhodri had friends— especially old ones. It had always seemed to her as if the wizard traveled alone through life, communicating as little as possible with his fellows and preferring to remain aloof and observant.

"How will I find this man . . . Hedric, you said?"

Rhodri smiled, as if aware of some great joke, but he did not laugh. Rhodri never laughed. "It won't be difficult to locate Hedric. In fact, you will find him at Osfonin's court. He is the High Wizard to the king—a very prestigious position in that country."

Wizard? Athaya groaned inwardly. *Not another one.* "Are the two of you very close?"

Rhodri paused briefly before he replied, as if the question required a more complex answer than a simple yes or no. "Hedric and I have known each other a great many years. But without boring you with the dull details of my youth, suffice it to say that Hedric was my teacher. It's been many years since we've spoken—we had a slight falling-out at one time," he added darkly, furrowing his brow, "but I hope he will be pleased to hear from me again.'' Rhodri clasped his hands tightly together until the tips of his fingers grew white. The subject of his old friend was clearly an intense one with him.

"I'll give him your letter as soon as I can," Athaya said, silently wishing she could avoid having anything to do with the intrigues of magicians. She bent down to tuck the scroll in the saddlepack Tyler had left with her.

As she slid the scroll inside the leather bag, the corbal crystal she wore on the silver chain around her neck slipped out from under her shirt and dangled freely in the bright, morning sun.

As if an arrow had pierced his skull, Rhodri instantly clutched his head between his hands and let out a piglike squeal of pain. He staggered drunkenly away from her, gasping for breath, and weakly slid to his knees in the dirt.

"Put it away!" he shouted harshly. "Get it out of here! Cover it up with something!"

Startled by Rhodri's reaction, it took Athaya a few seconds to compose her thoughts and hide the crystal. She hastily tucked the gem back inside her shirt and held her palm tightly over it, gazing with unexpected amazement at the sight of the powerful wizard cowering at her feet.

What do you know? she thought, cocking a brow. *It really works.*

"Ventan gave that to you, didn't he?" Rhodri asked with uncharacteristic sharpness. He rubbed his temples, massaging away the throbbing pain. Then, under his breath, Athaya heard him say, "Damned, meddling priests!"

The wizard rapidly regained his composure once the offending crystal was out of sight. He got to his feet and brushed the dirt from his robes, and only a slight shallowness of breath and a faint crease in his forehead revealed any signs of his recent agony. His expression was no longer angry, but repentant. "My apologies, your Highness. I didn't mean to speak rudely to you, but the corbal causes me much pain. Please forgive me."

"I'm sorry," Athaya said politely, though she admitted inwardly that she had actually found the incident quite fascinating. "The archbishop thought I might need the crystal for protection once I get to Reyka."

"I'm sure he did," Rhodri murmured out of the corner of his mouth. "But you needn't fear the 'evil of wizards,' as I'm sure he described it. I am afraid our dear archbishop is most unnat-

urally fearful of a people that never did a thing to harm him.
The Lorngeld are not an evil race, your Highness, although even
I will admit that just as there are good and bad human beings,
there are also good and bad wizards.''

''And which are you?'' she asked without thinking. Such
boldness never would have occurred to her before, but now that
she possessed a corbal crystal, it seemed quite easy.

Rhodri tilted his ivory head to one side. ''That is for others
to say. I do what I can, and leave the judgments to those I serve—
my king and God.''

Athaya lowered her eyes, ashamed at herself but angry with
Rhodri at the same time. He'd said just the sort of unobjection-
able thing she knew he'd say, and it made her feel foolish and
spiteful. But his answer was strangely lacking in conviction, and
Athaya found it difficult to believe that he was as humble as he
appeared.

''I'm sorry again about the crystal,'' she murmured.

''Never mind that now,'' he replied distantly, turning away
from her. ''I was once taught that great magic commands a great
price. I suppose the pain of the corbal is part of a wizard's
payment.'' He turned back and offered her a respectful bow.
''Good day, your Highness.''

Athaya followed the wizard with her eyes as he headed toward
the Great Hall, his silken robes fluttering out behind him like
wings. He stopped at the bottom of the short flight of stone steps
leading into the Hall and then graciously moved aside. Athaya
let out a muffled groan. Coming out of the doorway to the Hall
were Kelwyn and Archbishop Ventan, and trailing along after
them, Dagara, Durek, and Cecile. Rhodri joined the party,
pointedly avoiding the archbishop and taking a place on Kelwyn's other side, and Athaya caught sight of Ventan subtly caressing the diamond-and-corbal ring on his left hand as the
faintest of grins played upon his pious face. Behind them, Cecile
walked with her arm intertwined in Durek's, chattering away on
a subject that neither her husband nor Dagara appeared to have
any interest in whatsoever.

Athaya heard the shuffle of footsteps nearby and turned to see
Nicolas skimming the wall of the barracks as he made his way
toward her.

''You should have made your escape while you could,'' he

said softly, with a furtive glance across the courtyard. "They've spotted you by now, I'm sure."

"And why aren't you over there with them?"

Nicolas shuddered, twisting his face into an exaggerated grimace. "Please, I've just had my breakfast. Father isn't so bad, and Cecile is a charm, but I just can't stomach Ventan, Rhodri, Durek, *and* Dagara all at the same time. The thought alone makes me nauseated. Speaking of being nauseated," he added lightly, "where's Tyler?"

"I heard that, you little scoundrel," Tyler said, popping out of the doorway to the barracks. "And if your father wasn't looking I'd make you pay for it." He picked up the saddlebag that he'd left in Athaya's care and slipped in a deck of cards, a pair of dice, and a small purse of coins.

"All the essentials for an arduous journey, I see," Nicolas observed, grinning.

"You wouldn't want us to get bored on the way, would you?"

"No, not at all. But knowing the two of you," he said, dropping his voice down low, "you'll find something to do to occupy all those cold, lonely nights."

Athaya flushed red and poked her brother playfully in the arm. But her good spirits were eclipsed the moment she saw Dagara break away from her companions and stride on ahead more quickly. She appraised Athaya with a critical, disapproving eye.

"You *are* taking along something more suitable to wear when you present yourself to Osfonin, aren't you?" she said, pursing her painted lips together. "He's going to be hard enough on you without your traipsing around his court looking like *that*." Her words did not reveal it, but Athaya knew that the queen was unabashedly happy that her troublesome stepdaughter was leaving for several weeks and would probably like nothing better than to hear that she had been thrown out of the Reykan court the moment she arrived.

Athaya bit back a nasty reply. She would be free of Dagara soon enough and could tolerate her for a few more minutes. But in spite of her stepmother's strict sense of propriety, Athaya felt very comfortable in her loose-fitting breeches and crisp, white linen shirt, and saw no reason to make a long journey even more uncomfortable by wearing heavy, voluminous skirts. Her hair was pinned up neatly with a silver clasp, and her soft leather boots were freshly polished. Were she one of Tyler's men, Dagara would have found her appearance quite acceptable, but as it was, the queen merely looked repulsed.

"You really should be taking a carriage," Dagara said, clicking her tongue. "It's much more seemly."

"And much more inconvenient," Athaya replied crisply. "It's a two-week ride to Ath Luaine as it is, and I don't want to make it a month just for the sake of appearances."

"I shall make sure her Highness looks most acceptable when we reach Osfonin's court," Tyler cut in, smoothing the queen's ruffled feathers. "But if I may observe, your Majesty, we should leave soon if we are to reach Evarshot by nightfall."

"That you should, Captain," Kelwyn said, as he, Ventan, Rhodri, and the rest of the Trelane family caught up with Dagara. "The rest of your men are ready and waiting for you."

Although Kelwyn said nothing to her directly, Athaya sensed that beneath his stern exterior he was satisfied that she was departing on her mission without making too much of a fuss. He studied her intently, taking in every aspect of her appearance and showing no displeasure with her choice of dress as Dagara had done. He was dressed casually himself today, clad in a plainly cut green jerkin and mantle over an embroidered white shirt and a soft-brimmed felt cap taking the place of his coronet. But despite his informal attire, he seemed weighted down with serious concerns. The lines of his face were notably more pronounced, and his bearing was stiff and self-conscious in her presence. For an instant, Athaya wondered if he was reconsidering sending her off to Reyka, but she did not give that thought much attention. She knew Kelwyn both as father and as king and was sure that in either role he would not change his mind.

If I didn't know better, I'd venture a guess that he's going to worry about me while I'm gone, Athaya thought. She had never seen her father look quite so unsure of himself before. But since he rarely displayed any real concern for her, Athaya knew that whatever his feelings were, he would not voice them.

Durek stepped forward and offered her an imperceptible bow. "Good-bye, Athaya," he said stiffly. Athaya accepted his words with a cold nod; she knew that he was only here because some strange sense of propriety told him it was his duty to see her off on her journey. *Always so conscious of duty, aren't you?* Athaya mused, with an unexpected touch of sadness. *But how could the heir to the crown be anything else?*

"I'll miss our chess games," Cecile told her. "It will be too cold to have them in the courtyard by the time you return." She released her husband's arm and clasped Athaya's hands in farewell, flatly ignoring Durek's sour look of disapproval.

Archbishop Ventan gave Athaya a brief blessing and wished her a safe journey. "God's hand be upon you, your Highness," he said, touching his fingertips to his heart, then to his forehead, and finally extending them toward her in benediction. They briefly exchanged a knowing glance, and when Rhodri wasn't looking, Athaya placed her hand over the corbal crystal tucked beneath her shirt and gave the prelate a quick wink of thanks.

"Hurry back, little sister," Nicolas said. He embraced her warmly and kissed her on the cheek. In her ear, he whispered, "It's going to be damned impossible around here until you and Tyler get home."

Nicolas took her arm and led her to the corner of the yard where the rest of Tyler's men were waiting to depart. Tyler strapped his saddlebag to his chestnut-colored stallion, while Nicolas held the reins of Athaya's gray palfrey as she hoisted herself into the saddle. The captain was just about to give his men the order to ride out, but he motioned them to wait when he saw Kelwyn abruptly separate himself from the others and come to Athaya's side.

"Be careful, and mind what the captain tells you," he said softly, once he was sure that no one else was listening. "Tyler's an experienced soldier and he knows what he's doing." The king turned to go, but he hesitated, as if unsure whether to say anything more. Then he cleared his throat and barely audibly he added, "What I've asked of you takes courage, Athaya. I think I'm almost proud of you today."

He turned on his heel and strode quickly away with a look of gruff embarrassment on his face. Athaya was genuinely surprised at this rare display of emotion, and when Tyler snapped the reins and led the party toward the main gates, she followed without a word, glancing back more than once at Kelwyn, who lingered in the courtyard until she was out of sight, trying not to look as if he was watching her.

Their first stop would be at the abbey of Evarshot, a small community of monks who, between their prayers, made a modest living by making and selling wines produced from their vineyards. Athaya had never been to the abbey, but Kelwyn was very fond of Evarshot's wines and had his steward keep the castle's storehouses well stocked with casks from the obscure little monastery. Her party would likely receive a warm welcome from the abbot in light of the king's patronage, and Athaya knew that by the end of their first day's ride, she would be grateful for a quiet evening of rest at the secluded abbey.

Athaya and Tyler rode at the head of the party, while the other dozen men trailed in orderly rows about ten yards behind them. The sky was cloudless, and everything Athaya saw seemed sharply focused on such a clear summer morning. As they rode through the flatlands east of Delfarham, they were bordered on each side of the dusty, pitted road by clusters of country folk taking in the harvest from their fields. August was a busy time for them, and if Athaya could trust her own judgments about such things, this year's harvest seemed to be a good one. The corn was abundant, and the villagers' carts were loaded down with huge sacks of it, ready to be threshed and milled into flour. Others followed behind the carts, binding the high-standing straw with cord. On the grassy hills in the distance, herds of cattle grazed under the summer sun, and a swineherd was leading his pigs to the edge of the woods to scrounge for acorns. As Athaya and her party passed by a splintered old mill, she could smell the tangy scent of the first of the season's apples being pressed into cider.

The people toiling in the fields took little notice as she and her escort party passed by, and Athaya was grateful for their lack of attention. She had made spectacle enough of herself these last few days and relished the all-too-infrequent feeling of relaxed obscurity that she loved so well. She felt envious of the peasants' simple life and smiled inwardly, wondering how many of them would truly believe her sentiments. Any one of the women in the fields would probably delight in the chance to trade places with her, but Athaya knew, as they perhaps did not, how inequitable a trade that might be.

Athaya and her escort party made many brief stops during the day to water the horses and nibble on the bread and cheese packed in their saddlebags. But despite frequent rests, Athaya was growing weary, and by late afternoon, after nearly nine hours of traveling, she began hoping that before long she would see the steeple of the abbey church at Evarshot come into view.

"How much longer, Tyler?" she asked, stifling a yawn.

"Oh, I'd say about two or three more miles. Tired?"

She nodded. "And my muscles are stiffening up."

Athaya turned around and looked at the first pale, pink streaks of the sunset. The sky was clear, and even at this early hour, she could see the faint outline of the moon over the low hills dotted with evergreens and clusters of maples. But there was something else, too—far back in the distance. Something moving. Against the dark green backdrop of a grove of pine trees on the ridge, a hazy, rippling motion caught her eye, like heat waves passing over the landscape. Athaya blinked and rubbed her eyes, wondering if the long day of riding was beginning to wear on her, but when she looked again, the faint patch of rippling air was still there, although it was no longer moving across the grove of trees as it had been a few seconds ago.

Athaya frowned. "Tyler, what's that?"

"What's what?"

"Look there—in the distance, by those pine trees over there. It's . . . shimmering. Like something moving."

"Mmm, I don't see anything," he said, straining his eyes to try and locate the shimmering thing. He shook his head, seeing nothing. "The light can be tricky at this time of day, you know."

Athaya let out an impatient sigh. "Tyler, it isn't my imagination. I know I saw something." She squinted at the grove of trees, furrowing her brows. "It's not there now, though."

"You're probably just tired, Athaya. I know I am. We should be at the abbey within the hour and then we can get some rest."

The sky had turned from pale pink to brilliant orange when Athaya, Tyler, and the twelve guardsmen rode up to the front gates of Evarshot Abbey. The stone structure was old and covered with thick vines, but the building was sturdy and the grounds were neat and obviously well cared for, with clusters of rosebushes lifting their heady scent into the cool evening air. In the distance, behind the abbey's dormitory, Athaya could see the grapevines winding their way around white latticed posts, and waddling down the cobbled path leading from the vineyard to the front gates was a short, rotund little man with tonsured gray hair. He was dressed in a homespun, hooded brown robe and trailed by a half-dozen similarly clad brethren.

As his assistants opened the iron gates, the monk spread his thick arms out and clapped his hands together with delight. A broad smile lit up his face.

"You must be Princess Athaya," he said, offering her as much of a bow as his girth would allow him. "A rider from Delfarham arrived yesterday to tell us you were coming. I am Abbot Thorne. Welcome to our humble abbey, your Highness. I hope you will find your stay here a pleasant one."

Abbot Thorne called out to his brothers who were lingering at a proper distance behind him and asked them to take the horses to the stables and to see that they were properly cared for. Athaya slid out of her saddle, wincing at the stiffness in her legs, while Tyler and his men unstrapped the saddlebags and handed the reins over to the waiting monks.

The abbot led them down a cobbled path that circled around the south transept of the abbey church toward the kitchens, the visitors' cloister, and the monks' dormitory. As they walked, the abbot chatted animatedly about the history of Evarshot and the daily routine of the monks living there. He briefly guided them through the sanctuary of the church, pointing out the new stained-glass windows in the chapels around the high altar, then he showed them the vineyards which produced the wines that the king enjoyed. Athaya was quite impressed with the abbey; the lawn was clipped and neat, and the gardens obviously tended to with loving care. Although life here would be somewhat dull, Athaya found the abbey a peaceful place well suited to its contemplative purpose.

"We live a relatively quiet life here," the abbot said without apology. "But it is what we love. Daily prayers and services, growing what we need to eat, keeping the grounds neat and clean—it's all quite uneventful."

"What's that over there?" Athaya asked. She pointed to a gutted old building surrounded by broken rock and charred wood. The smoky scent of burned wood, now wet and rotting, lingered in the air. The abandoned pile of rubble looked disturbingly out of place in the beautiful, orderly monastery.

The abbot sighed heavily, and Athaya noted taut lines forming in his cheeks. The subject was clearly not a pleasant one.

"That used to be our herbarium," Thorne told her wistfully. "It was destroyed last month when someone from the village delivered a Lorngeld woman into our care. It's very unsightly, I know, but I wanted it to remain there for a while so that my brothers and I could contemplate the fates of those less fortunate than ourselves. It isn't the first time that the Lorngeld have caused disturbances here, but alas, they cannot help themselves. In the poor woman's madness, the herbarium exploded and caught fire—shattered to bits by the force of her magic. One of our order—our herbalist—was killed." He shook his head sadly. "Perhaps the woman knew that the herbarium was where the *kahnil* is made."

"Does this sort of thing happen here often?" Athaya asked hesitantly, wondering how many herbariums would need to be built and rebuilt if a great number of the Lorngeld sought refuge here.

"Oh no, not really. I hear it used to, though, a long time ago. The diaries of past abbots are kept in our library and one of them from . . . oh, almost two centuries ago, says that nearly six hundred Lorngeld were brought here in one year alone."

"For absolution?"

"Of course," he said seriously, punctuating his words with a whispered prayer. "Even the Devil's Children can attain the glories of heaven if they are cleansed of their sins."

"Cleansed?" Tyler said, speaking for the first time since they had entered the abbey's precincts. "You mean poisoned, don't you?"

"My dear captain, we do not like to call it that," the abbot replied with a pained expression. "We prefer to think of it as a gateway—a gateway to salvation and the ecstasies of heaven."

Athaya caught Tyler's look of disdain and quickly changed the subject. She and Tyler had never actually discussed it, but she knew that he was not completely in favor of the concept of absolution, even though he knew the valid reasons behind it. Athaya thought that it would be a much more pleasant evening for all concerned if no one became enmeshed in a religious quarrel and she began asking the abbot relatively harmless questions about the number of monks living at Evarshot and the quantity of books in the abbey's library.

Just before they reached the double doors leading inside the visitors' cloister, Athaya heard a low, rumbling growl, and puzzled, she glanced back toward the gates. She saw a small dog— a spaniel pup, by the look of it—pacing in agitated circles around the lawn with its teeth bared. The pup barked several times, hopping up on its hind legs, but Athaya couldn't see whatever it was that was upsetting him. And then she noticed it again—that same rippling, hazy movement she'd seen earlier in the day, by the grove of pine trees. A small knot formed in her stomach as she watched the strange blur drift past the confused spaniel pup and float across the yard, skirting the perimeter of the abbey wall.

Athaya looked away and shut her eyes tight. *I must be more exhausted than I thought.*

"Come here, you little mutt," the abbot cried out good-naturedly. "Here, boy." After a moment's hesitation, the pup scurried across the grounds to the abbot, wagging its tail, but occasionally letting out a whine and darting its eyes across the empty courtyard.

"I keep telling Brother James that we don't need any more dogs about the place," the abbot muttered, scratching the pup behind one ear, "but they do help keep the foxes away."

"What's the matter?" Tyler asked her, seeing the worry lines on her forehead as she followed the abbot inside the cloister.

Athaya shook her head. "Nothing. I'm just tired, that's all." She gave him a convincing smile. There was no need to worry him—all she needed was a good night's rest, and then she would stop seeing things. *Especially things that weren't even there.*

If nothing else, the monks at the abbey were exceptional cooks, and Athaya was more than pleased at the supper set out before her. The mutton was moist and juicy, accompanied by onions, peas, beans, thick broth, fresh-baked bread with honey, and warm, spiced wine. The abbot and a handful of his higher-ranking brothers joined the royal party, listening to Tyler review the latest happenings at Kelwyn's court with the detached politeness of those who have long since lost interest in secular events. The captain only vaguely referred to the reasons for the princess's visit to Ath Luaine, but Athaya could tell by the monks' sidelong glances that they were well aware of the rumors of a Caithan alliance with Reyka and the tempestuous direction the arrangements had taken thus far.

When the bottles of Evarshot wine had been emptied, and the church bells tolled eleven o'clock, Tyler dismissed his men for the night and the abbot asked one of his assistants to show them to their rooms in the gatehouse. The captain and Abbot Thorne remained behind to ensure that Athaya was pleased with her room in the visitors' cloister, and once the abbot was assured that his services were no longer needed and that Tyler could find his way to his own bed in the gatehouse, he bid them good night and retired to his private quarters in the monks' dormitory.

"We should be on our way by dawn," Tyler told her. He lingered by the door to her rooms as if hoping he'd be invited inside, but knowing he would have to refuse even if he were.

"I'll be ready." She leaned forward to kiss him, but hesitated, hastily checking the corridors for spying monks. The torches set in iron sockets on the wall cast long shadows down the hall, but Athaya saw nothing. Then, in the corner of her eye, she caught a glimmer of movement against the wall farther down the hallway, as if the stones themselves were swimming from side to side. There it was again!

Now I know it's not my imagination, Athaya thought. Her breath caught in her throat and she tried not to react. Whatever the thing was, she didn't want it to know she had seen it. She turned her back on the rippling patch of space and faced Tyler, who was staring at her with his brows raised in curiosity.

"Don't look around, Tyler," she whispered in his ear. "I think someone's following us. And I think whoever it is has been behind us ever since we left Delfarham."

"But that's impossible," Tyler said worriedly. "Lieutenant Parr and the others would have seen any other riders on the road, and nobody came through the abbey gates after we arrived."

"No one we could see, anyway," she muttered. "Remember that shimmering thing I thought I saw in the pine trees this afternoon? I noticed it again when we were inside the gates. That puppy was barking at it—probably picked up the scent—but he was muddled because he couldn't see anything. I saw it again—just now."

Tyler stepped aside and glanced casually down the corridor. "Are you sure? I don't see anything."

Athaya slowly reached inside the collar of her shirt. "I have an idea," she said. "If this doesn't work, I'm as stumped as you are—but something tells me that it will . . ."

In one fluid motion, Athaya whipped off her corbal necklace and held it up close to one of the wall torches to give it light. A sharp yelp of pain echoed down the corridor, and suddenly the glimmering patch of air at the far end of the corridor began to take shape and become solid. Athaya's eyes widened as the figure came into view. It was a young man, his head topped by unruly blond hair and sporting a crisp, white-feathered cap. He huddled on the floor with his face hidden in his hands, whimpering softly. For a moment, Tyler stood rigid, stunned with disbelief, but then his soldier's instincts took over and he bolted down the corridor and grabbed the man by the shoulders, locking an arm securely around his neck.

"*You!*" Athaya shouted, her cheeks aflame with rage. Squirming under Tyler's tight grip was Jaren, the courier she'd met in the tavern two days ago. The same man who all but offered her a bed during any future travels she cared to make. She rushed toward him and snatched away the dagger from his belt, waving it threateningly in front of his face. "You wretched little—"

"Please!" he cried out, holding his hands up to shield himself from the gem. "Just put the crystal away!"

"Put it away? Not until you tell me why the hell you're following me. You *are* following me, aren't you?"

"Yes, yes, but let me explain . . ."

"Why don't you do that?" Tyler said, tightening his grip around Jaren's neck. The courier's face grew purple as he gasped for breath, although Athaya wasn't sure whether it was from Tyler's grip or the effect of the crystal.

"All right, I'll tell you everything," he pleaded, "just put away the corbal!"

With deliberate slowness, Athaya slipped the crystal into the leather pouch on her belt. The lines of pain on Jaren's face soon began to relax, and his breathing became more steady. She took the dagger—a fine, costly one, she noted, wondering who he'd stolen it from—and placed the tip of the blade underneath Jaren's tender chin and raised it up, forcing his head back.

"Now start talking," Athaya said curtly. "Or I might just tell Abbot Thorne that I've found another wizard in need of absolution."

CHAPTER 5

AT TYLER'S SUGGESTION, THEY MOVED JAREN OUT OF the corridor so as not to alarm any of the abbey's monks who might happen to pass by. Their reception at Evarshot would not continue as pleasantly if the abbot knew they had drawn a wizard into their midst, so Athaya waited while Tyler none too gently escorted Jaren inside her spartanly furnished suite and deposited him on a stool near the leaded glass windows.

Athaya set an oil lamp on the window ledge and handed the courier's weapon to Tyler for safekeeping. "Now let's hear what you have to say, Jaren. And it had better be the truth," she added, pointing to the pouch which housed the corbal.

Jaren slouched down and cupped his chin in his palms. "I was only following you because I had to talk to you," he said sullenly. "I never meant any harm."

"That's fortunate for you, my friend," Tyler said, narrowing his eyes. "Any attempt on her Highness's life will earn you a summary execution courtesy of King Kelwyn."

Jaren nodded, casting a remorseful look at the princess.

"So you know who I am?" she asked, somewhat surprised. Then, recalling their first meeting, she added, "You knew who I was the whole time and yet you propositioned me in a tavern?" *If nothing else, at least you have a lot of nerve,* she thought, holding back a grin as she caught sight of Tyler's indignant expression of jealous outrage.

Jaren averted his eyes, embarrassed. "I'm sorry about that, your Highness. I didn't exactly handle things too well that night and I never meant you to get the impression that I wanted . . ." He paused as he cast a nervous glance at the captain. "Well . . . that I wanted what you thought I did. I only came to you in the tavern because I wanted to speak with you privately and find out how receptive you would be to the idea of leaving Caithe for an extended period of time. I couldn't request a formal audience with you. In fact, I probably would have gotten myself arrested if I'd chosen that option once you found out what my business with you involved. I needed to find a way to convince you to come to Reyka with me, without going into too much detail about why. And when you made no secret of the fact that you weren't happy in Delfarham, I thought I might be able to persuade you to simply run away." Jaren let out a despondent sigh. "I guess I didn't take the right approach."

"Not really, no," Athaya said shortly. She rested her hands on her hips, leaning her weight on one leg. "And just what made you think you could convince the king's daughter to run off unescorted with a foreign courier she'd met barely an hour before?"

A heavy silence hung over the room as Jaren suddenly realized how ridiculous it all sounded from her viewpoint. He fidgeted in his seat, pointedly avoiding her gaze, and fixing his eyes instead on the leather pouch fastened to her belt. "You have to admit," he said at last, choosing his words carefully, "you're hardly typical of your kind."

Stern as she was trying to be, Athaya found it difficult to hold back a smile. *I'll grant you that much,* she thought. *And who knows? One more flagon of wine and I might have taken you up on the offer.*

"And besides," Jaren went on, "*you* didn't know that *I* knew who you were. I was just talking to you the same way I would anyone else. Not that any of this makes a difference now. Once I found out you were going to be leaving for Reyka anyway, I used a simple cloaking spell to follow you here. It makes a person invisible. Or at least it's *supposed* to," he added dryly. "I was waiting for your captain to retire so I could speak with you alone. I wanted to give you my master's message before you arrived in the capital."

"Your master?" she asked, puzzled. The only person she knew in the Reykan capital was Felgin, and she sincerely doubted that the prince would have sent a messenger to seek her out after the way she'd treated him during his visit to Caithe. But even if he had, why wouldn't he have sent a letter, instead of having Jaren sneak around Delfarham under a magical cloak of invisibility? None of it made any sense, and Athaya was beginning to suspect that the courier—if indeed he *was* a courier—was lying.

"Do you expect me to believe any of this?" Athaya asked angrily. "It's totally illogical. You came here to ask me to come to Reyka at the same time that Kelwyn orders me to go there and you want me to believe it's a mere coincidence? Who sent you to me?" she demanded. "Who are you working for?"

"Master Hedric, my Lady," Jaren said respectfully. "The High Wizard to the king."

Athaya drew back apprehensively. She did not like the sound of this at all.

"Do you know this Hedric?" Tyler asked her, clearly not believing a word that Jaren was saying, but noting Athaya's worried look of recognition.

"Not personally. He's a friend of Rhodri's, so I'm not sure I *want* to know him. Rhodri asked me to deliver a letter to him when we got to Ath Luaine."

"I am Master Hedric's personal secretary and assistant," Jaren continued. "He wanted me to bring you to Reyka to see him. Of course," he added sourly, "we had no idea at the time that Kelwyn was planning to send you right to our doorstep, or I would have saved myself the trouble—not to mention a nasty lump on my head courtesy of your tavern friends—and simply stayed at home. One of Osfonin's personal couriers could have delivered his letter to your father. But we had no way of knowing this would happen. Hedric's futures aren't always reliable."

Athaya frowned. "His futures? What are you talking about?"

"What he can see of the future," Jaren said, somewhat taken aback at finding anyone who did not understand the ways of the Lorngeld. "It's very difficult—only the best magicians can do it on a small scale, and even then, they're not always accurate. Hedric was able to see enough—in a present-time view, of course—to know he had to meet you, but he couldn't predict that you'd be coming to Ath Luaine in the near future. Oh, he had vague sensations that you might come someday, but couldn't pinpoint exactly when and he knew he had to speak with you before it was too late."

"Too late? Too late for what?"

Jaren shook his head, tight-lipped. "That is for him to explain, my Lady."

Athaya let out an impatient sigh. This conversation made no sense at all, and she could feel a fit of temper coming on. "Well, what *did* he want you to say to me?"

Jaren cast a sidelong glance at Tyler. "Your Highness, this is a somewhat delicate matter. May I talk with you alone?"

"Anything you wish to say to me, you can say in Captain Graylen's presence."

Tyler said nothing, but the smug expression on his face was speaking for him. *So there, you miserable little wizard.* He toyed with Jaren's dagger, purposefully letting the lamplight gleam on the well-honed blade.

"Very well," Jaren said, obviously displeased. "Although there are some things that Master Hedric prefers to explain to you himself, I can tell you that your meeting with him is most urgent. Hedric has been concerned with the plight of our fellow Lorngeld in your kingdom for many years and wants to speak with you about bettering their lot."

"Me? Why me?" Athaya sighed impatiently, wishing that she would simply wake up and find that Jaren's existence was all a bad dream. "Why wouldn't he want to petition Kelwyn directly? My father is already trying to relax the laws governing the Lorngeld and pressuring the Church into doing away with the rite of absolution."

"Oh? I wasn't aware of that. Hedric will be pleased to hear it."

"Listen," Athaya shouted, pounding her fist against the wall, "I don't give a damn what this fellow Hedric is pleased to hear or not. I've spent a long day on the road and I'm tired. I want to get some sleep, not stay up and listen to your cockeyed stories all night. Now you either tell me what the hell Hedric wants with me, or I might just see to it that you never get back to Ath Luaine at all."

"It is not for me to say," Jaren told her firmly, showing more fortitude than he had thus far. "Hedric made that quite clear. My only duty is to see that you come. The future of the Lorngeld in your country depends on it."

Athaya rolled her eyes in total disbelief. "Future of—listen, Jaren, the Lorngeld *have* no future; it's as simple as that. And just how did Hedric think you could persuade me to go to Reyka and listen to his insane ramblings if he wouldn't let you tell me why I was supposed to go?"

Jaren said nothing, but he wriggled in his seat with acute discomfort. Athaya suddenly realized that as a wizard, he probably had many methods at his disposal for making her follow him to Reyka, had she refused to go. Perhaps it would be best if she didn't press him too far—at least not until she had had a good night's rest and could think her situation through more clearly.

Athaya scowled at him. "It's very lucky for you that I happen to be going to Ath Luaine anyway, because I'll tell you this—if I had a choice in the matter, nothing you could say would persuade me to do it. So don't go getting all proud of yourself for succeeding in your mission, Jaren, because you didn't."

She turned to Tyler, who had been listening to their conversation in a puzzled silence. "Tyler, I want you to take our friend here to your rooms for the night and keep an eye on him. And take this with you," she said, handing him the pouch with the corbal in it. "Just to make sure he doesn't try to slip out of here. We're going to spend the rest of our journey together, Jaren," she said to the young wizard, "and I hope, for your sake, that when we get to Ath Luaine, I find that everything you've told me is true."

At her signal, Tyler led Jaren away. The young messenger followed him obediently—probably because the captain stood nearly a head taller than he did—and to her surprise, he even turned to offer her a courteous bow as he left the room. Despite her rough warning, Athaya had a feeling that Jaren would not try to run away or cause any trouble during the rest of the journey, but she would have Tyler and his men keep a close watch on him just to make sure.

Athaya slumped down on the stiff cot, weary beyond measure. She looked through her saddlebags for a packet of looca, badly in need of the tobacco's mind-calming effects. Talking to Jaren had jangled her nerves, and she needed something that would help her relax and forget.

But the more she rummaged through the pack, the more angry she became. In a matter of minutes, her belongings were scattered about the floor like so many rushes. She found her looca-pipe, but there wasn't a single shred of tobacco to put in it.

"Damn. Of all things to forget," she muttered, rudely tossing the satchel away. For a moment, she considered sneaking out to the abbey's storehouses—surely they would have an adequate supply of looca if Lorngeld were sometimes brought here—but the thought of trying to explain her presence there if she were caught gave her pause. Still, she could feel herself growing more anxious, and it would only take a small amount to fill the pipe . . .

Luckily, the decision was made for her when she spied a large flagon of Evarshot wine that the monks had left for her refreshment. Yes, that would do as well. She gulped down a generous cupful as if it had been the first liquid she'd seen after days in the desert. Once the calming effects of the wine began to take hold, she drank another cupful, refilled the goblet again, and then lay back on the cot with her eyes closed.

I knew it, she thought, rubbing her temples as if trying to ease away Jaren's memory. *I just knew this trip was going to turn into a total disaster.*

"I think we'd better stop there for the night," Tyler said, pointing a gloved hand at a small cluster of buildings huddled against the mountain foothills. "It's early yet, but we probably won't find another town until well after dark."

By the sixth day of their journey, they were almost to the seacoast road which skirted the mountains and wound its way northward to the border wall separating Caithe and Reyka. The villages were small and sparse in the distant corners of Caithe, and one took shelter wherever it could be found.

Athaya nodded. "Fine with me. I could use a few extra hours of relaxation. Maybe we could even make use of those cards and dice you brought along."

"Only if we don't play for money," Tyler said firmly. "You've wheedled far too many crowns out of my purse already."

"Coward," she teased.

They followed the thin dirt path—it could hardly be called a road—through the fields of wheat and corn, to the outskirts of the village. As they drew closer to the settlement, Athaya was struck with the sense that something was very wrong, but she couldn't exactly put her finger on what it was. Around them, carts and baskets lay unattended in the fields, and Athaya realized for the first time that it was quiet—unnaturally quiet for this time of day—and that no one was in sight.

"That's odd," Athaya said, scanning the empty fields; "there's easily two hours of daylight left, but no one's out working. Look, even the sheep and cattle have been taken in for the night."

"Is it a holiday?" Jaren asked, equally disturbed by the deserted landscape.

Tyler shook his head. "Holidays aren't allowed during harvest. There's too much work to be done." With a worried look, he added, "There could be sickness here."

"Possible," Athaya said, unconvinced. "Come on, let's find out what's going on. If no one's here, we'll have our choice of accommodations for the night." She snapped the reins and urged her horse ahead, coming to a stop where the path widened to form a street just outside the town.

"This is peculiar," she said. "Look—no one's around the well, and there's no smoke coming from the baker's chimney. Even that tavern looks closed. There's somebody out in that cemetery behind the church over there, but other than that, it's as if everything just shut down all of a sudden."

Athaya glanced over at Jaren, about to ask him his opinions, and she saw him staring straight ahead, his eyes slightly glazed, as if he were in another world entirely.

"Jaren? Are you all right?"

"They're coming this way," he said vacantly, in an eerie, monotone voice. Athaya doubted he even heard her speak. He blinked his eyes several times in rapid succession and then abruptly came out of whatever sort of trance he was in. His face was strained and pale. "There is madness here, your Highness," he whispered.

Before Athaya could speak, the sound of low, rhythmic chanting rose into the evening air. It started softly, from a distance, and then grew louder as it came closer to them. Athaya felt a prickling sensation ripple down her back, and she had a sudden, inexplicable urge to flee. Jaren, however, pushed on, leading his horse to the source of the voices, and she followed him blindly, not knowing why.

It was then that she saw the steady stream of oil lamps, carried by the villagers as they wound their way down the distant hillside and approached the town. The village itself was not large, and judging by the number of people in the procession, Athaya guessed that every man, woman, and child was taking part in whatever ceremony was taking place. Then, with a sharp intake of breath, she realized what was about to happen. She reached over and touched Jaren's arm.

"Jaren, we'd better go. You don't want to see this. We can find another place to stop for the night."

He pulled away from her roughly, ignoring Tyler's look of cautious warning. "No, your Highness," he said, his voice as firm and resolved as Athaya had ever heard it. "I'm well aware of what's happening here, and I'm staying."

Jaren rode ahead, leaving Athaya, Tyler, and the others to trail after him, while Tyler more than once complained that Jaren was certainly causing his share of problems on this trip, and he, for one, would be glad when they all reached Reyka and could be free of the young wizard's disruptive company. They followed him through a twisted street to another edge of the town and moved their horses off the road to allow the procession to pass by.

The woman was striking. Her skin was tanned to a golden brown, and she was clad in a flowing gown of lightweight white wool. Rich locks of auburn hair fell freely down her back, and her head was crowned by a garland of dried flowers tied with colored ribbons. But amid her beauty, the woman's feet were bare, bleeding from the cuts of the stones she walked on, yet she was oblivious to the pain.

In moments, Athaya knew why. The woman was glassy-eyed, lurching forward in a stupor, unaware of everything around her. When she passed directly in front of her, Athaya picked up the scent of looca-smoke clinging to the woman's clothes and hair. Looca was pleasant and relaxing in small quantities, but too heavy a dose caused blackouts and a complete numbing of the mind, and if abused for too long, a slow, decaying death. The woman in white had been given just enough to make her pliable, but she was still lucid enough to be able to walk without assistance.

In front of her, a handful of women with baskets gracefully scattered rose petals on the ground, occasionally whispering words of encouragement to her as she trudged on. The woman was flanked on either side by two young men, one with similar coloring who seemed to be her brother, and another with red-rimmed eyes, who Athaya guessed was her husband. And behind them, in a seemingly endless line, the people of the village

followed, singing strangely joyous songs and clapping their
hands in celebration, even as they wiped tears from their eyes.

Jaren latched on to the end of the procession, lingering just
behind an old woman toting a small child in each of her withered
arms. Athaya and Tyler followed after them, the captain ordering
his men to wait in the town square by the well. The men obeyed
without hesitation; intriguing as the ceremony was, they had all,
like Athaya and Tyler, seen it often enough that it had lost its
novelty.

Separated from the town by a shallow creek was the village
church, and it was here that the procession ended. The villagers
streamed inside the tiny stone structure, which was already well
lit in anticipation of their arrival. The church bells chimed mer-
rily, as if for a wedding, and Athaya found the contrast revolting.
Jaren slid off his horse and tied the reins to a wooden post, but
as he turned toward the church, Athaya also dismounted and
hurried forward to restrain him.

"Jaren, there isn't anything you can do. Please, don't go in."

"I already know I can't help her," he said, "I touched her
mind as she passed by. What she still has remaining of a mind
is in total chaos—the madness is too far advanced. I could have
helped her . . . weeks ago, perhaps. But not now."

"Then let's leave. There's no point in staying."

"No point?" he cried harshly, yanking his arm away.
"They're my people, Athaya. I care what happens to them even
if you don't." He turned on his heel and strode up the flat, stone
steps into the sanctuary, disappearing behind the weather-beaten
oak door.

Athaya was quick to follow him, leaving Tyler with the horses.
The church was already warm from the press of bodies and the
heat from the candles, and Athaya found it unpleasantly stifling.
She found Jaren leaning against the back wall near a stone pillar
with his hands folded tightly across his chest, viewing the proceedings with an expression of complete disgust.

The white-clad woman was kneeling on a cushion at the base
of the altar steps. Her chin drooped down against her chest, and
her slender arms hung limply at her sides. Before her was the
village priest, a lean, bony-fingered man with silver-gilt hair.
He was dressed in a black, cowled robe belted with white rope
and had his back to the congregation. Holding his hands aloft,
he called out the invocation.

"Almighty God," the priest began, his voice strong and over-powering in the confines of the small sanctuary, "Father of all mankind and maker of all things; you who take away the sins of the world, hear us this day as we beseech you to receive our prayers. We do earnestly confess and lament our manifold sins, which are grievous in your sight, O Lord, and beg your mercy upon us as we ask that you forgive all that is past and grant that we may serve you and please you hereafter, to the honor and glory of your holy name. Hear then, O Lord, this prayer of pardon."

The priest bowed his head and paused for a moment of silence.

"Beloved children of God," he continued, lowering his hands and turning to address the people. "We are gathered here in the sight of God to smite the Devil in his attempts to reclaim the earth for his treacherous designs. We are gathered here to proclaim God's rightful rule over this world and all her people, to proclaim our loyalty and submission to His word, and to sing our praises to Him in gladness." The priest extended his hands toward the white-robed woman.

"This child before you comes forward to denounce the Dark Angel and all of his minions by renouncing the gift given to her by Satan upon her birth, who, in his eternal evil, seeks to lure his children back to him through the temptations of magic. For as she forsakes her life, so she finds her life, and as she meets death, so shall she conquer death, and dwell in the house of the Lord forever."

And the people responded in unison, "This we beseech you, O Lord."

"Who brings forth this woman for the sacrament of absolution?" the priest asked. The red-eyed man Athaya had seen at the procession stepped forward. His hands were shaking noticeably as he placed them on the woman's shoulders.

"I do," he said, his voice breaking with tears.

"Do you freely deliver her into the care of God's holy Church, such that her soul may be cleansed and her spirit transported unto God?"

"I do."

"Then sing in joyful gladness, people of God, for on this day we honor this blessed martyr and declare her victory over Satan, now and forever."

The congregation began to sing a verse from an ancient hymn

while the black-robed priest turned to the altar. From the rear of the church, Athaya could not see what he was doing, but she did not have to see. She knew. And so did Jaren, by the look of desperate fury on his face.

When the singing was done, the priest turned to face the congregation and lifted up a silver chalice. The cup was lovingly polished and reflected the soft gleam of the candles set upon the altar like a mirror. "O Heavenly Father, bless this cup, and bless her who shall partake of it, for in so doing she partakes of your divine nature, and guide her soul to you, since she willingly chooses the path." The priest motioned the woman to stand. "Now rise, my child, and take this cup and do not wish it to pass from you, for what you do now is good in the sight of God."

The priest came slowly down the altar steps to stand directly before her. He reached out and took off her crown of flowers, setting it aside on the altar rail. Throughout the ritual, she had been silent and oblivious, staring with unblinking eyes at the altar before her, and Athaya doubted that the young woman had any idea where she was, or what was happening to her.

The priest raised the chalice to her lips. "Now drink, my child," he urged, "and defeat the Devil's grip on you."

The rim of the cup touched her lips, but just as she appeared about to drink, the woman jerked back and let out a high-pitched wail of terror, as if she'd suddenly awakened from a nightmare to find that everything in her dreams was horribly real. She stumbled backward, her eyes wild with terror, and her arms flailing helplessly as she tried to squirm out of her husband's grasp. She let out another scream, this one more hideous and pitiful than the first, and Athaya was forced to look away. Jaren, however, stared straight ahead, his eyes fixed on the gruesome scene before him as if he'd made a wager he would not look away, and was determined to win it.

"Behold!" the priest called out, his words ringing up against the stone walls. "Satan himself cries out through her! He knows he is defeated and has lost another soul to God!"

The priest quickly motioned to two of his assistants, waiting in the shadows in readiness for this sort of event, and with their added help, they managed to hold the woman down so she would not escape.

"Michael! Michael! *Make them let me go!*" she screamed,

looking around frantically for her husband. But Michael, knowing her for lost, stepped back from the altar area to seek refuge with his friends and family. He watched with vague acceptance as the priest's assistants held his wife's head rigid, and the priest himself lifted the chalice to her lips and forced her to swallow the *kahnil*-laced wine.

The congregation watched in silent expectation as her body was immediately overcome with spasms. A low, mournful moan escaped from her throat, and she fell to her knees, clutching at her abdomen in terror. Her shoulders shook violently, as if she was chilled to the bones, while frightened, hopeless tears coursed down her cheeks. Only once did she glance back at her husband, her eyes filled with confusion, unable to understand why he had done this to her. He turned away, incapable of meeting that gaze, and sank down into one of the pews, burying his face in the shoulder of a friend while his body was racked with muffled sobs.

The woman's eyes rolled back so that only the whites remained, and soon she began laboring heavily for breath. The poison was doing its work well. After only a few agonizing minutes, she gasped once, as if knowing the end had come at last, and her body went limp. The priest's assistants lowered her weight onto the floor, laying her on her back before the altar, her hands crossed over her breast. Her body twitched one last time, but then was still.

"Behold, O Lord," the priest called out. "We have acted according to your laws and delivered this woman's soul unto you, thus saving her from the temptations of Satan and the eternal fires of hell. Bestow upon her soul the blessings of life everafter and fill her with your grace and heavenly peace."

Extending his hands toward the people, he gave the benediction.

"The peace of God, which passeth beyond all human understanding, keep your hearts and minds in the knowledge of the Lord God, and may the blessings of the Father Almighty be upon you and stay with you this day and forevermore. Amen."

"Amen," the people said. And at the priest's invitation, the congregation in the sanctuary broke out into song, joyfully celebrating another victory over Satan.

Spitting out a curse, Jaren stormed out of the sanctuary, his face red with fury. Athaya followed after him, worried that he might do something reckless. She was leery enough of wizards as it was and was doubly concerned about an angry one. Once outside, Jaren snatched up the reins of his horse and led it away, taking the road that wound past the cemetery behind the church. Athaya trailed after him hesitantly, motioning Tyler to come, too.

"Look there!" Jaren shouted at Athaya, wheeling around to face her. "Do you see that? Her grave is ready and waiting. Even the headstone has already been carved! Oh, how efficient you all are about death!"

Athaya gazed across the unshorn grasses of the cemetery, beyond the rows of aged headstones to where a freshly dug grave awaited the woman's body. The evening had changed to night while they had been inside the church, and the sight of the open grave under the darkened sky made Athaya shiver with dread.

"How can you let these atrocities go on?" Jaren cried out. His hands were curled into tight, white-knuckled fists, and he shook them at her in rage. "You, of all people—a member of the royal house itself. You, one of the—" He broke off, struck speechless with anger. "Your duty is to rule and protect your people, not hunt down and *murder* them!"

"You forget yourself, Jaren," Tyler warned him, stepping forward. "As long as we are on Caithan soil, you would do well to remember to whom you are speaking and treat the princess with respect."

"*Respect?* What would any of you know about respect? None of you have any respect for life—I've clearly seen *that*! Dear God, I think Master Hedric is wrong," he raved on, clutching his head in anguish. "There is no hope here. There can't possibly be . . ."

In one furious motion, Jaren swept himself up into his saddle and urged his horse into a full gallop, heading blindly out of the village as his horse's hooves kicked up dust and stones in his wake. Tyler quickly moved to go after him, but Athaya waved him to stop.

"Let him go," she said, watching Jaren rush from the village in a frenzy, plunging into the gloomy darkness of the night. "He'll come back." Turning back toward the town, her head hung in exhausted dejection, she added, "Let's get the others and find rooms for the night."

CHAPTER 6

✳✳

A THAYA AND HER ESCORT PARTY REACHED THE SEACOAST
road the next morning. The air was fresh and scented
by salty breezes, and white sand beaches, dotted with
shells and strands of seaweed, swept up the shoreline like a
crescent moon. The cry of gulls overhead and the muffled
thumping of hoofbeats on sandy soil were all that interrupted
the rhythmic sound of white-capped waves lapping the shore.
Athaya shaded her eyes from the glare of the sun on the water.
The beauty of the scene before her was almost enough to erase
the gruesome memory of the previous evening from her mind.

Shortly before midday, Athaya saw Jaren's familiar gray-and-
white palfrey trailing about a quarter mile behind them on the
road. She asked the men to slow their pace a bit to give him a
chance to catch up, but the young wizard seemed determined to
follow behind at a distance, slowing his pace to match theirs,
avoiding their gaze by keeping his eyes focused on the ground
in front of him.

"I'm going to see how he is," Athaya said to Tyler. "Keep
up this pace for a while—we'll be right behind you." She drew
her horse aside, allowing the captain and his men to pass by,
then backtracked down the road until she was beside Jaren.

"Are you all right?" she asked. Athaya felt genuine sympathy
for him. Despite the problems Jaren had caused for her so far,

she was truly sorry that he had witnessed yesterday's ceremony at the village church and she could understand, to some extent, how desolate and helpless he must have felt.

"I'm sorry about losing my temper last night," Jaren said softly, without looking up. "I had heard stories about your custom of absolution, but I'd never actually seen it. I just wasn't ready for the brutal reality of it."

"Where have you been all night?"

He shrugged his shoulders casually. "In the loft of an old barn. I used a cloaking spell to slip inside, and the owner never knew I was there."

"That talent must come in awfully handy," she remarked. Then she furrowed her brows, suddenly realizing that with such magic at his disposal, a wizard could go almost anywhere unnoticed. With a twinge of fear, it dawned on her that Rhodri would have been able to attend any number of private council meetings to which he was not invited, and no one, with the exception of Kelwyn himself, would have ever been the wiser.

"Is it a hard spell to learn?" she asked, pushing the irritating subject of Rhodri out of her mind.

"No, not really. All you have to do, in essence, is concentrate on not being seen. Of course, the thought processes governing your concentration are important. They're an integral part of a wizard's training."

Athaya shook her head. "It's so strange to hear you talk about training the Lorngeld," she said. "With the exception of my father, I've never met anyone who would dare advocate such a thing. I was always taught—"

"Yes, I know what you've been taught," he cut in, with a look of pained exasperation. "You've been taught that the Lorngeld are a condemned race of people, who get their magic from Satan and can only save their souls by killing themselves. Sounds a bit illogical to me, if you don't mind my saying so. According to your own scriptures, suicide is a sin. But of course, it isn't really suicide, is it?" he added harshly. "Your people either think they're dying an honorable martyr's death, or are so drugged with looca-smoke that they don't realize what's happening to them."

Athaya opened her mouth to contradict him, but hastily swallowed her ill-mannered comment. After a moment's thought, she wasn't even sure she wanted to contradict him. While she did not agree with everything he said, she had to grant him a right to be heard, and one corner of her mind, she realized, wanted very much to hear what he had to say.

"And what is their crime?" Jaren went on, full of passion. "If a person comes down with the pox, do you condemn them for it? No, you send for a physician and try to cure the sickness. If you can't comprehend it any other way, think of the *mekahn* as an illness, and guiding the magic through the proper channels is the cure. Without such training, the Lorngeld die. Should you deny them a cure simply because you find their affliction distasteful?"

Athaya averted her eyes, disturbingly confused. Put in those blunt terms, Jaren made the whole of the Caithan Church seem misguided and cruel—like a brotherhood of executioners hiding beneath a cloak of piety. She wondered what her father would think of Jaren, since Kelwyn was the first monarch in nearly two centuries who did not rigidly support the Church's teachings on the Lorngeld. But then she remembered that Kelwyn had already met the young wizard, if only briefly, since Jaren was the courier who had delivered Osfonin's green-ribboned letter—the letter that had prompted this journey in the first place.

"The *mekahn* . . . I've never heard that term before," she observed.

"That's our name for the mind-plague—the madness that comes over the Lorngeld if they are not trained. Do you call it something different here?"

Athaya shrugged. "We don't call it anything at all. To be honest, I'm not entirely sure what it is. But I don't think the priests know much about it either. I'm sure Rhodri knows—and my father, perhaps—but I never thought to ask them."

"Well then, Athaya, I'll give you a short lesson," he said. His voice was clear and clipped like a tutor's, and Athaya wondered if Jaren's role as Hedric's assistant meant that he spent a good bit of his time training his fellow Lorngeld. "In the ancient Reykan language, the word *mekahn* means 'time of change.' It surfaces in early adulthood, though not at the same age for everyone—rather like adolescence in that regard—but it usually comes when a person is . . . oh, around twenty or twenty-one. Unusually poor or good health can affect the timing one way or the other, but twenty is the average. You can think of it like adolescence in a sense, but the *mekahn* signals a mental change, not a physical one. In any case, left unchecked, the *mekahn* continues for about six months, until the person afflicted either learns to channel his power, or, in the worst cases, succumbs to the madness. It's important to begin training early, while the person is still alert and lucid. If the *mekahn* is too far advanced—as it was with that woman in the village—then the mind becomes too confused and decayed and unable to comprehend and learn the things it needs to know to save itself.''

Jaren paused to give her a chance to ask questions if she wanted to, but she motioned him to go on. Even though she could not comprehend much of what he was saying, it intrigued her in a morbid sort of way.

"If you don't see the early signs, then later on the person starts having bad dreams—violent ones, usually. They often feel destructive and reckless, and a lot of them turn to drinking or inhaling looca-smoke to try and calm themselves down. It's the destructiveness that frightens people. The violence is a result of the mind's reaction to what it knows is happening to it on an unconscious level. That's probably why the priests in your country assume that magic is evil and that it comes from the Devil. When people are afflicted by the *mekahn*, they seem out of control—'possessed' by a power greater than themselves. And in one sense, I suppose that's true.''

"But what exactly is it that makes them go mad?''

"It's hard to explain exactly—especially to someone who isn't a Lorngeld—but try to think of it this way. It's as if you're hearing voices whispering to you, only you can't understand what they're saying. Early on, the voices are quiet enough that you can ignore them, but as time goes on they get louder and more frantic and start screaming at you instead of just whispering. And the untrained Lorngeld can't understand what's happening. Unless they learn to touch that part of their mind and interpret what the voices are trying to tell them, the constant, psychic clamoring drives them mad.''

Athaya shuddered. The whole idea sounded frightening and repulsive. "How can you tell if someone's got it? Or is going to get it?''

"I'm afraid there's no real way of knowing before it happens. In most cases, you can't tell whether a person is Lorngeld or not until the *mekahn* sets in. It's possible, however, in the most powerful adepts, to recognize the signs and begin early training, since their powers usually bubble up sporadically before the *mekahn* becomes too strong. They usually find themselves doing things unconsciously that it takes a trained wizard diligent practice to master. People like that are often much harder to train—it takes longer to direct their power into the proper channels—but in the end, the results are astounding. Adepts like that are extremely rare, however. Hedric was one, although he's close to seventy now and his powers are beginning to fade.''

"I take it there's no magic spell to cure that?'' she asked offhandedly.

"Not yet,'' Jaren replied with a smile. "Wizards may have a gift for magic, yes, but they age the same as everyone else. But as to the rest of your question, it's often difficult to spot the very early stages of the *mekahn*. I knew when my time was coming when I began feeling moody—happy one day, depressed the next. I had a lot of energy, but I didn't seem to want to actually go out and do anything. Of course, those kinds of feelings are common enough in people not of the Lorngeld, especially young people, so it's no small task to know the difference. But in my case, I started spending hours, sometimes days, alone in my rooms brooding about how miserable everything was. Later, I started to suffer bouts of insomnia and would wander around the manor at night without any idea of where I was going. Then, after I started breaking things, my father realized what was happening and sent me to Hedric for training.''

"Your father—is he a wizard, too?''

"No, neither of my parents are.'' Jaren noticed her frown and clarified the matter for her. "The talent for working magic has nothing to do with blood or heredity. It's not like blue eyes or blond hair or illnesses that run in families. It's a gift—like a flair for music or painting. Don't you see? You and I may both have a pair of hands, Athaya, but that doesn't mean that our inborn talent for—well, let's say playing an instrument—is the same. The tools may be identical, but not the gifts for using them. Do you understand?''

Athaya nodded, but hesitantly. "I think so.''

"I used to play the harp when I was younger,'' Jaren continued nostalgically, "but for all my practicing, I was never very good. I just don't have an ear for music. But there is a musician at Osfonin's court who can play the harp like an angel—who can move you to tears with the beauty of his music. I have hands, just as he does, but I know I could never use them to play like that. I simply don't have the gift.'' Jaren looked profoundly sad for a moment, then gave a soft, bittersweet laugh. ''But that's the tale of my life, I fear. I'm passably fair at most things, but I'm not an expert in any one of them.''

''And does that hold true for your magic as well?''

Jaren flinched, as if she'd made a move to strike him, and Athaya felt her cheeks grow hot with embarrassment. She had not meant to hurt him. She was sure that whatever else his deficiencies, magic was doubtlessly the area in which he excelled. Apparently such was not the case.

''I'm afraid so,'' he said. ''My position with Hedric stems more from the fact that my father is the Duke of Ulard than because I'm a proficient magician. My talents aren't deficient, mind you,'' he added, salvaging a bit of his pride, ''but they're just average—nothing very outstanding about them.''

''Consider yourself lucky,'' Athaya told him, turning her mouth up in a half smile. ''Besides chess, card playing, and getting into no end of trouble, I've yet to find anything that I have even *average* talents for.''

Jaren laughed aloud, and the traces of sadness on his face vanished. ''Come now, I can't believe that. I've never met a princess yet who wasn't unbelievably good at something.''

''There's a first time for everything, Jaren,'' she remarked lightly. ''My lack of proper accomplishments has been a source of friction between my father and me ever since I can remember. And Dagara only encourages it. Sometimes I think she goes out of her way to convince him I'm worse than I really am.''

''The proverbial evil stepmother, I take it?''

''The original mold. And she's spread her venom to my older brother, too, who actually used to like me until she told him that it was quite improper for him to do so. My other brother, Nicolas, can't stand either one of them, so we tend to keep close company and bemoan our respective fates. But why am I telling you all of this? You probably know more about me than *I* do.''

''I doubt that, Athaya,'' Jaren said with sudden solemnity. ''But I think I understand you—at least a little.'' He gazed at her more intensely than he had ever done before, and the world suddenly seemed to fall silent, except for the sharp crying of the gulls. ''You're not very happy being the daughter of a king, are you?''

She gave a thin, dismissing laugh. "What do you mean by that?"

"Are you?" he repeated gently, not taking his eyes off her.

Athaya said nothing at first and turned her eyes toward the sea, watching the waves calmly wash the shore. Then she looked ahead at the uniformed guardsmen riding a short distance in front of them, and at their captain, who had his face turned toward the breeze, letting the sun warm his skin and the winds ripple through his golden hair.

"No," she murmured finally. "No, I don't suppose I am."

"I think I know how you feel about him," he said, gesturing ahead at Tyler. "I saw the way you looked at him in the corridor at Evarshot, when you thought no one else was around. You're in love with him."

Athaya looked up sharply. She had been so distracted by Jaren's sudden appearance at the abbey that she'd completely forgotten what he'd seen.

"You needn't worry about me," Jaren told her, picking up the train of her thoughts. "I'm not about to make any further trouble for you. But it might soothe Prince Felgin's ego a bit to hear that you weren't enthusiastic about marrying him because you loved somebody else rather than because you hated him personally."

Athaya drew in a quick, gasping breath. "Jaren, promise you won't say a word about this to anyone. And not to Felgin, either. I can't have this getting back to my father. There's no telling what he'd do. He's quite fond of Tyler as a guardsman, you understand, but not as a prospective son-in-law."

"I won't say anything," he assured her. "But I think *you* should. Felgin isn't as bad as you think, Athaya. In fact, he's trustworthy and loyal and quite a good friend of mine. He can be a bit of a scoundrel sometimes, but all in all, he's respectable enough. If you told him you were in love with someone else and asked him to keep that information confidential, I have no doubt that he would."

Athaya thought back to the prince's six-week stay at Delfar Castle in early summer. Despite Tyler's claims to the contrary, she had found Felgin conceited and condescending, and unless he was an exceptional actor, not at all the type of man Jaren was describing. "Somehow I never got such a good impression of him," she muttered.

"From what I heard, you didn't give him much of a chance," Jaren scolded good-naturedly. "He may be a prince, but Felgin's ego bruises easily and he was more than a little hurt by your cold reception."

Athaya let out a single, harsh laugh. "I find that very hard to believe." Then, with a curious, sidelong glance at Jaren, she added, "Did Felgin tell you that?"

"Not at first. In the beginning, he was all full of bluster, telling everyone how insulting you were so he could get their sympathy. It worked, too, by the way," Jaren added dryly. "But later, after he and I sat down alone together and had a few rather large mugs of ale, he told me that he thought you were beautiful and intriguing and wished that you would have liked him better. At times, he almost made it sound as if it was *his* fault that you two didn't get along. But he'll never admit that publicly. In fact, I think he even regretted confiding in me the next morning— once he'd sobered up a bit. If he knew I was telling you this, he'd probably have my head."

Athaya squeezed her eyes shut, as if sensing an approaching headache. "Wonderful," she moaned. "I didn't think it was possible, but now I feel even worse about all this than I did before. Now I *really* don't want to see him again."

"Oh, he won't be too hard on you," Jaren said with a smile. "Neither will the king, I'll wager. Osfonin knows his son too well to believe everything he says, including all of his complaints about you."

Athaya sighed heavily, wishing that she could simply erase the prince's visit from history and start again. "It wasn't so much that I disliked Felgin personally—although I did find him unbelievably pompous at times—but I probably would have reacted that way to anyone showing an interest in marrying me."

"Except Tyler, I take it?"

"Except Tyler," she said with a wistful smile. The smile was short-lived, however, and quickly changed to an expression of futility and pain. "I just wish I wasn't in such an awkward position. I sit alone for hours sometimes, wondering why I couldn't have been born into a family without any money or titles, so I could simply marry who I want to and live the way I want to, without being burdened with responsibilities and duties that I never even asked for and certainly don't want."

Jaren regarded her with profound seriousness. "It's always

difficult to try and fight against one's duty, Athaya. But some people are born to it and some aren't. That's the way of things."

"Now you're starting to sound like Tyler," she said with a scowl.

"I'm sorry. This must be a sore point between you. But I'm sure you're not the only one who resents the life that's been thrust upon you. I'm sure there are a fair amount of peasants in the fields who don't much like being poor and I'll bet there are a good number of young men being trained for military service who'd much rather spend their time reading books or writing silly poems to their sweethearts. And the same holds true for the nobility—even the royal house. Think of your own family, Athaya. Are you so certain that your father truly *wanted* to be a king, instead of doing it because it was his duty?"

"I'm not sure," she said, surprised that she'd never considered that possibility before. "He's my own father, but it amazes me sometimes how little I really know him."

"It's often the case, Athaya, that the extent to which you know those around you reflects the extent to which you know yourself."

Athaya opened her mouth to speak, but said nothing. Jaren's remark disturbed her more than she cared to admit. The idea of peering into her own soul frightened her. She was too afraid of finding out something about herself that she did not want to know.

Jaren was silent for a long time. He listened to the gulls and the relaxing rhythm of the waves and breathed deeply of the tangy sea air, while Athaya rode quietly at his side, immersed in thought.

"Your talk of Kelwyn reminds me of something," he said at last. "I should compliment you on catching me completely off guard back at the abbey, which, incidentally, isn't always quite so easy to do as you made it seem. I never expected that you would feel the need to carry a corbal crystal with you in light of the fact that your own father is one of my people."

"He most certainly is *not*," she replied indignantly. "No Trelane has ever carried the tainted blood of the Lorngeld." The moment the words escaped her lips, she flushed crimson, realizing the extent to which she had unintentionally insulted him.

He gave her a reassuring smile. "That's all right. Old prejudices are hard to break. But as I told you before, it doesn't have anything to do with blood.''

"Well, whatever it is, Kelwyn doesn't have it,'' she declared. "Corbal crystals never bother him. Archbishop Ventan has a ring of tiny corbals that he wears all the time, and my father has never said a word about it. And besides, he's almost fifty years old and he never went through the *mekahn*, so how can he possibly be a Lorngeld?''

Jaren frowned, at a loss for an answer.

"Kelwyn wasn't born with his powers,'' Athaya explained matter-of-factly. "They were given to him by Rhodri—a friend of Hedric's.''

Instantly, Athaya knew she had said something wrong. Jaren's face turned white, and Athaya saw him waver in the saddle, as if struck by a ringing blow on the head. His hands gripped the reins with sheer desperation, and his lower lip was trembling. He opened his mouth to speak, but nothing came.

"Jaren, what's the matter? Are you ill?''

"Are you sure about this?'' he choked out, his voice breaking.

Athaya shook her head, utterly bewildered. "Only if what I was told is true. It was some sort of ritual. I don't know much about it—it took place before I was even born. Why? What's the matter?''

Jaren laid a palm over his eyes, so wrapped up in his own thoughts that he seemed to forget she was there. He looked frighteningly pale, as if he were about to faint. "Dear God, it's worse than you thought, Hedric,'' he mumbled to himself, burying his face in his palms. "It's worse than any of us thought.''

"What's wrong?'' Athaya urged him, unnerved by his reaction. "Please tell me.''

But despite her pleas and one petulant royal command—issued before she realized that as a Reykan citizen he was not obliged to obey her—Jaren would tell her nothing. He was unnaturally silent for the rest of the day, speaking only when necessary, and even then, only in curt, monosyllabic responses. Athaya could not persuade him to come with her when she quickened her pace to join the rest of the riding party, so she left him trailing along behind to work through whatever problem was tormenting her.

"How's he doing?'' Tyler asked her, when she rode ahead

and caught up with him. He turned around and gave Jaren a cursory glance just to assure himself that the wizard was staying out of trouble.

"You mean about last night?" she said vacantly, staring straight ahead. "Oh, the absolution ceremony gave him a bad shock, but I think he'll be all right." She did not add that he was now even more upset by a new, more harrowing development. A problem that did not involve a poor peasant woman in an obscure little village, but was centered around the king of Caithe himself.

CHAPTER 7

✸

TOWARD THE END OF THEIR LAST DAY OF TRAVEL, ATHAYA was so anxious that she could barely eat a bite. Sensing her discomfort, Jaren chatted with her, trying to calm her down and to persuade her that she had nothing to fear from Osfonin. It worked to some extent—she'd been able to choke down a large slab of cheese by midday—and so he continued with his banter, pointing out landmarks as they rode past them, and telling her a bit of history about the towns they stopped in. Athaya was grateful for his attention. Jaren had become much more animated once they had crossed the border into Reyka, and while he occasionally slipped into long periods of silent brooding, Athaya did not think he looked as tormented as he had after their conversation on the seacoast road and assumed he had discovered a solution to whatever was troubling him.

As the pastel colors in the sky announced the approaching sunset, Tyler reined his horse in beside her. "Jaren says we'll be in Ath Luaine in another hour or so."

Athaya nodded reluctantly, conscious of the hollow feeling in the pit of her stomach.

"You'll do fine," he offered, giving her one of those smiles that warmed her so. "Osfonin's a fool if he drives someone as pretty as you from his court. I'll tell him so myself."

"Promise?"

"Promise. Just as long as I can say it from an open doorway with my sword drawn," he added wryly.

Athaya laughed aloud, comforted at knowing that whatever happened, Tyler would always be there for her. Sometimes it was just a word or a look, but Athaya was constantly amazed by his uncanny way of knowing exactly how to cheer her during the bad times. *Of course,* she admitted inwardly, *I've certainly been through enough of them to give him plenty of practice.*

They reached the outskirts of the city as sunset was at its peak, and the multicolored sky gave added beauty to an already lovely city. Ath Luaine was tucked into a valley between a range of majestic crags covered with high, golden grasses, now purplish in the evening light. The slate-tiled roofs peppering the city landscape gleamed softly under the dying sun, and Athaya could hear the soothing bells of the cathedral echoing through the hills. The entire scene was spectacularly dominated by the series of whitewashed, crenellated towers of the castle, and Athaya could see the standard of the royal house of Ben-Astri fluttering in the gentle breeze high atop the tallest peak.

Once inside the city walls, Jaren led them through the confused mass of winding streets, slowly heading up a steep hill toward the main gates of Glendol Palace. Neat, timber-framed homes lined the road on each side, their jetties leaning forward as if whispering secrets to one another across the cobbles. The shops were still open, and the streets were clogged with people bickering over the price of potatoes and turnips and trying to wheedle last-minute bargains out of the store owners before closing time. Athaya found it odd that while the cityfolk took notice of the rare sight of Caithan soldiers in their capital, they did not appear to be much amazed by it. Fingers pointed and whispers flitted through the crowds, but only a handful of people interrupted their business to watch Athaya's small procession pass by, and more often than not, she thought with a touch of injured pride, the people seemed to be paying more attention to Jaren than they were to her.

I suppose I haven't lost all of my desire for notoriety, she mused.

The road ended before the massive palace gatehouse, taller and more intimidating than the one at Delfar, with a gold-rimmed, enameled plaque over the gates proudly displaying the king's coat of arms: *sixteen eaglets, azure, between a cross gules, on a field argent.* It was a more inviting crest than that of the Trelane family. The eaglets' wings were raised in a gesture of welcome, not like the imposing black lions back home, and for a moment at least, Athaya felt less trepidation than she had before.

Blue-cloaked sentries with crisp white surcoats snapped to attention as Jaren directed Athaya into the palace courtyard, and the moment they were inside, a handful of stableboys and servants hurried out to take the reins of the horses and carry the saddlepacks and satchels for the arriving guests. They bowed respectfully to Jaren as they passed by, and Athaya had to hold back a look of surprise, so accustomed was she to regarding the young man as a troublesome courier and not the son of a foreign duke.

The courtyard was nearly deserted, and judging from the sounds of laughter and conversation drifting across from the Great Hall and the faint scent of roast venison lingering in the air, Athaya guessed that they had arrived during the evening meal. She felt immensely relieved. With the king occupied at supper, it was likely that her meeting with him would be delayed until tomorrow. That would give her time to bathe and change, and more importantly, try to think of what to say to Osfonin.

Then she saw a solitary figure strutting casually across the yard, and her stomach wound itself into a tight knot. The haughty, swaggering gait was disturbingly familiar, and the dark, bearded face all too memorable. He strode directly toward them, wearing a costly fur-trimmed mantle accented by an elegantly simple gold collar. His brown eyes gleamed with self-assuredness as he assessed every member of Athaya's party, stopping to rest a lazy moment longer on the princess herself.

"Jaren, welcome back," Felgin said, offering the young wizard a friendly pat on the back. "Hedric's been fussing ever since you left—swears he can't find anything without you."

"Don't believe a word of it," Jaren replied, laughing softly. "He only says that to make me feel useful."

Felgin gestured to his guests. "I take it that the Caithan delegation has arrived?"

"Yes, your Highness. I'm sure you remember—"

"Introductions are hardly necessary, Jaren. I remember Captain Graylen distinctly. His skill with a sword impressed me when I observed him drilling Kelwyn's young recruits last June.

And as for the princess,'' he added with a low-pitched, almost ominous laugh, ''she and I are already quite well acquainted.''

Athaya felt her face grow hot, but the prince spoke again before she could think of anything appropriate to say.

''You've come right on time, my friends. Supper is just being served. If you'll all follow me, I'll take you in and present you to the king.'' Felgin courteously extended his hand to Athaya, and after a moment of embarrassed hesitation, she took it, not knowing what else she could possibly do. ''Come, my Lady,'' he said, leading her toward the Great Hall with a renegade twinkle in his eye, ''my father and I are most anxious to repay your recent hospitality.''

Stepping inside the Great Hall at Glendol was like stepping back a century in time. It was rustic and ancient and had probably been the primary residence of the Reykan royal family long before the plans for Delfar Castle in Caithe had ever been drawn up. The atmosphere here felt steeped in inexpressible tradition. The trestle tables were strewn with flowers, not the expensive white linen that Athaya was accustomed to, and the tabletops were covered with hundreds of fat, white candles. The room was unusually bright, however, more so than Athaya would have thought possible by mere candles, and then she noticed a cluster of palm-sized red balls hovering in a circular pattern above the center of the room. The strange lights let off a bright, reddish glow that mingled with the golden gleam of the candles, like the colors in an autumn sunset.

Or the glow from the fires of hell, Athaya thought, knowing the lights must be some sort of magical creation.

Tyler and his guardsmen were directed to a table in the rear of the Hall by the castle steward, and Athaya gave him a desperate look of farewell as Felgin led her away toward the royal dais. Knowing that Jaren was only a few steps behind her gave little comfort, and although she knew she should be thinking of something more useful, the only thought running through her mind was that she had not been given time to change out of her riding clothes and was to greet the king of Reyka clad in dusty leather leggings, with her hair windblown and tangled. And even though Tyler often told her that she looked just as lovely in Nicolas's outgrown clothes as she did in her own fine gowns, he was not

the one she had to worry about impressing at the moment—
Osfonin might not be so accommodating.

In the center of the dais was a burly, muscular man clad in a
blue velvet overgown trimmed with marten's fur. He reclined
against a carved oak chair, laughing heartily at the conversation
of the fair-skinned woman, also in blue, sitting on his right. The
king and queen both wore thin gold coronets studded with sapphires and spoke to each other with a mixture of words and
gestures that revealed a long and intimate acquaintance. To their
left sat an aging, white-haired man in a striking robe of emerald
green, whose crooked cherrywood staff leaned casually against
the wall behind him. *That's got to be Rhodri's friend, Hedric,*
Athaya thought, seeing Jaren skirt around the edge of the table
and whisper something in the old man's ear. The old man stared
at her without blinking, as if amazed to see that she could walk
without assistance, and Athaya felt the heat of his gaze upon her
as Felgin brought her to the foot of the low steps in front of the
dais.

When the king caught sight of her, he immediately broke off
speaking to his wife. His former good humor vanished from his
face. He glared at Athaya through dark, probing eyes, and the
muscles in his face were taut and rigid. Thick fingers tapped
rhythmically on the tabletop, letting the ruby signet ring on his
left hand sparkle in the candlelight. He did not look at all surprised to see her.

"Father, I would like to introduce to you Princess Athaya
Trelane of Caithe," Felgin announced. "Princess Athaya, I
present his Majesty, Osfonin of Reyka."

Osfonin judged her with the intense, confident silence of a
man well aware of his power to intimidate others. With calcu-
lated slowness, he pressed his palms on the table and drew himself up and strolled step by step away from his chair and around
the edge of the table. His large hands were clasped behind him
as he walked, the fingers slowly lacing together and drawing
apart. He came down the dais steps and stopped barely a foot
in front of her.

"So. You are Kelwyn's daughter," he said in a rich, baritone
voice that filled the tense silence in the hall.

"I am, your Majesty," she said, inclining her head to him.
Had she been wearing a gown, she might have curtsied, but

because she was clad in old riding clothes, she thought that such a gesture would be ridiculously inconsistent. "I bring—"

"Kelwyn's ill-mannered daughter, from what I've heard," he continued harshly. His thick brows furrowed until they formed a single, bushy line across his forehead.

Athaya balked, but only momentarily. She had expected a reaction like this. "Yes, your Majesty," she said. She could feel her muscles trembling, much as she commanded them not to, and she felt feverish from the sudden heat. Osfonin did not look away and studied her intensely with angry eyes. In childish desperation, she wished that she could be anywhere on earth except where she was at that moment, but then it struck her that those were the same sentiments she frequently expressed while brooding in her rooms at Delfar. What was it about royal palaces that made her consistently anxious to get out of them, when ambitious young men and women in every kingdom spent the better part of their lives hoping they'd be allowed in?

"You are the young lady whom Kelwyn suggested that my son take as a wife, in order to form an alliance between our two lands?"

"Yes, your Majesty," she said again, increasingly wary.

Osfonin pointed an accusing finger in her face. "And you are the same young lady who made a mockery of my son, the Crown Prince of Reyka, and thus insulted me by doing so? You are the young lady who treated him without due respect or courtesy? Who baited him and argued with him and showed him no hospitality in your own home?"

"Only when he deserved to be treated so, your Majesty," she replied unflinchingly, tilting her chin up. "Which, I might add, was most of the time." She cast a sidelong glance up at Felgin, who disengaged her arm from his with subtle dispatch.

The king's eyes flashed, and he drew himself up sharply as if to reach for a weapon. Athaya stood firm, meeting his eyes with stubborn resolve. If Osfonin was going to hate her anyway, then she preferred that he at least hate her for being rude and disrespectful instead of meek and cowardly. Although she could not see where Tyler was sitting, Athaya could feel his presence in the back of the hall and knew he would, at this moment, be burying his face in his hands with his eyes closed in futile resignation, wondering when she would ever learn to keep her opinions to herself.

Then, with a complete change of expression, Osfonin slapped his palm on his thigh and leaned back to send a hearty peal of laughter ringing up to the rafters of the hall. His formerly angry eyes were bright and merry, and his face flushed red with good cheer.

"Well said, Princess Athaya," he said amid his chuckles. He shook a finger at his son. "Ah, Felgin, you are indeed a rascal. I suspected that you deserved at least some of the punishment she gave you."

Osfonin laughed again, a strong laugh from deep inside, and even Prince Felgin tilted his mouth up into a half grin.

"You are brave, Athaya," the king went on. "And, I believe, as outspoken as Felgin described you. I like that. Only cowards and fools waste their time peppering their opinions with so many platitudes and compliments that it's nearly impossible to know *what* they think. If, indeed, they think anything at all." He stepped back and retrieved his silver goblet of mead from the table and said, "Let me formally welcome you to my court, Princess Athaya. I hope your stay with us shall be a long and happy one."

With these words of acceptance, the queen and the other nobles gathered in the Hall relaxed into an attitude of welcome. The king drank to her, and following his lead, everyone in the spacious hall lifted their cups to her also.

Athaya was relieved, but not quite as much as she thought she should be. She had not expected Osfonin's quick forgiveness, and it gave her the strong impression that the Reykan king knew something she didn't and could therefore afford to be gracious. And although she hated to ruin the pleasant reception she was enjoying at the palace, she had come to Reyka for only one purpose, and as Tyler would have said, had to see her duty done.

"I've come to deliver a letter from my father," Athaya said, trying to keep the anxiety out of her voice.

Osfonin gave a dismissing wave of his hand. "Yes, yes. I expected that Kelwyn would be sending a reply to my letter. And I will give it the attention it deserves. But I have had a long day's hunting and have worked up a voracious appetite. I never do business on an empty stomach," he added, patting a slightly bulging stomach, "as you can well see."

The king clapped his hands, and the servants quickly filed out of the hall toward the kitchens to fetch the first course of the meal. Osfonin motioned to the end of the dais, where Hedric sat with his young assistant. "Jaren told us you would be arriving tonight, and so we have prepared the finest meal that Reyka could offer you."

Athaya threw Jaren a puzzled look. In all the time they had traveled together, she had not seen him write a letter, or hire a courier to ride ahead to Ath Luaine ahead of them. "Jaren told you?"

"Yes, about two days ago," Osfonin said casually. "He sent us word with his sphere."

She nodded her head in mute acceptance. *I'm not even going to ask about that one.*

Felgin led her around the dais to an empty seat beside the queen, then went to the far end of the table to join Hedric and Jaren, with whom he immediately engaged in hushed conversation.

"Good evening, Athaya, and welcome to Ath Luaine," the queen said, inclining her crowned head to her. "I am Ysell, and this is Felgin's sister, Princess Katya." She motioned to the woman next to her—a red-haired beauty who looked a few years younger than Athaya, but whose pale blue eyes sparkled with the mischief and boundless energy of a child.

They all exchanged polite greetings, and Athaya answered the usual questions about the conditions of the roads and the weather during her journey. The queen seemed interested in all of her responses, no matter how unexciting they were, and the kind attention quickly made Athaya feel like an old friend who has merely been away for a while, instead of a stranger newly arrived at a foreign court.

A few minutes later, when Ysell had turned away to speak to the king, Katya leaned close to Athaya as if to tell a secret. "Felgin tells me you have brothers," the red-haired girl remarked. "Do you like them?"

Athaya was taken aback by her guileless candor and couldn't help laughing aloud. "Which one of them?" she asked.

Katya smiled knowingly. "Mmm, so it's like that, is it? I think brothers are wretched most of the time, don't you? I have two, but I like my sisters much better. Do you have any sisters?"

"No, just two brothers. Nicolas I love—he's funny and charming and never treats anything with more seriousness than it deserves. My oldest brother Durek . . . well, he's rather stodgy and narrow-minded."

"I know the type. So wrapped up with knowing he's going to be king one day that he forgets how to be a human being. Felgin used to be that way, but he's getting better." Katya motioned to a servant to come and fill Athaya's cup of mead. "Well then, if you have no sisters of your own, I'd be delighted if you'd think of me as your sister. Who knows? Someday you just might be."

"Perhaps," Athaya said, not wishing to talk at length on that subject. She was not sure what to think or feel about her situation with Felgin at the moment, having been caught off guard by Osfonin's good humor and now Katya's open friendship, and she looked forward to the time when she would be alone in her rooms and could think everything through more clearly—if she could stay awake that long, of course. Already the sweet, honeyed wine was making her drowsy.

"Frankly, the more Felgin went on about how rude you were, the more I knew I was going to like you," Katya said dryly, as she glanced quickly down the table to where her brother sat engaged in conversation with Jaren and Hedric. "That one needs to be knocked down a few pegs. He gets too full of himself sometimes, prince or no prince."

"I heard that, Katya," Ysell said. The queen turned around and looked scoldingly at her daughter through thick, brown lashes.

Felgin's sister let out a small puff of a sigh. "Oh, Mother, you know it's true."

"Ah, but that does not mean you need to reveal all our faults to our guest," Ysell said, her lips curling up in amusement. "She will think us a very bad-natured family indeed and may set out for home again before she's even had her dessert."

Athaya was more than impressed by the rest of the meal, dessert included. She'd eaten next to nothing that day, so worried had she been about her reception at the palace, and she sampled every dish set before her. Her plate was filled time and time again with roast venison and mutton, partridge and goose, salted herring, an abundance of vegetables, and exotic varieties of sweets that she had never tasted before. From time to time she glanced at Tyler, sitting in the rear of the hall with his men, laughing and telling tales with the off-duty palace sentries, already at home among their Reykan brothers-in-arms.

When the sweet trays were emptied, Osfonin, who could now have anything except an empty stomach, was ready to attend to business.

"If you'll come with me, Athaya, we shall retire to my audience chamber and I will read this letter you have brought me. I know it is late and that you must be tired, so I will not keep you long."

Athaya went to fetch the letters from Tyler and, taking the captain's wishes of good luck with her, followed the king through a curtained doorway behind the dais and into a cozy, well-lit chamber. The walls were decorated with symmetrical arrangements of swords and daggers, and the gleaming steel glowed softly in the candlelight. Osfonin sat in a high-backed oak chair near the fireplace, and behind him, resting on his cherrywood staff, was the green-robed old man she had seen Jaren whispering to earlier. His eyes never left her, as if he were a physician studying the color of her skin for signs of illness. Athaya sat down on a cushioned bench across from them, clutching the scrolls of parchment tightly in her hand.

"Jaren may have told you about my wizard, Hedric," Osfonin said respectfully, gesturing to the old man in flowing green robes. The wizard folded his gnarled hands in front of him and bowed as low as he was able.

"I am honored to finally meet you, Princess," Hedric said. Athaya was surprised by the youthful clarity of his voice—not trembling or broken, but strong and confident. "I have been seeking you out for quite some time."

Athaya smiled by reflex only—she had no idea what Hedric was talking about. When Jaren had first told her that Hedric wished to speak with her, she couldn't imagine why, but now she suspected that it involved Kelwyn, and the way he had assumed his magic power. Jaren had certainly reacted violently to that piece of information. But Athaya had no time to worry about that now, especially since it was probably just a simple misunderstanding. With communications between the two kingdoms being almost nonexistent until very recently, it would not be at all surprising if much of what the Reykans thought of Caithe, and its king, was based on wild rumor and hearsay.

She handed the sealed letter to Osfonin. "Before you read this, let me apologize for it in advance. I suspect Kelwyn only wrote that letter to force me to come here and humble myself in front of you. In one respect, he was right. I did act unforgivably rude to your son, not so much from anything he did, but because I knew it would annoy my family. I . . . wasn't very fond of the idea of getting married, I'm afraid.''

"Many young people are not," Osfonin observed, "but few get little say in the matter. Ysell found the situation equally distasteful when her parents suggested she marry me." The king chuckled softly to himself. "But things changed. As I'm sure they would with you and my son. Felgin can be boorish and insufferably conceited at times—traits that my wife will gladly tell you he inherited from me—but he will be a good king when his day comes. Perhaps an even better one than I am, because of his talent for magic," Osfonin added, unable to suppress a touch of paternal pride. Then he went on more seriously. "From what Hedric tells me about your religion in Caithe, I can understand your reluctance to marry one of the Lorngeld.''

Athaya felt her cheeks grow pink. She would have preferred to avoid that delicate topic, especially in the presence of a powerful wizard like Hedric. She had no desire mistakenly to offend someone whose powers she had no knowledge of, and who might have the ability to send her back to Caithe in a substantially different form from the one in which she had arrived.

"You needn't say a word, Princess Athaya," the king said, sensing her discomfort. "I do not condemn you for your feelings. But I fear they stem more from ignorance than otherwise, and during your stay with us, I will do my best to persuade you that you are misinformed.''

As the king broke the letter's seal and began to read, Athaya stood up and handed the second scroll to the green-robed wizard. "I have another letter, too. For you, Master Hedric.''

The wizard's thick, white eyebrows went up slightly as he took the proffered scroll. He retreated to a far corner of the room, his robes rustling softly like leaves in a gentle summer breeze, and pored through the letter with his back turned to Osfonin and Athaya. Then, after several minutes of heavy silence, Athaya saw him draw himself up and methodically crush the letter into a ball with his slender fingers. He snapped the fingers of his other hand to summon a reddish globe of fire—a globe like those she had seen lighting the Great Hall—then placed the letter in his fiery palm and watched it slowly burn to ashes.

"Who writes to you from Caithe?" Osfonin asked lightly,

setting Kelwyn's letter aside. "Not a friend, I hope, from the way you treat his letters."

"An old pupil of mine named Rhodri," Hedric said softly, his shoulders sloping down from some unseen weight. He wiped the ashes from his palm and curled into a low-backed cushioned chair, his face expressing a mixture of sadness and simmering outrage. "Perhaps you remember him."

Osfonin nodded somberly. "Ah, yes." The king said nothing more.

Leaving Hedric alone with his thoughts, Osfonin pointed to Kelwyn's letter. "Your father seems rather upset with me," he remarked, without any malice or offense.

"May I speak plainly, your Majesty?"

"From what I've heard of you, Princess," he said with a gleam in his eye, "that is something that you are long accustomed to doing."

Athaya laughed softly. She liked the Reykan king more than she'd ever expected to. "I don't think my father is upset with you at all. I think he's upset with me for ruining his plans. I can assure you that Kelwyn is sincerely interested in forming a friendship with you and your people and that any anger you sense in his letter was probably meant for me and simply misdirected at you."

"Perhaps," Osfonin said. "But before you offer any more of your own explanations, let me tell you what I think. My contact with the Caithans has been limited over the years, but I do know that ever since the time of King Faltil, Caithe has been without any centralized control. For nearly two centuries, your noble houses have been squabbling among themselves and dividing the country into their own petty kingdoms. Kelwyn has devoted himself to reuniting the provinces and now that he's finally succeeded, he wants me to know that Caithe is finally a force to be reckoned with. Am I right?"

Athaya was genuinely surprised. Osfonin was as well versed in the goings-on in Caithe as she was herself, if not more so. "That may be so, your Majesty, but please don't interpret it as a threat. I don't think that's what my father intends."

"No, I don't believe he does. Although there are others who wish he would threaten me a bit, aren't there?"

Athaya averted her eyes. So he knew about that, too. "Yes. My father has been under constant pressure by his bishops—and by my brother Durek when he dares to suggest it—to launch a crusade against Reyka for allowing the training of Lorngeld.''

Osfonin shook his head with dismay. ''I'll never understand why your priests think that wizards are somehow barred from heaven. Why? The power that they have can be nothing else than a gift from God—a mark of divine favor.''

The idea was so different from what she knew, yet so simple and logical and strongly believed, that Athaya found she could say nothing to refute him.

''You may be surprised to hear this, but we in Reyka have been concerned about Caithe for quite some time. Not so much politically,'' he pointed out. ''I must admit that it is somewhat relaxing to have my neighbors warring among themselves. It assures me that they will have no time to plot against me.''

Athaya couldn't help laughing at the king's casual logic, and Osfonin was pleased that she was not offended by his remarks.

''We are more interested in the issue of the Lorngeld in your country,'' he went on. ''You don't realize how much it distresses us to know that those with the God-given power of magic are being systematically executed. I know, I know,'' he said, seeing her about to contradict him, ''you call it absolution. But that is not how we view it here. I may not be of the Lorngeld myself, but Felgin is, and so is my great friend Hedric. I am sympathetic to the needs of their brethren in your country. I shall send a letter back with you saying that very thing to Kelwyn.''

''He will be glad. My father does not hold with the Church's beliefs on the issue of the Lorngeld and is already trying to do away with the idea of absolution. He would welcome your support.''

''Assuming he's not still angry with me for telling him that Felgin refused to marry you. But I have learned much since I wrote that letter,'' he added obliquely, gazing first at Hedric, who remained in pensive silence in the corner, and then looking squarely at her. ''Perhaps Kelwyn and I can discuss this marriage again.''

Athaya felt a sickly feeling in the pit of her stomach. Without intending to, all she seemed to have done was unearth yet another reason why Caithe and Reyka should be allies, making it even more likely that she would be pressured into a marriage she didn't want. She was fumbling for something she could say to put the idea of a marriage out of Osfonin's head—wouldn't a written treaty suffice?—but just then there was a sharp rap on the door, and Prince Felgin stepped quietly into the room.

"With your leave, Father, I'd like to have a word with the princess when you've finished."

Osfonin nodded. "Certainly. Our business here is done for now." The king got up and placed Kelwyn's letter into a walnut box on the mantel. Then he crossed the room and set a hand on Hedric's tired shoulder. "Come on, you old wizard, and stop that sulking. Tell me about Rhodri's letter as we walk to my rooms."

Hedric got up to follow him, then turned back. Athaya didn't know whether it was Rhodri's letter or some other worry, but he gazed at her with acute concern. "I must speak with you at length tomorrow, your Highness," he said. There was a marked degree of urgency in his voice. "There is much we need to discuss about the Lorngeld in your country. And about you in particular," he added solemnly.

Athaya suddenly wished she had an excuse—any excuse—for avoiding this meeting, but she had not been in the palace long enough to have made other plans. "Well, I—"

"Please. I would not ask if it were unimportant. I . . . don't wish to alarm you," he added carefully, "but it is truly a matter of life or death."

Whose? she asked inwardly, but did not voice the question for fear the wizard might answer it. "All right," she told him politely. "I shall be at your convenience."

Nodding, Hedric turned away slowly, as if reluctant to leave her unattended. Offering a few words of farewell, the king guided him out of the chamber, and Athaya was left alone with Felgin. They had never been alone together, not even during his visit to Delfarham, and Athaya could not imagine why he sought her out now. Perhaps he was not exactly sure himself, since an uncomfortable silence hung in the air between them for several moments before the prince spoke.

"I think it's time we made peace between us," Felgin said at last, sitting stiffly in the chair his father had vacated. He shuffled his boots distractedly on the carpet, and the polished black leather reflected the light from the fire like a dark mirror. "Actually," he added, relaxing his shoulders, "it was Katya who suggested that I speak to you. I'm afraid that, despite her youth, she has much more good sense than I do."

Felgin ran his fingers through thick, dark hair in a gesture that made him seem charmingly unsure of himself. At that moment, Athaya saw a glimpse of the Felgin that Jaren had described to her, and it was a surprising contrast. This was certainly not the same brash young man who had swaggered his way through the halls of Delfar Castle looking down his nose at everyone, and whom she had haughtily ignored except to contradict or insult him. This prince looked far less imposing as he reclined in his father's chair struggling to think of what to say next, and his eyes showed honest sincerity instead of contempt. Athaya was disarmed by his change in manner and decided that if Felgin could show some humility and maturity, then so could she.

"I'm the one who must apologize, Felgin," Athaya told him. "I have no excuse for the way I treated you. I was—"

"Only trying to get me back for the way *I* was acting?" he concluded with a smile. "Don't deny it just to spare my feelings, Athaya. I think we were both the victims of bad first impressions, and everything we did after that only made it worse."

"I'm sorry about the chess match," she offered. "I shouldn't have suggested playing for money. I know that's the only reason your men stayed to watch."

"You hit a sore spot with me that time," he admitted. "I don't like to lose—I guess princes are used to people letting them win—and I especially didn't like being beaten in front of my entire retinue. So," he added wryly, "what did you do with the fifty crowns you won from me?"

Athaya grinned guiltily. "If you really want to know, I took it to the gaming tables in Delfarham. Doubled my money that night, too."

Felgin belted out a hearty laugh—one that clearly marked him as Osfonin's son. "You amaze me, Athaya. I've met plenty of young ladies who can sing and dance and work wonders with a needle, but until now, I've never met one who excelled at games of chance. Are there any other talents you're hiding from me?"

"No. I don't have very many. And you're already familiar with my talent for offending people. I've perfected that one over the years, I'm afraid. You're not exactly the first suitor I've driven off."

One side of his mouth tilted up in a smile. "Are you saying that you make a habit of this sort of thing?"

"Ever since my father started trying to marry me off to get

me out from underfoot. Not that I didn't mind leaving, but I just didn't want to go as the wife of any of the young men he was suggesting." She saw one of Felgin's eyebrows go up and quickly clapped a hand over her cheek. "Oh, I'm terribly sorry," she said, laughing with embarrassment. "You see? I've done it again. I didn't mean—"

"I know what you meant," he said, chuckling softly. "Never fear. I know what it's like to be pressured into marrying. Maybe more than you do, since I'm my father's heir. He hasn't said so yet, but I think he's started to worry that I'm never going to settle down and raise a few sons."

"And are you?"

"Oh yes, eventually. I'm only twenty-seven, you know. Old for an unmarried prince, yes, but not old enough to want to give away my freedom quite yet. I'm hoping the call of duty will silence itself for a little while longer."

Duty. Why does that word seem to pop up in every conversation I have? Athaya thought sullenly. Even Tyler was given to reminding her of what her duties were as the king's daughter, and sometimes she became so infuriated by the word that she vowed never to speak it again.

"Perhaps I'd better go now and let you get some rest," Felgin said, moving to go.

Athaya held up her hand. "No, wait. I think I owe you an explanation," she said hesitantly. "Jaren thought that I should tell you something . . . he said I could trust you to keep a confidence."

Felgin cocked his head to one side. "I may be a boor, Athaya, but I'm a very trustworthy one."

Athaya couldn't help but smile. The prince was making this easier than she'd dreamed it could be. "I wasn't hateful to you because I disliked you, Felgin," she told him, leaning forward. "It's just that . . . you see, I'm in love with someone else."

"Ah," he said. There was a faint glimmer of relief and salvaged pride in his eyes. "I take it your father disapproves of him?"

"No, not really. But he doesn't come from a noble family. His father is the steward for a lesser earl in southern Caithe. Respectable enough, but not likely to earn his son a chance to marry into royalty."

"That's unfortunate," Felgin said. Then, after a long pause, he said, "I will say nothing of this—I realize how delicate these kinds of situations can be." He gave her a warm, grateful smile. "I'm glad Jaren persuaded you to tell me. He's got a great deal of common sense, you know. And he's a practical sort—a good man to have in a crisis. I can't tell you how many times he's talked my father out of giving me hell for one thing or another. Perhaps he's already told you about my scurrilous tendencies," Felgin added, with a grin that convinced her once and for all that the rumors were true. "Yes, we've been friends ever since he came here to train with Hedric . . . oh, five years ago."

At the mention of Hedric, Felgin seemed to close himself off from her slightly, as if he'd mistakenly stumbled onto a topic he was instructed to avoid. He leaned back and steepled his fingers, suddenly quiet, and studied her for several minutes.

"Will you answer a question truthfully for me?" he said with abrupt seriousness.

"What is it?"

Felgin bent over and rested his elbows on his thighs. "Do you think—in all truth—that you are going to be able to marry this man you love?"

A heavy silence settled over the room, broken only by the soft crackle of the fire and the distant buzz of conversation from the people still lingering in the Great Hall. Athaya absently smoothed the ends of her hair, still tangled from the day's ride, and wondered where Tyler was at this moment.

"I dream about it . . . I hope . . ." Her words trailed off. No one had ever asked her that question directly before, and she realized for the first time how much she had been avoiding answering it, even to herself.

"But do you really think, deep down, that you'll be his wife someday?" Felgin asked again.

Athaya could feel her eyes grow moist with hot tears and she dug her fingernails into her palms to keep from crying. "No," she whispered, unable to meet Felgin's gaze. "I don't think he believes it either. He's already told me that he'll understand when the time comes that I have to marry someone else."

"Ah. Then he must truly love you." Felgin rose slowly, and paced in a wide circle around the room, rubbing his bearded chin and trying to think of the right thing to say. Athaya turned away to wipe a tear from her eye, not wanting Felgin to see her, but she knew she could not hide what she was feeling—the red rims around her eyes had already given her away.

"You can still love him, Athaya," the prince said at last. "There's nothing wrong with that. But you're going to have to face the fact—as he does—that a marriage between you is virtually impossible. And if you defy your family's wishes and run away with him, it would cast a bad light on your father. People would assume that if he can't control his own daughter, he probably can't control a kingdom, either. I'm sure you don't want that."

"Are you saying that I should agree to marry you?" she asked, looking up at him with puzzled suspicion.

"I didn't mean that. To be frank, I wouldn't like knowing that I was only second best. It may sound selfish—"

"No. It makes perfect sense," she said, blinking back a tear. "And I'm selfish enough to want to put what I want ahead of everything else. Ahead of my duties as Kelwyn's daughter." *There's that damned word again,* she moaned to herself.

"I'm sorry. I didn't mean to upset you like this." Felgin let out a wisp of sad laughter. "I came in here to make peace with you and all I've done is irritate you again."

"It's not your fault," she reassured him. "You were just telling me what I should have realized a long time ago. I suppose it's just hard . . ." She choked on the words and looked away. "It's hard to face the fact that I'll never have the only thing I ever really wanted. It's hard to give up on your dreams that way."

Felgin placed a hand on her shoulder. "After a time, Athaya, you'll have new dreams. Ones that can be reached."

Athaya nodded, but could not bear to believe him. Perhaps someday she would realize he was right, but for now, she refused to give up hope. Didn't the minstrels' songs tell how nothing was out of reach when two people were in love?

Unfortunately, songs written by starry-eyed minstrels held little relevance for Athaya at the moment. Now that it appeared she was more than welcome in Ath Luaine, and that neither Osfonin nor Felgin held a grudge against her, the chances of her becoming the prince's bride were increased substantially. And knowing that Osfonin wished to assist Kelwyn in his efforts to eliminate the rite of absolution in Caithe, the prospect of a marriage to seal such a pact held even more advantages for both lands than it did before. It would soon be apparent to both monarchs that there was no logical reason why their children's wedding should not take place. And although Athaya had a powerful reason of her own, she knew that in the larger scheme of things, what she desired for herself, and for Tyler, would be outweighed by what her duty required of her.

CHAPTER 8

※❈※

L ATE THE NEXT MORNING, ATHAYA LINGERED OVER HER breakfast in the Great Hall with Tyler, sharing the platter of bread, cheese, and cold bacon that was set before them. The Hall was sparsely populated at this hour, except for a few servants sweeping up the rushes and setting fresh candles on the table, and Athaya was pleased at the chance to speak with Tyler in relative privacy.

"Osfonin insists we stay until at least the end of the month," she told him. "In fact, he made a joke about the snows coming early this year, and us not getting home until April."

"Can't say I'd mind," Tyler remarked. "Lars and I were talking last night—he's the guard captain here—and he's already offered to show me around the city and tell me where all the best fishing holes are. Friendly fellow—I'll swear he knows more off-color jokes than anyone I've ever met. Except you, of course," he added with a grin.

Athaya would have liked to swat that smirk pleasantly off his face, but refrained in deference to the handful of servants still milling about the hall. "You can thank Nicolas for that," she said. "He taught me everything I know."

"A bad influence, that boy. Remind me to thank him when we get home." Tyler picked up the fresh loaf of bread and tore

107

off a large chunk. He offered her the loaf, but she refused it. Then he noticed that she had barely touched her meal.

"What's the matter? Don't you like the idea of being stuck here until spring? Surely you can't be that anxious to get back home."

Athaya shrugged, absently pushing a piece of bacon around her plate with the tip of her knife. For some reason, she wasn't happy with the idea of staying on in Ath Luaine, although she openly admitted that it was better than anywhere else she'd been lately, especially home in Delfarham. One part of her wanted to be here in Reyka, another part wanted—for some strange reason—to go back to Caithe, and yet another, more indefinable part didn't particularly want to be anywhere at all.

"It's not that, exactly. It's a pleasure not having Durek and Dagara all over my back, or Rhodri skulking through the halls with his eyes on everything. But there's something odd going on around here, and I just can't figure out what it is."

Tyler dipped his bread into a pot of honey and stuffed it into his mouth. "What do you mean?"

"I thought that I was going to get one hell of a cold reception when we got to Ath Luaine," she said, slicing herself a piece of dark yellow cheese. "But what happened? Osfonin welcomes me with open arms, Katya's offered to be a sister to me since I don't have any, and Felgin . . . did I tell you? Felgin stopped by last night to apologize for the way he behaved during his visit. I'm not complaining, mind you," she pointed out, "but I think it's awfully strange. I feel as if I have some sort of disease and everybody is being nice to me because they know I'm going to die any minute and they all feel sorry for me."

Tyler laughed aloud. "Oh, come now, Athaya, you're just imagining things."

"That's what you said when I saw Jaren following us to Evarshot," she said, waving her knife in his face.

Tyler broke off another piece of bread, but instead of soaking it in honey, he slowly crumbled it between his fingers, letting the fluffy white crumbs scatter across the tabletop. "So you talked to Felgin last night . . ." he began offhandedly. "Did he say anything about the marriage?"

Despite his casual attitude, Athaya could tell from the tightness in his voice that Tyler was much disturbed. She kept her eyes carefully lowered. "He didn't say much, but I don't think he's crazy about the idea either.'' All at once, her breakfast looked more inviting than it had a few moments ago, and she ate with sudden energy, not so much out of hunger, but out of a strong desire to avoid a delicate and painful subject.

''There's more to it, isn't there?'' Tyler asked, pushing his plate away. ''What else did he say to you?''

''It's nothing, really,'' she said reassuringly. ''We just agreed that neither one of us wanted to be pushed into anything.''

She could tell from his skeptical expression that he wasn't convinced. But what could she tell him? She didn't want to go through the most upsetting part of last night's conversation all over again, when Felgin had forced her to admit to herself that her secret hopes for marrying Tyler were little more than cloud-castles. She just couldn't bear to talk about that, not yet. It made her happy to let Tyler have his own hopes for a little while longer, even if hers had been damaged beyond repair.

''You don't have to worry about hurting my feelings, Athaya. It's not as if I never expected the subject of the wedding to come up again. But he obviously said something that upset you.''

''Tyler, please. I'm not upset. I just don't want to discuss it now.''

''All right. I'm sorry I brought it up,'' he grumbled, slumping back in his chair. ''But you've always talked to me about things like this before.''

''That has nothing to do with it. I just—''

''Never mind,'' he said curtly. ''Apparently it's none of my business.''

''Oh, stop being childish. If it's not your business then who the hell's is it?''

Tyler was silent for a long time, absently picking off bits of bread and rolling them up into tight little balls of dough. The muscles in his tanned face were taut, and he stared so intently at a knot of wood on the tabletop that Athaya thought his gaze might burn a hole right through it. Then he refilled his ale cup and drank it down in a single gulp.

''It's hard, you know,'' he said at last. ''Listening to everyone talk about who you're going to marry and knowing they're not talking about me.''

''I know,'' she whispered, wishing above all else that she could embrace him here and now and soothe away his cares.

"But don't you dare say what I think you're about to," she said quickly, shaking her finger at him as he started to continue.

"Say what?"

Athaya twisted her face into a grotesque grimace. "Duty calls."

"I won't," he replied. "I think I'm getting sick of hearing that, too."

A flash of white caught the corner of her eye, and she looked up to see Jaren slip through the doors and make his way toward her. Athaya almost didn't recognize him at first, having never seen him in such fine clothes before. A green velvet doublet fit snugly over his white ruffled shirt and hose, and the buckles on his shoes were glittering gold. His normally unruly hair was combed neatly back and topped by a soft-crowned cap, and his collar was adorned by an unusual cross-shaped brooch inlaid with emeralds. This Jaren was every inch a duke's son in his understated elegance, and Athaya had to admit that he was very handsome indeed.

"Careful, Athaya," Tyler whispered in her ear, as if he'd just picked her thoughts out of the air. "I'm a jealous man."

"You've made that more than obvious," she said lightly. But somehow she sensed that Tyler wasn't joking. He hadn't taken well to Jaren and tended to be cool and distant to him, as if he knew he should be suspicious of him for something but couldn't quite figure out what.

Jaren did not take a seat at the table. He looked more withdrawn and formal than usual, and Athaya sensed that he was here on some sort of official business and not simply for social reasons.

"Master Hedric would like to see you now, if it's convenient," he told her.

Her muscles tensed up immediately. She had been expecting this, but the hope had still lingered in the back of her mind that perhaps Hedric would forget about her and that she would be able to go about her business in Reyka without getting involved in the old magician's intrigues. *But I may as well get it over with,* she thought, realizing that if she were going to stay in the palace until the end of September, it would be next to impossible to avoid the old wizard.

She said good-bye to Tyler and followed Jaren across the main courtyard and through a small arched door at the base of one of the castle's towers. They climbed a drafty spiral staircase, much steeper and narrower than the ones Athaya was used to at home, and stopped before a weathered oak door on the topmost level. Hanging from a nail in the door was a cross-shaped symbol made of silver, almost identical to the one Jaren wore on his collar.

Inside, the chamber was a mess. Every inch of it was cluttered with books, jars of herbs, pieces of colored cloth, and cast-off quills with ink-stained tips. Athaya could barely make out the shape of a writing desk underneath the pile of scribbled papers strewn on top of it, and the floor was littered with droplets of hardened wax, bits of half-burned candles, and scraps of parchment with unfamiliar symbols hastily sketched on them. It was a stark contrast to Rhodri's apartments, which were so orderly and clean that Athaya wondered at times whether anyone actually lived there at all.

Robed in black, Hedric sat at his worktable, flipping through the ragged-edged pages of a leather-bound book. When he heard his guests arrive, he laid a strip of gold cloth across the page and set his book aside with haste.

"Princess Athaya, please come in," he said, rising excitedly out of his chair. "Please excuse the clutter. I'm afraid wizardry isn't always a tidy occupation. Come, sit here beside me and make yourself comfortable." He motioned to a gnarled chair that seemed to be formed out of thick, twisted branches, giving off the distinct impression that, having been a chair long enough, the varnished wood was slowly transforming itself back into a tree and taking root in the floor of the tower chamber. To Athaya's surprise, the chair was much more comfortable than it looked and seemed to mold to her body like a cushion as she reclined in it. *I suppose magic has its more mundane uses*, she mused.

"I have waited a long time to find you," Hedric said. In stark contrast to last night's ominous mood, today his cheeks were flushed pink with anticipation, as if he'd just come in out of the cold. He noticed the blank look of puzzlement on her face and added, "But my talk must sound strange. I will have to start at the beginning and explain everything to you. Let me offer you some wine before we start. Jaren, would you be so kind?"

Athaya gladly accepted the goblet of burgundy liquid that Jaren handed to her. Perhaps the mollifying effects of the wine would make her feel less nervous. She felt off balance and unsure of herself in this place, and it was a feeling she did not like.

Hedric swirled the wine around his own cup and sat back down behind his worktable. "I believe that Jaren has told you a little about why I wished to see you."

"He said that it was about the Lorngeld in Caithe. Something you wanted to do to help them. Frankly, I don't really see what I have to do with it."

The old wizard smiled at her, swollen with mysterious pride, with the look of a father who's found the perfect husband for his daughter and is just about to break the happy news.

"I plan to tell you exactly how you can help," Hedric said. He took a sip of his wine and set the cup aside. "You have a unique destiny, Athaya. You should be proud. Opportunities to achieve truly great things are rare and come to only the chosen few."

Great things? she thought, stupefied. *I can't think of a single great thing I've accomplished in my entire life, except perhaps the time I beat Durek fair and square at an archery match when I was twelve years old. Everything since then has definitely been relegated to the realm of the mediocre.*

"The Lorngeld in your country have been persecuted for two centuries," the old man began, lacing his slender fingers together. "You say that your father shows an interest in changing this, and that is good news. But how can this situation be changed, you ask? Only by allowing those born with the gift to live and instructing them in its use.

"When I was a younger man, I saw little hope for the Lorngeld in your country. Oh, yes, occasionally one of them would cross the border wall or hire a ship to Reyka, fleeing from absolution and hoping to find someone to help them. And when such people come to us, we take them in. But more often than not, the *mekahn* is too far advanced by the time they reach us, and we can do nothing to save them from their fate. From time to time, wizards from this country—myself included, back in my younger, more adventurous days—journey to Caithe in search of our brother Lorngeld, taking the chance that they could be persuaded to emigrate and learn to use their magic. But it is a dangerous task, and many promising young wizards have been arrested and burned by your countrymen for 'the spread of heresy.' "

"But if they had magic, why didn't they use it to fight back?" Athaya asked, baffled at the seeming stupidity of it.

"And destroy their enemies? No, I fear that would have only given your priests the evidence they needed to prove that the Lorngeld were truly evil and bent on destruction. We feel it is best to do what we can without the use of magic, or we risk the death of our own cause. It is a poor solution, I know, and only a handful of your people have been helped this way. It is like taking a few buckets of water out of the sea in an effort to stave off the rising tide, and it does little to solve the inherent problem. What the Lorngeld in your country need is a person of position—of power, from their own homeland, one whom they can trust to guide them. I have been searching for signs of such a person for many years, but have found nothing. But now," he said, his eyes sparkling, "now that has all changed."

Athaya looked aside at Jaren, but his face was carefully controlled, revealing nothing.

"I saw the first traces of your presence last spring," Hedric continued. "I didn't know it was you, of course. Not then. All I could pick up was a hazy image. But I knew that whoever it was, he or she had great power, and was highly born—the kind of person whom people would listen to and follow."

Suddenly Athaya was overwhelmed by a flood of dizziness and she felt her fingers begin to shake. She stared at the old wizard with disbelieving eyes, gaping at him, but her shock quickly changed to fear and trembling anger and she gripped the armrests of the chair so hard she thought they might splinter into fragments. "I don't think I like what you're implying," she said.

Hedric went on as if she had not spoken. "Your people need— forgive the overblown term—a 'savior.' Someone to take the lead in founding places of learning for the Lorngeld. Someone to preach against the Church in your country and lead a movement to change its teachings. You can be the champion of your people, Athaya. As a member of the royal house, your words will be heeded. And you are powerful. You possess the potential to be one of the most powerful wielders of magic of this age— one of the greatest of the Great Masters. You have a unique ability, a destiny, a God-given opportunity to give an entire race of people a chance to live and to work the kind of change that few people have ever done, or could ever dream of doing!"

Athaya's head reeled, and her vision started to blur. This was all a nightmare—a horrible, ugly nightmare—and she wanted to wake up and have it be over. She felt sick and confused and felt the urge to flee—to run as far away from this place as she could go. She rose out of her chair slowly, afraid she would lose her balance, and steadied herself on the armrest.

"You're crazy," she said bluntly.

"You must accept the challenge, Athaya. You are the chosen one."

"Good Lord, listen to yourself!" she cried, gesturing wildly with her hands. "Do you hear what you're saying? You're making me out to be the daughter of God Himself!"

"We are all sons and daughters of God," Hedric replied, priestlike.

"You know what I meant," she snapped, her voice breaking with anger. "I don't have to stay here and listen to you try and make me something I'm not. I don't know what you're up to or why you're doing this to me, but nothing you're saying is true." She wheeled around to face Jaren with livid, accusing eyes. "You knew about this all the time, didn't you? I suspected that there was something you all knew that you weren't telling me. That's why everybody's been so damned nice to me, isn't it?"

"They are simply showing the respect that is due to a powerful adept like yourself," Jaren told her. "Especially one who is royal-born. That is the highest honor one could hope for."

"Now I understand why everyone's suddenly so keen on my marriage to Felgin again. You've got them all convinced I'm a Lorngeld, and now I'm a much more valuable commodity to you than I was before!"

"Athaya, please try to calm down."

"I don't want to calm down, damn it all!" she cried, swatting away the hand that Jaren reached out to her. "Why should I calm down when you've just insulted me! I don't have to stand here and listen to you two rave on about some fantasy you've both invented in your half-baked wizard's brains. *If* you'll excuse me—"

Athaya bolted out of the tree-chair, stormed to the door, and grabbed onto the iron latch. She'd had enough of this insane talk for one morning—for one lifetime! She yanked back on the door with one hard pull, but a sharp pain shot up her arm when the door did not budge. Two more furious tries yielded the same result, and in desperate outrage, she curled her hands into tight fists and struck them against the door as hard as she could. But nothing she could do would budge the door even a hairsbreadth, and she doubted very much that anyone would hear her if she cried out for help.

Her ragged breathing steadied, and she turned around slowly, simmering with anger. "So we're going to play like that, are we?"

"I think you should stay and hear me out," Hedric said simply, without offense. "I didn't want to force you to stay, but you have left me no alternative. What I have to say is just too important. You must listen."

"I don't appear to have much say in the matter."

She sank sullenly back into the tree-chair, rubbing her bruised fists, and set her feet defiantly against the edge of the table. Snatching up her goblet, she drained off the last of the wine.

"Jaren spoke with me on the night you arrived in Ath Luaine," Hedric told her. "He told me what he knew about you, and I think we can give you more than enough evidence to convince you of what you are."

"You can try," she said with a shrug.

Jaren pulled his chair closer to hers and leaned forward on the table. "Do you remember the night in the tavern when that man accused you of cheating him at cards?"

"Of course I do."

"Well, he was right. You *were*."

"I was not!" she protested loudly, her cheeks growing hot from the blow to her dignity. "And what would you know about it? You weren't even there until—"

"I could pick up your spell halfway across town. You weren't being very careful about it. But that's to be expected with someone at your level."

"My level? What are you—"

"But I couldn't just walk up to you and blurt out that you were using magic, could I? That you were one of those 'mind-plagued wizards' everybody curses about? No, you didn't know you were doing it, but you were cheating all right. You were mentally guiding the cards so they came up in a beneficial order." Jaren laughed softly. "You must've driven that man crazy—he knew you were cheating, but he couldn't for the life of him figure out how you were doing it."

Athaya frowned and said nothing, although the coldly practical part of her mind was thinking that if this talent for fixing cards could be perfected, it would be very profitable indeed.

"And I saw you toss him down those stairs. No offense, Athaya, but he was almost twice your size—you never should have been able to hurt him as much as you did. But the *mekahn* sometimes causes sporadic bursts of strength. You didn't hit him that hard—your magic did. And another thing," he continued, not giving her time to protest, "just how did you walk past the sentries at Delfar Castle that night without them seeing you? There *were* sentries on duty, that night, correct?"

"Of course there were," she mumbled petulantly.

"Then why didn't they see you? I'll tell you why. Because you worked a cloaking spell. You concentrated so hard on not wanting to be seen that you rendered yourself invisible."

"This is ridiculous, Jaren," she said, rolling her eyes. "I wouldn't know how to work a spell—any kind of spell—even if I wanted to."

"You did it unconsciously. The part of the mind that every Lorngeld is born with told you how to do it. I saw you, Athaya. I'd been watching you with my sphere for the better part of the day, trying to find a time when I could approach you. I detected your spell, but none of the guards did. And another thing—"

Athaya moved to get up. This conversation was beginning to sicken her. "Jaren, this has gone far enough. I—"

"And how did you know I was following you to Evarshot?" he said, holding her back. "How did you see me in the corridor of the monastery?"

Athaya pushed his arm away roughly. "I saw something moving—like heat waves."

"But Captain Graylen didn't see it, did he?"

"N-no . . ."

"Athaya, listen to me. Only a highly trained wizard or an extremely powerful untrained adept would have been able to see through a cloaking spell. Assuming there were no mirrors around, of course, in which case anybody could have seen my reflection. And it's even difficult for a highly trained wizard to detect a cloaking spell unless he's looking for it. No, Athaya," Jaren told her, "it's not a question of whether you're a Lorngeld or not, it's a question of just how powerful a one you are."

"So if I'm a wizard, how come I haven't gone crazy?" she

shot back. "I'm twenty years old, right? And I feel just fine. I certainly haven't started blowing things up or starting fires or doing all those other things wizards do."

"Not yet," Jaren said ominously. "But you *have* been feeling moody and restless lately, haven't you?"

Athaya let out a frustrated sigh. "All right, I'll admit I've been feeling a little strange for the last month or two, but lots of people go through bad times. It doesn't mean they're all wizards! I've just been under a lot of pressure lately, what with my family badgering me all the time with talk about marrying Felgin, and Tyler—"

She cut off her words abruptly. She'd already said more than she should have about Tyler and wasn't so sure she trusted Jaren with the knowledge as much as she had before. And as for Hedric, she got the peculiar feeling that he would do whatever he thought necessary to force her into this role he wished her to play. She didn't put it past him to use Tyler as a lever to do it.

"And you've been having bad dreams, haven't you?" Jaren asked.

"Maybe. But even normal people have those."

"And you've been drinking and smoking looca more than usual, haven't you? That's very common to those approaching the *mekahn*. The dulling effects of liquor and looca-smoke help quiet the voices in your mind."

"And normal people get drunk sometimes, too," she said acidly. "And I don't hear any damned voices." Or did she? Where did that pressure, that restlessness, come from? Were there voices that spoke to her in a language she could not comprehend? But *voices*? The whole idea was ridiculous, and Athaya was growing more convinced that if she wasn't going crazy already, Jaren and Hedric were deliberately setting out to make her so, if only to prove their cockeyed theory.

Hedric shook his head, white wisps of hair floating around his face like mist. "I'm surprised that Kelwyn, or Rhodri especially, haven't seen the signs."

"How could they?" Athaya cried in sheer desperation. "There's nothing to see! And if you expect them to sit up and take notice because I've been irritable and depressed and troublesome, then you're out of luck, because I've been acting that way for the past ten years!"

Athaya stopped to catch her breath, but was not finished yet.

She had heard what they had to say, and now it was her turn to give them an earful. "And another thing—if I'm a Lorngeld, then why can I wear my corbal necklace? Would you like to see it? I've got it right here." She fingered the thongs of the leather pouch tied to her belt, and Jaren waved her hands away angrily.

"Leave that thing where it is!" Jaren shouted, his face flushed red with anger. "How dare you presume to wield a corbal in the presence of a Great Master!"

"Calm down, Jaren, it's all right," Hedric said calmly, almost amused by his assistant's outburst. "It's not as if nobody's ever used one on me before, you know. She had that pouch on her belt last night in Osfonin's chamber. I sensed the crystal's vibrations, but it wasn't too bothersome. I had . . . other things on my mind at the time."

"You knew I had it with me?" *Fat lot of good it does having a weapon against wizards if they know you've got it. So much for the element of surprise.* "But I had it with me at the monastery when I met Jaren. Why didn't he sense it?"

"My powers are more extensive than his," Hedric told her. "It is no slight on Jaren's part—I simply have the greater gift. The greater the ability for magic, the more sensitive one is to the corbal. The crystal gives off a sort of psychic sound. It's fairly quiet in the dark, or when enclosed in a case of some kind, but otherwise it makes a ghastly high-pitched whine that's extremely painful. The more highly trained and adept your mind is at magic, the more vulnerable it is to the interference of the corbal's vibrations."

"So if I'm a Lorngeld, then why doesn't it affect me?"

"Because you haven't been through the *mekahn* yet," he said simply, as if explaining why two plus two equaled four. "Magic has its price, and experiencing the pain of the corbal is a risk a wizard takes."

Magic has its price . . . where had she heard that before? No, it was *great magic commands a great price.* Rhodri had said it to her after he'd given her Hedric's letter. Did Rhodri have great magic? And if he did, what price had he paid for his power? Or was the corbal all there was?

Athaya slumped back in her chair, exhausted from arguing. "But no Trelane has ever been born a Lorngeld," she murmured.

"Are you so certain of that?" Hedric challenged her. "Many

families in your country—especially noble ones—are so ashamed
to reveal that their children have been born with the gift that
when the *mekahn* begins, they kill these innocents in the name
of mercy and put out the tale that they died of sudden illness. I
know this happens, Athaya. I've seen it. And if anyone tries to
hide them—or worse, tries to find a way to give them the magical
training they need to have—then they're rooted out and burned
as heretics for sheltering the Devil's Children.''

"And you want me to march right in and put a stop to it all
by myself, don't you? Just like that—poof!''

"I want you to accept what you are and do what you can for
your own people, Athaya. You have a duty to them.''

Duty! That hell-blasted word again!

"I am sick to *death* of everybody telling me what my duty
is!'' she cried out. "How in the hell do you know what I'm
supposed to do with my life when *I* don't even know yet? How
can you be so sure this 'savior' you're so obsessed with is really
me? Maybe it's somebody else! It has to be. This is all some
colossal mistake!''

"No, Athaya. I was very careful. I sensed a great power . . .
an unusual talent. And after what Felgin told me—''

"Felgin? What's *he* got to do with this?'' Did everyone in this
entire plague-ridden palace know about this except herself?

"In an indirect way, it was he who led me to you. He wasn't
sure. His abilities are not extensive, but rather more like Jaren's.
He thought there was something unusual about you after his visit
to Caithe, but he couldn't tell what it was. After we spoke, I
followed my instincts and used my sphere to focus in on you
and realized that you were the source of the power I'd been
seeking.''

Athaya rubbed at her temples, feeling a nasty headache coming on. "What in God's name are these damnable spheres
everyone keeps talking about?''

"A vision sphere is a tool for focusing your thoughts, observing things in other places, or trying to contact someone,'' Hedric explained. "You can look into the past, or see what's
happening at the present time in other places. Don't confuse a
sphere with the old myth about crystal balls. You can't divine
the future with a sphere. Well, some people can, but not very
well. Futures are very difficult and notoriously unreliable—even
I don't have much luck with them. But in any event, spheres

aren't difficult to create once you know how. Jaren used his to let me know what day you and your escort party would be arriving in Ath Luaine.''

"I didn't see you do that," she said, turning to Jaren.

"You wouldn't have. A wizard usually works his sphere in privacy. While you're using it, you're quite vulnerable to attack, since all your concentration is focused on sustaining the vision. Sphere-work tends to drain your energy as well, so you're less able to defend yourself if necessary. I certainly wouldn't recommend conjuring a sphere anywhere in Caithe—not where anyone can see you do it, anyway. And if you get pulled out of it before you're ready . . . well, it can be pretty unpleasant.''

Athaya was unexpectedly intrigued. "So you can talk to people with them?''

"Only if you want to," Hedric said. "It's extremely difficult to sense when someone is observing you with their sphere unless the observer willingly opens the channels of communication. Since you're curious, I can teach you to use one if you like.''

"What?'' Jaren blurted out, astounded that Hedric could have even suggested such a thing. "But she hasn't had a single day of training!''

"No . . . but I sense that her power may be greater than even I imagined at first. She just might be able to do it. I think that her unconscious mind knows more about magic than she does right now.''

Athaya shook her head resolutely. "Look, I don't want to learn how to use one. How can I? I'm not a Lorngeld, no matter what you seem to believe.''

"Ah, I see," Hedric said smoothly. "I understand. You're afraid to try because you know I'll be proven right.''

Athaya pursed her lips. "I knew you'd try to use that old line on me," she said. But she couldn't deny the effectiveness of his challenge. To refuse to try was an admission of fear, but part of her mind warned her that she had every reason to be afraid. And if she *could* create a sphere—assuming such a thing even existed—she might be forced to face the fact that Jaren and Hedric were right. And after last night, when Felgin had forced her to admit that she would never be Tyler's wife, she wasn't sure how many more unpleasant revelations she could take. *But why should I be unwilling to try?* the defiant part of her mind asked her. *It's not as if anything is going to happen. And I might be able to put an end to this absurd conversation once and for all.*

"Oh, for heaven's sake," she said, turning her eyes toward the ceiling. "All right, I'll do it. Anything to get the two of you off my back. Just don't get all upset when nothing happens."

"I won't," Hedric assured her. "I just want you to try."

"I might as well. I suppose nobody ever died from one of these things."

Athaya wished she hadn't seen the disturbing look exchanged by the two wizards. "Wait a second, what aren't you—"

"Don't worry, Athaya. We're both here to make sure nothing goes wrong," Hedric told her. "Now place your hands like this," he instructed her quickly, before she had a chance to change her mind. He folded his palms together as if he were at prayer. "And draw them apart about . . . this far, there, that's good."

Athaya felt incredibly foolish, not to mention a great deal more worried than she had been a moment ago, but she bit back her grumblings and followed the old man's instructions. What harm would it do to humor him?

"Just one caution before you begin," Hedric said, holding up a finger. "Whatever happens, don't take your eyes off the sphere before you've commanded it to disperse."

"Why not?" she asked apprehensively.

"Think of how you feel the morning after you've had way too much to drink," Jaren said, well aware that Athaya was more than familiar with the sensation. "Pulling out of a sphere too soon makes a bad hangover seem like a mild case of the sniffles."

"That'll do, Jaren," Hedric scolded lightly. "Let's not scare her off just as she's agreed to try it. Now think of something you wish to see, Athaya. It can be anything—a person, a place— anything. Just relax and concentrate."

Athaya stared at her upheld fingers for several minutes, and the longer she sat there, the more ridiculous she felt. What was supposed to happen, anyway? She didn't even know what a sphere *looked* like, much less how to conjure one. And besides, she couldn't think of anything in particular that she wanted to see.

Growing bored, Athaya let her mind wander at will, thinking how absurd this would all seem to Tyler when she told him about it later. The longer she sat motionless in her chair, the more idiotic she felt. Hedric gazed at her with rapt anticipation, while Jaren hung back, still skeptical. Yes, Tyler would find it all very amusing . . .

Then, without warning, she felt a tingling in her fingertips and had to fight to keep from pulling away in surprise. Thin streams of white fog drifted lazily out from the pads of her fingers, like smoke from a snuffed-out candle. They swirled gracefully, forming a tiny whirlpool between her hands. The fog grew thicker, molding itself into a solid ball as weightless in her hands as a bubble of soap.

"I don't believe it!" Jaren exclaimed quietly.

"Shh, don't break her concentration," Hedric whispered, waving him silent.

Athaya focused all of her attention on the sphere, so entranced by her creation that she'd forgotten all its implications. Jaren and Hedric's presence seemed to fade away into a misty background. An image began to take shape in the sphere, and she was amazed at its clarity—almost like a mirror. She felt as if she were no longer in Hedric's study, but floating on a cloud of smoke. The mist took on a greenish cast and melded into a picture, and Athaya saw a lush forest, the leaves of the trees tipped with the first touch of autumn gold. Bright sunshine spotted the ground as it peeked between the branches of the tall oaks, and Athaya could almost smell the lush green moss and damp earth. In the distance, she saw a group of riders on horseback, hooting with pleasure as they chased after a deer flushed from its thicket by a pack of noisy hounds. She recognized some of the men as being from Tyler's squadron, and leading the chase at the front of the party were Tyler and Prince Felgin.

Felgin? What on earth is Tyler doing with him? she wondered, staring at the image with puzzlement. They were laughing and joking together like old friends, and Athaya couldn't help but feel somewhat suspicious. Had Tyler decided to go on a hunt with the prince, hoping that Felgin would tell him more about his conversation with her the night before than she had at breakfast that morning? The idea of the two men becoming friends disturbed her, although she knew of no reasons why they shouldn't like each other.

"Can you see anything, Athaya?"

Hedric's voice was mildly distracting, like an insect buzzing in her ear, and gently pulled her back a bit from the light trance she was in. "I see—"

No, she did not want to tell him about Tyler; Hedric might wonder, and rightly so, why the guard captain was the first thing her mind chose to focus on. "I see the prince out hunting," she murmured.

"She's right! Felgin told me he was going out for a deer today," Jaren replied excitedly.

"That's excellent, Athaya," Hedric said. "You're doing splendidly. Now I want you to try extending your vision. Try to see something in Caithe."

She frowned as the image of Tyler and Felgin faded, and the sphere was again clouded with white mist. Unlike her ease with the first image, Athaya felt a wave of dizziness as the next scene began to come into view. But instead of the mirrorlike clarity of her previous vision, this one was badly blurred and clouded, shrouded in thick fog.

"Something's coming now," she said softly, squinting her eyes. "It's hard to tell exactly. Everything's hazy. But I think it's what I was trying for . . . yes, it is! It's Delfar Castle."

"Incredible," Hedric murmured. "What else?"

"I see the Great Hall," she said, furrowing her brow. "But nobody's there."

She concentrated on viewing other parts of the castle, but the only image that came to her was a group of three chambermaids in black gowns huddled in a corner of a hallway, speaking softly to each other as if afraid of being overheard. The image was still blurry, but Athaya could tell by the carvings on the wall behind them that the women were not far from the entrance to the royal apartments. They kept gazing worriedly toward the king's chamber, shaking their white-capped heads.

"Something's not right," Athaya whispered.

"Just don't look away, Athaya," Hedric urged her. "Fix your eyes on the sphere and keep concentrating. What else do you see?"

The vision swirled, and there was again another wave of dizziness; then she saw a great bed surrounded by sumptuous hangings. Heavy drapes shut out the sunlight, and Athaya could almost smell the thick odor of incense from the burners in the corner, clouding the room with perfumed smoke. And through the mists of the sphere, she saw Nicolas, his hair in disarray and his eyes rimmed with dark circles, as if he had not slept in days. He had one arm wrapped around Cecile's shoulders as he wiped away her tears, while Durek paced furiously back and forth across the carpet, only occasionally offering a word or two of comfort to Dagara, who looked terrified and alone, slouched down on a cushioned stool by the fire. Archbishop Ventan hovered near the foot of the bed like a jeweled vulture, his gold-threaded robes of office glittering garishly in the somber bedchamber as he intoned his prayers. And a few steps away, Rhodri was bent over the king, trying to find a way to rouse him back to consciousness.

"I'll never forgive this!" Durek cried out, his face scarlet with rage. *"Never!"*

"Durek, please," Nicolas said, his voice weak from exhaustion. "Not now. Think of Father."

"I *am* thinking of him, you imbecile! That's why I'm going to bring the full force of the law—"

"Your Majesty," Rhodri said to Durek, drawing away from the bedside. He was noticeably shaken. "The king is dead."

With a terrified gasp, Athaya closed her eyes and jerked her hands back from the vision. The sphere burst, leaving a soaplike film over her hands and spattering drops of liquid fog on the floor that hissed like drops of water on a hot griddle. Then, almost immediately, the pounding started—like a hammer inside her skull, just behind her eyes. She let out a low moan and doubled over, on the verge of passing out.

"Lay her down in the other room," she heard Hedric say, as Jaren lifted her up and carried her to a soft goose-down mattress in the wizard's inner chambers. She felt cool water splashing on her face and heard the faint clinking of glass jars. A warm coverlet was laid over her, and she felt Jaren's hand—it was too soft to be Hedric's—patting her cheeks and whispering her name, trying to rouse her.

Then the room begin to spin, and she felt herself slipping . . . falling off the edge of the bed and plummeting down into a foggy, swirling mist. She tried to cry out, but no words would come. Her throat was parched and dry, and her head pounded and throbbed and felt as if it would burst and spatter across the floor, as had the sphere.

And then there was blackness, and silence.

CHAPTER 9

✳✳

A THAYA STOOD IN THE REAR OF THE VILLAGE CHURCH watching the absolution ceremony. When the cat-eyed priest had called the invocation and delivered the prayer of pardon, he turned to mix the *kahnil* into the sacred wine. A white-robed woman knelt at his feet, her head thrown back to reveal the look of divine rapture illuminating her features. She wanted this, she had come to the altar willingly, now that the moment had come, she yearned to relinquish the Devil's gift and seek her reward in heaven.

The priest turned and offered her the cup, his green, slit-pupiled eyes never leaving his willing prey. The woman took the cup gladly. She lifted it up and said a prayer to God and raised the chalice to her lips.

"*No!* Don't do it!" Athaya screamed. "They're trying to kill you!"

She bolted up the aisle toward the woman, but the people rose out of their pews and blocked the way, hauling her back to the rear of the church. Her arms were pinned behind her by two strong men, and the condemning glares of the people were all upon her. But the white-robed woman smiled at her and said, "Do not fear for me. I do this of my own accord and I am joyful because of it. I do not wish to accept the gift, and as my priest tells me, I will only find my life by losing it."

125

"But the priests are wrong!" Athaya cried, desperately trying to squirm away from the grasp of her captors. She turned her eyes to the circular stained-glass window above the altar, where the lifeless glass images of the saints looked down on her in silence. *"Why won't anyone listen?"* she cried out to them, her body racked with sobs. *"Why can't you help me convince them?"*

Then she saw the priest raise his hands aloft and she screamed aloud, for on the tips of his fingers were sharpened claws and the tips were soaked in blood, as if they had just finished ripping out the innards of a freshly killed beast. The woman lay dying at his feet—her face still lit with unearthly joy even while the spasms of death overwhelmed her—but the priest ignored her and silently stalked down the aisle toward Athaya. And just as he reached her, his feline hands extending toward her throat, the stained-glass window above the altar suddenly exploded into a thousand multicolored shards, showering the priest and his con-gregation with a knife-edged hail of angry glass, cutting their eyes and faces and arms until the aisle of the church ran red with their blood.

Athaya sat bolt upright, throwing her arms up to shield her-self. But the threat was no longer there. No glass rained down upon her. Everything was quiet, and she was safe and warm inside the dark confines of her bedchamber. The front of her gown was damp with sweat, making her shiver from the chill. She forced her breathing to relax and, as she did so, she became conscious of the dull, throbbing ache in her head.

"Everything's all right now, Athaya," said a soothing voice nearby. "You'll be just fine."

Ysell was arranging the heavy brocade curtains over the win-dow to keep out the light. She crossed the room, her velvet gown swishing softly on the carpet, and placed a cool hand on Athaya's forehead. "Good. The fever's gone."

The queen took a seat on the blue-cushioned chair next to Athaya's bed. "Hedric told me what happened. He says that breaking a sphere can be quite painful, but it usually doesn't cause this strong of a reaction."

It took Athaya a few moments to realize what Ysell was talk-ing about, since her mind was still fuzzy with aftershocks from her dream. Yes, she did remember something about a sphere, and something terrible it had shown her. Or had that been a dream, too? She sank back against the thick pillows, rubbing her temples. The less she moved about and the less she tried to think, the more bearable the pain behind her eyes became.

"I had the most horrible nightmare . . ."

"That's to be expected," Ysell said. "I've been with you for most of the night, and your sleep was very restless."

"Most of the night? What time is it?"

"Just past dawn. You've been ill for almost two days."

Athaya sat up in frightened surprise, but the quick motion made her head spin and formed black patches of blurriness before her eyes.

"Just lie back and relax," Ysell said, gently pushing her back against the pillows. "You're going to spend the rest of today right where you are. You're a bit weak yet and need another day's rest."

"But I don't want to sleep—" she murmured. Nursing a nasty headache was definitely preferable to drifting back into that dark world of nightmares.

Ysell patted her on the arm and moved toward the doorway. "Don't worry about that, Athaya. I'll mix you something that will help you sleep without being bothered by dreams. And I'll make sure to send word to your guard captain that you're awake and feeling reasonably well. He's a loyal man and he's been very anxious about you these last few days. Now you just lie still, and I'll be back in a few minutes."

The door closed without a sound, and Athaya curled up under her blankets, trying not to think about the stiff, cramped feeling in her stomach. She pushed the memory of the nightmare out of her mind, but it was quickly replaced by the events of yesterday—or had Ysell said it was the day before?—when she had lost consciousness. Hedric and Jaren had told her some ridiculous story about reforming the Church; of using her magic to lead her people to freedom. And she remembered holding a vision sphere in her hands, and seeing a vision of her father's bedchamber at home. His death chamber.

Damn Hedric and Jaren and their cockeyed stories! she thought angrily. *They're playing tricks on my mind and making me think I'm crazy.*

But the vision in the sphere had seemed real enough, and the memory of it haunted her. She had never felt the devotion to Kelwyn that she knew other girls had for their fathers, but the idea of his death shone a light into the farthest corners of her soul, stirring up long-ago emotions like dead leaves in an autumn wind.

She could vaguely remember when she was very young and had looked up to Kelwyn with a child's adoration, marveling at his glittering clothes and commanding voice, amazed and proud that this godlike man was her father. That was back in the days when she would try everything she could to please him—back before she knew he could never be pleased. But those days were long past. Since then, she had grown into womanhood and learned that her efforts were in vain and had shut away the pain of that knowledge in the dark recesses of her mind, hoping to forget and persuade herself it did not matter. But sometimes the hurt would not stay confined, and she remembered the times—the rare times—when her father would gaze at her in quiet desperation, as if he truly understood how much she wanted to earn his love, but knew deep in his heart, with sad resignation in his eyes, that he could not grant it. She wondered why. *Why? What have I done? What have I failed to do?* She would weep bitter tears of outrage, but quickly wipe them away with anger, calling herself a child for crying over such a stupid thing. And she would tell herself it did not matter, since his rejection would only hurt the more if she admitted to caring what he thought of her. Did she really care? Behind all the arguments and punishments, did she actually love him? She did not know. Perhaps she had . . . once. And perhaps part of her still did.

But no matter what her true feelings for her father were, she had certainly never thought about him dying, or what she would do or feel when he did. The vision *had* to be a bad dream, she told herself. A delusion. Her father had been in perfect health when she left Caithe. Yes, perfect health. But although she didn't want to believe what the sphere showed her, she knew that her mind would not be completely at peace until she confirmed that the magic globe had lied.

Between the shock of her recent nightmare and her broodings about her father, Athaya was now wide awake, and the darkness in the chamber was making her feel listless and gloomy. Moving slowly, so as not to aggravate her headache, she threw back the soft coverlets and slid her feet into a pair of soft leather slippers that had been set by her bedside. She padded across the carpet to open the heavy drapes that Ysell had closed earlier. As she crossed the room, she noticed that the drapes were rustling slightly, as if from a strong draft. *No wonder it's so chilly in here,* she thought. Shivering, she pulled back the curtains.

A soft cry escaped her throat and she reeled back sharply, as if struck full in the face by an icy wind. The glass from the window was completely shattered—blown out from the inside.

Trembling violently, she leaned on the windowsill, careful to avoid cutting herself on the shards of glass still clinging to the window frame. In the courtyard below her window, jagged pieces of glass lay scattered across the grass, reflecting the glare of the morning sun.

Athaya furiously swept the drapes closed and sank into a miserable ball on the floor. Her entire body was shaking, and she was overcome by a stream of confused and frightened tears. *There has to be another explanation for this,* she told herself, not wanting to accept the obvious one. *I am not going crazy. I am not. I am not!*

Ysell returned to find her there, huddled beneath the window with her arms wrapped around her knees. The queen set an earthenware cup on the bedstand and went to put her arms around Athaya's shoulders.

"I thought I told you to stay in bed," she scolded softly.

"T-the window . . . did I do that?" Athaya choked out, futilely trying to stop crying like a child in front of the Reykan queen.

"Only you can answer that. Was there anything about broken glass in your dream?"

Athaya nodded weakly, remembering the exploded stained-glass window and how the floor of the church was slick with blood. She glanced down to make sure the carpet in her room was not soaked red, but all she saw were bits of glass and a jagged tear in her slipper where she had stepped on one of the shards.

Ysell gathered her up, led her back to her bed, and covered her shivering body with downy quilts.

"It's frightening, I know," she said, tucking the covers around Athaya. "I am not a Lorngeld, so I haven't been through the *mekahn* myself, but I was with Felgin when his time came. He had a difficult time with it before he learned enough to take control of his power. I can't tell you the number of windows *he* broke!" Ysell added, laughing lightly.

"I'm just so confused," Athaya said quietly. "I never wanted this. I'm not even sure I believe it yet."

Ysell said nothing, but began to hum softly, reaching out to comfort her by stroking her hair with slender, fair-skinned fingers. It was a warm, maternal gesture that made her yearn for the kind of childhood she never had, and Athaya felt safer and more content than ever before.

"You're being so kind to me," she whispered. "I feel as if I'm one of your own children." Athaya closed her eyes. "I never knew my mother. She died a few days after I was born."

"Ah, that is sad." Ysell picked up an ivory-handled brush and began running it through Athaya's black hair. "But your father remarried, did he not?"

"Yes, twice. But from what I've heard, he never loved either of them. Not the way he loved my mother, Chandice. A long time ago—back when my oldest brother, Durek, was still being civil to me—he told me that Father was devastated when Chandice died, and that he never quite got over it. Of course, I have a hard time imagining my father loving anyone that much," she added sadly. "He's rather gruff and cold."

"Kings are, oftentimes. It is a difficult thing to bear the weight of an entire nation on one's shoulders. When Osfonin was young, he was not as merry as he is now. He was serious and reserved and had surprisingly little humor about him. But I have softened him a bit," she said with a knowing smile, "and now he's learned that being the king doesn't require that he also be a stodgy, unemotional old bastard."

Athaya laughed aloud. The young Osfonin sounded exactly like Durek.

"I wish my father would realize that," Athaya said. "Most of the time I think he hates me."

The gentle strokes of the hairbrush ceased, and Ysell gazed at her, suddenly serious. "He does not hate you, Athaya. More likely, he simply does not know how to tell you what he feels."

"I know what he feels. He feels that I'm an embarrassment to the whole family and he's ashamed of me. He wanted me to be the most brilliant, the most beautiful, the most talented young lady of his court. Someone he could be proud of and point to and say, 'That's my daughter.' " Athaya smiled wanly. "He didn't get his wish."

"It sounds as if he asked for the impossible," Ysell observed, with the cool serenity of one who is surprised by little. "Could he really have expected that such a wish would be granted?"

Ysell put the brush aside and reached for the earthenware cup on the bedstand. "Now drink this, Athaya. It'll help you sleep. And there won't be any dreams."

Athaya took a whiff of the gray, sludgelike concoction and wrinkled her nose. "What *is* this?" The thick liquid smelled like something scraped off the floor of a disreputable tavern, and didn't look much better.

"I think you're much more likely to drink it if I don't tell you what's in it," Ysell said with a twinkle in her eye. "But it will help you rest. It always worked for Felgin, although he complained about the smell far more than you did."

Athaya drank the mixture, glad that it didn't taste quite as bad as it smelled. It wasn't long before she began to yawn. Her eyelids fluttered and closed, and she had to struggle to keep from drifting off to sleep.

"Thank you for being here," Athaya said quietly, smiling. "And I'm sorry about the window."

"You're more than welcome," Ysell replied, gently touching her hand to Athaya's cheek. "You just get your rest. And don't worry about the window. I'll have it replaced right away."

Athaya opened one eye. "Maybe you shouldn't bother."

Ysell laughed musically and departed. In moments, soothed by Ysell's potion, Athaya fell into a deep, relaxing sleep. And there were no dreams.

The next day, Athaya felt fully recovered and was able to join Ysell and her family in the Great Hall for supper. She noted with great relief that neither Hedric nor Jaren was in the Hall that evening and she hoped that, wherever they were keeping themselves, they would stay there and leave her alone so that she could enjoy her supper. But she felt Tyler's worried eyes upon her throughout the meal; after supper was done and the servants began to clear the tables, Athaya said good night to the king and queen and skimmed around the edges of the Hall to speak to him.

"You had me worried," he said, as she sat down on the bench next to him, far enough away from the others that they would not be overheard. "Jaren told me you passed out—some sort of sudden fever. That's not like you."

"Did he say anything else?"

"No. That's why I was worried. You haven't been ill in years."

Athaya nodded, pleased at Jaren's show of good sense. Obviously Jaren realized that whatever Tyler knew or didn't know about her claims to wizardry was hers to decide. In light of her countrymen's prejudice against the Lorngeld, it would be safer for everyone not to discuss her "talents" too widely.

"I got the feeling that Jaren was hiding something," Tyler went on. "But I've always had that feeling about him—as if he's covering up something. What did he and Hedric say to you, anyway?"

Without thinking, she was just about to tell him when she suddenly bit back her words. Up until now, she could think of nothing that she hadn't confided to him . . . but this! This was totally different. Magic, whether it came from heaven or hell, had always seemed like a subject for priests and scholarly old men and it was one of the few things she and Tyler had never found the need to discuss at length. She had no way of predicting how he might react. She knew that Tyler had never openly condoned the concept of absolution, but simply accepted it as an unfortunate fact of life. How would he feel, knowing that she was one of the cursed ones? And with her marriage to Felgin growing more likely with each passing day, such news might be just the excuse he needed to put his love for her behind him once and for all, as he knew he would have to do eventually.

At that moment, Athaya felt very afraid and alone.

How can I tell you, Tyler? she cried inwardly. *You're the only good thing I've ever had, and I'm not going to risk losing you— not one minute before I have to. And I'm definitely not going to do it because of some bizarre story that Hedric and Jaren concocted in their spare time.*

"They just wanted to talk to me about the Lorngeld," she said, with as much casualness as she could. "Jaren said something about it that night at the abbey, remember? They're especially concerned about the rite of absolution. As you can imagine, they're violently opposed to the idea and want me to try and do something to stop it." That was fairly close to the truth. As close as she planned to get for now. Never mind that Hedric expected her to do it alone, by leading a crusade against the Church and exposing herself as one of the Lorngeld.

"You? That's odd—why don't they talk to Kelwyn?"

"Maybe because I'm here and he isn't," she said impatiently, eager to get off the subject. "Besides, what makes you think talking to me wouldn't do any good? I'm not totally incompetent, you know. I might be able to express their views to my father and persuade him to listen to what Hedric has to say."

"I didn't mean that at all, Athaya," he said, his voice edged with irritation.

"Well, it certainly sounded like it."

Tyler frowned skeptically. "You're awfully touchy about this."

"If I'm touchy, it's only because you keep badgering me."

"Look, Athaya, I just think it's damned peculiar that this fellow Hedric sends Jaren off on a five-hundred-mile trip to get you to come to Reyka—a trip he didn't even have to make in the first place—only to tell you something that he could just as easily have put in a letter to Kelwyn. Don't you find that a little odd? Unless there's a piece missing to this puzzle and there's something you're not telling me."

"For God's sake, Tyler, why are you so damned curious about everything all of a sudden?" she said defensively. "The day after we arrived here, you grilled me about a conversation I had with Felgin, and now you're after me about this. And that reminds me . . . since when did you and the prince become such close friends? You went out hunting with him a few days ago, didn't you?"

"What does *that* have to do with anything?" he asked, bewildered by the abrupt change of subject. "Felgin was going out on a hunt and asked me to come along; it's as simple as that. And I actually had quite a good time."

"I'm glad," she said blandly.

"For heaven's sake, Athaya, what's the matter with you? And what in God's name is so terrible about my going out riding with Felgin? Do you think I'm going to babble to him about how wonderful you are so he'll be that much more tempted to marry you? I'd never do that, although your father would certainly have wanted me to, if he knew I'd had the chance."

"I'm sure he would," she said, oddly disturbed by Tyler's friendship with the prince.

"Of course, if you command me not to befriend him, your Highness," he said, now coldly formal, "then I will obey you."

Athaya felt every muscle in her body grow taut, like bowstrings pulled too tight. She swore that if they were anywhere else but the Great Hall, she would have struck him. It did not happen often, but when Tyler was extremely upset about something, he would throw her titles up in her face and play the humble servant, well aware that it infuriated her far more than anything else he could ever do. It shone a glaring torch over the gulf which separated them and pricked like a thorn where she was most sensitive.

"That wasn't fair, Tyler."

"I don't care if it was fair or not. I'm only trying to help, but it's obvious that you don't want me to. And if that's the way you want it, I won't stand here and argue about it in front of a roomful of people. But I think something's going on around here, and whatever it is, you don't trust me enough to tell me about it."

Fuming, Tyler got up from the table, making a point of offering her an elegantly cold bow before he stalked away. Despite the carefully controlled look of calm on his face, she could see his hands curling into tight fists as he left the Hall. The sound of his angry footsteps echoed on the stone walls of the corridor outside the Great Hall before they quickly faded away.

Her shoulders drooping, Athaya slipped out of the Hall and somberly headed toward her chambers. She rarely argued with Tyler and she hated it each time she did—it always left her feeling empty and abandoned. Perhaps a good night's rest would clear both their heads, and they could talk more rationally in the morning. But she still was not going to tell him about her magic. That was something that a simple good night's sleep wouldn't allow him to accept as easily.

She almost groaned aloud when she saw Jaren lingering in the corridor outside her chambers. He leaned back against the wall, his arms folded across his chest, tapping the toe of his boot restlessly on the floor. Athaya quickly thought of going back to the Hall, but she was not quick enough. He had already seen her.

"Stay away from me, Jaren," she said as he approached. "I don't want to hear one single word out of you right now."

"You're going to have to," he said firmly. She had not noticed it before, but now she saw that his face was drawn and strained, and he looked badly in need of sleep. "You must come see Master Hedric again. Right away."

Athaya pushed roughly past him. "Absolutely not. And don't even bother asking again, because the answer will still be no."

"You only heard part of what he had to tell you before—"

"Before what? Before I passed out and was sick in bed for three days? No, Jaren, I'm not getting involved in any more of his stupid magic tricks. I'm not coming with you and that's final."

She opened the door, hoping to slam it in his face, but as she threw it closed, Jaren held up one hand and made a quick sign with his fingers. The heavy door stopped dead, as if it had hit a doorstop.

"It's important, Athaya," Jaren said, dropping his voice down low. "Very important. And I can make you come if I have to."

Jaren's veiled threat only made her angrier. "Would you two simply leave me *alone*?"

"It has nothing to do with you this time!" he shot back. He grabbed hold of her wrist and drew her back out into the hallway. "It's about Kelwyn."

Athaya felt as if the ground had dropped out from under her feet, and Jaren's face seemed to swim before her eyes. The vision she had seen in her sphere came back with horrible clarity. Up until now, she had persuaded herself that it had only been a delusion, a horrible nightmare, but that reassuring belief had just been brutally snatched away from her.

Athaya clutched the doorframe for support, and her voice was barely above a whisper. "He's dead, isn't he?"

"Follow me," Jaren said, leading her away from her chambers. "Master Hedric will explain everything."

CHAPTER 10

✼✼✼

ONCE AGAIN ROBED IN BLACK, HEDRIC WAS AT HIS WINdow gazing pensively at the stars when Athaya and Jaren arrived in the tower chamber. The room was quiet—abnormally quiet—and even the fire burned silently, without a crackle. Jaren moved to the windowseat, sinking down into the moonlit cushions. With a slight gesture of his white hand, Hedric invited Athaya to sit as well, but she was too worried to relax and merely leaned against the back of Hedric's tree-chair, nervously tapping her fingertips on the varnished wood.

"Jaren says something's wrong with my father. What is it? He can't be dead . . . he was fine when I left home." It had not even been three weeks since she rode out of Delfar Castle, but suddenly it seemed much longer, as if she'd been gone for months. To her own surprise, and perhaps for the first time in her life, she desperately wanted to be home to make sure everything was all right. The vision of Kelwyn's death had shaken her, and the strained look of worry on Hedric's face did nothing to lessen her fears that something was very wrong in Caithe.

"Your father is alive," the old wizard said wearily, as the firelight made shadows on his weathered face. "But I will not lie to you, Athaya. I don't think he will live much longer."

Athaya stared straight head, unmoving, and everything around her seemed to fade into a misty, dreamlike background. "I don't understand," she murmured. "Is he ill?"

Hedric sighed deeply. "If he has not succumbed yet, he will—to the mind-plague. I fear there is little hope."

"But that's not possible!" she said, too stunned to be angry. "How can the *mekahn* strike him? He's nearly fifty years old and he's not even a Lorngeld!"

"I know. That is the tragedy of it. Were he of the Lorngeld, he would be able to save himself. But now . . ." Hedric's voice drifted off, and he and Jaren exchanged a brief look of sad understanding.

"On the night you arrived in Ath Luaine, Jaren related to me what you told him during your journey here—that Kelwyn's power was not his own and had been bestowed on him through a magic ritual. I had suspected that for quite some time, but I was never sure of it until now. In order for you to understand your father's situation, I need to explain to you the method by which he assumed his power. It was done through what we call the 'rite of assumption.' "

"I've never heard of that before," she said, realizing only after she'd spoken how ridiculously obvious that fact was. Why would she have any knowledge about some arcane wizard's ritual? Up until a few days ago, the only thing she'd known about magic was that people unfortunate enough to be born with it went mad and died, destroying themselves with their own magic. She had never needed or desired to know more.

"I wouldn't have expected you to know of it," Hedric said, lowering himself into the high-backed chair at his worktable. "The ritual has been forbidden for almost two hundred years."

A forbidden ritual. That phrase struck a familiar chord in Athaya. Yes, she remembered hearing vague rumors that Rhodri used some form of forbidden knowledge to grant Kelwyn his powers, but she had never thought anything about it until now. Magic had always been a part of the Kelwyn that she knew—he had possessed it before she was ever born. She had never been much interested in how he obtained it. And since he rarely used his magic now that there was relative peace in Caithe, it was easy to forget that he possessed it at all.

"Why forbid such a ritual?" she asked at last. "If someone's willing to take the risk, what's the harm?"

She saw Jaren dart a quick look to Hedric. The old wizard's

jaw tensed and he drew his shoulders back, looking more angry and awesomely powerful than Athaya had ever seen him. "Because it is wrong for those not born of the Lorngeld to obtain the powers that God chose not to give them. The Lord has his own purposes for choosing who is to be bestowed with magic and who is not. We cannot meddle with His decisions. Such meddlings have dangerous consequences, and the Circle of Masters—that body which monitors the actions of the Lorngeld throughout the Continent—forbade the ritual because of what happened the last time it was used."

Athaya frowned. "The last time?"

"Yes. In the time of your King Faltil, two centuries ago. It was this ritual that ultimately caused the Time of Madness."

Athaya's eyes widened in terror. She hadn't attended to much as a child, but she did know her history. She remembered the stories about rampant death and destruction and how the Lorngeld literally tore Caithe apart with their uncontrolled magic. It had been nothing less than a holocaust—thousands of the Lorngeld gone insane, causing fires, explosions, sickness, and death all around them as they slowly succumbed to the mind-plague. The idea that the blackest era in her country's history and her own father's fate were tied up in the same tale frightened her beyond anything she could imagine.

Jaren, who had been sitting silently beneath the window, picked up the story's thread from Hedric. "King Faltil persuaded a young wizard/friend of his to perform the ritual by telling him how much better a king he could be with the power of magic at his command."

Athaya shook her head, confused. Something was not right. Either her memory was faulty, or the histories she had been taught as a child were not entirely accurate and true. "But wait— I thought Faltil was a Lorngeld to begin with."

"No. That's simply the conclusion that your historians made, once Faltil was dead. Faltil was not a Lorngeld, but he was jealous of them—intensely jealous. They had a power that he didn't and that infuriated him. He wanted the power of magic badly, and when his wizard-friend, Senal, told him about the new discoveries concerning the rite of assumption, he realized he'd found a way to get it. Faltil convinced Senal to give him his power by telling him that it would be a noble sacrifice—that as king, he could use magic to do far more good for his people than the wizard himself could, not being of royal blood. And in return for his gift, Faltil promised to reward Senal with lands and titles and wealth beyond his wildest imaginings."

"I'm confused. You mean the wizard had to give up his *own* magic?"

"One cannot create power where it does not exist, Athaya," Hedric explained softly. "Power can be transferred, but only God can create it. And it is not our right to give it to those whom God has not chosen."

"So what happened to Faltil's friend?" she asked, wondering what sort of terrible revenge Hedric's God would exact on those who gave away the gift that He had bestowed on them.

Hedric leaned forward, folding his hands together. "Senal was an idealist and devoted to his country. And he was more than a little proud to be involved in such a grand scheme. So he agreed to perform the rite. Faltil must have been persuasive indeed, to convince Senal to give up his power—his very essence. It reminds me of the old tales about selling one's soul to the Devil," Hedric added with a frown. "But apparently Senal thought the sacrifice was worth it. He thought that Faltil would be a great king and, of course, he also thought of the honor he might get for himself by being the one who made it all possible. Faltil no doubt used his friend's vanity against him. But he had to make sure Senal was willing, for power cannot be taken from a wizard unless he gives it freely.

"The rite was done very secretly, so that no one would ever know that the king's magic was merely borrowed from another man and not bestowed by God. But once the king got his power and learned how to work a few spells, he betrayed Senal. He didn't use his magic for the good of his people—instead, he began to seek out and destroy every trained wizard in Caithe, so he alone would have the knowledge of magic. And he succeeded. The Lorngeld that fled here to Reyka during that time told of the inquisitions and burnings . . . of how Faltil persuaded other wizards to turn against their brothers and destroy them, so that they would be sole custodians of the art of magic. And once his minions had done this, Faltil turned against them, too. When the scourge was over, Faltil was the only wizard in Caithe, and there was no one with the power to oppose him."

A glimpse of pain appeared on Hedric's weathered features before he went on, as if he had personally known some of those ancient Lorngeld and still grieved for them. "With the wizards in his country dead, there was no one left to train those Lorngeld who reached the *mekahn*. They succumbed to the madness and left destruction in their wake, burning forests and towns, destroying fortresses that had stood for hundreds of years, calling storms, and casting spells of sickness. I'm sure you remember the stories. And it would not be so different today, but for your rite of absolution. That is what keeps the violence in check—by killing the Lorngeld before they can do much damage. But in those days there was no such thing, and the priests didn't know what to do.

"No wonder your Church grew afraid of them and called them the Devil's Children. It certainly would have seemed that God was using Faltil as a means to destroy them. And Faltil encouraged this, pushing his priests and bishops to preach against the Lorngeld. He loved his power too much to share it and did not want a single one of the Lorngeld to be schooled in the use of magic. Such a one might challenge and defeat him. So to protect himself against the scourge he'd begun, he told everyone that his magic had been given to him by God, and that God had instructed him to use his power to rid the land of the Devil's Children and their mad destruction."

Athaya's mind was spinning from what she'd been told. It all seemed too fantastic to be real, but in another way, it all made awful sense. She had been taught that Faltil was a Lorngeld, and as such, had caused the ruin of his country. She had not been told that he was an inherently evil man—a man born without magic, but subject to human greed and jealousy. But whether the historians at that time truly believed Faltil was Lorngeld or not, they had decided to teach posterity that he was, and Faltil was blamed for all the misfortunes that befell Caithe during those dark times. Ever since then, the Lorngeld had been marked as a dangerous threat to the peace. And what had Faltil done? *Nothing short of mass murder*, Athaya thought. *Just like the Church and all its babble about absolution. Oh, but how soon I forget*—that *method of murder is of a properly approved kind.*

"But what about this friend of his—Senal?" Athaya asked. "Didn't he do anything?"

Jaren shook his head. "Senal realized what he had done, but it was too late. He protested violently, but without his magic, he was powerless to act against the king. Faltil took back Senal's lands and titles and had the former wizard tried for treason, for daring to speak out against the king and for being so presumptuous as to claim that *he* had given Faltil his magic, and not God.'' Jaren's face grew solemn. ''Senal was executed shortly after that.''

''Senal paid a high price for what he had done,'' Hedric said. ''And after he was dead, the Circle of Masters decided to outlaw the practice of power transferral. The rite of assumption had only been perfected a few years prior to Faltil's reign, and all of its destructive properties were not yet known.'' Hedric looked away, absently staring at the stars twinkling outside his window. ''And I hope they never shall be.''

''I'm still confused, Master Hedric,'' Athaya said, using his title for the first time. ''I was taught that Faltil died of the mind-plague. If he wasn't a Lorngeld to begin with, what happened?''

''Your historians assumed he was a Lorngeld because he *did* die of the madness. But that did not take place for several years. Faltil enjoyed his power for a time, watching the Lorngeld in his country—the same people he took an oath to protect—being winnowed out and murdered. Those who spoke out against the atrocities were burned as heretics. But after twenty years went by, and the magic began pressing upon his mind, Faltil was powerless to stop it. And in his case, the madness was not gradual, surfacing over the course of six months or so, as with a normal Lorngeld. His was quick and intense, overpowering him in a matter of days. It grew steadily worse, until finally, as you know, he died when his magic went completely out of control and he set himself on fire.''

Athaya felt her stomach churn. Such a death was too terrible for her to imagine. Her forehead broke out in beads of sweat at the thought of the hot flames, the greasy, sickening smell of charred flesh, and the agonizing pain of stripping off flaming clothes and peeling off blackened skin as well.

''If Faltil's death accomplished any one thing, it was to teach the Lorngeld more about the nature of magic and the mind than we had previously known. First, we learned that the act of giving away one's power is surprisingly simple; a wizard at any level of training could do it. The difficulty lies in preparing the mind of the receiver—in constructing the framework within which he'll work his magic. Not being born with that element of the mind, it needs to be added before the power can be bestowed.''

"Like needing a pitcher to put the water in?"

Hedric smiled. "Something like that. You see, in the Lorngeld, this framework—we call it our 'paths'—doesn't develop until approximately twenty years from one's birth, and thus the onset of the *mekahn*. Until that time, the power remains relatively latent in the mind. But in cases where magic is transferred, the framework is there and so the power can be used right away. Its adverse effects on the mind don't appear until about twenty years after the magic has been bestowed. No one really knows why it happens. Perhaps the falsely constructed framework simply can't handle the magic once it matures. In Faltil's case, he was a young man of twenty-eight when the ritual was performed, and so the madness struck him when he was close to fifty.''

Athaya shivered, as if caught in a cold draft. "Just like my father," she whispered.

"I'm afraid so. The twenty-year process began when Kelwyn assumed his power. Since you tell me his magic was bestowed on him about a year before you were born, and that you are now twenty, the *mekahn* is imminent in him—if not somewhat overdue. Indeed, it has already begun in you, and seems to be nearly halfway through its course, judging from the way your dreams have begun spilling over into the real world—yes, Ysell told me about the window. But for you, there is hope. You can be taught to manage your power. When the time comes for Kelwyn, there will be no way to stop it.''

"But isn't there something we can do?" she cried desperately. "If my father is going through the *mekahn*, can't he be trained? That's what stops the madness, isn't it?"

"Not in this case, Athaya. Since your father is not a Lorngeld, he does not possess that part of the mind which can be trained to comprehend his magic. He was not born with it, as you were. The ability to understand—to truly understand—what magic *is* cannot be passed from one person to another. It's a gift—a sixth sense.''

Athaya's face was lined with tension as she strained under the weight of everything she had been told. "None of this is making *any* kind of sense, sixth or otherwise! If he can't be trained, then why can't he use his magic *now*?"

"Kelwyn's power has never been true," Hedric explained.

"He casts his spells like a child who recites memorized verses, oblivious to their meaning. Your father was given the tool for magic, but not the gift for using it. It was as if Rhodri had given him a harp and taught him how to pluck out notes by rote, but without any knowledge of how to arrange them to make music. Faltil's magic was much the same. Senal gave away his instrument—his power—but retained the gift for using it, even though the gift was rendered useless. It must have been horrible for him to watch what Faltil was doing with his power, knowing he could do nothing to stop it, knowing that his own gift was useless—like a master harper with all the music playing in his head, but whose hands have been cut off."

Athaya slumped down in the tree-chair, leaning forward with her head cupped between her hands, as if trying not to pass out.

"I don't understand," she murmured. "Rhodri told everyone that because my father isn't a Lorngeld, the madness wouldn't affect him."

"That's because Rhodri was much too self-confident," Hedric said, his mouth twisting up in disgust. "He was convinced that Faltil's adverse reaction to the ritual was because of Senal's incompetence in preparing the king's mind to receive the power. Rhodri wanted to try it again and prove that there was no reason to forbid the transfer of power from a Lorngeld to a non-Lorngeld. In the letter you brought to me from Rhodri, he told of his success with Kelwyn and that over twenty years had passed since he'd taken on his power with no signs of the madness. He wants me to petition the Circle of Masters to revoke the law concerning the rite of assumption and has asked me to meet with them and persuade them to hear his case. But I refuse to do such a foolish thing. I'm afraid Rhodri began gloating over his success a bit too soon."

Athaya felt a hot tingle of anger ripple through her. "Are you trying to tell me that Rhodri knew all along that this ritual could kill my father and yet he went ahead and *did* it? He endangered the life of the king for the sake of some stupid *experiment*?"

Hedric nodded regretfully, but his jaw was firm from anger. "I'm afraid Rhodri has little respect for the life of his king and even less for the lives of his subjects. In fact, I think the only people Rhodri has ever respected are those who make up the Circle of Masters. He has always wanted to join our number. Over time, it became an obsession with him."

The old wizard shifted his weight in his chair and winced at the stiffness in his joints. Then the lines in his cheeks subsided, and his face took on a nostalgic, almost sad expression.

"Rhodri was one of the most brilliant pupils I ever trained," Hedric said, letting out a wistful sigh. "Remember when I told you that I used to go to Caithe and look for Lorngeld who would agree to be trained? Well, Rhodri was one of the ones I found. His parents were tenants on a small estate within a few days' ride of the Reykan border. They couldn't bear to see their son taken away by the Church and poisoned, so when I arrived, they told him to go with me. He was about nineteen then, I think—in the early stages of the *mekahn*. His talent was obvious even then, so I brought him back here and taught him everything I could. He was an unusually quick learner, even though he tended to be overly proud of himself. He liked knowing he could work spells that were out of the range of most wizards. I'm convinced that if he actually *did* get the rite of assumption to work flawlessly, he'd never tell anyone how he did it. He's much like Faltil in that respect.

"But while I noticed these things, seeing Rhodri each day as I did, most of the other Circle members did not. The others I knew at that time—most have since died, God rest their souls—were amazed at his proficiency and skill. Rhodri had a great gift for magic and was told so on many occasions."

The old wizard let out a sharp, mirthless laugh. "Unfortunately, he took all the compliments a bit too seriously and began thinking he was smarter than all of his teachers. In one respect he was right. Judged on technical proficiency, he could have been one of the Great Masters. But his biggest failing was in the area of ethics . . . of knowing how and when it is acceptable to use one's powers. That sense of ethics is what distinguishes a true Master from other wizards. When Rhodri was taught about the rite of assumption, what it had done to Faltil, and why it was forbidden, he was wildly anxious to test it. He was understandably furious when I told him he couldn't. It is sad in a way," Hedric added, shaking his head. "Brilliant as he was, he could never understand that just because something *can* be done, doesn't mean it *should* be done."

Athaya could feel her head begin to pound. This was all too much to comprehend. "If you knew Rhodri was going to try something like this, then why didn't your damned Circle do anything to stop him?'' she asked, suddenly overwhelmed with anger that, knowing what they did, neither Hedric, nor Jaren, nor any other wizard in Reyka had made a move against him.

Jaren's face went red with anger. "*Damned* Circle? Do you have any idea who you're insulting? I'll ask you to show some respect for—"

"That's enough, Jaren," Hedric said shortly, cutting him off with a wave of his hand. "I think Athaya has enough to worry about right now without your making her feel worse."

Jaren thrust out his lower lip defiantly and slumped back down in his seat, simmering in silent outrage.

"I argued with Rhodri about it several times," Hedric said. "I tried to get him interested in other things besides the rite of assumption, but he became obsessed with trying it, probably because he knew it was the one thing I told him he couldn't try. Our friendship was near the breaking point when we heard that one of the Circle had called a meeting to propose the name of a new member. Knowing his reputation among them, Rhodri was convinced he was the one we were considering. A few weeks later, the Circle met to vote on the new candidate, which, indeed, was Rhodri. But a unanimous decision is required, and Rhodri's nomination was overturned by one vote." Hedric paused, curling his fingers around the edge of the table. "Mine."

Rhodri's words echoed through Athaya's mind. *We had a slight falling-out at one time.* That had certainly been an understatement.

"What happened?" she asked quietly.

"The day after I told him the results of the election, he was gone. He simply disappeared. It was months before I discovered he was in Caithe—he was very adept at shielding himself from my sphere with wards. And then I started hearing rumors about Kelwyn's magic and about the unusual success he was having quelling the civil war. I heard that he could touch the minds of his lords to see if they were being truthful when they swore their oaths of loyalty and that he always seemed to know just where his enemies were hiding and how many men they had . . . the result of sphere-work, most likely. Once I began hearing those things, I started to suspect that Rhodri was involved."

"And you didn't *do* anything?" she cried, outraged by the wizard's seeming carelessness.

"I did all I could, Athaya. I tried to contact Rhodri with my sphere, but someone—I wasn't sure whether it was Rhodri or Kelwyn—kept Delfar Castle tightly warded against me, and I could see nothing. I even wanted to go to Caithe and try to talk to Rhodri, but the Circle of Masters forbade me to go, knowing that in your country I could have easily been arrested and executed simply for being a wizard. Rhodri took an incredible risk going there himself. I have no idea how he managed to get an audience with Kelwyn and make his offer of magic. But apparently the risk paid off—for Rhodri at least. Until now."

Hedric held up his hands, palms up. "And, the Circle told me, if the ritual had been performed already, what could I have done? I might have been able to persuade Kelwyn to give back the power he took, but give it to whom? Some poor unfortunate who would go mad himself when the time came? Again, ethics," he said with a shrug. "And on top of everything else, I didn't know at that time if Rhodri had given Kelwyn his own power, or enlisted the help of a third party. The Circle also brought up the very real possibility that Kelwyn was born one of the Lorngeld, and that Rhodri had simply trained him, hoping that he would put an end to the rite of absolution in Caithe. Kelwyn was close to thirty at that time, and although extremely rare, it is not unheard of for the *mekahn* to appear that late. In lieu of anything else, we accepted that, hoping it was true, and that Rhodri's common sense had steered him along the right path. Later on, once we heard that there was a wizard in Kelwyn's court who was instructing him in magic, we were even more convinced that Kelwyn was a Lorngeld and that Rhodri was simply training him."

The old wizard sighed dejectedly. "Obviously, we were wrong. Rhodri must have found someone willing to give up his magic for Kelwyn. Of course, in Caithe, I can't imagine that finding someone willing to get rid of his magic would have been all that difficult."

Athaya frowned. "Now that I think of it, Rhodri never said where the power came from. He only said that the ritual gave it to Kelwyn."

"I'm sure that the person who gave up his power was encouraged to be silent about it. Can you imagine the rioting that would take place if the Lorngeld in your country suddenly found out that there was a way to get rid of the so-called 'Devil's gift'?"

Hedric paused, and folded his hands in his lap. "What Rhodri still does not understand is that even if his plan actually worked—even if Kelwyn suffered no ill effects of his power—I would still cast my vote against Rhodri for Circle membership on purely ethical grounds. But ambitious as he is, perhaps he would simply wait for me to die . . . who knows? He's waited twenty years already. He might be willing to hold out for a few more."

"I just don't see why my father has to pay for Rhodri's insufferable egoism!" she cried, furious both with Rhodri and at whoever it was that had cursed her father by giving away his own magic.

Hedric clasped his hands in front of him. "Magic commands a price, Athaya. Not even a king is exempt from that. And the larger the gift, the more it must be earned."

"Well, it certainly doesn't sound as if Rhodri paid any sort of a price at all," she snapped. "From what you tell me, he's gone from being a poor farm boy to a powerful wizard who sits in my father's court waiting to see if his experiment is going to work so he can earn himself a place on your precious Circle. And while he waits, he does nothing to help Kelwyn in his work to abolish the rite of absolution. He delights in being the only one in Caithe besides the king who knows how to work magic—just like Faltil."

"Faltil paid for his magic," Hedric said. His eyes took on an ominous cast. "As will Rhodri."

"And my father?" she asked, her hands shaking.

Hedric did not look away as she thought he might, but held his gaze on her. "I'm sorry, Athaya. I'm afraid that in Kelwyn's case, he will pay for using magic that was not rightfully his by birth. But the situation may not be as tragic as it seems right now," he added. "It's likely that the rite of assumption, in addition to giving Kelwyn his power, was also responsible for your being born a Lorngeld. It could also account for your extraordinarily high level of power. I'm not sure how, exactly—Faltil never had any children after he assumed his magic, so we have no way of knowing if they would have been born with the gift or not."

"Good God, listen to yourself!" Athaya cried, bolting out of her seat and slamming a fist on Hedric's worktable. "You expect me to believe that my being born a mind-plagued wizard is supposed to make up for my father going crazy and dying some

sort of horrible death? That's the most callous, nonsensical thing
I've ever heard in my life! And how do I know you're not lying
to me about my own supposed magic? How do I know that the
sphere I created wasn't your handiwork—or Jaren's? How do I
know that everything you've been telling me isn't a pack of
damnable lies?''

She knew her accusations weren't true, but her frustrations
were pent up so tightly that the words tumbled out uncontrollably. Athaya could feel hot tears stinging her eyes when she was
finished and angrily brushed them away. It was too much for
her to take—everything was just too much. She felt as if she
were slipping into a dream world—an unreal place full of nightmares and sordid tales, where everything she used to believe in
suddenly wasn't valid anymore. But something wouldn't let her
escape, something wouldn't let her run away to hide from what
Hedric was telling her. But whatever that something was, she
hated and despised it for keeping her here and wished that she
had never come to Reyka, nor ever heard of the Lorngeld and
their hell-spawned magic arts.

Her hands began to shake, and her eyes flickered hungrily to
the row of herb jars on Hedric's shelf, wondering if one of them
might contain any looca—at least enough to make her forget
everything she'd just been told.

''I don't know why I'm listening to *any* of this!'' she shouted,
turning her back on Hedric and clutching her head between her
palms. ''You're just trying to make me crazy. Both of you! And
I wish—''

Suddenly there was a loud clatter of noise as one of the herb
jars on Hedric's shelves flew from its place and smashed against
the far wall, showering the floor with scraps of broken pottery
and greenish-brown powder.

Athaya gasped and covered her eyes. ''I wish both of you
would leave me alone!'' she cried, frightened by what was happening to her and knowing she could not control it. *''Stop doing
this to me!''*

Another jar slid off the shelf and crashed to the floor, filling
the room with a stench like rotten eggs. And another jar quickly
followed—and another, until the floor was littered with earthenware shards and scraps of dried leaves and roots. Athaya was
unaware of them now, however, too wrapped up in her own
tortured thoughts to realize what was going on around her and

paying no attention to Hedric calmly shuffling across the room to clean up the half-dozen broken jars. She fell back into the tree-chair, striking the armrests with her fists, trying to fend off the alien emotions overtaking her.

Jaren gripped her shoulders hard and began to shake her. "Athaya, stop it! Try to take control!"

"Let go of me," she said, trying to squirm out of his grasp. "I can't take control—everything's falling apart—I don't know what to do . . ." She babbled on, unaware of what she was saying and only barely aware that she was speaking at all. It was as if she had lost control over her very self, and some demon-child inside her was governing her actions and her words. Distantly, she heard the panes of glass in the window begin to rattle, on the verge of exploding as if battered by a forceful wind. The room seemed to fade away, as if she were drifting off into some other world, and Jaren's grip began to grow weak and insubstantial, as if he were a mere shadow.

Then she felt a sharp sting, definitely not from any shadow. She clasped her hand to her cheek, now hot with pain from where Jaren had struck her. Gradually, like being roused from a drunken stupor, her mind began to clear. The room appeared real and solid to her again. The blackness had gone. Hedric looked up from where he hunched on the floor tidying up, and after raising a brow at Jaren, went back to his work, satisfied that she was all right. Jaren, however, looked almost sheepish as he backed away from her, hiding his hands behind his back.

"I'm sorry I had to do that, Athaya," he said. "I had to break your concentration. Sometimes there's no other way."

Athaya rubbed her cheek, easing away the sting. "I can't argue that it worked," she said, offering him a half smile to let him know she wasn't angry. In fact, she had to admire him for having the gumption to openly strike a foreign princess. "I feel better now. Thanks." She took a deep breath, and grimaced from the rotten-egg odor still lingering in the air. "I'm sorry about the jars."

"Don't worry about it," Hedric told her, tossing a handful of pottery pieces into a basket in the corner. "I've grown used to this sort of thing over the years. Jaren had quite a fondness for breaking things when he was going through the *mekahn*. So did Felgin, as I recall. It's very common."

"I don't know what came over me. What you said about my

father—it just struck something inside me. I couldn't control it."

"Your mind is straining under the pressure of your magic, Athaya. It will be hard for you to have complete control over your actions until you've mastered your power. And that will take time—the greater the gift, the more difficult it becomes to control." He approached her and laid a hand on her shoulder. "But as to the issue of Kelwyn, please believe that I didn't mean to sound callous. I am saddened by this more than you know. Kelwyn has been one of the greatest of the Caithan kings. He is the first king in two centuries who has sympathized with the Lorngeld. His death will be a blow to them. From what I gather, his eldest son does not share his views and will likely let the persecutions continue."

Athaya nodded glumly. "Durek hates Rhodri and all the Lorngeld. He can accept Father because he wasn't born with the power, but he tends to agree with Archbishop Ventan that the Lorngeld are cursed. He was livid when he found out Kelwyn was considering my marriage to Felgin." Despondent, Athaya slouched forward and cupped her cheeks in her palms. "I just can't believe this . . . I wish I knew if he was all right."

Then she thought of something. She didn't want to try it, but it seemed as if there was no other way.

"I could use a sphere—my sphere—to see him, couldn't I?"

No! her mind cried out in protest. *What on earth are you saying, you fool! You're starting to accept the fact that you have the power. And if you believe anything strongly enough, it just might come true. Be careful what you wish for . . .*

"You can try," Hedric said. "But without formal training, your visions are bound to be inaccurate. If you like, I can try to see him for you. But I can't promise you I'll be able to—I tried a few days ago, right after your last attempt at sphere-work, but Rhodri must have had the castle spelled against me. I couldn't see anything. Unfortunately, that could be a sign that something has started to go wrong, and that Rhodri is trying to keep anyone on the Circle from finding out."

"That's not good enough!" she said in a commanding, royal voice, ignoring the fact that among wizards, Hedric probably outranked her to no small extent. "I have to see it for myself. I have to know that what I saw before wasn't true. I have to know he isn't dead!"

Hedric wheeled around quickly, his eyes flashing. "Is that what you saw?"

Athaya nodded, and Jaren drew in a sharp breath. "You don't think she was seeing futures, do you?" Jaren asked his master, stunned.

"Doubtful," the old wizard replied hesitantly, obviously annoyed with Jaren for tactlessly voicing the ghoulish suspicion, even though his trepidation indicated that he probably shared it. "Athaya, what you saw in your sphere can hardly be construed as truth. Your power is untrained. You can't trust it to be reliable. And you've openly admitted that you and your father have never gotten along. I expect that you merely projected into the sphere some deep-rooted fears that Kelwyn would die before you made your peace with each other, and thus, your mind created a false vision."

"Then there's only one thing to do." In one fluid motion, she pulled herself out of the comfortable tree-chair and headed for the door.

"Wait, Athaya—" Jaren called out. "Where are you going?"

"To see Osfonin," she said firmly. "To tell him that I must leave Reyka immediately."

"But you can't go now!" he sputtered. "The *mekahn* has already begun in you, and there's no way of predicting how quickly it will progress. Master Hedric already told you that you're halfway through your time. Don't you know what that means? You could be risking your life by leaving. You've got to stay and learn to use your magic before you go back to Caithe!"

Athaya narrowed her eyes. "And leave my father to die?"

Hedric rose to his full height, fixing his gaze on her the same way he had when she had first arrived at the palace. "If you go now, Athaya, you will only see to it that you die with him."

Hedric's ominous prediction shook her for a moment, but she remained adamant. "Master Hedric, you don't understand—"

"You are the one who does not understand, Athaya. You know what untrained magic can do. Do you think yours will be any different? As an adept, you may do even worse damage than most."

Athaya sighed impatiently. "Then I'll come back. I'll make sure he's all right, and then I'll come back."

Hedric shook his head solemnly. "You would never return in time. Even now you are in danger. Breaking a window and some crockery are trivial compared to what can happen in the late stages of the *mekahn*. Were you to remain untrained for even another month, the results would be disastrous.''

''But my father—''

''You can do nothing to help him,'' Hedric said, sincerely regretful. ''And it will be dangerous for you there now. You must not fall into the hands of your Church. They will try to destroy you if they know what you are. And Rhodri could pose a danger as well,'' he added. ''Not simply because of your power—although I can't imagine he'd like knowing he has a rival in Caithe—but because he might perceive you as a threat. You could expose what he's done to Kelwyn and ruin him.''

''But everyone already *knows* what he's done.''

''They know Rhodri gave him power. But they don't know that the ritual all but doomed him. Listen, Athaya, I know how Rhodri thinks. This 'experiment' means everything to him, and he'll take action against anyone who interferes with it. If he discovers your power, then it won't take him long to realize that I already know about it, too. And if he notices a change in your behavior toward Kelwyn, he'll start worrying about what I've told you concerning the rite of assumption. He might fear that you'd tell everyone how he purposefully endangered Kelwyn's life for his own ends. All his claims about wanting to help the king reunite his country using the gift of magic would be seen as the lies they were. The suspicion alone would ruin whatever sort of benevolent reputation he's managed to cultivate for himself, and once Kelwyn began suffering from the *mekahn*, your charges would be proved true, and Rhodri's deceit would be obvious. Your priests would have more proof that magic is evil, and Rhodri would be lucky to get out of Caithe with his life.'' Hedric regarded her seriously. ''And he'd have you to thank for it.''

''Then that's a risk I have to take,'' Athaya said, full of determination. ''Master Hedric, I'm sorry. I'm not sure I can explain it any better than this, but I simply have to be there with him. My father and I . . . we haven't been the best of friends. If there's even a chance that he's going to die, I have to be there.''

She paused before she left and turned her eyes toward the window to gaze at the stars—the same stars which glittered over Delfarham, five hundred miles away. ''I have to say I'm sorry,'' she whispered, speaking not to Hedric or Jaren, but to herself, and the stars, and whoever or whatever the god was that had put them there. "I have to make my peace with him before it's too late."

CHAPTER 11

✳✳

As Athaya had expected, Tyler was suspicious when she told him they were leaving Reyka immediately without offering any explanations as to why. He did not press her for a reason—probably knowing she would refuse to supply one—but the next morning, as he hitched his leather saddlebags to his mount in preparation for their departure, he cast several anxious looks in her direction. Whenever their eyes met, however, he quickly turned away, suddenly remembering that he was upset with her for such secrecy.

Knowing she could do little to ease his mind at present, Athaya let him get on with his work as he organized his men in preparation to ride out of Ath Luaine. She didn't want to worry him by telling him that she feared for her father's life; Tyler was staunchly loyal to Kelwyn, both as a guardsman and as a friend, and would be concerned about him the whole way home. But more important, how was she supposed to explain the reasons behind her fears?

It's all very simple, Tyler. I'm a wizard, you see, and I had a magic vision of Kelwyn's death.

She could see it now. He would raise his brows into bushy arches and widen his eyes, then frown and tuck his thumbs into his belt, as he always did when trying to decide whether she was teasing him or not. And then he would conclude that either she

154

had been brainwashed by Jaren and Hedric, or had gone crazy herself. And if he found out it was true, and that she was born with magic—had she finally admitted that at last?—then it would never be the same between them. *Perhaps I underestimate him*, she would think at times. He might understand. But she wasn't ready to take that big a risk, not yet. If she lost Tyler, then she lost the rock to which she clung when things were at their worst, and without him, she knew she would be swept away and drowned by events beyond her control.

As she waited for Tyler to ready her horse, Osfonin, Ysell, and Katya clustered around her, offering their kindhearted farewells. Across the courtyard near the stables, Felgin gave final orders to the Reykan escort party who would ride with Athaya and her men as far as the border wall. Like the royal family, Athaya was tightly wrapped in a heavy, fur-trimmed cloak to ward off the morning chill, and judging from the gray, low-hanging clouds overhead, it would likely rain before midday. But instead of worrying about the threatening skies, Athaya pondered how different this departure was from the day she left Delfarham three weeks ago. Today she felt as if she were truly leaving home and wondered when, if ever, she would return.

"Here is my letter to Kelwyn," Osfonin said, handing her a large scroll tied with green ribbons, the same ribbons that had made her heart sink when she'd seen them applied to his last letter to Kelwyn. "It basically states that I have reconsidered your marriage to my son and think it a fine idea. We can begin negotiating the betrothal contract as soon as he likes. Oh, and I've said nothing of your magic. That is something he should hear from you. But I think he will be very proud, Athaya." The king's face was sad for a moment. "Perhaps the only one in all of Caithe who could be."

"I'm grateful for the hospitality you've shown me, your Majesty." She smiled at him self-consciously. "I honestly thought you were going to hate me."

Osfonin let out a merry laugh. "Impossible! How could I possibly hate someone with the ability to work Felgin up into a lather as much as you did? I must admit to being angry at first, but Hedric and I had a long talk about you after he'd begun to realize your potential for magic. Considering that you were dealing with the troubles that go along with the initial onset of the *mekahn*, your aversion to marriage in general, and my son's disgust at realizing that the tales about absolution in your country weren't simply exaggerated fables, it's a wonder that your and Felgin's first meeting wasn't more of a disaster than it was.'' Osfonin chuckled lightly. "But that's all history now. I'm glad to hear that you and he are on friendly terms now.''

"Yes," she said, glancing over toward Felgin, who was speaking with one of the blue-liveried Reykan guardsmen. If anyone had told her a few months ago that she would soon be friends with the Reykan prince, she would have laughed and bet a purse of silver crowns against it. "I think Felgin is as charming as his father.''

"Come now, you must think better of him than that," Ysell teased. "Have a safe journey home, my dear," the queen told her, giving her hand a gentle squeeze. "And remember what I told you. Your father does love you, he just can't show it. Perhaps," she added quietly, "you both suffer the same affliction.''

The wind whipped up, sending the first of the autumn leaves scattering over the gravel in the courtyard, so Osfonin ushered his family indoors and bade Athaya a final farewell. As they entered the Great Hall, a gray-cloaked figure emerged from it and came toward her, sweeping the dried leaves from his path with the tip of his staff. His eyes drooped down in sadness, and the deep lines on his ancient face were tensed with a subtle look of dread. Athaya did not have to ask what was on his mind.

She waited for him to speak first, but he did not.

"I'm sorry, Master Hedric. I know you and Jaren think it's wrong of me to leave, but I just can't stand by and do nothing while my father is in this kind of danger.''

"I understand, Athaya. But that does not mean I approve. I cannot condone what you are doing.''

Athaya slipped her hands inside the folds of her cloak, agitated by Hedric's calm condemnation. "Is it so wrong?" she asked softly. "Is it so selfish to want to try and make amends with my father before it's too late? For all I know it may already *be* too late. Can't you understand how I feel?''

"I do," he said, looking at her squarely. His face was clouded with foreboding. "But ask yourself this. Isn't it more selfish of you to focus your attentions on one man, rather than the thousands of people who need you? For Kelwyn you could do nothing. For them, you could work miracles.''

Athaya winced, as if in pain. "Please, Master Hedric, don't put such a burden on me. I just can't face that right now."

"You will have to face it eventually. And perhaps at a much more urgent time." Hedric sighed weakly, and his aged shoulders drooped. "But I will say nothing more. The future will speak for itself."

Athaya frowned, disturbed by the implications of his words, but she quickly tried to put them out of her mind. She had too many other things to think about to be distracted by Hedric's ominous premonitions. The only thing that nagged at her mind was her surprise at how easily he seemed to have forfeited the argument. He certainly had the power to make her stay in Reyka if the situation was as urgent as he thought it to be.

"Have you any messages you wish me to take back to Caithe?" she asked, eager to find a less controversial subject.

"Only one. To Rhodri." The old wizard's features changed, and for the first time that day he looked truly angry. "Tell him that I know what he's doing," Hedric said darkly. "And tell him that I will not honor his request. I will not talk to the Circle on his behalf. Just tell him that."

Then his gaze softened, and he looked at her as if knowing he would not see her again. "Good-bye, Princess. I hope you can live with the choice you've made."

Hedric shuffled away, leaning more heavily on his staff, and Athaya stood alone in the windy courtyard. The air was cooler than it had been, and she wondered how much longer the rain would hold off. She glanced up at the blue pennons over the castle gates, snapping briskly against the slate-gray sky, and shivered as a sudden burst of wind bit through her woolen cloak.

"Apparently God doesn't like the fact that you're leaving either. He's sent us rain to convince you to stay a while longer."

Athaya started at the unexpected voice and turned to see Prince Felgin standing beside her. Unlike herself, he barely seemed to notice the cold and wore no fur-lined gown over his wool jerkin and linen shirt.

"Felgin—good morning. Is the escort party almost ready?"

"Almost. One of the horses you brought with you from Delfarham has a stone bruise on one of his hooves, so I asked the stablemaster to ready one of mine for you to take instead. It won't take long."

"That's kind of you. Ty—uh, Captain Graylen will be upset

if we leave too late. He wanted to be underway shortly after dawn so we'd make it to the coast by nightfall.''

"Tyler . . . he's a good man," Felgin said. He glanced approvingly toward the stables where the captain was inspecting the sleek bay gelding that he would be taking back to Caithe. Then, with a subtle tilt of his head, the prince added, ''But I expect you already knew that.''

Athaya felt her heart stop for a moment. Felgin's face was difficult to read, but she thought she detected a hint of amusement in his features. There was a gleam in his eye that had not been there before, and the corner of his mouth turned up just slightly.

"That reminds me—I have something for you," he said, reaching into the folds of his jerkin. He drew out a small velvet box and handed it to her.

Athaya was genuinely surprised and felt her face grow warm. "Oh, Felgin, you didn't have to—''

"I wanted to. And I think you'll like it.''

She looked inside the box and found a round, silver locket suspended on a delicate chain. The outside of the locket was set with tiny emeralds and seed pearls, and inside! Athaya gasped when she opened it. The soft image of a face appeared, hovering in the air between the sides of the locket. It was barely the size of her fingertip but held a better likeness than any painting could hope to capture—not flat and dimensionless, but full and unbelievably real, so much so that she expected it to speak. It was the image of a man—staggeringly lifelike, but made of magic mist and air, by Felgin's deft touch.

It was an image of Tyler.

"How did you know?" she said, her voice breaking with unexpected emotion.

"We wizards have our ways." He arched his brow slyly and made her smile. "But in truth, I didn't use my magic at first. I happened to mention you when the captain and I were out riding, and I sensed that his devotion to you went beyond what a guardsman usually feels for his royal charges. I touched his mind—perhaps it was presumptuous of me to do so without asking, but I never stopped to think. His feelings for you were so strong that I picked them up easily. I hope you're not angry.''

"No, it's all right," she said, snapping the locket closed. The image of Tyler folded away inside the silver sides. "I'm sure he'd understand. And thank you. It's a beautiful gift.'' She was deeply touched, amazed that Felgin truly understood and sympathized. But hadn't Felgin been the one who had made her see that marrying Tyler was impossible? Why would he then go to such great pains to give her a gift that would always remind her of the one she loved?

"But why?" she whispered. "I thought you said—"

"As I told you before, Athaya, just because you cannot marry him doesn't mean you cannot still love him. I wanted to give you something—as a memento of your journey here. I could think of nothing that could mean any more to you than that."

Felgin shrugged, trying to sluff off the embarrassment he felt by such a display of tenderness. "Hedric helped me to set the spell that's used to create the image—it's rather difficult and usually takes two wizards to do it well. All it took was a tiny bit of the captain's essence to activate the image. It won't hurt him," he assured her. "And it's rather like taking a drop of water from the ocean. He'll never know that drop is gone. I was going to ask Jaren to help me with the spell, but I thought it might mar the image. I sense that he isn't quite as fond of Tyler as I am and I didn't want his thoughts to adversely affect the spell." Felgin smiled warmly. "Ah well, perhaps he's just a bit jealous of the captain. I can hardly blame him—I'm a bit jealous, too. Why, Tyler's captured the heart of the loveliest woman in Caithe!"

With a smile, she put the locket around her neck and tucked it inside her shirt. She no longer wore the corbal necklace as protection against wizards. She had long since put the crystal back in its pouch and tucked it in the bottom of her saddlebags, realizing that at least in Reyka there was no one to fear.

It was then that she saw Jaren crossing the courtyard with a well-stuffed satchel slung over his shoulder. He'd left off his noble dress for a casual leather jerkin and boots and wore a simple felt cap tilted slightly over one ear.

"Well, it's about time, you little varlet," Felgin called out. "They're just about to ride out."

Jaren gave him a brief nod and disappeared inside the stables, barely glancing at Athaya. *That's a bad sign,* she thought. She shifted her weight to her other foot, wondering how long it would take before Jaren launched into the same speech as his master had, trying to persuade her not to leave. But in truth, it appeared that he had no interest in saying anything at all to her and was upset that she had not taken Hedric's word as law and done what he had wanted her to do.

"I suppose I'd better go," she said, strangely reluctant to leave Felgin. "We should try to get as far as we can before the rain starts."

"Then I bid you farewell," he said, taking her hand and brushing it with a kiss. After a pause, he added, "Be careful, Athaya. I'll worry about you until you return."

"I will. And thank you—for caring." She gave his hand a gentle squeeze and watched as he drifted away, blending into the crowd of mounted men clustered against the wall of the stables, away from the biting wind.

Jaren stood apart from them in a deserted corner of the courtyard, fastening a drab brown cloak around his shoulders with a brass clasp. He offered no greeting when Athaya approached him, and gazed at her blankly, waiting.

"I thought you were going to let me leave without saying good-bye."

"I wouldn't do that," he said casually. There was an odd gleam in his eye—a defiant gleam. Athaya did not like it.

"I know I've said some awful things to you these last few days, but I want you to know that I didn't mean to offend you. It's just that I had a hard time accepting what you and Hedric were trying to tell me. I'm still not sure I completely accept it yet—that could take some time. But it was nothing personal."

Jaren nodded. "I know."

"What you were—"

"Say no more," he said, holding up his hand. "Apologies aren't necessary. Besides, I'd hate to see you waste a fine speech." He gave her a confident smile—too confident. "I'm going back to Caithe with you."

Athaya felt her stomach drop sharply. "You're *what*?"

"You heard me. Since you refuse to stay here and learn how to use your magic, I'm going back with you to make sure you learn it there. Hedric and I talked about it last night and decided it was the only solution."

"B-but you can't!" she sputtered. "*We* can't! If anyone at home finds out about this we'll both be in two hells' worth of trouble!"

"There's no use arguing, Athaya. I'm coming with you and

that's final. I have to teach you what I can before your magic starts going out of control. I know my powers aren't very extensive—your abilities require training of the kind that Hedric or another of the Great Masters could give you—but I'll have to do for now.''

He turned on his heel and went inside the stables to fetch his horse, but Athaya followed quickly behind, angrily kicking patches of straw out of her way. ''Jaren, listen to me—''

''You can't let your power go to waste, Athaya! You can't let your *life* go to waste. I won't let you just give up and let the madness take you. I know it doesn't seem like much of a threat now, but it's going to get worse. You can't simply assume that like any horrible thing, it can only happen to other people.''

Athaya clutched her head, trembling with a dozen confused emotions all battling for release. ''Why is my life so blasted important to you, anyway?''

''Because I—''

He broke off, suddenly flustered, and changed whatever he had been about to say. ''Your people need you too much, Athaya. The Lorngeld in your country need someone to lead them— someone in a position of power. Kelwyn won't have time—''

''Would you stop calling them *my* people?'' she said, trying not to shout. ''I don't know whose they are. Maybe they're God's and maybe they're the Devil's, but they're sure as hell not *mine*!''

''How can you turn your back on them, Athaya? How can you turn your back on people like me, and Hedric, and Felgin—and yourself, for God's sake!'' Jaren's hands curled into tight fists. ''I just wonder if you'd be this uncaring if it were Tyler who needed your help and not just a mass of faceless strangers. Would you walk away from him, Athaya? Would you leave *him* to die?''

Without a moment's hesitation, Athaya whipped the back of her hand furiously across his face. ''How dare you speak that way to me!'' she cried, her breath ragged with outrage. ''You have no *right*!''

''I have every right!'' he shouted. ''The life of every Lorngeld in your country depends on it, and I'll damn well do whatever I can to make you *see* that.''

Athaya ordered him to be silent with a quick, threatening gesture. ''Keep your voice down, will you? Tyler's right outside, and I don't want him knowing about any of this, do you hear me? You breathe one word of this to him, and I swear I'll have your head. I mean it," she said, gritting her teeth. "Now get away from me and leave me *alone*. The last thing I need is for Tyler to come in here and think we're having some sort of a lover's quarrel!"

Jaren flushed deep crimson, but Athaya could not tell whether it was from anger or embarrassment. But whatever it was, she did not care. If Jaren were to fall dead at her feet this very instant, she could easily step right over him and leave him to rot without a single look back.

Turning sharply on her heel, she stalked away and went to her horse, snatching the reins away from a frightened-looking squire. She edged the gray palfrey toward the main gates, brooding in silence while she waited for her escort to join her.

Tyler was at her side a few minutes later. "Give the word and we'll go," he said. He looked back at his men, neatly lined up in six pairs and flanked at the rear by Osfonin's guardsmen. Then he frowned and tightened his jaw in sudden outrage.

"Wait . . . what the hell is *he* doing back there?" Tyler said. He pointed toward Jaren, who lingered at the rear of the party on a chestnut stallion, and flashed him a look of pure hatred.

"He's coming with us," Athaya said curtly, avoiding Tyler's questioning glare.

"What? But Osfonin already gave us an escort as far as the border."

"No, Tyler. He's coming all the way to Delfarham. And before you say one single word, yes, I already tried to talk him out of it."

Tyler let out an impatient breath. "Did he say why he's coming?"

Oh, of course he did, Tyler. He's going to teach me all about magic so I can lead a great crusade against the Church. Isn't that just wonderful?

"He . . . uh, wants to talk to Kelwyn about the Lorngeld. You know, like I told you before. Hedric is sending him as a sort of envoy."

Tyler furrowed his brow, clearly suspecting that he wasn't being told the whole story. "The men won't like it, you know. They were suspicious enough of that wizard when he joined us at Evarshot and they sure as hell won't like having him with us all the way back to Delfarham."

"I don't care what they like, Tyler," she snapped. "Kelwyn

doesn't pay them for their opinions. They take orders from you, not the other way around."

After a moment's hesitation, Tyler inclined his head to her, stiffly formal. "Yes, your Highness."

The rain began after they were barely a quarter hour's ride from the palace, but despite the fat, heavy drops pelting down on her, Athaya paused at the top of the ridge overlooking Ath Luaine to take one look back at the Reykan capital. When she stood on this same ridge a week ago, taking in her first glimpse of the city, her only worries were of Osfonin's wrath and whether he would humiliate her for the way she had treated his son. But now, instead of being free of her cares, she was plagued by even greater ones—whether her father would be alive when she returned to Caithe, and what would happen to her if anyone were to know that she had been born with the power of magic. And worse, she feared that despite her defiant words to Jaren, part of her mind was already considering the unthinkable idea of learning to use her power, and thus accepting the Devil's gift.

CHAPTER 12

ATHAYA SPENT HER LAST NIGHT IN REYKA IN A DILAPIDATED old inn that huddled in the shadow of a high-peaked crag a few hours' ride from the border. It didn't look too disreputable—she had been in worse places—and after a long, cold day of slogging through the muddy roads along the seacoast, she was grateful for the plain, hot broth and stringy mutton joint that the innkeeper provided. Long after Tyler and his men had retired to their rooms on the second floor, Athaya remained in the corner of the common room, determined to finish off a rather large flagon of wine as she tried to sort out the conflicting emotions warring in her mind.

Was it really so selfish, putting her father's needs ahead of her own? Was it wrong to delay her own need for schooling in the uses of magic until she could patch the tattered relationship between herself and Kelwyn? If the Lorngeld in her country had suffered ever since the time of Faltil, what was another few days, or weeks, or even years? And why was their plight suddenly *her* responsibility? That made her the angriest of all. Oh, yes, Hedric had his answers for that. He seemed to have answers for everything.

"Care to share any of that?"

Jaren slid into the chair across from her and filled an earthenware goblet from her flagon. He glanced at the rushlight in the wall socket above their table, now nearly burned down and starting to smolder. "It's late—why are you still up?"

"I might ask you the same thing."

Jaren swirled the wine in his cup and took a long draught. "I just wanted to see how you were feeling." He paused and offered her a tentative smile. "I also wanted to find out if you were still angry with me for following you back to Caithe uninvited."

"I don't know," she said with a shrug. "I don't feel anything right now. I'm just . . . numb. Maybe it's the wine." She set down her goblet and buried her face in her hands. "I just want this whole thing to be over. And no," she added reluctantly, poking her eyes over the tips of her fingers, "I don't think I'm all that mad at you anymore. Although sometimes I think I *should* be."

"You'll find I can be just as stubborn as you are about some things."

Athaya tilted the corner of her mouth up in a half smile. "That's becoming more than obvious."

With a soft hiss the rushlight above the table sputtered and went out, leaving them cloaked in darkness. Glancing up in annoyance, Jaren snapped his fingers, and a ball of red fire appeared in his hand, glowing softly. It was exactly like the globes she had seen lighting the Great Hall on her first night in Ath Luaine.

"What are you doing?" she said anxiously, trying to hide the red light with her palm. "Put that thing out!"

"We're not in Caithe yet, Athaya," he said, commanding the ball of fire to hover over the table. "It's just a witchlight. If you like, I can show you how to make one."

Athaya shook her head and reached over to grab a candle from another table. "I've never found anything wrong with plain old tallow. And besides, it's much less pretentious."

"Come on, it's easy. All you have to do is follow the path to the spell."

Athaya looked at him skeptically. "Path?" she said, vaguely remembering Hedric using that term before. "What are you talking about?"

"The paths in your mind," he told her matter-of-factly. "They lead to where your spells are kept."

"But I've never created one of these lights before. How can

a spell already be in my mind if I've never learned it in the first place?''

"The spell has always been there," Jaren said simply. "You were born with it, same as me. And as for the path, you'll see what I mean once you try it. It sounds complicated, but it's really just the method you use to explore your mind and find the magic you want. Sooner or later, you'll find the right path, and once you do, you'll be able to work the spell. You've already done it unconsciously a few times."

Athaya frowned, discomfited by the idea that her mind had elements to it that she wasn't aware of and couldn't always control. "But wait," she said. "What if I take the wrong path?" She had no idea what would happen if she did, but she was fairly confident that it would not be pleasant.

"Don't worry—you won't be able to. Until you master the simple spells, your mind shields you from being able to access the harder ones. Otherwise, you could start casting spells you don't know how to stop. That's part of what happens when the *mekahn* advances too far. The natural shielding breaks down, all the paths start crossing and blocking each other, and it eventually becomes impossible to straighten them all out again."

"What about people like my father who weren't born with magic? Do they have paths?"

"People born without magic don't ever develop them," he said. "Your father has them, but his paths aren't natural—they were constructed for him prior to the ritual that gave him his power. Rhodri had to build them artificially. I'd expect that Kelwyn's magic is fairly limited because of that. I'd venture to guess that he can only work the spells that were specifically implanted during the rite of assumption. But you should be able to locate any spell you want, since you have all the paths. Why don't you try it?"

Athaya blinked disbelievingly. "What? You mean right here?"

"Why not? I went into my paths in order to make my witchlight. I wasn't there more than an instant—it's instinctive for me by now—but I was there. It's nothing near so exotic as going into a trance or some such thing. Those kinds of theatricals are usually reserved for charlatans and swindlers," he added dryly. "No one else will be able to tell that you're doing it, and you'll still be conscious of everything around you."

Athaya rested her elbows on the table, trying to take in everything she'd been told. "I don't know . . . it sounds hard."

Jaren shrugged casually. "So did walking when you first tried it. But for a wizard, working spells is as natural as walking. And once you learn, you don't forget. Now, why don't we give it a try?"

"We?"

"You'll need a trained wizard to help you get started. I have to help you find the doorway that leads into your paths—you won't know what to look for yet, but I will. You also need to have someone with you when you're learning your way around the labyrinth of paths in your mind, so you don't get lost. Everyone's paths are slightly different, but their general pattern is the same. I'll be able to explain more about it once we've gone in."

"You'll be inside my mind?" Athaya asked hesitantly. She wasn't sure she liked that idea at all. "You'll be able to tell what I'm thinking?"

"Only if you want me to," he assured her. "It's almost impossible to force a thought-reading on another wizard if he's purposefully trying to shut you out. I—or rather, my mind—will be there with you to show you how to maneuver through the paths. I won't be able to pick up your thoughts unless you let me."

Athaya was growing confused. Magic was becoming more complex than she'd ever imagined. "I wish I'd started learning about this sooner. Then maybe I wouldn't feel so overwhelmed."

Jaren nodded sympathetically. "It would make everything easier if people like us could be taught how to use their paths before the pressure of their magic becomes a threat. Unfortunately, it can't be done. Paths don't even start to develop until just before the early stages of the *mekahn*, so there's no way anyone can learn to use them in advance." He gave her an encouraging smile. "Ready to try?"

"I guess so. Just don't let me get lost."

"I won't. I wouldn't want you to get flustered and start setting off spells by accident. Now just follow me, and we'll begin."

Without closing her eyes, Athaya waited nervously for something to happen. At first she felt nothing, except the foolishness that comes with trying to see something that wasn't there. But then she felt the cool brush of another presence—like a feather tickling the inside of her skull—and she flinched in surprise.

Don't pull back, Athaya, it's only me, she heard Jaren say calmly, though his lips never moved. *I'm going to look for the doorway now. Just think about your paths and try to see where I'm taking you.*

For a few moments she saw nothing except the soft glow of Jaren's witchlight hovering above the table and the mundane sight of the inn's common room. But it seemed darker somehow, as if she were looking at it through tinted glass. Then she saw another image—a faint scene superimposed over her normal vision. In her mind's eye, she felt herself walking through what looked like a dimly lit cave. The walls were smooth and shiny, like polished ebony, and though she knew her body was not physically in the cave, she could feel soft earth under her feet. She was in a large room walled in by stone and saw no doors leading out.

I think that's it, Jaren thought.

Athaya could not see Jaren in the caves with her, but she could sense his presence. She followed his voice, ever conscious of the cool, strangely comforting feeling in her mind that he was there. He guided her toward a smooth slab of gray stone, one shade lighter than the other walls. Above them, Athaya could make out faint symbols carved into the wall above the slab, but they held as much meaning for her as a string of words written in an unknown language.

Command the door to open, Athaya. Just think of what you want it to do. It has to obey you.

Hesitantly, Athaya willed the stone to move aside and was amazed to see that it did so. In her mind's vision, she watched the stone roll silently to one side, revealing a huge entryway to a series of twisted passages, all leading to other caves. Some of the corridors were blocked off, and others were only half constructed, like the walls of an unfinished cathedral. Jaren led her down one of the finished corridors—a path that was more brightly lit than the others—and they stopped near a small recess in the wall. The stone was etched with the same kind of symbols she had seen over the entryway, but they seemed to form a familiar pattern, in a language she knew, yet did not know.

Now try to create a witchlight, Jaren said. *The spell is right here.*

But . . . how?

Just listen. You'll know.

She concentrated on the symbols, listening, and trying to let their meaning speak to her. She heard no physical sounds, but sensed the whispering all the same—it was all around her, like the soft roll of ocean waves and the rustling of leaves in a summer breeze. Fixing her eyes on the wall of etched stone, she snapped her fingers. She felt a warm tingling sensation in her palm, but no fireball appeared.

That's all right, he said patiently. *Try it again.*

Biting her lip, she opened her mind to the array of symbols and snapped her fingers again. This time, a faintly burning ball of fire appeared in her palm.

"Look!" she said, her eyes wide open in disbelief. Suddenly the image of the paths was gone and she saw nothing except the inn and the fireball in her hand.

Jaren couldn't keep a giddy smile off his face. "That's wonderful!" he whispered, watching as Athaya released her witchlight, allowing it to hover next to his. He sat back in his chair and smiled with pride at his pupil's quick learning.

A few minutes later, as she and Jaren basked in the glow of the double witchlights, a buxom young girl with a mass of grubby blond curls sidled up to their table and refilled their flagon of wine.

"A couple of wizards, eh?" she cooed. With only a cursory glance at Athaya, the wench batted her eyes at Jaren. "We don't get too many of your kind in here—there's only two in the whole village. And neither one of 'em is as fine-lookin' as you." She laid her hand boldly on his chest and leaned over him, her abundant breasts straining against the thin laces of her bodice. "How's about I show you a little of my own magic? *If* you know what I mean . . ."

The tips of Jaren's ears turned red as he averted his eyes from the girl's bosom.

"Er—no thanks." Then, not knowing what to say next, he pointed to Athaya and added, "I'm with her."

The girl's lower lip poked out in a pout. "Too bad. But if you change your mind, my name's Lorna, and my room's just off the kitchen." She winked at him and strode away, purposefully swaying her hips from side to side.

Athaya leaned back, and for a moment, gazed at Jaren as if she'd never met him before. He was a boyishly attractive young man, to be sure, but Athaya had grown accustomed to regarding him as an annoying disturbance most of the time and never as a potential bedmate. It was difficult for her to imagine a woman making such blatant advances toward him, and it was even more difficult to comprehend that the serving girl had not been attracted by his appearance alone, but by his magic.

"Do you get offers like that all the time?" she asked, one eyebrow cocked in amusement.

Jaren shrugged. "It's happened before."

"Enjoy it while you can," Athaya said dryly. "Women aren't going to throw themselves at your feet like that once we cross the border into Caithe tomorrow." She motioned toward the red witchlights, still glowing above the table. "One little gesture like that could get you roasted like a goose on a spit."

Conscious of the warning behind her words, Jaren shook his head in dismay. "It's all so inconsistent. If the Caithans believe that magic is evil, why do they respect Kelwyn so much? Why can they excuse the fact that he uses so-called 'Devil's magic'?"

"You can thank the Church for that, strange as it sounds. They couldn't very well come out and accuse the king of heresy— well, I suppose they *could* have, but nobody was willing to be the first to risk it. So Archbishop Ventan managed to convince the Curia that Kelwyn should be excused for his dabblings in magic since he only did it out of devotion to his country. And now it's become accepted that he was willing to do anything for his land—including risking his soul. My father openly admitted that kings had tried and failed for two hundred years to reunite the Caithan provinces, and that if magic was the only solution, then he was going to use it. But you know," she added thoughtfully, "I believe that it's true. My father may be a lot of things, but he isn't an evil man. He only wants what's best for Caithe."

"Unlike his ancestor, Faltil," Jaren murmured, running his finger around the rim of his goblet.

"Not everyone approved of his magic at first. From what I've heard, my mother was very much opposed to the idea of his accepting the powers. She was afraid he'd be damning himself."

"Your mother . . . you've never mentioned her before. What was she like?"

"Chandice? I don't really know—not firsthand, anyway. But I've been told I look a lot like her. Apparently she and my father were completely enamored with each other. They were only married for about eight years when Chandice died, though. Some sort of sudden fever.''

Jaren lowered his eyes sadly. ''Maybe that was part of the price.''

''The what?''

''The price of his magic. Maybe that was God's way of exacting payment for the magic Kelwyn was using. By taking away the woman he loved.''

Athaya folded her arms across her chest with a look of disgust on her face. ''If that's the case, Jaren, then you and Hedric believe in a very petulant, cruel God.''

Jaren said nothing and slowly sipped the rest of his wine.

''I don't see why God would want to punish a king for trying to do what's best for his subjects,'' Athaya went on. ''After all, if God Himself gave Kelwyn the divine right of kingship, then why punish him for doing the duty he was born to do? Despite whatever differences I may have with him, I truly believe that Kelwyn is a good king. He's just . . . not a very good father.'' Athaya cupped her chin in her palms, suddenly exhausted. ''And I suppose I haven't been the best daughter a man could want, either,'' she added quietly.

On that gloomy note, Athaya wished Jaren good night, more impatient than ever to be home again.

Moonlight streamed through the stained-glass windows as Athaya processed up the aisle of Saint Adriel's Cathedral. The entire sanctuary was decked with blossoms, perfuming the air like a spring garden. In her hands she held a bouquet of sweet-smelling white roses that tumbled down to her feet like a skirt of petals. Her gown was the finest thing she'd ever worn—a stunning fantasy of white satin sewn with seed pearls and diamonds—and a translucent white veil cascaded down her shoulders from a jeweled coronet. Smiling, she listened to the chimes in the bell tower ring out in celebration.

Her family watched her walk up the aisle from their pews near the high altar. They all looked so happy—so proud. Durek had an uncharacteristic smile on his face, and at his side, Cecile dabbed tears from her eyes. Nicolas gazed at her with deep emotion, and Dagara—yes, even Dagara—smiled and nodded in satisfaction.

And then she saw him, and a warm rush of joy swept through

her. Tyler waited for her on the steps before the altar, dressed
in a splendid fur-trimmed coat of white satin. His hair shone in
the candlelight like polished gold, and his head was capped by
a white, plumed cap. His eyes sparkled more than the jeweled
collar and belt he wore, and Athaya knew him for more than
just a man. There was something divine in him today, and in
only a few more moments—a few more seconds—he would be
hers.

She stood beside him near the altar and the music of the chimes
ended. Leaving his pulpit, Archbishop Ventan moved to his
place near the altar. He was clad in a snowy white cassock and
crowned with a golden miter. He held a gilt-edged prayer book
in his hands, and a red silk ribbon streamed over the pages,
marking the page from which he would read. If only he would
begin! Athaya could wait no longer to hear him say the words
she'd always dreamed of hearing. *Do you, Athaya Chandice
Theia Trelane, take this man* . . .

The archbishop lifted his hand and the congregation fell silent. A hush of rapt anticipation blanketed the crowded sanctuary.

"Almighty God," Ventan invoked, "Father of all mankind
and maker of all things; you who take away the sins of the world,
hear us this day as we beseech you to receive our prayers. We
do earnestly confess and lament our manifold sins, which are
grievous in your sight, O Lord, and beg your mercy upon us as
we ask that you forgive all that is past and grant that we may
serve you and please you hereafter, to the honor and glory of
your holy name. Hear then, O Lord, our prayer of pardon."

Athaya frowned. The words . . . they were wrong. Ventan
was reading the wrong litany. She had attended enough wed-
dings to know that the sacrament of marriage did not open with
a prayer of pardon. She gave a questioning glance to Tyler, but
he seemed to have noticed nothing and stared straight ahead,
his eyes strangely glazed with tears. But they did not look like
tears of joy . . .

Ventan droned on, and his words were becoming muffled.
Athaya could not hear what he was saying. Something was terribly, terribly wrong.

It was only then that she saw the crown on Durek's head and
realized that Kelwyn was not there. And Cecile wept, and Nic-

olas held her close to comfort her, and Dagara smiled even more.

The archbishop closed his prayer book and turned to pick up the chalice from the altar.

"Who brings forth this woman for the sacrament of absolution?"

She felt Tyler's hand fall gently upon her shoulder. His lower lip trembled as he said, "I do."

"No!" Athaya screamed. The bouquet of white roses slipped from her fingers, and she dug her nails into Tyler's fine coat, tearing off the jewels carefully sewn there. "How could you? How could you *do* this to me?"

He wrapped his hand tightly over hers—so tightly that she could not squirm away. Taking a step toward her, his boot crushed the tender blossoms of the bouquet at his feet. "I do this because I love you, Athaya. Because I cannot bear for your soul to be damned. How can we spend our eternity together if I am in heaven and you are not? I can see that, even if you cannot. It's for the best, my love. All for the best . . ."

"You said you wanted to *marry* me," she whimpered, dazed with fear.

"Yes. It was the only way. I knew you would try to flee otherwise." The tears were gone from his face now, and he looked at her sternly. "Save yourself, Athaya. Drink the sacred wine. Be waiting for me in heaven when my time comes."

"Yes, you must drink the wine," Durek echoed from his pew. "For the good of Caithe, and for your brother, its king."

"You must," Dagara said, her vicious smile revealing sharpened teeth, like fangs.

"You must," Cecile said, weeping uncontrollably.

"You . . . you must," Nicolas said, hesitating.

Archbishop Ventan came closer, clutching the chalice with a hungry gleam in his eyes. "Listen to them, my child. Listen well. They know what is best for you. Your mind is almost lost to you now, and you cannot make your own decisions. Your family is only trying to save you—"

"No! You're wrong! All of you! Tyler, please—*please* tell them!"

She let out a piercing shriek as Tyler turned his face to her. She saw tiny licks of fire in his eyes as he pulled her toward the altar, and he looked like Satan himself, his skin red and blistered. He threw her down before the archbishop and forced her head back.

"Give her the wine, Archbishop," he growled. "Get it over with quickly."

Athaya desperately tried to twist her face away, but Tyler's grip was too strong. *"I won't!"* she cried, even as the chalice was poised above her lips.

Without warning, a clap of thunder split the air, and a great bolt of lightning lit the sky, sending streams of colored light through the stained-glass windows. The wind began to howl, shaking the very foundations of the cathedral, and Athaya heard torrents of rain pounding down furiously on the slate-tiled roof. The rain fell hard and fast, and soon her slippers were soaked as the water flooded the sanctuary, pouring in from every door and leaking through the stone walls. The huge double doors at the end of the nave flew open, and gusts of icy wind bit into her skin.

But Tyler held her firm, ignoring the storm, and commanded her to drink from the chalice.

Then the hands that gripped her began to shake her violently. "Athaya, come out of it!" she heard a voice say. The voice was distorted and strange, like that of a man who has lost his tongue as punishment for some ill-chosen comment. "Athaya, wake up!"

Her eyes snapped open, and she saw a white-clad figure bending over her, holding her down. "Let go of me!" she screamed, kicking at him as she struggled to get away. *"Let go!"*

"Look at me!" he cried. "Don't you know who I am? It's me, Jaren."

"Jaren?" she said blankly, as if she'd never heard the name before. She blinked a few times, trying to clear her vision. She felt strange—not yet awake, but not asleep, as if she were drifting in some half-real world. Suddenly the thunder wasn't quite as loud, and the rain began to slacken as the storm moved off to the east. The wind began to die away, but she could still hear the grating sound of branches scraping against the wooden shutters. The cathedral was fading away, and she saw it only partially now, as if through a thick fog.

"Athaya?"

She shook her head, trying to dispel the remnants of the vision. "Who . . . what happened?"

Jaren placed a hand on her forehead, testing for fever. "The thunder woke me. I could tell by the sound of it that it was a magic storm, not a natural one. It was too . . . hollow."

The storm . . . the cathedral . . . the flood . . . yes, she remembered it now. She was going to be married . . . and her whole family was there. And the more she thought of it, the more real it became, until Jaren began to dissolve before her eyes, and the vision of Tyler returned, holding the poisoned chalice.

"Stop!" she cried, slipping back into the nightmare. "Jaren, make them let me go! All of you, leave me alone!" She opened her eyes, but saw nothing of the room at the inn, only a crowded sanctuary, battered by a storm. "Let me go! I won't drink it! My God, Tyler, how *could* you?"

Jaren pinned her down against the pillows, calling her name, but his voice sounded faint and distant. Athaya reached out for him, her arms flailing wildly against her mind's images of Tyler and the archbishop, and she desperately wanted to cling to Jaren, to keep herself from slipping away and drowning in the poisoned wine . . .

"Athaya, listen to my voice. Pull yourself out of it—don't let it take control. Fight it with everything you've got!"

The words meant nothing. She could barely hear him now, and the sound of his pleas was overwhelmed by the chants of the people in the cathedral, screaming for her death. *The wizard must die,* they cried over and over. *The Devil's Child must be destroyed!*

Then she felt a sharp sting on her cheek and knew that someone had stuck her, but in her mind's confusion she did not know from which world the blow had come.

"What in the name of God is going on in here?"

With a sudden jolt of fear, Athaya jerked her head toward the voice. Tyler stood in the doorway, the harsh glare of rushlights in the corridor beyond bathing his features in sickly yellow light. His doublet and hose were hastily donned and hanging in disarray, and he gripped the splintered doorframe with white hands, his face a picture of wild and furious outrage.

"*You!*" Athaya shouted, pointing an accusing finger at him. "How could you? How could you turn me over to them?"

Tyler crossed the room with two swift strides. He grabbed Jaren by the collar of his nightshirt, yanked him away from

Athaya, and hurled him fiercely against the wall. Then he saw the red welt on her cheek, and he boiled over with rage, slamming his fist into Jaren's stomach.

"What the hell are you doing to her?" Tyler shouted, pulling Jaren forward and hurling him against the wall a second time. "What are you up to, you sniveling little wizard?"

"Tyler, stop it!" Athaya said. "He was only trying to . . . to . . ." *To what?* What had he said? Something about a storm, wasn't it? But there was no thunder now. All she heard was the soft patter of the rain and the sound of the wind blowing the storm clouds off to the east.

Tyler clamped his hands around his captive's throat like a vise, and Jaren gasped for breath as he futilely tried to escape from the captain's ironlike grip. "You're using your magic on her, aren't you?" He shook Jaren roughly from side to side like a rag doll. "What do you want with her? And more precisely, why did you have to come to her bedchamber in the middle of the night to get it?"

"Let go of him, Tyler!" Athaya shouted. "That's an order!"

Tyler winced, as if jabbed by a needle. His grip around Jaren's throat relaxed, enough to let him breathe, but not enough to let him escape.

"What's he done to you? He's trying to turn you against me, isn't he?"

She clutched her temples, feeling the steady pounding of an approaching headache. "Stop being so irrational," she snapped. "That has nothing to do with it."

"How can you say that?" He turned a killing glare onto Jaren. "I ought to take you outside right now and—"

Athaya cut him off with a sharp wave of her hand. "You lay one hand on him and I'll report you to Kelwyn the minute we get home. Do you hear me?"

Tyler stared at her, his eyes wide with stunned outrage. He released Jaren, who fell limply to the floor gasping for air.

"Athaya, you can't mean—"

"Captain, you are *dismissed*!"

The moment the imperious words had escaped her lips, she wished she could take them back. But it was too late. Clenching his teeth, Tyler spun on his heel and stalked out of the room, slamming the door behind him with such force that Athaya thought it would fly from its hinges. A second slam followed a few minutes later, as Tyler reached his own room.

Thoroughly drained of energy, Athaya fell back on her straw pallet and wiped away bitter tears with the sleeve of her sweat-soaked gown. She heard Jaren moan softly, still doubled over with pain from the captain's onslaught. Opening his eyes just enough to see, he crawled to the edge of her pallet and leaned against it, trying to regain the breath that Tyler had almost completely squeezed out of him.

"Are you all right?"

He nodded weakly. "I will be . . . in a few minutes."

Athaya listened to his breathing gradually grow steady. She heard the soft sound of raindrops spattering against the mud outside the inn. "The storm—it was real, wasn't it?"

"Magic, but real," he said, gulping down a mouthful of air. "You called a bad one. Half the roof on the other side of the inn was blown clean off, and the valley's almost flooded. I guess that's why Tyler was here—to see if you were all right. Either that or he heard you screaming."

"And now God only knows what he's thinking." Athaya scowled. "He certainly didn't like finding you here. Especially dressed like *that*."

Jaren pulled the rumpled nightshirt over his knees. "I'm sorry, Athaya. I always seem to cause trouble for you, don't I?"

"I won't argue that," she replied with a weak smile. "But it wasn't your fault Tyler stamped out of here in such a huff. I never should have snapped at him like that." Athaya let out a heavy sigh. "I just don't want him to know, Jaren. I'm too afraid of what he might think."

"Is what he's thinking *now* any better?" Jaren asked, his voice touched with annoyance. "He's convinced that I'm using my magic on you against your will. Either that, or he thinks I was trying to get from you what I could have had from that serving girl earlier."

Athaya hung her head in defeat. "I'm sorry. I just can't tell him yet. I'll explain everything to him someday, but not now. Not yet."

"Then when? After he finds out by accident? It's bound to happen, you know. And if you start spending a few hours a day learning your spells from me, he's definitely going to think there's something going on between us."

Athaya let out a sharp laugh. "That's ridiculous. Tyler knows I'd never be interested in anyone else."

Jaren paused before he spoke, banishing an unmistakable look of disappointment. "I understand your reasons for not wanting him to know you're a Lorngeld, Athaya. But let me just ask you one thing. If he won't accept you for what you are, then is he worth it? Does he deserve what you feel for him?"

After a few moments of pointed silence, Jaren got to his feet and left, closing the door softly behind him. Athaya almost called after him, ready to answer his challenging words, but then she remembered the murderous look on Tyler's face as he stormed from her chamber and fell strangely quiet, suddenly unable to respond to Jaren's challenge with confidence.

Damn him! she thought angrily. *I hate you, Jaren. Stop holding up mirrors and making me see things I don't want to.*

Athaya slept no more that night, but curled up on her pallet and listened to the lonely sound of the wind, moaning like a dying man outside her window.

CHAPTER 13

✳✺

"**S**EE THAT GATEHOUSE, JAREN?" TYLER SAID, GES-
turing toward the lime-washed towers of Delfar
Castle coming into view at the end of the street.
It was the first time he had spoken to the wizard since finding
him in Athaya's rooms at the inn two weeks before. "And do
you see those long, metal pikes on top of those gates? Make one
false step while you're here and you just might find your head
impaled on one of them."

Jaren said nothing, wilting under Tyler's glare. The captain
made it clear that he would not consider it an entirely bad thing
if Jaren got caught using his magic. Athaya gazed at the towers
as well, but she wasn't looking at the pikes. She breathed an
audible sigh of relief that no mourning banners had been raised
over the turrets. Kelwyn was still alive. There was still time.

"Jaren isn't staying at the castle," Athaya announced, irritated by Tyler's threats. "He can find a place to stay here in
town. There are usually rooms to be let behind the dyer's shop—
the one near Oren's tavern."

"Of course there are," Tyler said, wrinkling his nose. "Have
you ever smelled the place? Not much demand for rooms that
stink of a day-old chamber pot, especially by a man of Jaren's
lofty station." His face was devoid of expression, but his tone

made it clear that he considered such a place ideal for the wizard.

Athaya did her best to ignore his sarcasm, even though he did have a point about the smell. The dyes used to color much of the cloth woven in the city were often made from a base of urine, and while the color was spectacular once it had set, it took numerous rinsings to rid the wool of its stench.

"I think it's a good idea for Jaren to stay away from court until I can tell my father why he wants an audience," she explained. "Not to mention explaining why he showed up six weeks ago masquerading as a courier." *And never mind the fact that he isn't going to have an audience with Kelwyn at all, but is going to need a more private place than a guest chamber in Delfar if he's going to teach me how to work spells.*

"How considerate of you to look after his well-being," Tyler said with exaggerated courtesy. "With your leave, I'll ride ahead and let his Majesty know we're back. Lieutenant Parr," he called back to his second-in-command, who rode with the rest of the squadron about ten yards behind him, "take over for me here."

Without giving Athaya a chance to voice her permission, Tyler snapped the reins and spurred his horse ahead, leaving a cloud of dust in his wake.

Athaya detached herself from the remaining guardsmen long enough to rent Jaren a small, not-too-dingy set of rooms behind the dye shop. Then, leaving him to whatever amusements he could find in the capital city, she turned her thoughts toward home. For once, she did not dread the idea of being there again, and it was a strange but welcome sensation.

Since Tyler had ridden ahead to the castle, Nicolas was there to greet her when Athaya passed through the main gates and drew up in front of the stables. She slid off the saddle and embraced him warmly. "I missed you, Nicky," she said, lifting off his green felt cap and tousling his hair.

"You don't know how good it is to have you back, little sister. With you gone, Dagara had to have someone else to pick on and she chose me."

"You're more than welcome to take over that office," Athaya said. She unhitched her saddlebags and slung them over her shoulder and handed the reins over to a waiting groom. Throwing his arm around her, Nicolas gave her a good-natured squeeze and led her across the courtyard toward the Great Hall.

"Tyler rode in not long ago, but he barely spoke two words to me. He was in an awful snit." Nicolas paused for a moment, waiting for an explanation that did not come. "What's the matter—you two have a fight?"

Athaya's footsteps faltered. She stared straight ahead, expressionless.

"Sorry, I didn't know. I'll try another subject, although I'm not sure if it'll be much better. How did it go with Osfonin?"

"Surprisingly well. He didn't throw me out or insult me after all."

Nicolas shook his head with mock solemnity. "Dagara will be disappointed to hear that."

Athaya couldn't help but smile. "Then she'll be even more disappointed to hear that Felgin and I parted on good terms." She placed her hand over the locket he had given her. "That reminds me, I have a letter from Osfonin for Father. Where is he?"

"Closed up in another meeting with the Curia. He's not having much luck with them, though, and it's starting to make him irritable. Archbishop Ventan doesn't usually oppose him like this, but he refuses to give in when it comes to the subject of absolution. And even though he doesn't have any say in their final decision, Durek has been making it quite clear to the other bishops that he sides with Ventan."

"That doesn't surprise me," she said, shaking her head. "It truly amazes me how Father can be so fond of Durek when they rarely agree on anything—especially *this*."

"True. If being contrary with Father is a way of earning his respect, then it's you he should be worshiping, not Durek."

Athaya gave him a good-natured poke in the ribs.

"Listen, Nicky, do me a favor, will you? I expect I'll be busy for the rest of the day, so would you give something to Archbishop Ventan for me as soon as his meeting is over?" She reached into the bottom of her saddlebag and handed him the pouch containing the corbal crystal. "Tell him thank you, but that I won't be needing this anymore."

"What is it?" Nicolas said, unlacing the leather thongs. He slid the gem into his palm, and suddenly Athaya felt a dull throbbing behind her eyes. The pain wasn't so bad that she couldn't hide it from Nicolas, but she was unpleasantly startled. She hadn't expected to be affected by the crystal. But judging from what Hedric had told her, the pain would increase the more proficient a magician she became. And with what little she knew of magic at this point, the aches she felt now were only a faint hint at what was to come.

"It's a corbal crystal. Ventan gave it to me for protection. It's uh—supposed to keep wizards from using their power. It gives them headaches. Muddles their thinking."

Nicolas laughed dryly. "If you ask me, our friend Rhodri is muddled enough. At least lately. He's been acting odd for the last few weeks. He spends all his time closeted away in his rooms, reading old books, drawing pictures in the air, and mumbling to himself. If that isn't muddled, I don't know what is."

Athaya followed her brother into the Great Hall, where she saw Dagara, Durek, and Cecile sitting together in front of the center fireplace watching little Mailen play with a pair of cloth puppets. When the boy saw her, he quickly thrust his toys aside to come wrap his arms around her legs and squeal a greeting.

As soon as Athaya had disentangled herself from Mailen's grasp, Cecile got up and offered her a friendly hug. "I want to hear all about your trip," she said with a smile, paying no attention to her husband's look of disapproval as she welcomed Athaya home. Unable to suppress her curiosity, she added, "Is it true that wizards are everywhere in Reyka?"

"Please, Cecile," Durek scolded. He pulled Mailen away from Athaya and set him back down in front of his puppets. "Why should you want to know anything about a bunch of damned wizards? I can't believe you'd ask such a silly question."

Cecile tossed back her blond curls. "As you like, Durek. But I'll only ask her later when you're not around."

Durek scowled at her, but said nothing.

"Has Father been well?" Athaya asked, directing her question to no one in particular.

Dagara flinched, as if someone had pricked her with a needle. "Why do you ask?"

"Oh, it's nothing really," she said casually. "I just had a bad dream the other night that he was sick, that's all."

Cecile laid a finger to one side of her chin. "Now that you mention it, he has been rather moody and—"

"Don't be ridiculous," Durek said, cutting her off. "I'm sure that doesn't mean a thing." He let out a caustic laugh and added, "Athaya's been moody her whole life and *she's* healthy enough."

Dagara laughed aloud while Athaya choked back an ill-mannered comment. She refused to let them goad her into saying anything uncivil. She had enough on her mind to worry about without adding yet another family squabble to the list.

"Your father wants to see you the moment he dismisses the Curia," Dagara announced, her eyes glittering darkly. "He's anxious to hear about your meeting with Osfonin."

Athaya nodded. She would have loved to launch into a florid speech about how friendly the Reykan king was, and how much she had liked his family, but she remained silent. Let Dagara enjoy her spitefulness for a few minutes longer. It would only hurt the more when she found out that Athaya had not been humiliated by the Reykans, but welcomed to their court with open arms.

"Come back in about an hour," Durek said. "Father's meeting should be over by then."

Giving Mailen a pat on the head, Athaya left the Hall and went back out to the courtyard, with Nicolas following close behind.

"What did Cecile mean when she said Father's been acting moody?" she asked.

Nicolas shrugged. "He's been a bit edgy. Something's bothering him lately—probably his problems with the Curia. By the end of the day he'll forget something you just told him that morning. And you never know what sort of a mood he'll be in, either. One day he'll be fine, and the next—" Nicolas rolled his eyes. "Say the wrong thing and he'll bite your head off."

Athaya felt a cold shudder ripple through her. Nicolas didn't know it, but he was accurately describing the initial stages of the *mekahn*. And no one in her family, no one in the entire castle—save one person—knew the source of her father's symptoms.

"I'll see you later," Athaya said, stepping up her pace. "There's someone I want to talk to before I see Father."

Athaya had been to Rhodri's chambers only a handful of times and had hated the experience each time. She expected today to be no different.

She used the iron door knocker to announce her presence,

and a few seconds of silence passed before she heard the wizard's muffled voice give her permission to enter. The outer chamber was unusually cluttered, with open books and scraps of paper scattered all about. Rhodri sat in the corner at his writing desk, reading a large leather-bound book by the light of an oil lamp. His face was lined with vague apprehension. Athaya couldn't put her finger on it, but something was different about the wizard today. She could feel it in the air. He was agitated about something and had lost his usual marblelike composure. He seemed more fallible than usual, and more human than Athaya had ever seen him. But Athaya wasn't sure if she should be less afraid of him because of it, or more so.

"Ah, your Highness, please come in," he said genially, trying to cover whatever thoughts were distracting him. His false smile only made him look more uncomfortable. "Welcome home."

"I'm sorry to disturb you, but I brought you a message from your friend Hedric."

Rhodri slid off his stool with unexpected agility. His sapphire eyes glistened with anticipation. "Yes? What does he say?"

"Well, I don't really understand the message, but he told me you would," Athaya explained, feigning ignorance as best she could. "He said to tell you that he knows what you're doing, but that he cannot honor your request."

Athaya saw Rhodri's fingers curl inward, as if he were about to make a fist, but then he relaxed them. His eyes were glassy and cold. "That's all?"

"That's all. Does the message make sense to you?"

"Oh, yes," the wizard said darkly. "Perfect sense." Rhodri sat back down on the stool behind his writing desk. He drummed his fingertips angrily against the smooth oak desktop, and his lips moved slightly, as if muttering silent curses.

"You and Hedric must know each other quite well," Athaya remarked with well-crafted innocence. "He mentioned that he used to teach you magic."

"Did he?" Rhodri said, arching one eyebrow. "I'm surprised he'd admit to that. Hedric and I . . . well, we had a difference of opinion several years ago. The letter I asked you to deliver was the first communication I'd had with him in over twenty years."

"Did you have an argument?"

Rhodri laughed softly. "Something like that. I'm afraid that Hedric finds me a bit fanatical in my beliefs. But that is because he is so intolerably rigid in his. Anything would look extreme by contrast. You see, he didn't approve of my bestowing magic on your father twenty years ago. And the message you brought tells me that he still doesn't approve, even after I told him how well Kelwyn has done with it. He's given his people the first years of peace they've had in centuries. Ah, but Hedric's a stubborn old ox . . ."

Rhodri tapped the tips of his fingers together. His gaze grew more intense, more determined, and he seemed to forget that he was not alone in the room. His voice took on a hard, angry edge. "But one day he'll see. I'll find something that no one has ever done before. Then he can't deny me. I'm just as worthy as he is to be one of the—"

He broke off, suddenly conscious that he might be saying too much. "Forgive me," he said smoothly, smiling at her. "I'm sure you are not interested in my past dealings with Master Hedric."

Athaya was careful to sustain a look of polite bewilderment on her face, as if she understood nothing of what he was saying. Unfortunately, she did understand—all too well.

"I think it was noble of you to share your magic with my father," Athaya said, hoping to goad him into correcting her assumption. She knew she should avoid the subject, but she simply had to ask. If her father was in danger because of someone else's magic, then she wanted to find out who that person was and what had become of him. And she promised herself that it would be the first and last time she ever talked to Rhodri about such things.

Rhodri gave her an indulgent smile. "I'm afraid you're mistaken, Athaya. Much as I'd like to deserve your compliment, I should tell you that I still have all of my power. I don't expect you to be able to fully understand this, but all I did was transfer magic from someone who didn't want it to someone who did. It was quite simple."

"Then whose power did my father get?"

Rhodri paused for a moment before he began, but to her relief, he did not look at all suspicious of the question. "Did you ever hear of a friend of your father's named Donnely? Stefan Donnely? You wouldn't have known him. He was killed in the war before you were even a year old. Sad," Rhodri added with an unconvincing air of sympathy. "Donnely was only twenty-five at the time—just a few years younger than your father. He thought that since he was past the age when the Lorngeld's madness usually strikes, he was not one of them. Then, when his mind began to weaken, he was terrified that his friends and his family would be afraid of him and despise him. That was about the same time I was telling your father of the ritual which could give him power. Everything worked out beautifully. Kelwyn got the power he needed to help his country, and Donnely freed himself from a fate he did not want."

"It's too bad that he never lived to see the good things that Kelwyn was able to do with his magic," Athaya said wistfully. "He would have been proud."

"Yes, too bad," Rhodri said flatly, clearly having no real opinion on the subject.

Athaya put her hand on the door handle. "I'd better go. Father's expecting me."

As if he were the higher-ranking of the two, Rhodri gave her a nod of dismissal and went back to his books. Athaya slipped silently out of the room, feeling fairly confident that he would ascribe her inquiries to simple curiosity.

The soft tolling of the chapel bells told her that it was nearly time for supper. Kelwyn should have dismissed the Curia by now and would be waiting to see her. She wanted to deliver Osfonin's letter and talk with him privately about her time in Reyka. And more important, she needed to begin the difficult task of making a peace between them that was long overdue.

CHAPTER 14

✖

ATHAYA WAITED IN QUIET AGITATION, PACING BACK AND forth across the anteroom to her father's audience chamber. After leaving Rhodri's rooms, she had changed her riding clothes for more feminine attire, donning a plain but elegant gown of dark blue velvet embroidered with silver thread, and setting a jeweled circlet atop her head. The skirts of her gown swished softly on the carpet as she walked, and her fingers were busily fraying the ends of the ribbons that bound Osfonin's letter to Kelwyn. The meeting with the Curia had been over for nearly a half hour, but as yet, her father had not called for her. She did not want their discussion to be postponed until after supper, but it was growing late. Kelwyn's courtiers were already gathering for the evening meal in the Great Hall, and Athaya could hear the low buzz of their conversations on the other side of the wall.

After a few more minutes of waiting, the door to Kelwyn's chamber opened, and a red-liveried squire came out and bowed crisply to her. "The king will see you now."

Athaya entered the chamber with the same nervousness she always experienced when faced with speaking to Kelwyn alone. He had a gift for intimidation unlike anyone she'd ever known. *A fine quality in a king*, Athaya thought, *but an aggravating one in a father.*

Kelwyn was standing by the window, staring out across the sea. Thin beams of silvery moonlight poured into the dimly lit chamber, illuminating the few streaks of gray in his hair. When he heard her come in he turned and gazed at her softly, with emotion. Athaya felt strangely warmed. Her father had never looked at her that way before, and at that moment, she believed that Ysell had been right after all.

He did love her.

"You're back," he said quietly, coming to stand beside her. A warm smile lingered on his face. "You've been away a long time."

"We had a lot of rain, and the return trip took longer than expected." She paused, unsure of what to say next. How could she even begin to tell him what had been on her mind these last few weeks? How was she going to explain that she came home from Reyka after staying only seven days because she feared for his life? And more, what could she say to narrow the gap that separated them, the gap that had existed ever since she could remember, and try to make amends before it was too late?

Perhaps I should tell him about my magic, she thought suddenly, feeling a spark within her. *We could do it together.* By openly refusing to give his daughter up for absolution, Kelwyn could make a strong statement against the Church and show his resolve to help the Lorngeld. The idea excited her. With Kelwyn's backing, she might be able to do what Hedric had asked of her by helping to free the Lorngeld from their miserable fate, while at the same time forging a long-needed bond between herself and her father.

"I worried about you while I was gone," she said, conscious of what a spectacular understatement that was. "Have you been well?"

Kelwyn leaned his weight against the side of his desk. "Well enough," he said with a shrug, as if he thought it an odd question. "I missed you, of course."

She handed him the green-ribboned scroll. "I brought you a letter from Osfonin. He says he's anxious to help you change the Church's views on the Lorngeld in any way he can."

"Ah. That is good news," he said absently. He set the scroll aside without looking at it.

"He . . . also says he is reconsidering the idea of my marriage to Felgin."

She expected that Kelwyn would be delighted with the news,

knowing that all his hard work to renew relations with the Rey-kans had not gone to waste. She was completely unprepared for his violent reaction. He gripped the edges of the desk, as if bracing himself for a fall, and the color vanished from his face.

"Your *what*?"

Athaya knitted her brows with bewilderment. "Surely you remember about—"

"My God, how could you *think* of such a thing?" he said, with fearful desperation in his voice. "You can't marry him!"

Athaya's mouth hung open in stunned confusion. She had been sent to Reyka for the express purpose of trying to undo the damage she'd inflicted upon the marriage negotiations and to clear the way for an alliance between the two lands. And now he was worried that she had succeeded?

"But I thought you sent me to—"

She cut herself off abruptly, shocked by the look on his face. He was more haggard and afraid than she had ever seen him, and his eyes were locked into an expression of stupefied disbelief and horror. Twice he looked as if he were about to speak and twice he stopped himself short with confusion. He wrung his hands together anxiously, then ran his fingers through his hair, tangling it.

"I don't understand how you could do this," he cried. "Didn't you tell him you were in love with someone else?"

Athaya felt a sharp twist in her stomach, as if the floor had suddenly dropped out from beneath her feet. How could he possibly have known about Tyler? *How?*

"Are you feeling all right, Father?" she asked softly, un-nerved by the way he stared at her. His face was lined with worry, and his puffy eyes were bright red around the edges.

"You're not going to marry him, are you?" Kelwyn de-manded harshly.

Athaya shook her head, baffled by the course of their conver-sation. "Not if you don't want me to," she replied. What had happened in her absence to have changed his mind so com-pletely about her marriage to the Reykan prince?

Kelwyn was appeased and grinned. "Good, good, good. It's all settled then. No wedding."

Without knowing why, Athaya was suddenly very much afraid of him. Not even when he used to shout at her with such fury that the entire court would turn their faces away in embarrassment did Athaya ever feel so ill at ease in his presence. During those public scoldings, she could insulate herself with anger, telling herself over and over that only a hateful and pompous man would humiliate her so. But for this new kind of attack Athaya had no defense. How could she fight against a weapon she could not understand? She felt exposed and powerless and she hated that feeling above any other.

Her mind quickly groped for an excuse—any excuse—to get out of the chamber. There was danger here—danger of a kind Athaya could not comprehend.

"You look pale," she said, trying to sustain an outward show of calm as she backed toward the door. "Why don't I send for your physician?"

"But you can't leave again!" he cried, his voice shrill with hysteria. "You've only just come back!" Kelwyn lurched forward and gripped her by the wrist with such force that she let out a sharp cry of pain. She tried to squirm out of his grasp, but he would not release her.

"Please, you're hurting me!" The smooth skin of her forearm was burning under his grip, and her fingers, one by one, were slowly growing numb.

He pulled her close to him, and she was amazed at his strength. His eyes were desperate and pleading. "You can't go! You just can't—"

"Father, let me go!"

His grip suddenly slackened. "Why did you call me that?" he asked, his brows furrowing. A shadow of doubt clouded his features. "Don't you know who I am? Certainly in only twenty years you cannot have forgotten?"

Athaya detected a hint of anger in his voice. A king's voice, which despite all logic, said: *Give me the answer I wish to hear, but pray to God that it is not a lie.*

"Of course I haven't forgotten," she said smoothly, hoping that he would somehow explain what it was that she was supposed to remember.

Athaya was surprised at how easily he accepted her words. He let go of her arm and moved to the table in two swift strides, reaching out for a pair of silver goblets and a flagon of wine. His hands shook wildly as he poured, and the liquid spotted the white linen tablecloth like drops of blood. He picked up the cups and spun around quickly, not seeing how the wine sloshed out of them and stained the costly Cruachi carpet. His eyes were glazed with a kind of unearthly rapture, and he gazed at Athaya in sudden adoration, like a peasant boy who has caught his first glimpse of his king and thinks him a god.

Kelwyn thrust one of the cups toward her. "Here, drink with me. We must celebrate!"

Celebrate? Celebrate what? The fact that you're acting like an imbecile? Athaya stopped herself short as the horrible realization came over her.

An imbecile . . . or a madman.

Oh no, she thought, as she felt her heart skip in its rhythm. *Dear God, not yet. Not yet . . .*

Kelwyn forced the goblet into her hand and gestured toward the windowseat. "Come sit here with me. Ah, we had many happy times here, did we not?"

Hesitantly, Athaya sat down beside him and sipped her wine. It was a fine vintage from Evarshot, but it had no taste for her. She would have given anything at that moment to know what thoughts were in her father's tortured mind, but she humored him in silence, unwilling to risk incurring his wrath, or worse, a dose of misdirected magic. In his current state, Athaya suspected that his geniality could switch to fury in an instant. Perhaps later there would be a chance for escape, but for now, she dared do nothing.

She felt the cold touch of her father's hand on hers as he gently caressed her cheek. "It was here that I asked for your hand and it was here that you accepted me. Oh, Chandice, you are beautiful still. It is as if you never left."

Athaya's blood ran cold, and she saw the wine in her goblet swirl violently from her trembling hands like a miniature tempest. For a moment, she forgot to breathe.

"I've missed you so much. So much," he said. He reached out and ran his fingers through her hair, gazing at her lovingly. But not with paternal love—with the love of a man for his wife— a wife dead for twenty years.

Athaya tried not to flinch from his touch, afraid that it would anger him. Everything suddenly became clear—horribly clear.

No wonder he had not wanted her to marry Felgin. He thought she was intended for *him.*

He leaned close to her, forcing her back against the wall. "I'm so glad you've come back," he whispered, winding a lock of her hair around his finger. Then, before she realized what was happening, he pressed his lips against hers, drowning out her cry of protest. She felt his tongue inside her mouth, probing gently, and was conscious of his fingers exploring the laces of her bodice, trying to expose her breast. In a burst of sheer panic and revulsion, she pushed him away with all her strength, fighting back the tears which stung her eyes.

Kelwyn frowned at her, openly hurt and displeased. "What's the matter, my love?"

Athaya swallowed hard. *Careful,* she cautioned herself. *Be careful. He doesn't know what he's doing.* "I . . . I just can't," she blurted out.

Her father smiled indulgently. "Ah, you always were shy, little one. But that will pass in time. After we are used to one another." He laid his hand on her thigh, gently caressing the smooth velvet of her gown.

Athaya took a deep breath to steady herself, trying to fend off the panic she felt rising within her. Kelwyn was lost in his own world, unaware of who she was or what he was doing. His time had come too soon. She would never be able to explain to him all those things she had hurried back from Reyka to say. All she could hope for now was to escape his presence before he forced himself upon her, by strength alone, or with the help of magic.

"Please," she said, shrinking away from him. "I've had a long ride and I'm tired."

Suddenly angry, Kelwyn snatched his hand away, as if burned by a hot iron. "I should not be so pleased to have you back, you know," he said, his voice dropping down an octave. His smile was gone, and he glared at her with calm intensity. "You went away without a word to me, and I missed you so terribly that I—"

His eyes narrowed dangerously, until they were no more than two milky white gashes across his face. "I think that now, dear Chandice, I should hate you."

He stood up so quickly that Athaya gasped with fright. Her instincts told her to reach for a weapon—any weapon—but the cool, rational part of her mind warned her not to be such a fool as to openly threaten the king. She had seen this look on her father's face—the hard line of his jaw, the flared nostrils, the eyes that glittered like cold jewels. It was a murderous but powerful look, one that was often on his face in the early years of the civil war, when he was forced to declare a death sentence on former friends who turned against him. Athaya felt ice in her veins, and her eyes focused on the way his hands rhythmically opened and closed, as if trying to fight the impulse to snatch his daughter—or his wife?—by the throat and strangle the life from her.

"Look at what has become of me since you left!" he shouted, his voice echoing from the timber rafters. "I'm wretched and alone. I married twice again, but neither wife could please me. Especially not the dragon who currently wears the queen's crown," he added maliciously. "My eldest son is cold and heartless, and I hate myself for loving him; my youngest son is a fool who thinks he can sing and joke his way through life like a jester; and my daughter—gads, my daughter! She's as bad as a Sarian mercenary—gambling and brawling in taverns, swearing like a common footsoldier, and doing the opposite of anything I tell her to do just to spite me. Every time I look at her, I see you, Chandice. God, she looks just like you. Her eyes, her hair . . . but to see her acting the coarse way she does," he said, his hands tightening into fists, "I cannot bear that. It's an insult to you!"

Kelwyn's voice rose in pitch, until it became shrill and broken. "I wanted to love her, for your sake, Chandice. I wanted to, but I can't. She's an embarrassment to me. To me and all of Caithe! If you had stayed, she would have grown to be sweet and gentle, and attended to her music and her books. She would have grown to be just like you. But you deserted us, you hateful little bitch, and now we are all in ruins!"

He whipped his hand across her face in a blind fury, hurling her to the floor. "You never loved me. How could you have loved me and left me alone all these years?"

Athaya's mind swirled in confusion as she tried to ease away the pain from Kelwyn's blow. Her father slipped in and out of time, one moment believing himself a bridegroom, and the next recalling that he had married three times and fathered three children. But of one thing he was constantly sure—that Chandice had not died, but had deserted him and had now come home again.

He hauled her up roughly from the floor, prepared to strike her again.

"Father, please listen!" she pleaded. "It's me, Athaya!"

His hand stopped in midair. Spasms of confusion rippled across his face, and his fingers began to tremble.

"Athaya?" his voice was suddenly small and weak, and he sounded bewildered and frightened, like a lost child. He stared straight ahead, unblinking. "Then where is my wife? Where is Chandice?"

"Chandice is *dead*!" she cried out in agonized frustration. "Don't you remember? My mother died twenty years ago, right after I was born!"

A tense silence hung over the room. The only sound was of her own ragged breath as she fought to control the tears that welled within her. Why couldn't she make him see? What did she have to do?

Kelwyn nodded faintly. "Ah, yes. Little Athaya." His eyes met hers, and for the first time, he recognized her for who she was. There was no trace of love in his eyes, as there had been when she'd entered the chamber. No, that gaze had not been for her, but for her mother. Now his eyes were cold, reflecting the same resentment, the same disappointment that Athaya knew all too well.

"Yes, now I remember, Athaya," he said with dark calm. His voice was slurred, as if he were drunk. "Chandice is dead. *And you killed her*."

Kelwyn backed away, oblivious to the look of horror on his daughter's face. Then, with his face twisted in anger, he raised his hands and sketched a pattern in the air with his fingers.

Instantly, Athaya felt as if someone had wrapped a thin rope of nettles around her neck and was tightening it with excruciating slowness. Her hands clutched at her throat, trying to loosen whatever magic thing was assailing her, but there were no nettles, no rope. There was nothing, except the pain of sharp thorns digging into her throat. Thorns that were not there and drew no blood, but pierced her skin as the invisible rope tightened and forced her breath from her lungs.

She tried to cry out, but nothing would come. Nothing but the gurgling sounds made by a hanged man, dangling from the end of the noose.

Her vision blurred, but she could see Kelwyn's hazy image standing over her as she sank to her knees. He was smiling—smiling like a demon as he watched her die, and once she heard him let out a thin peal of vengeful laughter. Athaya began to panic as she gasped futilely for breath. She felt herself on the verge of passing out and fought the urge to sink into black oblivion, knowing that the moment she did so she was dead.

Then she saw nothing but darkness and felt herself slipping away . . .

But in the darkness, she saw the vague outlines of cavern walls, faintly lit. In sheer desperation, she searched the paths for a spell that would stop Kelwyn's onslaught. She looked for the doorway to her power, and when she found the gray stone, she commanded it to roll aside and admit her into the mental labyrinth. The stone moved quickly from the force of her command, and she ran wildly through the passageways, looking for something—anything—to counteract her father's spell.

Many of the darkened corridors were closed to her, but she had no time to wonder what kinds of spells were hidden there, out of her reach. She stumbled ahead, trying not to slip away into unconsciousness, and suddenly found herself in a small room whose walls were covered with symbols, like those she had seen when trying to create a witchlight. Desperately, she concentrated on the strange drawings, opening her mind to them and commanding them to tell her what to do. And without knowing how or what she did, she pointed her fingers toward her father and whispered words she had never heard before.

"Ignis confestim sit!"

Kelwyn's magic cord of nettles released her at once, and she gasped for air, filling her starving lungs. But then her muscles froze as she heard her father cry out in agony, his voice splitting the air. She opened her bloodshot eyes to see what she had done and clamped her hands over her mouth in utter horror.

He was writhing on the floor, trying to struggle out of the greenish, snakelike coils of lightning that bound him. The ropes of green fire seemed to have a life of their own—a life Athaya had given them—and curled around his arms and legs hungrily, tormenting him. Sparks flew from the coils, filling the air with a sharp crackling sound and the pungent scent of seared cloth and flesh. Kelwyn's eyes were wild, like those of a stag who knows the hunters have him cornered, and he threw his head back and screamed aloud from the pain.

"Stop!" Athaya cried out, commanding the lightning to disperse. "Leave him alone!" But the fiery coils kept streaming from her fingertips, avoiding her body and winding themselves tighter around Kelwyn, squeezing out his last breath.

And then, in one last moment of lucidity, he looked up at her with eyes filled with confusion and dread, and said, "Athaya, no! *Please, no!*"

Tears welled in her eyes, and she was frozen—helpless—watching him plead with her to release him and not knowing how to do so. She had only wanted to make amends . . . to apologize. She wanted to tell him that she loved him, in spite of not knowing how to show it. She wanted him to know that she did not hate him. Now she knew that he had never despised her, but only felt pain when he looked at her, knowing both how much similar, and tragically different, she was from his beloved Chandice. But no matter what she told him now, he would never believe her.

Assuming he lived to hear her explanation.

"God in Heaven, what are you doing?" The door to the audience chamber crashed open, and Durek's voice boomed across the room. "Stop it! Athaya, do you hear me? *Stop it!*"

Athaya wheeled around and lowered her arms, and the green lightning abruptly faded from her hands. Released from his prison of fire, Kelwyn's body convulsed and went limp. He let out a weak sigh and lay motionless at her feet.

If she could have had anything at that moment, Athaya would have wished to vanish forever. In the doorway were Durek and Rhodri, both staring at her in wordless shock. But while Durek's eyes reflected swollen outrage, Rhodri seemed afraid—deathly afraid—as if he had been openly threatened. The sight of her magic had shaken him deeply. But Athaya paid little mind to either her brother or Rhodri.

Standing behind them, his face frozen with horrified disbelief, was Tyler.

Durek came toward her, his face purple with rage. "My God, you're one of them, aren't you? Those Reykans have made a mind-plagued wizard out of you!"

"They didn't do anything to me!" she protested through her tears. "It's . . . just the way I am . . ."

Her brother turned around and made a sharp gesture toward Rhodri. "Damn it, get over there and try to do something for the king. Tyler, see if you can help."

Averting his eyes from her, Tyler hurried to Kelwyn's side and cradled the king's head in his lap. Rhodri bent down over Kelwyn and tested for a pulse, but kept one eye fixed nervously on her, rapidly trying to assess her power. She could feel the wizard's gaze as if it were a palpable thing, and it was hot and intense, like a flame. But Tyler would not look at her, keeping his eyes focused on the king, and Athaya could only wonder if it was merely due to shock, or stemmed from pure revulsion.

Durek pulled her roughly away from where Kelwyn lay, afraid her very presence was a danger to him. "You're mad, that's what you are!" Durek shouted at her. "You've gone completely insane, just like all the others."

"But he was—"

"He wasn't doing a damned thing! You *attacked* him!"

"He attacked me first! He was trying to kill me!"

Durek tightened his jaw in disgust. "Don't expect me to believe such a pitiful excuse, Athaya. Come now, you're a much better liar than that."

"You don't understand," she said, burying her face in her hands. "He thought—"

"So you finally got pushed too far, didn't you? What was it? Did you bring home bad news from Reyka? Did Father threaten to exile you? Damned if he shouldn't have, the way you bait him all the time. Is this your way of getting even for all the times he punished you? All the times he made you pay for your impertinence and bad temper? Was this your solution? Murdering your own father? Murdering the *king*?"

"He's still alive," Rhodri said softly, putting his fingers to the veins on Kelwyn's throat. "But he's very weak."

Durek glared at her murderously. "I swear, Athaya. I swear on everything that's holy—if you've killed him, I'll make you regret the day you were ever born."

Athaya sank to her knees in defeat. *I already do, Durek. Oh God, I already do.*

Her head was spinning in confused agony, but of one thing she was sure. She could not stay another moment in this room. Much as she wanted to remain until she knew if her father would live, it was too dangerous. If he died, Durek would have her arrested for the unspeakable crime of murdering the king. But even if he survived, it was a foregone conclusion that, sister or no, Durek would notify Archbishop Ventan that he would be needed to administer the sacrament of absolution, before anyone found out about her gift of magic, and the Trelane name was tainted with scandal.

And what of Rhodri? What might he do, knowing that she had

obviously brought back more from Master Hedric than a simple message for his former pupil? Seeing her power and knowing she had met with Hedric, Rhodri would inevitably realize that her naive questions of a few hours ago had been full of purpose. It would not take him long to conclude that she knew about the risks that the rite of assumption entailed and knew that Rhodri had never bothered to warn Kelwyn of them. And if he suspected her of trying to interfere with his experiment of magic—his painstaking attempt to display his skill to the Great Masters—he would stop at nothing to ensure that she never interfered again.

Athaya's eyes darted quickly around the room. She had to escape—but how? The door out of the audience chamber led through the anteroom and directly into the Great Hall, by now crowded with people awaiting their supper. She was certain to be restrained by someone—surely Durek, Rhodri, and Tyler were not the only ones who heard Kelwyn's cries. Yes, someone would entrap her.

Athaya's breath caught in her throat. *Yes, they would entrap her. But only if they could see her.*

Without making a move, she prayed to whatever god might hear her that her cloaking spell would work as well today as it had before. She had cast the spell unconsciously before; she doubted she could find it in her paths while purposefully looking for it. But even if she could, she had no time to try, and she hoped that her mind could be trusted to act of its own accord and cast the proper spell.

The moment Durek turned his back to her to check on Kelwyn, she began. Concentrating as hard as she could, she closed her eyes and thought of nothing else except the wish not to be seen. She banished all other thoughts from her mind and willed herself invisible, thinking of mist and air, and in less than a minute, she felt as if a thin blanket had settled over her, and her limbs felt light and weightless.

She opened her eyes tentatively. Her body was still visible—to her eyes at least—and she felt her hands shaking, afraid that the spell had failed. Careful not to make a sound, Athaya inched her way toward the door. She watched Rhodri closely as he tried to rouse the king into consciousness. She did not know whether he would be able to detect her spell or not, but she took no chances and moved as quickly as she could, eager to get out of his dangerous presence.

Then Durek turned back and started. His eyes bored right into her and through her, as if she were not there.

"Where did she go?" he demanded, trying to cover his fear with anger. "Damn it, where is she?"

Rhodri jerked his head around and scrambled to his feet. "She's under a cloak!" Athaya heard him say as she bolted out of the room. "Mirrors! Quickly, you'll need mirrors!"

Athaya ran blindly through the Great Hall, past tables full of people who were sipping their wine and chatting with each other, oblivious to her presence. Behind her, she heard Durek's voice echoing up to the rafters as he shouted out orders to his guardsmen.

"After her!" he shouted. "Seal off every door and gate and bring her to me the minute you find her. Damn it, Captain, do you hear me? Don't just stand there—*move*!"

Stumbling over the rough stones, Athaya fled out of the Hall and into the courtyard, unaware of the cold night air biting through her gown. The moon was now covered by clouds, and there was nothing to light her way.

She bolted through the main gates just moments before the warning horns were sounded and the guards lowered the port-cullis with a thundering crash, the iron-tipped spikes at the grille's base spearing brutally into the earth like knives through flesh. Her breath was nearly gone, but she could not stop now, even though the cobbles bit into her soft leather slippers and bruised the soles of her feet. It began to rain, and the cold droplets spattered in her eyes and turned the earth to mud.

Hysterical, confused, and shaken to her very core, Athaya ran out into the night through the darkened streets of Delfarham, crying but unseen, like moaning wind.

What have I done? she thought. *Oh God, what have I done?* And she was conscious that, for the first time, the real world had become far more terrifying than even her worst nightmares.

CHAPTER 15

✽✾✽

ATHAYA POUNDED HER FISTS AGAINST THE DOOR, IGNOR-
ing the thin splinters of wood cutting into her hands.
The rain was coming harder now, and she shivered from
the cold wind that threatened to turn the rain to sleet and ice.
The alley was slick with mud. She had slipped and fallen several
times on her way, and her once-fine gown was now soiled beyond repair. Her hair was wet and tangled under the jeweled
circlet, and her eyes were red and swollen.

"Let me in! For God's sake, let me in!"

She heard a frantic rush of footsteps and the metallic swish
of an iron latch being hastily thrown back. Jaren opened the
door and pulled her inside the warm, dry room. Stumbling over
the threshold, she threw her arms around his neck, clinging to
him in quiet desperation. She buried her face in the soft linen of
his shirt, staining it with her muddy tears.

"Help me, Jaren." Her voice was broken with sobs. "Please
help me. It's so terrible, what I've done. So terrible . . ."

After a moment's hesitation, Jaren slipped his arms around
her and held her close, stroking her wet and tangled hair in an
effort to calm her. Slowly, he guided her to a low stool near the
fireplace and covered her with a thick, dry blanket. He reached
out and brushed a strand of wet hair from her eyes.

"Easy, Athaya. Calm down. You're safe now."

Jaren lifted off her circlet and laid it on the table, and the sparkling jewels looked strange against the scratched and pitted wood. He went into the small bedroom and emerged with a soft cloth soaked in water and he bent over her, gently wiping away the mud from her face. She closed her eyes, trying to forget what had brought her here, and fixed her thoughts on the smooth, relaxing sensation of the cloth as it brushed her cheeks and forehead. Although her clothes were thoroughly soaked, the water felt refreshing on her skin, and Jaren's unhurried touch was calming and hypnotic.

"I tried to look in on you a few hours ago, but I couldn't get through. Rhodri must still have his wards up." His voice was low and comforting and full of concern. "Tell me what happened."

Jaren leaned against the edge of the table, listening intently and taking in her every word. He did not interrupt her, but let her go on at her own pace, patient with her sporadic tears. When the blanket over her shoulders was soaked through, he took it away and gave her another and added another log to the fire.

Athaya's hands shook wildly as she spoke, although she was not sure if it was from the chill or from shock. She felt empty—so empty—as if she had been twisted inside out. She told him about Kelwyn's madness, and his delusions of Chandice, and how he had attacked her, and how, not knowing what else to do, she had struck back.

"I killed him, Jaren. My father's dead and it's all my fault."

"You don't know that for sure," Jaren said softly. "You said yourself that he was alive when you left."

"But he isn't now—he couldn't be. You weren't there. You didn't see what happened." Athaya broke off, and her face was lined with painful memory. "You should have seen the way he looked at me, Jaren," she added in a whisper. "It was horrible. He was begging me to stop, and I just couldn't. He died thinking I hated him when all I wanted to do was say I'm sorry." She struck her fists against her thighs in frustration. "Damn it all, I thought you said I was safe. I thought you said that I'd be protected from casting spells I can't stop!"

Jaren regarded her seriously, his brows forming a solid line across his forehead. "It's possible that the *mekahn* is farther advanced than Hedric thought. Your shielding could be starting to break down."

"I knew it," she said, burying her face in her hands. "Durek was right. I am going crazy."

"No, Athaya. You're not crazy. And you're not going to be, either." He reached out and tucked a lock of hair behind her ear. "But you are in need of some intense training. If you can master a few basics, the risk of madness will be completely gone. But you'll still need to learn control. That only comes with time and practice."

"But there *is* no time!" she said. "We've got to get out of here right away!" She looked wildly around the room, as if expecting the crimson-clad men of the King's Guard to burst in any moment, even though she knew they had not seen her slip through the main gates.

Jaren knelt down on the floor beside her and clasped her hand. "We'll be fine right where we are. And you're not going anywhere until you've gotten ahold of yourself. Besides, by now your brother's probably got dozens of soldiers out looking for you. The safest place for us right now is here. If we tried to leave the city tonight, they'd be sure to spot us. Especially if Rhodri told them how to see through a cloaking spell with mirrors."

"But if we stay, won't Rhodri be able to find us with his sphere?"

"I don't think so. I warded both rooms shortly after you left this afternoon. Still," he added worriedly, "from what Hedric has told me, Rhodri is a much stronger magician than I am. I know it's a lot to ask right now, but it would help if you could reinforce my wards. With both of us spelling the place against him, I seriously doubt he'll be able to detect us. And as for anyone who isn't a Lorngeld, they won't even bother looking here. The wards will send a subtle, psychic message that the rooms are empty, and to go look somewhere else."

Athaya felt drained and exhausted, unsure if she had the strength to stand much less work a spell she'd never tried before. But she also knew that Jaren was right. Tyler and his men would be combing the city for them, and if they tried to escape, they wouldn't get far. The best thing they could do was put up whatever magic defenses they had and wait until the guardsmen had given up their search. Then she and Jaren could get out of Delfarham once and for all.

"Show me what to do."

Jaren took her to the far corner of the small room, empty except for a broom of twigs and a thick coating of dust. Athaya hadn't noticed it before, but now that she was calmer, she saw that the walls of the room glistened, as if covered with dew. Curious, she reached out and touched the splintered walls, and they felt like they'd been brushed with a thin coating of oil.

"Now just relax and let me step you through it," Jaren said.

A few seconds later, she felt the cool touch of Jaren's presence in her mind as he helped her search through the paths, looking for the place in her mind where the warding spells were kept. The labyrinth was not as dark as it had been before, and for the first time, Athaya was able to see that the corridors did not all look alike. The walls were narrower in some, the ceilings higher in others, and because of the brighter light, the symbols etched in the stone were more readable.

They took one wrong turn and had to double back when they found their way blocked by a wall of polished stone; despite Athaya's trepidation, Jaren explained that every wizard's paths were patterned slightly differently, and it was nothing to worry about. *But I must say,* he added, his thoughts echoing in her mind, *you have more open corridors than I've ever seen in anyone before.*

He stopped abruptly, and Athaya was conscious of standing on a warm patch of soft, rust-colored sand. She was overwhelmed with the sensation of being safe and warm, as if she were wrapped in a silk cocoon where nothing could harm her.

This is it, Jaren told her. *Now just follow me and do what I do.*

Shifting her concentration to the world outside her paths, Athaya watched Jaren spread his hands out and touch the walls of the room—the real room—with his fingertips. Then he pressed his palms together, as if in prayer.

"Periculum absit," he whispered. The corner of the room glistened brighter, with a silvery glow like starlight.

Athaya repeated the movements and words after him, paying close attention to every movement so she would remember how to work the spell again, if need be. They went through both rooms, enacting the simple ritual in every corner. The act of casting the warding spells helped take Athaya's mind off her harrowing experience at the castle, albeit temporarily, and she felt more relaxed when they had finished.

"That ought to do it," Jaren said. He admired their work, unabashedly proud. The walls gleamed like moonlight on snow-covered earth.

"How long will the wards last?"

"About a day," he said. He pulled a three-legged stool out of the corner and sat down next to the fire. "Don't worry, we can work the spell again when they start weakening."

Athaya pulled a chair away from the table and sat down next to him, letting the heat from the flames warm her face. "What did you mean when you said I had a lot of 'open corridors'?"

"You know how some of the caves are open to you and others are blocked off? Well, you have an unusually high number of open passages for a wizard with your level of training. It makes more sense once you know that every Lorngeld is born with all the magic that it's possible to know already in his mind. But the greater the gift for magic, the more spells a person can get to. Hedric estimates that even the greatest wizards only tap into about fifty percent of their potential, which tells you just how much uncharted territory is still out there. I've only been helping Hedric train wizards for a few years, and most of them have paths like mine—all the basic spells, and a few open corridors to the more intricate ones. But you have lots of open passages in addition to the basic ones."

"And what does that mean?"

"That means, Athaya, that you have more potential than any-one I've ever met. You might be able to discover spells that nobody has ever heard of before."

A shadow passed over her face. "Like the rite of assumption?" she asked darkly.

"No, not exactly. That particular spell isn't very difficult. Anyone should be able to do it—theoretically, at least. As Hedric said, the tricky part lies in constructing paths for the person getting the magic. The actual spell used to transfer power is simple. Dangerously simple. But for all the trouble that ritual has caused, I wish it never existed to begin with. I'm glad it's forbidden."

"If it causes that much trouble, why on earth would you teach people that it exists at all?" Athaya asked, astounded that such a complex situation had an amazingly simple solution. "If you ask me, all you're doing is creating your own problem and then complaining about it."

"I know I'm going to sound like Hedric for saying this, but it's not our place to suppress knowledge. That route almost inevitably leads to disaster. Hedric believes, as I do, that only when something is fully understood can it be rightfully condemned. All magic comes from God and must have some purpose, even if it's only to see how well we can avoid using it. Wizards must know why certain spells should not be cast. It's all a part of their ethical education. You'll get to that later," he added. "Not to tell them about the spell at all would be wrong. Chances are good that many wizards would discover it on their own, and, by no crime except that of ignorance, cause no end of damage."

"Rhodri caused a fair amount of damage and he knew what he was doing," Athaya pointed out. "So did that fellow Senal—the one who gave his magic to Faltil."

"I can't deny that. But what we don't know is how many of those incidents might have been repeated if knowledge about the rite of assumption had been suppressed, and it was left to chance as to who would discover how to work the spell on their own. And the very fact that they'd never been taught about it would make it awfully tempting to experiment with. Without knowing any better, wizards could begin to transfer power away from those to whom God gave it, to those of their own choosing. They'd be all but playing God themselves, deciding who should have the power and who should not, and that would be meddling of the worst kind."

"Just as Rhodri did," Athaya finished quietly. She gazed somberly into the fire. "I wish I knew what's happened to my father."

"Well," Jaren said, growing more serious, "if, as you said, Durek's got Rhodri looking after Kelwyn and trying to find some sort of magic cure, he can't be paying much attention to his wards. We might be able to get through and see something."

"Let me try. After all, I'm the one who needs the practice," she added wryly.

Jaren nodded. "As you wish. But if you feel a headache coming on that probably means the wards are still in force. Don't push too hard or you'll hurt yourself."

Taking a deep breath for relaxation, she held her palms up a handspan's width apart. She focused her attentions on her fingertips, and before long, her mind obeyed her wishes and she felt the familiar tingling sensation. The sphere came quickly, swirling into existence at her command. It was clouded with a grayish haze at first, and Athaya felt her heart sink, fearing that Rhodri's wards were still at full strength. But then she felt a slight twinge behind her eyes, like the faint hint of a coming headache, and soon an image began to take shape as she passed through the weakened wards.

Gazing intently into the weightless orb hovering between her fingers, she reached out to her father, concentrating on his image as she looked into the swirling mist. In seconds, she saw an image begin to take shape. It was the king's private bedchamber. The brocade drapes were closed, and the room was poorly lit. Athaya saw clouds of incense coming from the burners in the corner, filling the room with perfumed smoke. Then she saw Kelwyn hidden under a mass of quilted coverlets, and she gasped at the sight of him.

His hair had gone white—white as Hedric's—and he looked like a man twice his age. His face was pale and drawn, and his arm was white against the deep blue quilts like a crescent moon on a winter night. Thin wisps of breath escaped from cracked and bleeding lips. Athaya choked on her breath as she realized, with unspeakable pain in her heart, that the man who had once struck fear in her with only the slightest glance was now nothing more than a living corpse.

In the rear of the room she saw Nicolas, tired and haggard, with his hair in wild disarray. He had one arm wrapped around Cecile's shoulders as he wiped away her tears. Durek, clad in a blood-red doublet the color of his cheeks, paced furiously back and forth across the carpet, and Dagara was slumped on a cushioned stool by the window looking terrified and alone. Archbishop Ventan stood at the foot of the bed in his gold-threaded robes, rotely whispering prayers, and Rhodri, his face as white as Kelwyn's hair, bent over the king, trying to find a way to rouse him back to consciousness.

"I always knew she was the Devil's child," Dagara muttered to herself. "So willful, so obstinate. She always did hate him. They never got along."

Cecile looked angrier than Athaya had ever seen her. "How can you say such a cruel thing? I'm sure this is all some ghastly misunderstanding."

"I'll never forgive this!" Durek cried out, his face scarlet with rage. *"Never!"*

"Durek, please," Nicolas said, his voice weak from exhaustion. "Not now. Think of Father."

"I *am* thinking of him, you imbecile! That's why I'm going to bring the full force of the law—"

"Your Majesty," Rhodri said to Durek, drawing away from the bedside. He was noticeably shaken. "The king is dead."

Athaya drew in a sharp breath. Her vision blurred, but it was from the tears welling in her eyes, and not the failure of her sphere. She had to fight from pulling away from the image too soon.

You've been wrong so many times in your life, she told herself angrily. *Why did you suddenly pick this time to be right?* She blinked a few times, and teardrops ran gently down her cheek.

Ominously calm, Durek made a smooth gesture, and Athaya saw Tyler step into view.

"Captain, bring me a pen and parchment."

"What are you doing?" Cecile asked, trembling as she let go of Nicolas's arm.

Durek drew his shoulders back, and his eyes glittered like ice. "I am going to draw up an official order for the immediate arrest of one Athaya Trelane, on charges of high treason."

In the corner of the sphere, Athaya saw Tyler flinch noticeably, and he almost dropped the inkwell as he handed the writing implements to Durek.

Nicolas's eyes bulged. "No! You can't possibly—"

"I can do what I like, Nicolas," Durek snapped back. "I am the king now."

"Durek, for God's sake, she's our sister!"

"I can't help *that*," Durek said, his eyes narrowing.

"And she is a Lorngeld, your Majesty," Ventan cut in smoothly, careful to use Durek's new title though he'd held it less than a minute. "Her magic is evil."

Rhodri made no retort to the archbishop's remark, but remained silent and thoughtful, all too aware that he was in a delicate situation. Athaya could understand why. With Kelwyn dead, he was certain not to be welcome in Durek's court, and he would definitely want to avoid anyone finding out that Kelwyn's death was indirectly his fault.

Durek scrawled a few hasty words on the ivory parchment. "Rhodri, give me Father's ring."

The wizard did as he was told and slid the signet ring from Kelwyn's bloodless hand. Durek took it and dipped it in wax, sealing the order.

"Captain, take this and round up a search party," Durek said, thrusting the paper into Tyler's hands. "Conduct a complete search of the city and scour the countryside within a ten-mile radius. She can't have gotten too far on foot in only an hour. When you find her, bring her directly to me. Preferably alive," he added darkly. "But use your own judgment." Durek clenched his teeth in quiet rage. "She has a great deal to answer for."

Unable to take any more, Athaya willed the sphere to dissolve. The misty orb faded, and Athaya wiped the dewlike residue on her skirts. She squeezed her eyes closed and wished that the entire world would go away and stop tormenting her.

"I knew it. I knew it, Jaren. He's dead, and it's all my fault." Jaren lowered his eyes. "I'm sorry, Athaya. Truly."

"I'll never forgive myself—"

"There's nothing to forgive," Jaren said. "Don't blame yourself for this. I know you might not believe this now, but your father wouldn't have lived much longer, even if you'd never come back from Ath Luaine. And he might have done a lot of damage and hurt a lot of people once his magic went completely out of control."

"I saw him die," she said, as if unaware that Jaren had spoken. "It was the same. Exactly the same as what I saw before."

"Before?" Jaren asked with a puzzled expression. "When?"

"That time in Hedric's study. That's what I saw right before I passed out."

There was a long, silent pause. "Are you sure it was exactly the same?"

Athaya nodded. "Exactly. Only I saw more this time."

"Futures," he said, thunderstruck. "That day in Hedric's study . . . you were seeing futures. And you had no training at all!"

Athaya felt a flutter of apprehension. "Is that good?"

"Good?" he said, wide-eyed. "Athaya, you don't realize how rare a talent that is. Even Hedric can't do it very well, and only a handful of the Great Masters can claim to have any reliability

with future readings. Futures . . ." he repeated to himself.
"That must be why you saw through the wards . . ."

"Well, I don't care a damn for seeing futures if I'm going to
see things like this!" she blurted out angrily. It was better not
to know about the future at all than discover something disastrous was going to happen. "I wish I'd never learned how to
make a sphere at all." She folded her arms across her chest and
stared sullenly into the fire. "But I never did learn, did I? How
did I make a vision sphere that first time? I didn't know a thing
about paths then. And for that matter, how did I do it just now?"

"The same way you did the other things, I suppose. Rear-
ranging the cards in the tavern, working a cloaking spell to sneak
out of Delfar. Something tells me that your unconscious mind
knows a lot more about working magic than your conscious one.
The trick is going to be getting both of them to work together
so you'll have control over your spells. That's the trouble with
gifted adepts like you—the more power you have, the harder it
is to control." Jaren paused for a moment to think. "I'll bet
that's why you couldn't stop the fire-spell you cast on Kelwyn.
You were trying too hard. The minute Durek walked in and
interrupted your train of thought, your unconscious mind took
over and the spell dissolved."

"Durek," she said, remembering her vision. "He sent Tyler
out after me. To arrest me. Oh, why did it have to be him?"
She shook her head in quiet resignation. "You should have seen
his face, Jaren. He hates me now. I just know it."

"I'm sure that's not true," Jaren said. But his voice lacked
conviction, as if he didn't want to fully believe his own words.
He set an earthenware cup in front of her and poured her a
generous serving of wine. "Here, drink some of this. It'll help
you relax."

Athaya's lower lip trembled as she drank the rich, red liquid,
and a look of profound sadness came over her. "I don't know
what I'll do without him. I remember when Father first gave
him his commission three years ago," she said, smiling wistfully. "I'd go out to the lists and watch the men at their war
games and I'd pretend that I was there to watch Nicolas, but I
really went to see Tyler. And I think he liked the attention, too,
because he always tried to show off whenever I was there."

Each time she drained off the wine in her goblet, she refilled
it from the flagon. She drank absently, not from thirst, but from

a desire to numb her mind and deaden the grief that tormented her.

"Tyler was the first man I ever fell in love with," she went on, talking as much to herself as she was to Jaren. "I always knew that my father would choose my husband for me, but I couldn't help what I felt for Tyler. It took him a lot longer to admit he loved me. He knew how impossible it all was and that he'd lose his commission if anyone ever found out there was something between us. Even though we never—" She broke off and her cheeks turned pink. "Well, that doesn't matter now."

Athaya finished off the rest of the wine in her goblet. She glanced up at Jaren, who had been patiently listening to her, without a word. He looked tired and alone, wrapped up in thoughts he didn't seem inclined to share.

"Thanks for the wine," she said. "I feel better now."

Jaren lifted up the bottle, now almost empty. "You should," he observed, offering her a half smile. "Now why don't you go in the other room and rest for a while. And get out of that wet gown before you catch your death. You can put on a few of my things until I can slip out tomorrow and buy you something else to wear. After all, you'll never get back to Reyka this time of year without something a bit warmer than that," he said, gesturing to her ruined gown.

"Reyka? What are you talking about?"

"We certainly can't stay here. And you definitely need a teacher of Hedric's ability, not mine." Before she could mouth a word of protest, he added, "But we'll talk about that later. Right now you need to rest."

"I couldn't possibly sleep after everything that's happened. It sounds silly, but I'm just too exhausted to sleep."

"I'll take care of that," Jaren said cryptically. "Just go and put on some dry clothes, and I'll be in after a few minutes."

With a puzzled frown, Athaya obeyed him. She went into the bedroom and searched through Jaren's saddlebags, pulling out a soft shirt of embroidered silk. It was large enough on her to act as a makeshift nightshirt, and she put it on and laid her velvet gown on the floor to dry. It felt good to be out of her wet clothes, and Jaren's shirt was smooth and warm against her skin. She buried herself under tattered wool blankets, trying to find a comfortable position on the hard pallet of straw, and a few minutes later, Jaren knocked softly and came in.

He perched himself on the edge of her bed, careful not to draw too close. Then he reached out and laid his palm across her forehead, as if testing for fever. "Just relax," he said, his voice low and hypnotic. "Close your eyes."

Soon she felt his familiar, gentle presence in her mind, like the touch of a cool feather. She thought she heard him speaking, but the whispers didn't form words, only a soft, rhythmic pattern of sound that lulled her into a feeling of security and warmth. Suddenly she was overwhelmed with exhaustion and began to lose her awareness of where she was and of Jaren's presence next to her.

Sleep well, Athaya. His voice echoed in her mind, and she felt as if she were floating—drifting on a calm sea. Just as she was poised on the verge of unconsciousness, she thought she heard Jaren say something else, but the words were little more than vague whispers, and she slipped away, unhearing, into a deep, dreamless sleep.

When she awoke, Athaya saw that the door was slightly ajar, and a weak ray of light filtered in from the outer room. She threw off the wool blankets and went to the doorway. Jaren was still awake and sat motionless on the three-legged stool near the fire, staring into the flames. An iron pot was suspended over the fire, and he absently swirled the contents with a wooden spoon, showing little interest in whatever he was concocting. His head drooped down listlessly, and Athaya was sure he had stayed awake while she slept to guard against danger.

"What time is it?"

Jaren jumped and spun around, dropping the wooden spoon on the floor.

"Sorry. I didn't mean to startle you."

"I didn't think you'd wake up so soon," he mumbled distract-edly. He wiped off the spoon with a rag and set it on a hook near the fireplace. "It's just after midnight. You only slept for a few hours."

Judging from the way he turned away from her, Athaya got the distinct impression that she had interrupted some very se-rious thinking on Jaren's part. But perhaps he was simply em-barrassed at seeing her clad only in one of his shirts, with her legs bare and her hair falling loosely over her shoulders.

Jaren fetched two bowls from a narrow shelf above the hearth. "Are you hungry? I made us a little soup."

Athaya glanced into the pot and took a whiff of the steaming broth. "I didn't know you could cook."

"I can't," he said with a self-deprecating grin. "Wait'll you taste it."

With a smile, Athaya sat down at the table while Jaren set out the two bowls, laid a thick slice of black bread in each, and dished out the hot broth over it. Jaren picked up a fat, white candle from the mantel and set it in the middle of the table, centering it inside the jeweled circlet that Athaya had abandoned there.

"There," Jaren said proudly. "I'll bet we're the only ones in the city with such a costly centerpiece to our table."

Athaya laughed softly and took a tentative taste of the broth. "It's not bad at all," she said. "But I'm so hungry that even boiled leather would taste good right now."

Jaren arched an eyebrow. "I'll try not to take that personally."

Athaya ate the simple meal ravenously, recalling that she'd had nothing to eat since early that day, before she had even reached Delfarham. *Had that only been this morning?* she thought. Only one day, and her entire life had been turned upside down. This morning she was Princess Athaya, bringing news of a Reykan alliance to her father. But now, even though she could still claim her royal title, she was little more than an outlaw, with her brother and his guardsmen combing the city for her.

She was suddenly aware of the silence in the room and of the way that Jaren stirred his soup without eating it. He stared absently at the circlet in the center of the table, watching the candlelight sparkle on the rubies and sapphires embedded in gold. Their eyes met briefly, and they both looked away self-consciously. Clearly they each had something to say, but were both hoping the other would go first.

"I don't know how I can thank you," she said finally, when Jaren showed no signs of speaking. "You're risking a lot to look after me, and I appreciate it."

Jaren nodded slowly. He looked somewhat disappointed, as if he'd been hoping she would say something else. "Master Hedric told me to keep an eye on you. That's what I'm doing."

"It isn't just that, though, is it?" she asked, leaning closer to him. "There's more to your involvement in this than just making sure I live long enough to become this . . . this 'leader' that Hedric wants me to be, isn't there?"

Jaren collected the dishes and began scraping the remains back into the pot. "What do you mean?" he said, turning his back to her.

"I think you know."

His hands stopped their motion, and Athaya saw that they were shaking.

"Jaren, look at me." Her voice was soft, but gently commanding.

He turned to her reluctantly, and when he did, she saw complete vulnerability in his eyes, as if she'd looked into his very soul. She saw pain in his eyes—a pain she understood all too well. It was the pain of knowing that everything he wanted was out of his reach, whether it was the desire to work great magic—much greater magic than his skills would allow—or the desire to have her love him in return, and knowing that she could not, because she suffered her own pain in loving Tyler, all too aware that he was out of her reach. Or she was out of his . . .

"It's nothing to be ashamed of," she said, trying to keep her voice from breaking. "I know—"

"What's that?" he said sharply, cutting her off.

A sudden wave of nausea rippled through her. In the distance, she heard the sharp clatter of hoofbeats echoing on the cobbled street.

Jaren hurried to the door and pressed his ear to it. The hoofbeats stopped dangerously nearby, and in seconds, Athaya heard the sticky sound of booted feet stamping in the mud outside the door.

"Quick, get in the other room," Jaren whispered urgently. He pulled her up out of her chair and pushed her toward the bedroom. "The window next to the bed leads out into the street. If there's trouble, I want you to get the hell out of here. Don't worry about me."

Athaya shook her head, confused. "But won't the wards keep them out?"

"Wards keep magic out, Athaya, not people. We only set them a few hours ago—they should be strong enough to send a subtle message to whoever is out there that no one is here. Still, we'd better not take chances." He unhooked the dagger from his belt and handed it to her. "Take this, just in case."

"But what if you need—"

"Don't worry," he said intently. "I'm no master wizard, but I've got a few other weapons at my disposal."

"But I—"

"No arguments. *Go!*"

He all but shoved her into the next room, and she heard the soft clink of an iron key as he turned the lock.

Jaren couldn't have gone more than three steps from the bedroom door when Athaya heard the crash of the outside door being kicked open. She heard a pair of heavy footsteps slowly crossing the floor with grim determination. And then came the cold sound of a steel blade being drawn from a scabbard.

Every muscle in her body tightened when she heard Tyler's voice, low and threatening. "All right, Jaren," he said. "Where is she?"

CHAPTER 16

✖✖

"**D**IDN'T YOU HEAR ME?" TYLER DEMANDED.
"Where's Athaya?"

The bedroom door was not snug in its frame, and Athaya could see a fraction of the outer room through the crack. Tyler threw off his sodden cloak and tossed it aside, revealing the burgundy-and-gold uniform underneath. He looked powerful and intimidating next to Jaren, who was plainly clad in drab brown riding leathers and was noticeably shorter and less muscular.

Jaren's voice was surprisingly calm. "What do you want with her?"

"That's none of your damned business," Tyler said, backing Jaren roughly against the wall with the point of his sword. "And don't even bother telling me she isn't here. Unless that's *your* piece of jewelry in the middle of the table."

Jaren glanced at Athaya's circlet, gently twinkling in the firelight. But his eyes quickly turned back to the blade that hovered mere inches from his throat.

"You're behind all of this, aren't you?" Tyler said. "Every damned bit of it. You knew about Athaya all along, but you didn't tell anyone. What did you plan to do? Use her magic to get rid of Kelwyn and spare yourself the blame? Is that what you Reykans are up to?"

"I'm only trying to keep her from being put to death by your misguided priests!" Jaren burst out, trying without much success to keep Tyler's accusations from riling his usually calm temper. "Athaya has incredible potential, but she needs to be protected until she learns how to control it."

Tyler grimaced as if with a mouthful of sour wine. "Is that what you were doing that night at the inn? The night I found you in her room? It certainly didn't look as if you were protecting her *then*."

"Captain, I can explain everything if you'll stop ranting and raving like a jealous husband and just listen to me."

Crimson with rage, Tyler raised his blade to strike. "Why, I ought to—"

In one fluid motion, Jaren lifted up his hand and whispered a word under his breath. Athaya instantly detected a circular patch of shimmering air hovering around his hand like a shield. Tyler's sword struck it, and in the midst of a shower of blue sparks, the blade glanced off to one side. Blinking his eyes in disbelief, Tyler stumbled back from the magic shield.

"Now, Captain," Jaren said with a glint of determination in his eye, "can we discuss this more rationally?"

Biting on his lower lip, Tyler rapidly assessed his opponent, circling him like a wolf. Athaya could tell from the look in his eye that he was trying to think of a way to defend himself against a weapon he had no knowledge of, but it was obvious that he could think of nothing. Then Tyler noticed the door leading to the next room, and with a flash of victory, he turned on his heel and stalked toward it, his sword still drawn. Athaya's heart beat wildly as she watched him approach and she held Jaren's dagger tightly in her hand, fervently hoping that she would never be forced to use it.

Jaren gestured again, and the moment Tyler reached out for the doorknob, his hand struck another translucent shield. He yelped in pain as blue sparks laced around his wrist, winding their way up his arm until they finally disappeared. Tyler turned and gave Jaren a withering glare.

"I repeat my question, Captain," Jaren said simply.

Tyler ignored him. "Athaya, it's me!" he called out, careful not to get too close to the shielded door. "What is he doing to you? Are you all right?"

"She won't answer you," Jaren said, shaking his head. "Assuming she's still there, of course."

It was all Athaya could do not to respond to Tyler's pleas. She could hear the desperation in his voice, but she dared not say a word, still unsure whether he was here to help her, or if he'd come to bring her back to Delfar in chains. He had been a member of the King's Guard for years and knew that duty must be done, no matter how unpleasant. Athaya knew what she wanted to believe, but she was in much too dangerous a predicament to let her heart start ruling her better judgment, no matter how much it hurt inside.

"Athaya, are you there?" Tyler said. His voice was weaker and edged with pain.

Hearing nothing but silence, his expression changed, as if he realized at that moment that he had failed. He looked from the door, to Jaren, and back again, his face lined with defeat. Then his shoulders sagged, and he gazed at his gleaming sword with regret, knowing the fine weapon was all but useless against Jaren's magic.

"All I want to do is find her before the others do," he said, almost pleading. "I'm not going to let them throw her into prison! I'm not going to let them kill her!"

"How can I be sure of that?" Jaren countered. "How can she? You're the captain of Durek's guard. Yes, I know that Kelwyn is dead," he added, seeing Tyler's look of surprise. "And so does Athaya. And she also knows that you were given orders to have her arrested and that you'd be risking your commission, not to mention your life, if you disobeyed them."

"I just want to help . . ."

"In spite of what she's done?" Jaren said with deliberate harshness. "In spite of the fact that she's responsible for the death of the king? The man you've sworn to protect?"

Tyler wheeled around furiously. "It's got to be a mistake! Athaya would never have deliberately attacked him. She told Durek that Kelwyn threatened her first. But we never saw it, and Durek didn't believe her."

"And you do?"

Tyler looked him squarely in the eye. "I have to believe it, Jaren," he said quietly. "I just have to."

Jaren nodded slowly, weighing the captain's words. It was deathly silent for several minutes. The only sounds in the room were the soft crackling of the fire and of Jaren's soft boots brushing against the rushes on the floor as he paced in a wide circle.

"You have two choices, Captain," he said at last. "You can share your thoughts with me, so I can tell whether you're being honest or not, or I can hold you here as long as it takes for me to get Athaya to safety." Jaren took a step toward him. "Which is it?"

Tyler eyed him skeptically, hesitant to involve himself with magic. "Share my thoughts? What are you talking about?"

"Let me into your mind willingly, so I can test your sincerity. I could force you to open up against your will if I had to, but that would be unpleasant for both of us—especially for you."

Tyler scowled. That idea clearly did not appeal to him. "I should know better than to trust you, but I don't have much of a choice, do I?"

Jaren shook his head. "No, Captain, you don't."

"Just what is it you're going to do?"

"You won't feel a thing, except maybe a slight tickling sensation. That's all. It's not difficult. From what I hear, Kelwyn used to do it all the time, to find out if his nobles were lying to him when they swore their oaths of fealty. All I'm going to do is read your thoughts and make sure your intentions toward Athaya are really what you say they are. Just one thing before we start," Jaren added, motioning to Tyler's sword. "Do you mind putting that thing away? It's rather distracting."

Reluctantly, the captain slid the blade back into its leather scabbard. He took off his sword belt and laid it across the table beside Athaya's circlet.

"Now sit over here, Captain, and just try to relax."

Tyler lowered himself into a pockmarked old chair by the table, and Jaren stood behind him, whispering for him to breathe deeply and let the tension out of his muscles. Tyler flinched when Jaren first laid one palm across his forehead, but after a moment he closed his eyes and tried to relax so the wizard could do his work.

Athaya bit her lip nervously, listening to the rhythmic breathing of the two men as Jaren searched Tyler's mind for the truth. She could not help but remember what Jaren had said to her the night she had conjured the storm. *If he won't accept you for what you are, then is he worth it? Does he deserve what you feel for him?*

Please, Tyler, she thought, closing her eyes as if to pray. *You're all I have left now . . .*

A few minutes later, Jaren drew back and let his hand fall limply to his side. He let out a small sigh, speaking both relief and disappointment. "I believe you, Captain."

Jaren gestured toward the door with his finger, and Athaya suddenly heard the lock trip open.

"You can come out now, Athaya. It's safe."

Setting Jaren's dagger aside, Athaya rushed from the room and let Tyler sweep her into his arms. He held her tightly, as if afraid the moment he let go, she would slip away from him again.

"Thank God you're safe," he said, digging his fingers into her hair. "I can't tell you what I've been through tonight . . . wondering if you were all right . . ."

Athaya blinked back a tear. "How did you know where to find me?"

"I didn't know for certain. But when you told me this morning that Jaren wasn't going to stay at the castle, I remembered you saying that there were usually rooms to be let behind the dye shop near Oren's tavern. I just prayed that they hadn't been rented to anyone else, or I wouldn't have had any idea where to look for you." He cupped her cheek in his palm. "And don't worry about the other men. I arranged to search this part of town myself, so no one else should be bothering you."

Athaya smiled gratefully and brushed his cheek with a kiss. Then she caught sight of Jaren pacing back and forth across the front doorway, rubbing his chin distractedly. Every so often he reached out to touch the walls on either side of the door, wiping away the oily residue on his sleeves.

"What are you looking for?"

Jaren shook his head in puzzlement. "I just don't understand how he got through two sets of wards. They're still at full strength."

"Sets of what?" Tyler asked.

"Spells to keep people away," Athaya told him. "I'll tell you all about it later."

"Now that you mention it, I did feel something strange earlier. When I was outside the door, I could have sworn that no one was in here. I was convinced of it. I almost rode on and searched somewhere else, but I knew I couldn't leave without making sure and confirming it with my own eyes. I never would have forgiven myself if I hadn't checked, and you'd been here after all.''

Jaren cleared his throat noisily. ''Well, I'm sure you two have things to talk about. Why don't I just disappear for a while?'' He slipped into the bedroom and emerged with his cloak draped over one arm. Athaya saw the slender blade of his dagger peeking out from the folds of the woolen cloak.

''Where are you going?'' Athaya said. ''You can't leave—they'll find you!''

''Who? Rhodri? You're forgetting, Athaya, that he doesn't even know I exist. And as for any of Tyler's guardsmen, they're looking for you, not me.''

''But the ones that went to Reyka with us will recognize you,'' Athaya cautioned him.

''I might have already taken care of that,'' Tyler said to Jaren. ''I knew there was nowhere Athaya could go except to you, and even though I didn't think you could be trusted, I didn't want anyone else finding her before I did. And since I knew my men didn't trust you either, I took advantage of it. I don't know if it worked or not, but I told all the men in my squadron that you were a Reykan envoy come to see Kelwyn, and since you were a wizard, you would have been spying on us with your magic.''

''How flattering,'' Jaren said dryly.

''No offense—but I think it worked. I told them that you would have slipped out of the city the minute you knew what had happened, fearing you'd be blamed. They don't expect to find you here, or within twenty miles of here, for that matter.''

Jaren shrugged. ''Even if I do run into them, I can cast a simple cloaking spell. And if they have mirrors with them, I'll just make sure I see them first and get out of their way. Don't worry—I've got a little experience at avoiding people who are after me.'' Jaren laughed softly to himself. ''Ask Felgin about Braiden Hall sometime.''

''About where?'' Athaya said.

''Oh, it's just a quaint little story about how the two of us made a very hasty departure from an estate in northern Reyka after Felgin got caught seducing an earl's daughter. It was quite a while ago—back in the prince's more impetuous days.''

''And what were you doing there with him?'' Tyler asked, arching a brow.

"That's none of your business," Jaren replied with a grin. "But did I mention that the earl had *two* daughters?" With a flourish, he flung his cloak over his shoulders and clasped it around his neck with a silver brooch. He tied his purse to his belt and made sure that his dagger was secure in its sheath.

Tyler followed Jaren to the door. "Thanks for taking care of her," he said, extending his hand. "I'm sorry I didn't trust you before, but—"

"No apologies necessary, Captain. After all, I didn't trust you either." Jaren shook his hand, then glanced over his shoulder at Athaya, his gaze softening. "At least now we know we're both on the same side."

Jaren leaned close and whispered a few words to Tyler that Athaya could not hear. Tyler nodded, seemingly pleased, and gave him a friendly pat on the shoulder.

Then Jaren rattled the latch on the door. "You can lock up the place if you want. I won't need a key." He bade them good night and slipped away into the dark alley.

Tyler latched the door and turned to face Athaya, his brows forming a good-natured frown. "Now that he's gone, would you kindly explain to me what you're doing wearing his clothes?"

"There's nothing for you to look so suspicious about," she scolded lightly. "My dress was soaked through, and I needed something to wear."

"Mmm, that's an old tale," he said, looking down at her through his lashes. Then he smiled and held out his arms. "Come here, you little wench."

He wrapped his arm around her and led her to the fire, and they sat down together to warm themselves in front of the flames.

"So that's what all this secrecy was about," he said, folding her hands inside his. "All those things you didn't want to tell me."

"I just couldn't tell you, Tyler. I didn't know how you'd take it. I didn't want to scare you away."

"The only thing you could do to scare me is tell me that you don't love me anymore." He stroked her hair, absently twisting it around his fingers. "I don't care what the priests say about magic being evil. If you have it, it can't possibly be. Which reminds me . . ."

Tyler reached inside his doublet and drew out a piece of parchment, folded over and sealed with wax. With a look of disgust, he hastily flung the paper into the fire.

"I can't believe Durek did such a thing," Athaya whispered, as the warrant for her arrest curled inward and turned black.

"You're not the only one who feels that way. Cecile won't even speak to him, and Nicolas . . . my God, I've never heard Nicolas so angry in my life. He had a vicious fight with Durek right before I left. Durek all but threatened to have him locked up if he didn't shut up and leave him alone."

Athaya looked up with apprehension. "Nicolas . . . does he understand?"

"Oh, don't worry about him. He was as stunned as I was when he heard what happened, but we talked about it and sorted everything out. And do you know what he said to me? He said, 'I'm glad my sister's a wizard. Maybe she could learn a spell that would turn Durek into a human being.' "

"That sounds like Nicky," she said, laughing while a tear of relief slid down her cheek. "What else is going on that I should know about?"

"Probably just what you expected. Durek's convinced that you murdered Kelwyn in cold blood, and Dagara—as usual—is in full agreement with him. And as for Archbishop Ventan, he's going around making pious speeches against the Lorngeld and demanding that you give yourself up for absolution."

"That doesn't surprise me," she said sourly. "What about Rhodri?"

Tyler frowned. "I'm not sure. He's keeping a very low profile. What's the matter? Do you think he might try to come after you?"

"It's likely. He won't like knowing that he isn't the only wizard in Caithe anymore." *And he definitely won't like knowing that his twenty-year experiment on my father has just been brought to an abrupt conclusion.* Athaya shook her head worriedly. "Jaren was right. I'm going to have to get back to Reyka as soon as possible."

"Back to Reyka? Why?"

"It will be safer for me there until I finish learning everything. Jaren's taught me a few spells, but he says I need Hedric to help me with the harder things."

"Was that what Hedric wanted to see you about? Did he know you were a Lorngeld the whole time?"

Athaya nodded. "He knew before we ever got there. Apparently he thinks I've got a lot of potential, and since I'm a member of the royal house—a member in dubious standing at the moment," she pointed out dryly, "he wants me to start a crusade to abolish the rite of absolution. He thinks I'm going to be some sort of savior or something."

"That's quite an assignment."

"It *was* quite an assignment," she said firmly. "I'm afraid Hedric will have to find someone else now. I might have been able to do something for the Lorngeld while my father was alive, but with Durek on the throne, I can't possibly do what Hedric is asking of me. I'm all but an outlaw in Caithe. Durek won't be able to keep news of this from getting out, and once that happens, I'm certainly not going to get anyone to believe that I want to help the Lorngeld."

"Don't underestimate yourself, Athaya. The word of a Trelane carries weight. No one can ever take your name away from you."

Athaya took a deep, unsteady breath as she fought off her tears. "But why should they believe anything I say? I've just killed the only king in two hundred years that showed any interest in the Lorngeld at all. All I've done is give the Church more fuel for their fire. 'Look at what the evil magician has done!' they'll say, and everyone will think I'm just the same as Faltil, wanting no one else to have power but myself."

"Stop saying that you killed him, Athaya. Jaren already told me that you weren't in control of your magic. Kelwyn's death was an accident. A horrible accident." Tyler paused before he went on, and his expression changed to one of calm resolve. "But if those are the kinds of things that are going to keep happening if you don't practice your magic, then there's no question of what you have to do. I don't care what the Church says. You have to go on and finish your training. To hell with absolution. I want you to live, Athaya. I want you to live, and be what you were born to be."

Athaya couldn't speak for several minutes. She was too overcome with inexpressible emotion—with the feeling that the impossible had suddenly come to pass. A few hours ago, she expected never to be happy again, but now Tyler was here with her—and more than that, he accepted her for what she was and loved her just the same.

"It's so hard to believe—even now," she said finally. "There's still part of me that can't quite believe the things I can do. But back in Reyka, when I first heard—my God, I couldn't even deal with it myself, much less try and explain it to you." Athaya leaned against him and rested her head on his shoulder. "That's why I never talked to you about it. But it was so hard not to tell you. Especially when I saw that look on your face the night you found Jaren in my room. The look in your eyes . . . it was horrible. But there was nothing going on between Jaren and me," she added quickly. "That storm—I conjured it by accident in my sleep, and he came in to try and stop me."

Tyler was quiet for a moment, wrapped in thought. "He's in love with you, you know."

Athaya looked up, but she wasn't surprised. She had already realized that Jaren's feelings for her were growing beyond friendship, but what did surprise her was that Tyler had obviously known long before she did.

"How can you tell?"

"Simple. He looks at you the same way I did, back when I was deciding whether it would be a good idea to fall in love with you or not." Tyler smiled wanly. "Logically, of course, I knew it wasn't a good idea at all, but I couldn't help doing it anyway."

"And aren't you glad you did?" she teased, stroking his cheek. Then, more seriously, she added, "Jaren's been so kind to me . . . so patient. And I care for him as a friend. But I'm not in love with him."

"I know. And so does he," Tyler added. "He's not trying to come between us. That's what he told me right before he left."

Athaya ran her fingers down the smooth wool of his doublet, toying with the thin leather laces. "I wish I'd never hidden any of this from you. Can you forgive me?"

Tyler leaned over and touched her cheek with a kiss. "Just promise me that there won't be any more secrets between us. I love you, Athaya. There's nothing you could possibly tell me that would change that."

Athaya returned his kiss, but then pulled away distractedly. She'd just thought of yet another complication. "But what will we do now? I have to leave . . ." Her voice trailed off. After all this, how could she possibly leave him behind now?

Tyler shrugged casually. "Well, while you're off having magic lessons, I suppose I can ask Felgin for a post in Osfonin's guard."

Her eyes lit up with unexpected joy. "You'll come with me?"

"Did you think I wouldn't?"

"But Durek . . . your commission . . ."

"I swore loyalty to Kelwyn, not Durek," he said firmly. "I don't mean any offense to your brother, but I know I couldn't serve him with the same sincerity as I did his father. Frankly, I can't serve a man I don't like. No, there's nothing for me here now. I want to be where you are."

Athaya held him close to her, bubbling over with happiness. At this moment, only hours after her panicked flight from Delfar Castle, everything had suddenly made itself right again. She leaned against him, basking in his warmth, and wished that she could spend the rest of her life right here beside him.

Tyler reached inside the collar of her shirt, twirling her hair between his fingers and stroking the soft flesh of her neck. When his fingers brushed against the silver chain she wore around her throat, he lifted it up, and examined the costly locket.

"What's this?"

"Felgin gave it to me. Look inside."

Tyler snapped open the locket, and his eyes widened as he saw the image—his own image—appear before his eyes. "It's so real," he said in awe. "I feel as if I'm looking right into a mirror."

"Remember that first day in Ath Luaine when I didn't want to tell you what Felgin and I talked about? Well, we talked about you. I didn't mention your name at the time, but I told him I was in love with someone else. He realized it was you on the day you went hunting with him. That locket was his way of saying that he understood how I felt about you, even if I had to marry him eventually."

Suddenly Athaya gasped aloud and she clapped a hand to her cheek. "Tyler—my God, do you know what this means? Oh, why didn't I see this before!"

He snapped the locket closed, and the image vanished. "See what?"

"I don't have to marry Felgin," she said, trembling with enthusiasm. "I don't have to do anything anymore! Don't you see? I'm free, Tyler." She shook her head, staggered by the realization. "Osfonin may like me personally, but he certainly isn't going to want me to marry his son now. And once word of this gets out, Durek wouldn't be able to marry me off to a Sarian mercenary if he wanted to. Tyler, don't you understand? It isn't just a dream anymore. We can get married the minute we get to Reyka. There's nothing to stop us now!''

Tyler stared back at her, uncomprehending. Then, like a slow sunrise, his expression of disbelief changed gradually to acceptance and finally to unabashed ecstasy. He let out a high-pitched whooping sound as he scrambled to his feet. Lifting her up off the floor, he swung her around so hard that she felt as if she were flying. Without music, they danced a few steps together, laughing with merriment.

"I just know Osfonin will give you a commission in his guard," Athaya said, rattling on without restraint. "Felgin already said how talented he thought you were. And we can buy a little house in Ath Luaine and have a family . . ."

"Assuming, of course, that I agree to marry a girl without a dowry," he said with mock solemnity, stopping their silent dance.

"Oh, stop it," she said, poking him playfully. "I've got the only dowry you could want. I'm in love with you."

Tyler gave her a firm hug and smiled. "Then how could I ask for anything else?"

In the distance, Athaya heard the bells at Saint Adriel's toll three o'clock. The real world had intruded upon them, and the spell that had enchanted them was suddenly broken. Reluctantly, Tyler released her.

"It's late—I'd better get back."

Moving with haste, as if afraid he would change his mind, he picked up his cloak from the floor, still damp from the rain, and began smoothing out the wrinkles. Watching him, Athaya knew that she could not let him go. Not yet. She reached out and took the cloak from him, and laid it across the edge of the table. Wrapping her arms around his neck, she pulled him close to her and kissed him deeply.

"Don't go," she whispered, her voice thick with desire. "Stay with me."

He drew in his breath slowly, as if he didn't quite believe what he had heard. "Athaya, are you sure?"

"There's no reason not to. Not anymore."

Tentatively, he slid his arm around her waist, still not ready to accept what was happening. "But wait—what about Jaren? He might be back—"

"Why do you think he left?" she said with a beguiling smile. She picked up the white candle from the table and without a word led him into the shabby bedroom.

"I suppose I can tell Durek that I was out looking for you all night," he said, his breath quickening as he closed the door behind them and slid the bolt to one side. "I'll just forget to mention that I found you."

CHAPTER 17

✷✳✷

A THAYA AWOKE LONG BEFORE TYLER DID, BUT SHE MADE
no move to disturb him. She lay silently beside him,
watching the soft rise and fall of his chest, and taking
in the scent of leather on his skin. His limbs were riddled with
faint scars from long-ago battles, and she traced the jagged,
whitened lines with her fingertips, quietly angry at whoever had
dared deal him those blows.

I can't believe you're really here, she thought. Even though
she could touch him, and feel his solid presence next to her, she
wondered if it was all a dream—a fantasy of her own mind. *It
is you, isn't it, Tyler? Not just a magic image, like the one in my
locket?*

She saw his eyelids flutter and open, and a smile broke across
his face. "Good morning," he whispered, his voice cracking
from hours of disuse.

She greeted him with a kiss, long and deep.

"I'd ring for the servants to bring us breakfast, but . . ."
Athaya scanned the spartanly furnished room and shrugged.
Then she turned back to him, gazing at the flecks of gold in his
eyes. "I'm so happy, Tyler. I've always dreamed of this—of what
it would be like to wake up next to you. But I never dared to
hope that it would really happen." She ran her fingers across
his chest, and down, underneath the blankets.

"We'd better not start," he said, reluctantly guiding her hand away. "This time I really *do* have to go. I've got to get back before Durek realizes I've been gone all night and starts asking questions." He turned the blankets back and picked up his shirt from the floor. "But don't look so sad, my love," he added. "We'll have the rest of our lives to wake up together. And then— I promise you—I'll be much more willing."

She watched him dress, lazily admiring him, watching the arms that had warmed her through the night slip inside the silky white shirt and tie up the laces of the burgundy doublet. She watched his lean, muscular legs slide into the woolen hose, then into snug-fitting breeches.

When he was ready to go, Athaya slipped into Jaren's shirt and followed Tyler to the outer room.

"Well, look who's here," he said softly, motioning across the room with amusement. Jaren was curled up in a snug little ball on the floor in front of the fireplace, his cloak draped over him like a blanket. His boots were folded up under his head as a makeshift pillow.

"He can't be very comfortable," Athaya remarked.

"He's not," came the muffled voice from under the cloak. Jaren rolled onto his back, wincing at the stiffness in his muscles. "But his bed was otherwise occupied."

Tyler chuckled to himself. "I think that's my cue to leave. Take care, Athaya," he said, giving her a quick kiss. "I'll try and come by tonight and let you know what's happening. And I'll bring you some decent clothes while I'm at it."

He unlatched the door and went out into the alley, letting in a cold October breeze. Athaya waved good-bye, then quickly closed the door and began laying a fire. Jaren didn't move from his place near the hearth, but watched her go about her task in silence. His shirt and breeches were rumpled, his hair tangled and unruly, and he looked sorely in need of rest.

"Did you get any sleep at all last night?" Athaya asked, setting a pair of logs on the iron grate.

"Not much," he said, stretching his legs. He gave her a sidelong glance. "But more than you did, I expect."

She looked away and felt her cheeks grow warm. "Where were you?"

"At Oren's tavern. In one of the upstairs rooms."

"Upstairs?" Athaya said with surprise. She'd come all too

close to spending a night there herself not long ago, and remembered vividly what those rooms were like—squalid, cramped, and used by the city's whores. Surely *that* was not how he'd spent his evening . . .

"One of the girls offered her services, but I don't think she believed me when I said I wasn't interested. I ended up paying her something just to leave me alone and let me get some rest. But she must have been hoping I'd change my mind, because she undressed herself and fell asleep on the floor next to the bed."

Athaya shook her head with derision. "Why did you go to a place like that?"

"I didn't think your brother would send his men out looking for you in a run-down whorehouse," he said, propping himself up on his elbow. "But I'm afraid I overestimated his regard for you. A couple of soldiers showed up about an hour after I got there. Not to worry, though. I didn't recognize any of them, and the minute that they saw that the girl in my room wasn't you, they left."

Jaren sat up, rubbing his stiff back. "That reminds me. I brought you this," he said, motioning toward the plain kirtle of homespun wool hanging over the back of the chair. "It's not much to look at, but at least it's reasonably clean. It'll do until Tyler brings you something else."

"Where did you get it?" she asked. She held the dress up to her shoulders, checking it for length.

"Don't worry about that. Just see if it'll fit."

"But where did you get it?" she asked again, noting how he avoided her gaze.

He grinned sheepishly as he got to his feet. "I took it from the girl at the tavern. She was still asleep when I left."

"Oh, Jaren, how could you?" she said, laughing aloud in spite of herself. "That poor girl won't have stitch to put on when she wakes up!"

"One of the hazards in her line of work, I suppose," he said dryly. "And besides, it was for a good cause. The Princess of Caithe can't go around for the rest of her life dressed in one of my old shirts."

Athaya went into the other room and slipped on the rust-colored kirtle. The sleeves hung loosely on her and the skirt was a fingerlength too long, but overall, the fit was good enough. The cloth was coarse and scratchy, but at least it was warm.

"I've seen you look better," Jaren said when she emerged from the bedroom. "Hmm, maybe this will help." He picked up her jeweled circlet from the table and set it delicately on her head. "Perfect. You're the picture of incongruity."

Athaya cocked her head to one side and smiled. "I always have been."

She placed the soup kettle over the fire to warm up the remains of last night's meal while Jaren went into the next room to run a comb through his hair and splash cold water on his face. He was gone for several minutes and when he returned, he looked strangely altered. He sank down into one of the scarred chairs with a remote look in his eyes, as if his thoughts were far away.

"I assume Tyler's coming back to Reyka with us," he said, trying to assume an air of casualness.

Athaya stopped stirring the lukewarm broth and turned to him. "Yes, he is." She paused, watching Jaren pick absently at a piece of slivered wood. His tone had not deceived her.

"I'm going to marry him once we get there," she added.

Jaren didn't look up, but only nodded slowly as he traced a pattern on the tabletop with his finger. "Then I suppose congratulations are in order."

Athaya hung the spoon on its peg by the fire and sat down next to him. "Jaren, I—"

"You don't have to explain anything," he said quickly. "Please—just don't say another word about it."

He stood up abruptly and swept his cloak up from the floor and fastened it around his neck. "The shops probably opened hours ago. I'll go out and get us something to eat." Before Athaya could voice a word of protest, he slipped out the door and was gone.

Jaren returned an hour later with a handful of parcels wrapped in string—two loaves of black bread, a large round of goat's cheese, and a flagon of sweet-smelling wine. But their talk was sparse and stilted as they sat down to eat their meager meal, neither of them making any mention of their unfinished conversation that morning, but both uncomfortably aware of what wasn't being said.

* * *

Tyler returned that night, shortly after dark. The moment he arrived, Athaya knew that something was wrong. He was tense and distracted, and his eyes were surrounded by tired lines. He deposited a leather satchel on the floor and gladly accepted the goblet of wine that Athaya offered to him.

"What happened?" she asked. "No offense, but you look terrible."

"It hasn't been a good day," he said, gulping down his wine. "Durek's starting to get suspicious. He called me into the audience chamber today and asked me if I knew where you were. He figured that since I went to Reyka with you, I might know why you came back knowing how to work magic and where you might be hiding. And he also got wind of the fact that we brought a wizard back with us," Tyler added, shifting his gaze to Jaren. "I'm not sure which one of my men told him, but he's convinced that you're responsible for Athaya's sudden . . . abilities."

"What did you tell him?" Athaya asked worriedly.

"Nothing he wanted to hear, I'm afraid. I said that as far as I knew, Jaren was just a courier, and his being a wizard was just a coincidence you have to expect when dealing with Reykans. I'm not sure if he believed me, though. He made me swear an oath saying I didn't know where you'd gone."

Athaya stopped breathing for an instant. "Tyler, do you realize what you've done? Making a false oath to the king is treason."

"I know," he replied solemnly. "But so was failing to turn you over to him the minute I found you. It doesn't matter what I do now. I'll be in as much trouble as you are if anyone finds you here."

"Then I suggest we get out of this city as soon as possible," Jaren said. "Captain, how much longer will it take for the king to call off the search parties?"

Tyler rubbed his chin thoughtfully. "Kelwyn's funeral is in five days. I'd guess that Durek will busy himself with the search until then, but afterwards he'll be too occupied with the arrangements for his coronation to give it his full attention. And most of his guardsmen will be called back from their search parties to attend both functions."

"Good. The sooner we get out of Caithe, the better," Jaren said. "With all the people that will be flocking into the city to attend the funeral and the coronation, no one should notice us slipping out. In fact, it would be safest if we left during the funeral itself, while everyone's crowded inside the cathedral.''

Tyler nodded in agreement. ''I can talk to Nicolas and arrange for horses and provisions. And maybe he can pilfer us a small sum out of the royal treasury to get us as far as Reyka.''

Tyler and Jaren went on for several minutes making plans for their departure, but Athaya paid little attention to them. She got up and walked aimlessly around the room, sipping out of her wine goblet. The men's voices were little more than a low buzz as she tried to sort out the conflicting thoughts assailing her. She knew she had to leave Caithe—perhaps forever—but she could not escape the feeling that there was something still left undone. Something she had to do before she could depart with a clear conscience.

Then, in an instant, it slid into place, and she realized what it was she had to do. And she also knew that Tyler and Jaren were definitely going to object.

''How does that sound to you?'' Tyler asked, breaking her out of her reverie.

She turned to him distractedly. ''What?''

''Taking the sea route to Reyka. I know winter's coming, but there shouldn't be any problems with ice until at least November. Granted we can't set sail from here—Delfar Castle has a view of the entire bay and someone would be bound to notice our departure. But we can ride to Feckham and hire a ship from there.''

Athaya nodded absently.

''There's just one problem,'' Tyler said. ''I know Durek will want me on duty during the funeral. I'm not sure how I'll beg off so I can meet the two of you.''

''That won't be a problem,'' Athaya said firmly, reclaiming her seat at the table. ''In fact, I'd much prefer that you were there.''

Tyler shook his head. ''I don't understand.''

Athaya drained the wine from her goblet in a single gulp.

''I'm going to my father's funeral,'' she announced, setting the cup down heavily on the table. ''We'll leave for Reyka as soon as it's over.''

Jaren stood up so quickly that his chair toppled over on its side. ''You're *what*?'' he exclaimed in horror. ''But the cathedral will be mobbed with people. You'd be crazy to set foot in that place!''

"I'm a wizard," she said acidly. "I'm *supposed* to be crazy."

Jaren rolled his eyes in disbelief, but before he could voice a retort, Tyler cut him off. "Athaya, what are you talking about? You can't possibly—"

"Don't even bother trying to talk me out of it, because you'll be wasting your time." She paused long enough to get control of her thoughts, then continued more calmly. "I have to go, Tyler. I'm not going to change my mind. It's the least I can do for my father after what I've done. I have to tell him I'm sorry." She dug her fingernails into her palms to keep away the tears. "I have to say good-bye."

Tyler bowed his head, dropping his shoulders down.

"I know your father's death has been hard on you, Athaya. But there's nothing you can hope to accomplish by being at his funeral. I'm sure he'd never want you to endanger yourself that way. Your presence there won't make a difference."

"It will make a difference to me, Tyler," she said softly. "And besides, I can't leave without seeing Nicolas and Cecile one more time, even if they won't know I'm there. I have no idea when—or if—I'll ever be able to come back."

Jaren slammed his fist down on the table, suddenly more furious with her than he had ever been before. "How can you be so reckless!" he shouted. "This has got to be the most foolhardy thing you've ever done in your life!"

Athaya drew her shoulders back defensively. "Look—what are you so worried about? Tyler will be at the ceremony keeping an eye on everything. You and I can slip inside the cathedral under a cloaking spell, stay for a few minutes, and slip out again. No one will ever know we were there."

"Except Rhodri," Jaren observed. "He might be able to see through the spell. You seem to be able to see through mine well enough."

"Then we won't go anywhere near Rhodri. Besides, he won't be expecting us, and you told me yourself that it's hard to detect a cloaking spell unless you're looking for one."

Jaren's look of apprehension did not lessen, but Athaya refused to let it weaken her resolve. "And if you're afraid that my magic is going to go out of control again, then we have all week to work at it, to make sure it's safe."

"But I can't train you in a week!" he sputtered. "You'll need weeks, maybe months to get complete control over your spells—"

Athaya got to her feet and set her hands defiantly on her hips.

"Then I guess now is when we find out just how good of a teacher you are, Jaren. Because I'm going to that funeral, and that's final."

"But—"

"Forget it, Jaren," Tyler said. The corner of his mouth turned up in a slightly amused expression. "I've seen her like this before. The only way you'll get her to leave Caithe without going to Kelwyn's funeral is to put her to sleep with one of your spells and carry her off."

"I'm seriously considering it," Jaren said shortly.

Tyler laughed softly, somewhat mollified. "Actually, this may not be as much of a problem as we thought. If these 'cloaking spells' of yours make you invisible, then all you really have to worry about is Rhodri detecting them. And I have the feeling that he won't even be there. Considering the way Kelwyn died," Tyler added delicately, "Durek is bound to tell him that it would be best not to have any wizards in the church. In fact, I'll be surprised if Rhodri stays in Delfarham at all. Durek's always hated him, and I'll wager your brother will waste no time trying to get him out of his court."

"Oh, great," Jaren muttered to himself. "He'll probably head straight for Reyka."

"And even if something goes wrong with your spell, I can make sure that some of the doorways are guarded by those I can trust to say nothing of your presence there. I've heard some grumbling among my men—not all of them approve of what Durek's done to you. Some of them flat-out hate him."

"You see, Jaren?" Athaya said, holding her palms up. "There's nothing to worry about."

"Well . . . it sounds safe enough," he said reluctantly. "I still don't like the idea, but I think I understand why you want to be there."

Athaya smiled gratefully. "Oh, Tyler—one more thing," she said. "Don't tell Nicolas about this. He's in enough trouble with Durek as it is. Just tell him I'll send word from Reyka." She looked away wistfully. "I wish he could come with us. He always wanted to be at our wedding."

Athaya saw Jaren lower his eyes, but Tyler did not notice.

"I'll talk to Nicolas and tell him what's happening," Tyler said. "I'll also tell him that I'm planning an indefinite leave of absence from the Guards. After I've been gone awhile, he can make up a story explaining why I won't be back and have Durek appoint someone else to my post."

Tyler got to his feet. "But for the next few days, I have to at least pretend that I'm loyally serving Caithe's new king." He fastened his cloak around his shoulders. "I think it's safer for all of us if I don't come back here again. Not the way Durek's been acting."

Athaya nodded in agreement but couldn't help feeling disappointed.

Before Tyler left, the three of them quickly drew up a plan for the day of the funeral and decided on a place she and Jaren would meet Tyler after the ceremony. After Tyler assured them that he would take care of supplying horses and provisions, he gave Athaya a quick kiss on the cheek and motioned to the satchel he had left by the door when he'd come in.

"I brought a few things for you to wear—some of Nicolas's old castoffs that no one will miss. There's also a little bit of money so you can buy some decent food."

"Then I'll see you in five days," Athaya said, opening the door for him.

Tyler smiled broadly. "And after that, my love, I promise I'll never leave you again."

The next few days passed quickly. Jaren spent every spare moment drilling Athaya in the simpler spells and teaching her new ones. Each morning they reset the wards around the rooms, just in case Rhodri might be seeking Athaya with his sphere, and then they began work. Athaya fell into bed exhausted every night—Jaren had insisted that he was comfortable enough sleeping near the hearth—and she was grateful to find that her nightmares had all but stopped now that her control over her power was more reliable.

After four days of intense tutoring, she was able to move through her paths more quickly. She no longer had to visualize the cavern walls to locate the simpler spells, but found that they came to her by instinct. She created vision spheres with a minimum of effort, her witchlights were strong and bright, she found out how to open a locked door without a key, and she learned how to spark a flame to light a candle spontaneously, just as she had seen her father do on the night he told her she was traveling to Reyka. And above all else, she practiced her cloaking spell so that it would work flawlessly on the day of the funeral. Jaren was impressed with her skill, and try as he might, he could not break or see through her magic cloak of invisibility. He made sure she could sustain the spell for several hours at a time without breaking her concentration. During their small evening suppers he might never have known that she sat across from him at the table were it not for her goblet and knife hovering in midair as she ate.

On the night before Kelwyn's funeral at Saint Adriel's Cathedral, Athaya and Jaren gathered their few belongings in a satchel in preparation to leave the next morning.

"You've learned a lot these last few days," Jaren said, regarding his student with pride as he tucked a wax-covered round of cheese and a parcel of dried meats into the bag so that they would have something for supper the next night. "I think you've mastered more spells in four days than I did in four weeks! But don't expect your magic to work reliably all the time. You'll probably have a few false starts. After all, you didn't learn to walk without falling down a few times. Well, maybe *you* did, being a princess and all," he added wryly, "but most people make a few blunders at first."

"I've always been very good at those," she remarked, trying to hold back a yawn. Seeing her, Jaren was unable to stifle one of his own.

"We'd better get some sleep," he told her. "After that funeral is over, I want to put as much distance between us and Delfarham as is humanly possible." Jaren tied his satchel closed and tossed it into the corner, sending up a puff of dust. "Can't say I'll be sorry to leave this place, either," he added, brushing a stubborn streak of soot from his hose.

"Oh, I don't know," Athaya replied, letting the dirt on her own clothes remain where it was. "I'm getting to like it here."

Jaren regarded her with amused disbelief. "I think you're more exhausted than you look."

While Jaren tossed another log on the fire, Athaya poured a small cup of wine before going to bed, feeling suddenly wistful as her eyes fell across the dusty floor, the soot-stained walls, and the greasy goatskin that was stretched across the window, shutting out the moonlight. To her surprise, she was somewhat saddened at the idea of leaving the shabby little room behind the dye shop. This was the place she had begun to understand her magic and the place where she and Tyler had been together for the first time. It was odd, but she had been happier here than she ever had inside the relative luxury of Delfar Castle. By this time tomorrow she would be miles away from here, but wherever she found herself in the future, Athaya knew that she would hold fond memories of this little set of rooms, aware that it was in this squalid place that she had finally made peace with herself, and where her life had been changed forever.

CHAPTER 18

✳✳

ATHAYA RUBBED HER EYES AS SHE PRESSED HERSELF against the wall of the small side chapel near the cathedral's high altar. She and Jaren had risen well before dawn to make their way to Saint Adriel's before the worst of the crowds appeared and they had spent the last six hours silently waiting for the service to begin. The seats in the nave and transept had been filled to overflowing shortly after the church's doors opened that morning, and in all the noise and confusion, no one had noticed when she and Jaren slipped under cloaking spells and crept past the guards into the restricted altar area.

She had been glad to see the familiar faces of Tyler's guardsmen at the transept doors where she had entered the cathedral and was even more relieved to see that none of the men carried mirrors with them in addition to their usual complement of weapons. Durek was obviously not expecting her to attend today's ceremony.

Although the everyday services at the cathedral were impressive enough considering the stunning beauty of the place, it was on high occasions such as this when the building seemed almost unearthly. Huge clusters of roses were placed in every alcove and draped over the choir screen and altar rails like a canopy. If Athaya closed her eyes, she could almost believe she was standing in a garden, and half expected a cool summer breeze to

239

ripple through her hair. The golden ornaments on the altar were
polished to perfection, and candles softly burned from iron candelabras set near each pillar of the nave and transepts, around
the choir, and all along the arcaded galleries above. But most
beautiful of all was the midday sun streaming through the
stained-glass windows, colored rays of light making dappled
pools on the smooth stone floor like a mosaic. Athaya shook her
head with wonder. The last time she remembered seeing this
place so beautiful was on the day of Durek's wedding to Cecile
almost three years ago.

As she listened to the slow, doleful music echoing from the
great organ, Athaya turned her eyes to her father's coffin resting
on a low, silk-covered table in front of the altar. The casket was
draped in jeweled cloths, which sparkled by the light of dozens
of white tapers set in the elegant candelabras surrounding it.
Later, after the ceremony was over, it would be taken to the
royal crypt beneath the church, and the body transferred to a
tomb of stone until such time as a fitting memorial was built for
it in a chapel adjoining the sanctuary.

As the cathedral chimes tolled twelve o'clock, Athaya saw the
funeral procession beginning to make its way up the aisle. A
long stream of choirboys led the way carrying long white candles, and behind them came a dozen priests in crisp white robes,
slowly intoning the words of a mournful plainsong chant. Next
came the higher-ranking clergy, mainly the bishops of the Curia
whom Kelwyn had summoned only a few weeks before. It was
now common knowledge that Durek had dismissed the Curia,
much to that body's general relief. The bishops who controlled
the doctrines of the Caithan Church were eager to drop the dis-
concerting proposals regarding the Lorngeld that Kelwyn had
introduced to them, and the new king had invited them to remain
in Delfarham for Kelwyn's funeral before returning to their sees.

Behind the black-robed bishops, trailed by two small boys
who carried the hem of his train, was Archbishop Ventan himself. He was sumptuously clad in gold-encrusted vestments and
seemed nearly a foot taller under the jeweled miter. In inelegant
contrast, his jowls hung over the tight collar of his cassock, and
his cheeks were bright red, as if flushed with anticipation of his
role in the ceremony to come. He walked slowly, leading his
steps with his silver staff, curved at the end to resemble a shepherd's crook.

A fine shepherd, Athaya thought bitterly. *One who leads his sheep to their deaths with a string of lies and a simple cup of poison.*

Behind the archbishop, she saw her family heading toward their places in the pews near the altar. The royal box faced across the archbishop's pulpit, exquisitely paneled in linenfold, on the opposite side of the aisle. Biting her lip, Athaya noticed the golden circlet atop Durek's head and realized, perhaps for the first time, that her oldest brother was truly the king now and would exchange that circlet for the royal crown in a matter of days. He looked even more sober than usual and seemed to have aged several years since Athaya had last seen him five days ago. Beside him, Cecile dabbed her eyes with a white lace handkerchief, and on his other side, Dagara leaned back in her seat, resplendent in a new black velvet gown, and toyed with the massive rope of pearls around her neck. Nicolas sat next to her, his face turned away, apparently in no mood to speak to anyone.

I'll miss you most, Nicky, Athaya thought sadly. She wondered when—or if—she would ever see him again.

Then she saw Tyler's comforting presence as he stood guard over the royal family from a pillar beside the royal pews. He wore black bands of silk over his crimson uniform and surveyed the cathedral in his usual watchful manner. Athaya smiled inwardly. Little did Durek know that this was the last official function for which he could depend on the loyal guard captain, for in a matter of days, Tyler would be seeking employment with Osfonin of Reyka, treasonous as that might seem.

And as Athaya finished scanning the great sanctuary, she found, to her relief, that Rhodri was nowhere to be seen.

If we're lucky, she thought, *Durek's already gotten rid of him.*

After what seemed to be hours of waiting, Archbishop Ventan proceeded to the pulpit. He raised his hand—a hand so weighted down with jewels that Athaya was surprised he could lift it at all—and the organ ceased playing. The solemn chords softly died away under the graceful vaulted ceiling.

"Our Father in heaven, we come before you today to mourn the passing of your noble servant, and our beloved king, and to honor him with our presence and our prayers."

Ventan led the congregation in a short opening litany, and after a response by the choir, he began his lengthy eulogy, reviewing Kelwyn's twenty-one-year reign and meticulously reciting a list of his memorable achievements. Athaya noted with wry amusement that Ventan was careful to avoid mentioning how the king's magic assisted in these achievements and made no reference at all to Kelwyn's well-known plans for banning the rite of absolution for the Lorngeld.

Then Athaya squeezed Jaren's hand and began to move away. *I'm going up to the casket for a minute, but I'll be right back.*

Jaren made no response, but Athaya could sense his trepidation in the way he clung to her for several heartbeats before finally releasing her hand.

Athaya left the side chapel and passed, unseen, behind the archbishop's pulpit, careful to avoid stumbling over the red-cushioned faldstools flanking the altar on either side. The altar itself was covered with precious ornaments—gleaming gold and silver chalices and candlesticks and altar plates, all set on a dazzling altar cloth embroidered with gold and set with colored gems. She stepped slowly past the candelabras near her father's body, not wanting the flames to flicker in the draft of her passage. She knew no one could see her, but she felt dangerously exposed as she stood only a few paces from the pews where her family sat, close enough to hear Cecile's ragged breath as she wept.

Reverently, Athaya approached the coffin and knelt behind it on the soft carpet and ran her fingers over the jeweled cloth coverings.

I came to say good-bye, she whispered with her thoughts. *It was the least I could do.* She leaned her forehead against the casket, and felt her eyes grow moist. *I hope you can forgive me.*

Then she felt a slight tingling sensation behind her eyes, like the touch of a feather, and paused for a moment to see if Jaren had anything urgent to tell her. But he said nothing, and she continued with her prayers, comforted that he was there with her.

Father, wherever you are, please know I never meant for any of this to happen. I only wanted to be friends. I wanted for us to stop fighting with each other. When I came back from Reyka, I knew that you were in danger and I wanted to make everything right before it was too late. But I just couldn't.

Athaya closed her eyes tight and drew in a breath to steady herself. *You were right about the Lorngeld all along, you know. They—we—aren't an evil race as Ventan keeps saying.* She cast a glance toward the archbishop, now reciting prayers on Kelwyn's behalf as he committed the king's soul to God. *You were one of the few who believed that, even though everyone tried to convince you that you were wrong. But you showed them that magic didn't have to be evil. If only you'd had more time—then perhaps they would have listened. But I ruined everything,* she added, wiping away a tear. *And now, after what I've done to you, they think that the Lorngeld are more dangerous than ever.*

And that's got to change, she resolved.

Kneeling beside Kelwyn's coffin, Athaya slowly understood that the force of her magic would not have been so deadly if allowed to be channeled properly, if the Lorngeld were not constantly denied their gift, and if the havoc that Faltil had wrought could somehow be reversed. That was what Hedric had been trying to tell her all along. And she was in a unique position to do it, with the power of a royal name and the power of her magic both behind her.

She drew herself up slowly, and despite the occasion, felt a blanket of peace settle over her. Now she knew why she had been so compelled to come to the cathedral today. Being here had forced her to see that she had been wrong. Now, more than ever, she finally felt as if she had some purpose—some direction. A focus for her life that she had never possessed before. This was what she had been born to do, much as she might have tried to deny it. She had to continue the work that her father had started and find a way to put an end to the persecutions so that the Lorngeld could use the gift that had been bestowed on them.

I won't fail you, Father. I'll finish what you've started. And I'll make you proud of me. I swear it.

She bowed her head and said her last good-bye. Before she got to her feet, she felt the soft touch of a hand on her shoulder.

"I'm all right, Jaren," she whispered. "We can go now."

Then she heard the soft rustle of a robe brushing against the carpet behind her and she frowned. Jaren had worn no long robes today, but a short cloak over his doublet. And hadn't he said that he could not see through her cloaking spell? How had he known where to find her? A hot rush of terror flowed through her, and she drew in her breath sharply just before she heard Rhodri's voice.

You should be more careful, he said smoothly. His presence echoed through her mind—the presence she had thought was Jaren.

But how—

Lovely altar plates, aren't they? he remarked casually. Athaya turned her head aside in puzzlement, and quickly realized how Rhodri had found her. How could she have been so careless! Dimly, if she looked hard enough, she could detect the outline of her own reflection in the huge, costly ornaments.

You cast a strong spell, he added. *I'm impressed. If I hadn't been standing next to the altar myself, I'd never have caught your reflection.*

Then he had been there the whole time. He had touched her mind and heard everything she'd said. Athaya felt a shudder ripple through her limbs. She felt violated, as if she stood before him unclothed.

Getting to her feet, Athaya glanced worriedly at the archbishop and at her brother the king, quietly listening to his speech.

Oh, don't worry—they can't see either of us, Rhodri told her. *I cast quite a good cloaking spell myself, you know. I saw no need to upset the archbishop by letting him know I was here. Your brother seemed to think that my presence here would be inappropriate, but I had his permission to come if I kept out of sight. Despite what you may think, Kelwyn was quite a good friend of mine.*

Athaya could not see the wizard, but she felt his coldness beside her and the firm grip he had on her shoulder. Unlike Jaren, whose spell was weaker, Rhodri was completely invisible under his magic cloak. Athaya saw no rippling patch of air to mark his presence, and when he spoke, it was like being addressed by a spirit. Consciously shutting him out of her thoughts, she almost called out to Jaren, but then stopped herself short. Even if Rhodri had already heard that the "courier" she had brought back from Reyka was a wizard, he didn't show any awareness that Jaren was presently in the cathedral. But Jaren could have no idea of the danger she was in. He wouldn't be able to see through Rhodri's spell either!

So you want to lead your people to salvation, Rhodri said, emitting a droll little laugh. *How noble.*

She gritted her teeth. *What would you know about nobility? Nothing at all, I'm sure,* he replied lightly. *But who put you up to this great task, I wonder? Hedric, I imagine. He always was an incurable idealist.*

He only wants what's best for the Lorngeld. My God, they're your own people, Rhodri. Why have you done nothing for them? Why have you let the Church go on poisoning them, teaching people that their gift is evil? Why haven't you helped to train them?

Rhodri laughed again, a wheezy, mocking laugh. *Can her Highness have forgotten that teaching spells to the Lorngeld is strictly against canon law? Even Kelwyn wouldn't have allowed me to do such a thing until he cleared it with the Curia. He may have disagreed with his bishops, but he wasn't going to openly defy them.*

And you didn't do a thing to help him, did you?

I think you are failing to grasp one additional point, he went on, his voice dripping with exaggerated courtesy. *The more people who have a talent, the less that talent is appreciated. There wouldn't be anything special about a master musician if everyone could play a harp as well as he could, now would there?*

I see, she replied bitterly. *So instead of distinguishing yourself by hard work, you think it's better to simply kill off the competition.*

I've never killed anyone. Yet, he added darkly. *But I see no reason to encourage them.*

Never killed anyone? she retorted. She pointed angrily to the coffin, knowing that Rhodri could see only her dim reflection in the altar plates. *You did this! You killed him, Rhodri. I'm being blamed, but it's you who's responsible. You gave my father power that you knew would destroy him. Hedric told me so himself! You knew the ritual was dangerous, but you went ahead and did it anyway. And why? Because you wanted to prove yourself superior to Hedric. Because you were aching to be accepted as one of the Great Masters no matter who you had to destroy to do it.*

She caught his dim reflection in the polished plates and saw him glaring at her with quiet fury. But she did not care. She had nothing to lose now.

You may be a master magician, Rhodri, but you're a despicable human being. And I think the Circle will be able to realize that. Overwhelmed with fury, she curled her hands into tight fists. *Damn you for what you've done, Rhodri. I hope you burn in hell for this!*

Athaya threw her weight against him, striking out at him with her fists even though she could not see him. In front of the entire congregation—blind to her existence as they calmly listened to Ventan's prayers—she fought with him, not caring what he might do to her. He wrapped his hands around her wrists, trying to fend off her blows. But before he could work one of his spells against her, she heard him cry out as he stumbled backward into one of the heavy iron candelabras next to Kelwyn's coffin.

There was a flash of brilliant, orange light as the slender white tapers crashed down onto the coffin, swiftly igniting the sumptuous cloths draped over the casket. Burning hungrily, the flames licked the edges of the casket, slowly eating their way through the polished oak toward the shrouded body encased there.

Archbishop Ventan broke off his prayers and gaped at the flames in horror. The sanctuary erupted into a sea of frightened voices.

"This is God's judgment!" one of the priests cried suddenly, stumbling to his feet from his place near the pulpit. "He warns us against the evils of magic!" A low buzz of agreement rippled among the thousands of people gathered in the cathedral. For no one would have seen the struggle taking place between Athaya and the wizard, but only the inexplicable motion of the candelabra toppling on its side, as if pushed by the hand of God Himself.

Athaya clapped a palm over her mouth, horrified by what she had done.

Athaya, for God's sake what are you doing? Jaren's voice was almost hysterical, but she barely heard him. For at that moment she was struck motionless by the sight of the archbishop pointing an accusing finger directly at her, and realized that she had been so distracted by the sudden blaze that her cloaking spell had dissolved.

"The Lord have mercy on us!" Ventan cried out. "The Devil's Child is loose in the house of God!"

Gripping her wrist so hard that her fingers went numb, Rhodri dragged her in front of the burning altar. Then, counteracting his cloaking spell, he shimmered dramatically into view before the congregation, like a holy apparition.

"Behold, my Lord King," he said to Durek, raising her

numbed hand aloft. "Your sister is not content to merely murder your father, but she seeks to deprive his very body of decent burial by consigning it to the flames."

From his post near the royal box, Athaya saw Tyler's eyes bulge with terror. The halberd he carried slipped out of his hands and clattered noisily to the floor. Broken out of his stunned silence by the noise, Durek shouted for his guards to douse the flames. Never taking his eyes from her, Tyler gestured to two of his men, and they whipped off their cloaks and began beating out the fire that had nearly consumed the costly draperies and had started to feed on the oaken casket.

"Bring her to me, Rhodri," Durek said, his voice shaking from fury.

Jaren's voice came to her again, clear and strong. *I'm going to cause a few more diversions, Athaya, and then we're getting the hell out of here.*

Although he was standing several feet in front of the burning altar, the hem of Rhodri's gown suddenly went up in flames, and the wizard let out a loud yelp of pain. He released her and stumbled forward against the altar rail. The flames from his robe quickly spread to the flowers and velvet coverings placed there. Unnaturally fueled by Jaren's magic, the fire swept from the coffin to the edges of the costly altar cloths behind it, eventually chasing the archbishop from his pulpit and consuming the finely paneled wood.

In an instant, the scene was etched forever in Athaya's mind—an image of Rhodri snatching up the basin of holy water from the baptismal font and drenching his robe with it amid a flurry of angry curses—of Nicolas, choking from the smoke as he pulled Cecile from the royal box and down the aisle to safety. Of Dagara, stumbling out of the pew after them and trying to flee, only to have a lick of angry fire spit out at her from the casket and ignite the skirts of her black velvet gown—and of Durek, seeing the queen running blindly in circles as she squealed horribly like a pig at the slaughter, throwing his fine, fur-lined cloak over her and beating out the flames.

And then, like a final judgment, the circular stained-glass window above the altar exploded inward, showering the burning sanctuary with colored glass.

Shielding his head from the torrent of glass, Tyler stumbled over the altar steps to Athaya. "Come on—we're getting out of here."

Only a few yards behind him, she heard the sound of Durek's angry voice spewing out commands.

"Bring her to me, Captain! Bring her to me at once!"

Without looking back, Tyler seized Athaya's arm and yanked her in the opposite direction. Crushing the broken glass under their feet, they fled past the pulpit toward the chapel where Jaren waited, now uncloaked and in full view.

"Damn you to hell, Captain," came Durek's shrill voice, ringing up to the vaulted arches of the church. "This is treason! Do you hear me? *Treason!*"

Ignoring the king's frantic cries, Tyler and Athaya followed Jaren down the transept toward the pair of double doors. Throngs of people were in panic, desperately trying to escape the burning church, and Jaren, not knowing what else to do, quickly conjured a witchlight so that the people would draw back from him in terror and clear a path so that the three of them could pass.

Athaya was gasping for breath in the smoke-filled building when they reached the end of the transept. Tyler quickly reached out to push the doors open, but an angry shower of blue sparks lashed out at him, singeing the sleeve of his uniform.

"Damn!" he shouted, clutching at his injured arm.

Rapidly assuring herself that Tyler was not seriously hurt, Athaya turned to Jaren. "What's wrong? Why won't they open?"

"Rhodri's got them shielded!" Jaren said, punctuating his words with a muffled curse. He reached out to touch the polished wood, and while there was a new burst of magic sparks, Jaren was able to smother them as he furiously tried to find a way to counteract Rhodri's spell.

The door trembled in its frame as he concentrated on breaking the spell, but just as he opened it up far enough to allow a thin shaft of light to stream in from the outside, Jaren suddenly stumbled back and clasped his hands over his eyes in agony.

"No! Get out!" he shouted, gasping for breath. "Leave me alone!"

Athaya wheeled around in panic. "Jaren, what's the matter?"

"It's Rhodri . . . he's . . . in my mind . . ." Then Jaren let out a high-pitched cry and crumpled to the floor at her feet.

Athaya grasped Tyler's hand for support. They were cornered—backed against the immovable doors—and out of all the things Jaren had taught her that week, she knew of nothing that would counteract the shields that barred the door. And now, only a few steps in front of her, Rhodri stood motionless, his robes drenched in holy water and his face twisted by a thin smile of victory. Behind him, Athaya saw a gentle rain falling inside the cathedral. Fat drops of water spattered the ground from a cloud that hovered just below the vaulted ceiling, putting out the fires that Jaren had ignited.

Rhodri stepped forward, casting a look of disgust at Jaren. "You must be one of Hedric's students," he said, towering over him. The hem of his robe, now badly scorched, brushed against Jaren's face. "Let me guess. Your father is one of Osfonin's friends." When Jaren did not respond, but only gave him an angry glare, Rhodri clicked his tongue, and let out a low chuckle. "Yes, I thought so. Your resistance is pitifully weak. It's sad, in a way. In my day, Hedric would never have accepted someone with such mediocre talents as yours. He must be growing childish in his old age."

"What did you do to him?" Athaya demanded, kneeling on the floor beside him. The color had drained from Jaren's face, and his breathing was shallow and forced. With tortured slowness, he managed to get up on his hands and knees, but he was still unable to stand.

Rhodri shrugged carelessly. "Oh, he'll be all right. I just gave him a nasty psychic jolt. Paths are like caverns, your Highness. They echo. What I did was the equivalent of standing in the middle of the caverns and screaming as loud as I could. The effect can be quite painful," he added with cold detachment, as if he were speaking of something as trivial as a change in the winds. "But be warned, I can do the same to you if you attempt to escape."

Then Athaya saw Durek, flanked by six red-liveried guards, approaching them from the main body of the church. His fine velvet coat was dripping wet from Rhodri's magic rain, and droplets of water streamed from his hair and ran down his cheeks like tears. Athaya expected him to order her death at any moment, but to her surprise, he was not looking at her at all.

"Lieutenant Parr," Durek growled, his voice like the rumble of distant thunder. The vigilant young man trotted up next to him and snapped to attention. The king pointed an accusing finger at Jaren. "Is this the man you told me about—the courier from Reyka?"

"Yes, my Lord. He joined us at Evarshot, a day after we'd left for Ath Luaine."

Tyler cast a withering glare at his lieutenant, realizing it had been his trusted man Parr who had sidestepped his authority and informed Durek of the wizard's existence himself.

"I don't know why he decided to come back here with us," Parr continued, seemingly oblivious to Tyler's presence. "But on the day we left Reyka, I heard Princess Athaya arguing with him in the stables. I was too far away to hear most of what they were saying, but I did hear them mention magic."

"I remember him," Durek said, glaring down at Jaren. "He's the man that brought Osfonin's letter to Kelwyn back in August." He shifted his gaze to Tyler. "The same man, Captain, that you claimed had absolutely no connection to Athaya at all." His face flushed red with fury, like a boil about to burst. "You knew where she was hiding the whole time, didn't you? You knew that this mind-plagued wizard had been sheltering her and teaching her magic! And yet you deliberately *lied* to me." Durek stamped his foot on the floor like an angry child. "Damn you, Captain, I ought to take you out right now and have you hanged!"

Tyler met his gaze steadily, but said nothing. Athaya was glad. In Durek's present state, anything that either one of them said would inevitably be twisted out of context and used against them. But what could they say in their defense? Durek's accusations were all true.

"And *you!*" Durek went on, finally turning his attentions to Athaya. "Wasn't it enough that you killed Father? No! You had to come back and try your hand at the rest of us, didn't you? Nicolas and Cecile passed out from the smoke, and Dagara—" His face darkened dangerously. "She's been badly burned."

Athaya bowed her head, utterly defeated. Not even Tyler's presence next to her could comfort her now. If she believed herself in trouble a few days ago when she had fled the castle, it was nothing to the danger she found herself in now.

"Lieutenant," Durek said to the young man beside him. "Take these three out of my sight and lock them up. Rhodri, go with him," he added, motioning sharply to Athaya and Jaren. "I want you to personally make sure that these two can't escape using any of their tricks."

Ignoring Tyler's silent, condemning glare, Lieutenant Parr pulled Jaren roughly to his feet and clamped a pair of irons around his wrists. Two more of Durek's guardsmen fastened similar pairs of manacles on Athaya and Tyler, forcing their arms painfully behind their backs. Their eyes met only once, exchanging a look of silent resignation. And while they were being led out of the cathedral under the soldiers' watchful eyes, Rhodri followed close behind, smiling.

CHAPTER 19

✻✦✻

ATHAYA COULD ONLY GUESS AT THE TIME AS SHE HUD-
dled in the corner of the cramped, windowless cell in
the bowels of the castle. A thick, yellowed candle flickered from a scarred bedstand in the corner of the room, and
judging from the marks she had made on its side, she had been
here a little more than two hours. She estimated that it was late
afternoon, but without any windows to let in the sunlight, the
matter was academic.

Well, the accommodations could be worse, Athaya realized
with a sigh. At least the floor was stone and not earth. And there
was even a small chamber pot in the corner, though she had her
doubts as to how often it would be cleaned. She had also been
given a pot of ink, a quill, and several sheets of parchment so
that she could compose a confession of her crimes, but the ma-
terials remained stubbornly unused. All things considered, Durek had granted her a reasonably honorable confinement. Her
quarters were those reserved for more noble prisoners, most
recently the great lords sentenced to death for betraying Kelwyn
in the civil wars, and the walls were marked with half-finished
drawings and scrawled phrases—the last outpourings of those
former prisoners, now long dead.

It should have been so easy to escape. That was the most
frustrating part of all. She should have been able to trip the

heavy lock on the door and slip past the guards with a cloaking spell. But Rhodri knew all those things as well and had taken precautions. The guards in the outside corridor were armed with mirrors as well as swords, and Rhodri had placed powerful binding spells around the door so that Athaya could not go near it without feeling a hot, blinding pain inside her skull. She was careful to keep her distance from the thick, iron-studded door and glared at it hatefully from time to time as if it were Rhodri himself.

Before leaving her, Rhodri had obliged her with an exhaustive explanation of the technical properties of the spell, making it abundantly clear how much pride he took in his own skill and knowledge. He was fascinated by the inner workings of his magic but showed a blatant disregard for the purposes to which he put his powers, be they good or evil. She had felt a slight twinge when the binding spell was enacted, as if she'd been pricked with a needle from inside, and Rhodri had been happy to inform her that a small sliver of her own essence was required to key the spell specifically to her. Now, wizard or no, she was trapped inside the cell while everyone else could come and go at will, unharmed. She wasn't sure whether such spells were entirely ethical—spells that required a part of a person's very self to work—but she recalled Felgin mentioning something similar when he told her how Tyler's image had been placed inside the locket.

Athaya took out the delicate silver pendant and flipped it open, drawing comfort from the image of his face. If Hedric had indeed assisted Felgin with the setting of such a spell, there could be nothing dangerous or unethical about it. A tiny drop of Tyler's self kept the image alive, and Athaya was glad that even though he was being held in another part of the fortress, part of him, however small, was here with her.

Tucking the locket away, Athaya raised her palms and willed her vision sphere into existence, hoping to find out how Jaren and Tyler were faring. She balked at first; if anyone entered the room during her sphere-work and broke her concentration, not only would she suffer a painful backlash, but news of her latest act of conjuring would only find its way immediately back to Durek.

She smiled grimly. *But how could that possibly make things any worse?*

The sphere quickly swirled into existence at her command, lightly poised between her fingertips. Gazing into the misty globe, she concentrated on Jaren and tried to focus in on where he was being held. It took a long time before an image began to take shape, but she kept trying, drifting deeper and deeper into concentration. All awareness of the walls around her faded away as she lost herself in the swirling clouds.

And then she found him—and gasped.

Unlike her's, Jaren's confinement was less than honorable. He was imprisoned in one of the tiny cells on the lowest level of the dungeon—the place reserved for the most heinous of Delfarham's criminals. The walls around him seeped with moisture, and she saw the occasional movement of a rat skittering in the shadows. Shivering, Jaren sat on the dirt floor with his back against the damp stone, his hands securely chained to irons set in the walls on either side of him. His head hung limply against his shoulder so that his hair fell across his face. Every few moments she heard him moan pitifully, and he would arch his back and close his eyes against the pain, and then his muscles would go limp again. Then she saw the reason for his agony.

Around his neck, suspended on a silver chain, was Archbishop Ventan's corbal crystal—the same one she had taken with her to Reyka. And above him, keeping the crystal alive in the darkness, was a brightly burning witchlight.

Dear God, what have they done to you? she thought desperately. She remembered Rhodri's reaction to the corbal on the day she left for Reyka, and how, only at the threshold of her powers, she had winced at the corbal's power when she'd asked Nicolas to return it to the archbishop upon her return. She cringed at the thought of what Jaren must be going through and at the untold agony that the small purple gem was inflicting on him.

"Jaren, can you hear me?" she said. She had no idea whether she would be able to make contact through the sphere, but she seemed to remember Hedric saying that it could be done if the sphere-worker wished it. Jaren's eyes fluttered open briefly, but seeing no one in the little cell with him, he shook his head as if trying to banish a delusion. Every time he moved, she heard the menacing clank of the chains which bound his hands to the irons in the wall.

"Jaren—it's me. I can see you in my sphere."

"Athaya?" His voice was cracked and hoarse. He looked

blankly ahead with glazed eyes, like a blind man. Athaya had never seen him so utterly beaten before. "I can't hear you very well."

"Do you want me to try and touch your mind instead?"

"No—no, don't!" he protested suddenly. "You'll only get aftershocks from the corbal." He glanced down at the slender gem, then looked away with revulsion. "When the guards brought me here, Rhodri conjured the witchlight and left it behind. Once he was gone, the archbishop came in and put the crystal around my neck."

"Can't you put out the light?"

"No. I tried once, but I almost passed out. I can't use my power with the crystal that close. My paths—they're all crossed. It hurts, Athaya," he said, giving in to the torment. "Oh God, it hurts so much . . ."

Athaya bit her lip angrily, overwhelmed by helplessness. "Is there anything I can do?"

"It's no good. You wouldn't be able to put the light out from a distance. And even if you were right here with me, I doubt you'd be able to break Rhodri's spell." He paused for a moment to fight back a spasm of pain. "He's powerful, Athaya. Maybe even more than Hedric realized."

"If it hurts too much to talk, I can go . . ."

"No, please stay." Jaren tried to force his ragged breathing back into its natural rhythm. "Talking to you helps keep my mind off the pain."

Athaya saw the vision cloud for a moment, but she knew it was from the tears welling in her eyes, and not the fault of her magic. If only she could *do* something . . .

"Why you?" she asked, gazing at the crystal that glittered coldly by the light of the magic fire. "Rhodri's already admitted that he doesn't consider your power much of a threat."

"But I'm fully trained and you aren't," Jaren pointed out. "I can't overpower him, but I could still cause trouble for him. Maybe he wants to make sure I can't interfere with whatever plans he has for you. He isn't afraid of you—he knows that you've only started learning about your power. I've taught you a lot these last few days, but Rhodri's had years of practice and training. He's stronger than you are and he knows it."

And I know it, too, she thought miserably. In spite of everything she had learned, she was still only a beginner. Whatever untapped potential she possessed didn't matter at this point. Simple cloaking spells and vision spheres were not going to be enough to counter the power of an adept like Rhodri. And the stronger spells that she had worked unintentionally, like the coils of fire that had killed her father, were out of her conscious control. She wouldn't know how to work them if she wanted to. And who was going to teach her how to master them now?

"I wonder what Durek will do with us," she said, breaking the silence that had fallen between them.

"It depends. You might actually come out of this alive, just by virtue of being his sister. Maybe you can convince him that the fire was an accident. Tell him it was all *my* fault, for heaven's sake."

"He'd never listen," she muttered under her breath. "Durek's a pigheaded ass. And besides, I'm not going to make things worse for you than they already are."

Jaren briefly scanned his squalid little cell. "I don't think that's possible." He shifted his weight slightly, and Athaya could see by the whiteness in his face that each small movement was a torture to him.

"As for Tyler, who knows?" he continued, short of breath. "Durek might be lenient on the basis of his past service. He could spend the rest of his life in prison, but at least he'd be alive."

Athaya's heart sank. She couldn't bear the thought of being responsible for such a thing. Not on top of everything else. Death would be preferable to spending endless, empty years locked away from the world.

"And what about you?" she asked quietly. So far Jaren had made no mention of his own fate.

He didn't reply right away, but Athaya noticed that his expression had changed. He seemed resigned, as if he'd lost whatever hope he might have had. The muscles in his face stiffened as he tried to mask his fear.

"Your brother isn't going to let me walk out of here alive, Athaya. You might believe that, but I don't."

"Don't be ridiculous. There must be some way . . ."

Jaren closed his eyes and rested his head against the damp wall. "None I can see. Look at it from Durek's point of view. He thinks all magic is evil. He knows I'm a wizard, he knows I've been teaching you magic, and he knows that your magic is what killed Kelwyn. I'd say if he's got it in for anyone, it isn't you—it's me.''

"You can't just give up like this," she said. Although the words were strong, her voice trembled as she said them. Did she truly believe there was a way, or was that merely what she felt obligated to say to cheer him?

"I'm not giving up, Athaya. I'm being realistic. For the last few hours I've tried to think of something—anything—that can get us out of this, but I just can't.'' He clenched his teeth, furious at his own helplessness. "And even if a spell existed that would instantly transport us to Reyka, I couldn't work it with this damned crystal around my neck!''

He pulled against his chains as hard as he could, lashing out against the pain in anger. But the power of the crystal was too strong for him. He let out a shallow moan and slumped back against the wall, his strength completely gone. Tiny rivers of sweat ran down his face, soaking the collar of his shirt.

"Are you still there?" he asked weakly, on the very edge of consciousness.

Athaya had to strain to hear him. "Yes, I'm here.''

"Listen to me . . . listen carefully, please. Whatever you do, you've got to save yourself. No matter what happens to me, find some way to get out of here and get back to Hedric. He can . . . teach you . . .''

"But I just can't leave you here!" she cried, unable to believe what she was hearing. "And Tyler—''

Jaren shook his head firmly, and Athaya could see tears of pain rimming his eyes. "I know it will be hard, but if there's even a chance you can escape this, you must. You're too important. Your power is too great to go to waste. I've told you all this before . . .''

Athaya could feel her hands shaking, and the image in the sphere seemed to blur before her eyes. "I could never do that. Not after everything you've done for me.''

"Save yourself, Athaya.'' His voice was almost gone, and she could barely hear him. "That's all that matters. Do whatever you have to . . .''

He said nothing more. Arching his back, he let out a low cry, and his head dropped forward against his chest as he slipped away into blissful unconsciousness.

Athaya blinked back a tear, watching his breathing relax into a normal rhythm as he slept. Much as she would have liked to sustain the link between them—if only to assure herself that he was still alive—Athaya did not try to rouse him. At least he would feel no pain for a few hours.

The sphere clouded over, and the vision was gone. She felt alone and more frightened than she had ever been before. Not until that moment did she realize how much she depended on him. Jaren had always been there to help her understand the new direction her life was taking now that her potential for magic had been uncovered. She could trust him and confide in him, as if they had been friends for years instead of weeks, and she could not bear to think that it would be her fault if anything happened to him. He had risked so much for her that she felt it would be the supreme act of betrayal to flee and save herself and leave him to whatever fate Durek saw fit.

Instead of banishing the sphere, she attempted to locate Tyler next. She wasn't sure whether she would be able to speak to him—she suspected that only two Lorngeld could communicate with each other that way—but she had to make sure that he was all right and not in torment like Jaren.

Shifting all her concentration onto Tyler, she waited. At first she saw only hazy, half-formed images, like a fresco whose colors were faded from time, but then the vision came into focus. It was the royal audience chamber, and in the center of the room was Tyler, his hands securely fastened behind him. He stared straight ahead with a coolly detached look on his face and seemed oblivious to the two uniformed men lingering nearby, each holding a well-polished halberd.

Durek's boots made no sound on the carpet as he paced slowly in front of his captain, eyeing him coldly. "Perhaps you did not hear me the first time, Captain," he was saying, his voice low and ominous. "I have accused you of treason. How do you plead?"

Tyler was motionless as a statue. He fixed his eyes on the far wall and said nothing. It was as if he had no interest at all in what Durek was saying and was passively waiting for the king to finish his tirade and return him to his cell.

Durek shook his head in disgust. "Athaya's treachery I can understand. She always fought with Kelwyn—I'm hardly surprised at what she's done. And I'm not surprised that she brought back a wizard from Reyka to help her do it. But you!" Durek tightened his jaw and locked his gaze onto his wayward servant. "I trusted you, Captain. My father trusted you. I can't believe that you would betray us for the sake of two damned wizards!"

Athaya saw a flash of anger in Tyler's eyes, but still he would not speak. And it was clear that his silence was beginning to grate on Durek's nerves.

"My men have searched your quarters," Durek told him. "Oddly enough, everything was packed," he said, raising an eyebrow. "Almost as if you were planning to go somewhere. Somewhere like Reyka, perhaps?" His face clouded over. "And you were going to take Athaya with you, I gather? And that wizard?"

He tapped the toe of his boot on the floor, impatiently waiting.

"The wizard has been teaching her spells, obviously. You knew where he'd been hiding her, but you lied to me, and swore a false oath. Do you deny it?"

Again, he waited, but in vain.

"Damn you, Captain, I order you to speak!" he burst out. "You may be too damned stupid to save yourself, but will you say nothing on Athaya's behalf? You obviously care for her more than any of us have been led to believe." His lips curled down in distaste, as if that in itself was a crime worthy of punishment.

In the silence that ensued, Durek rubbed his chin with a faint smile on his face, confident that he had touched upon his opponent's weakness. "Her fate is not yet sealed, my friend," he said smoothly. "Persuade me to be merciful and I may only decide to imprison her for the rest of her life. It would be unfortunate if one of my first official acts as Kelwyn's successor was the execution of my own sister. I don't need a black mark like that at the start of my reign." He laced his fingers together, one by one. "The people tend to object to that sort of thing."

For the first time, Tyler met his gaze. But instead of being infused with hope, he seemed to be on the brink of losing his carefully guarded self-control. The veins in his neck were swollen with suppressed rage.

"I know you too well, Durek," he said, pointedly omitting the king's proper title. "You'll have her executed no matter what I say. You don't care what the people think of you. You never have. So don't tempt me with bargains that you don't intend to keep. It doesn't become you."

Durek's cheeks flushed red with outrage. But Athaya had seen that look before, and knew that her brother was not near so furious at the insult as he was at being caught in such a blatant lie. In one sweeping gesture, the king signaled for his guards to step forward.

"Get him out of my sight," he snapped, thrusting an angry finger in Tyler's face. "And put him in one of the lower cells—next to the wizard."

As the guards led Tyler out of the audience chamber, Athaya commanded the sphere to disperse. She couldn't bear to see any more. Thoroughly drained of energy, she lay back on her hard bed, resting her head on the flat, greasy pillow. She stared up at the soot-covered ceiling and absently looked for patterns on the blackened stone as if they were summer clouds.

Why are you defending me, Tyler? Why don't you tell him I had you under a spell and that you'd never have betrayed him otherwise? If nothing can be done for me, why don't you lie to him and try to save yourself?

But she knew he would never do it. In his heart, Tyler was a noble man, above the petty intrigues that were all too common in a royal court. As he had shown through years of loyal service in Kelwyn's army, he was willing to risk his life for what he believed in. That was something she had sensed the first time she saw him, and something that had drawn her closer to him, and made her love him. But now, when he risked his life for her, and not his king, Athaya was plagued with guilt and unworthiness and wondered, despite the pain it caused her, whether it might not have been better had they never met at all.

Athaya tried to sleep, but it was useless. Lacking anything else to do, she fixed her eyes on the yellowed candle on her bedstand and watched the soft, hot wax drip slowly down the sides and harden into pools at the base. A thin tendril of black smoke rose from the wick, giving off a sweet scent. Every so often she fanned the flame gently, watching the shadows on the wall flicker as it danced, and then grow still again. But suddenly she imagined faces in the flames—faces crying out to her, and if she tried, she could hear their voices. Voices without hope, like Jaren's. *Help us, Athaya. You have the power.* And Tyler was in the middle of them, staring straight ahead. He did not cry out as the others did, but suffered in silence. And then he smiled at her.

Shaking, Athaya snuffed out the flame with a sharp puff of

breath and hid her face in the pillow, futilely trying to shut out the world. It was then that she was conscious of the sounds from the outside corridor. She heard footsteps and the low murmur of voices. The jangle of iron keys rang out near the door, and a moment later, a large, robed figure filled the doorway clutching a slim, leather-bound book in his fleshy hands.

It was Archbishop Ventan.

As he stepped into the room, the torchlight glittered on the large, circular pendant he wore around his neck. *A Saint Adriel's medal, of course,* Athaya thought dryly. *How could I forget the holy man who founded the practice of absolution . . .*

"What do you want?"

Ventan offered her a placating smile. "I want to save your soul, your Highness. Even if you do not." He sat down on the edge of her pallet and ran his fingers across the smooth leather binding of his book. She did not have to look at its title to know what it was. Archbishop Ventan was an avid reader of the writings of Saint Adriel and frequently carried with him the noted *Essays on the Nature of Magic.*

"My soul is none of your damned business," she said, looking away.

"Your Highness, please believe me when I say that I hold nothing against you for the tragedy which took the life of your father. You cannot be blamed. Your will is not your own. Your thoughts and actions are being controlled by the Enemy of God."

"I'm in control of myself!" she shouted.

And a fine job I'm doing keeping myself out of trouble . . .

Ventan was undaunted by her protests. "The Devil has a strong hold on you—so strong that you cannot resist it. He tempts you with evil power—"

"My power isn't evil!" she snapped. "How can it be? Magic is a gift from God Himself!"

The archbishop drew back sharply, as if physically struck. The idea that magic could be anything but diabolical had obviously never occurred to him. Recovering, he narrowed his eyes. "Those are dangerous words for one in your position, your Highness."

"The truth is always dangerous, your Excellency. Especially to those who do their best to hide it."

To her surprise, Athaya was not afraid of him. She did not know from where the strength came, but it sustained her and gave her a level of confidence that she never expected to have a few short hours ago. She had never possessed any strong religious convictions before, but perhaps they had been hidden inside of her all along. The words flowed out of her easily, and she felt as if she had been inwardly rehearsing for just such a confrontation her entire life and was ready for it.

Ventan got up and walked in a small circle around the room, rubbing his chin as he planned his next method of attack. "If, as you say, the Lorngeld's power is not evil, then why is it destructive? Can you deny that the Lorngeld were the cause of our country's blackest era? Their insanity is evidence of the Devil's power over them. It is how the Devil calls to them and seeks them out. If the power is from God, as you seem to think, and you are His chosen people, then why would He wish your magic to wreak havoc on the earth that He created?"

A few months ago, she might have asked the same question. But now she knew what the answer was and wondered when that realization had actually taken hold.

"It's the price," she explained. "Magic commands a price. It is the trial of madness that keeps the Lorngeld from abusing their gift. It is what they must suffer to earn the power." She felt as if Hedric himself was speaking through her, and for the first time she understood—truly understood—the reason why magic must be paid for. That was the way it had to be. That was the proper order of things. For without trial, the gift is undeserved.

Ventan made a dismissing gesture with his hand. "Nonsense."

"But you use the same argument yourself," Athaya countered. "In your own sermons, you preach that we must suffer the miseries of life on earth in order to attain eternal life in heaven. It's much the same thing."

"It is not," he said, puffed up with offense at having his own doctrines compared to those of heretics. "You're only trying to make excuses for the evils caused by Faltil's magic. The Time of—"

"And you're wrong in that assumption, Archbishop," she went on. "It was not a Lorngeld who caused the Time of Madness. That was King Faltil's doing, yes. But he was not one of them."

Ventan's eyes threatened to pop from his head. If he thought she was talking nonsense before, he was clearly convinced of it now.

"What?" he said, almost laughing. "That's absurd. Every historian of that time recorded the events of those years and they all agree that Faltil was a Lorngeld and born with the curse of magic."

"They thought he was a Lorngeld because they didn't know what other conclusions to draw. Faltil's magic was given to him—just like my father's was—but he silenced the man who gave it to him so that everyone would believe his power came from God, as he claimed. But he only made that claim so he'd have an excuse to start his scourge—the same scourge that you and your Church are perpetrating to this day! Faltil was jealous of the Lorngeld and wanted to keep the knowledge of magic for himself. *That's* why he destroyed every Lorngeld he could find—not because he was 'doing God's work.' And of course there were years of destruction afterwards! The Lorngeld had never been denied their training before, so no one had any idea of what damage could be done once their madness was allowed to run its course. My people were innocent victims, Archbishop. Simple human greed was the ultimate cause."

My people, she repeated inwardly, struck by what she'd said. As many times as she had heard Hedric say it, she had never used that phrase herself until now.

Ventan shook his head in disbelief. "I cannot understand how you can believe such things," he said, raising his book in front of him. "Saint Adriel himself wrote that once Faltil had turned against his own kind to cleanse the land of magicians, he was struck down—punished by the Devil himself." Ventan flipped to a turned-down page and began to read. " 'And the Evil One smote the king for killing the Lorngeld so that their pernicious knowledge of magic could not spread and infect the world with its evil, as the Devil desired.' He also writes that—"

"Don't quote scriptures to me," she snapped. "That book you live by is nothing but the lunatic ramblings of a man who cared less for God than he did for making a name for himself in the king's court. Once Faltil was dead, his son wanted theological backing for the belief that the Lorngeld were evil, and so Bishop Adriel accommodated him by penning that book of essays you carry around with you and concocting the idea of absolving the Lorngeld of their sins by killing them. And now you honor him as a holy man? It's preposterous!"

"You *dare* to call Saint Adriel a liar?" he exclaimed, his cheeks purple with anger. "He was inspired by God to write—"

"He was inspired by the king's purse."

Archbishop Ventan sputtered with rage. "You speak heresy!"

"Your Church infuriates me!" she said, rolling her eyes. "No one can disagree with anything you say without being labeled a heretic. How can you be so damned sure you're so right about everything? Did God personally descend from heaven and reveal His word to you?"

Ventan drew his shoulders back and lifted the numerous folds of his chin. "I would never presume to claim such a thing!"

"Then how do you know? Answer that, if you can. How do you know that the Lorngeld aren't evil at all, but are God's chosen people, with divine work to do. Work they can't accomplish unless you let them? How will you ever know if you keep murdering them before they learn to master their talents?"

Archbishop Ventan got to his feet, his eyes blazing. "The Devil speaks through you. I will listen to no more of this." His face was rigid with resolve as he paced quickly back and forth across the room. Whatever compassion he had brought to this meeting was gone. "Your choice is simple," he said. "You must accept what you are. You must renounce the Devil's magic and consent to be absolved of your power."

Athaya folded her arms across her chest. "And if I refuse? Which, by the way, I have every intention of doing."

"Then your brother will command you to do so. If you refuse him, then you would be disobeying the king's own will, and thus guilty of treason."

Athaya laughed sharply. "Durek's already accused me of *that*."

"If you will not be absolved, then the king would have no choice but to punish you some other way and deny you your only chance for saving your soul. A trial would be inevitable, as would the verdict and the sentence."

"But either way I die."

"If you choose correctly, your Highness, your soul will still be saved. That is the most important thing."

"You don't give a damn about my soul!" she said, springing to her feet. "Putting it simply, I'm a threat to you and you don't like it. You can't stand the idea that I was born with the gift of magic and you weren't. That without even being a priest of the Church, I have been called to do His service. That's a right you want reserved only for you and your handpicked priests, isn't it?''

The archbishop gripped his leather-bound book tightly, as if hoping it would give him the strength he needed not to lose control.

''Your Highness, don't you see that I'm only trying to help you? I am not calling you evil, only he who enslaves you with magic. But the power itself must be destroyed, before it consumes your soul and condemns you to eternal flames.''

She gazed directly into his eyes. ''It's too late for that, Archbishop. If magic is evil then I'll burn for it. I won't let you poison me and that's final.''

A tense silence hung in the air between them for several seconds before Ventan shrugged in resignation. He had given up.

''Then you are lost,'' he said, and quietly left her cell.

It wasn't until he was gone that Athaya allowed herself to lower her shield of strength. Now that the confrontation was over, she felt drained and tired and let out a few sobs of relief that it was over. The battle was behind her—there was nothing that could be done now. She had voiced her opinions and now she would die for them.

Several hours after the archbishop left her, one of Durek's guardsmen brought her a tray of supper. It amused her to note how the young man kept his distance, fixing a watchful eye upon her as he set the tray down on the table. For no better reason other than she was bored, Athaya slowly lifted her hands and began making random signs in the air, pretending that she was about to place him under a spell. It was all she could do not to laugh aloud as he nearly stumbled over himself in a frantic effort to get out of the room.

After eating what she could of the meager fare, Athaya curled up under the tattered blankets and closed her eyes, and in a matter of minutes, slipped away into dreamless oblivion.

The next thing she was aware of was the slip of the lock and the creak of the door as it swung slowly open and closed again. Pulling the covers down from her face, she cracked open one sleepy eye and saw the hem of a black robe brushing the ground beside her. With a faint groan, she drew the blankets back over her head.

"If you've come back to get me to change my mind, Archbishop, then don't bother," she said, her voice muffled under the sour-smelling blankets. "I'm not going to consent to absolution."

She sat bolt upright when she heard Rhodri's low chuckle.

"Good morning, your Highness," he said smoothly, casting a disdainful eye over the stark little room. He folded his hands inside the sleeves of his robe. "I assure you that I am not here to espouse the archbishop's cause. In fact, I have a much different proposal for you. One I think you'll find most intriguing."

CHAPTER 20

RHODRI SAT DOWN AT THE SCARRED LITTLE TABLE IN THE center of the room and motioned for her to join him. She did so reluctantly, unnerved by the way his eyes glittered with confidence. He was elegantly clad in a high-necked robe trimmed with ermine, and pinned to his collar was a striking silver brooch in the same cross-shaped design as the enameled plaque she remembered seeing above the door to Hedric's chambers. His appearance made Athaya feel acutely uneasy, especially in light of her own bedraggled state. Her homespun dress was wrinkled from having been slept in, and her hair was tangled and smelled of soot and perspiration.

"I trust you slept well," he remarked. "Although I must confess that it's a bit drafty in here."

She shrugged carelessly, keeping her face devoid of expression. "I'll live."

"That, your Highness, is a debatable point at the moment," Rhodri observed, folding his hands in his lap. He cast a critical eye around the room. "But you should be grateful. It's much more comfortable here than down where your wizard-friend is staying. Jaren . . . is that his name?"

Athaya felt her muscles stiffen with rage. "What you've done to him is inexcusable, Rhodri. That crystal is killing him!"

"Yes, I assumed that you would try to locate him," Rhodri

said, pleased that she had acted according to his expectations. "Vision spheres are one of the first things a wizard learns how to use. But don't worry—the corbal won't kill him. It causes no physical harm, so theoretically he could stay that way indefinitely. The corbal's only effect is on his mind. He feels pain because the corbal tricks his mind into believing that it exists. Of course, real or not, the pain will drive away his sanity sooner or later."

"How can you torture him that way?" Athaya said, glaring at him with revulsion. "You know full well how much he's suffering. I saw the effect the corbal had on you at one time."

Rhodri held his chin up a little higher, his dignity wounded by having to admit such a weakness. "I'm not completely responsible for his situation, your Highness. The archbishop told the king about the crystal he possessed, and until such time as his Majesty decides what's to be done with your Reykan friend, he asked me to arrange everything so that Jaren wouldn't cause any trouble. I was merely obeying your brother's wishes."

"How noble of you," she said under her breath.

"But in any event, I didn't come here to discuss Jaren. He is a secondary problem at the moment." Rhodri picked up a quill from the table and absently began stroking the soft feather with his fingers. "You've caused quite a commotion in the city. I don't think I have to tell you that news of yesterday's incident at the cathedral is on the lips of everyone in Delfarham. I'd estimate that it will only take a matter of days to spread through the rest of Caithe."

Athaya lowered her eyes in shame. *For somebody who's always dreamed of running away to live in pleasant obscurity, I'm certainly making a name for myself.*

"Your brother, needless to say, is faced with a difficult situation," Rhodri went on. "Archbishop Ventan informed him last night that you refused to consent to absolution—the most convenient solution to the problem as they see it. And since the king knows how close you are to Nicolas, he's asked him to try and convince you to see reason. Needless to say, Nicolas used some colorful language during his refusal. He argues with Durek constantly. I suspect Cecile sides with him. She's being very careful to keep out of her husband's way lately. And Dagara is pressuring the king to move against you even more than Ventan is."

"Why are you here?" Athaya asked, having finally heard

enough. "To gloat? To try and make me feel worse about what's happened than I already do?"

"Not at all, your Highness. In fact, I've come to help you."

Rhodri set down the quill he'd been toying with and got to his feet. He walked in a slow circle around the tiny room with his hands folded in front of him and did not speak for several minutes. Athaya suspected that his silence was not because he wanted to choose his next words carefully, but because he wanted to frazzle her nerves even further. And much as she hated to admit it, his ploy was working well.

"I spoke with the king for several hours last night," he said at last. "We managed to come up with a way of resolving this situation. Your brother doesn't relish the thought of dragging you through an ugly and pointless public trial and would prefer to deal with this matter as quietly and privately as possible."

"I'm surprised Durek granted you an audience at all."

Rhodri smiled thinly. "Oh, he didn't at first—until I explained that I was trying to prevent you from causing any further trouble."

"And he probably believed that, didn't he?" Athaya pressed her fingertips against her temples, feeling the veins throbbing beneath her touch. "If he'd only *listen* to me—"

"I'm afraid you won't get a chance to speak with him yourself. He refuses to see you and has forbidden anyone from coming here without his express permission."

Athaya could barely control the storm clouds of rage swelling inside of her. "I don't know why he doesn't order you out of his court once and for all!"

"That's quite simple, your Highness," Rhodri said with a casual shrug. "Much as your brother dislikes me, he isn't about to send me away as long as you and that wizard/friend of yours are still around. He wants someone schooled in magic to protect him from the two of you. Besides, he knows as well as I do that he couldn't get rid of me unless I actually wanted to go. But enjoyable as it is here at court, I have no real reason to stay with Kelwyn gone. My work here is almost finished. Thanks to you," he added darkly.

"My father wouldn't have lived much longer, Rhodri. The *mekahn*—"

"Who told you that? Hedric?" Rhodri's lips curled down in disgust. "Hedric doesn't know a damned thing about it. Your father wasn't going mad at all. While you were away in Reyka, Kelwyn was a bit irritable and moody, yes, but no more so than he usually is when there's something preying on his mind. He was simply concerned with how you were progressing at Osfonin's court. That's all."

"You're wrong, Rhodri. You didn't see him that day. The day I got back . . ."

"No, and neither did anyone else," Rhodri snapped back with uncharacteristic haste—haste rooted in eagerness to deny an unpleasant truth. "You claim that he was mad, but there's no one to back up your story, *is* there? No, you'll not fool me so easily. Everything was going just as I planned. Kelwyn was showing no signs of the madness. No signs at all. I didn't make the same mistakes that Senal did, when he performed the rite of assumption on King Faltil. I did everything to perfection. And it was working, Athaya. Working beautifully. But you killed him before I could prove that to the Circle. You ruined twenty years of my work, your Highness. Twenty years." His eyes narrowed dangerously. "And you're going to pay for that."

"Revenge, Rhodri?" she said, inwardly pleased at having caught him in such an obvious lie. "And you said you were here to help me."

"Yes. That's the beauty of it." A disturbing smile crept over Rhodri's face, and for a moment he looked as if he would laugh aloud. "I can do both at the same time."

Athaya sensed a hollow emptiness in the pit of her stomach. Whatever Rhodri's plans were, she dreaded them even more now that she had a few moments ago.

"I'm going to offer you a way to save yourself," he said, returning to his seat at the table. "If you agree to what I'm about to suggest, then I can offer you your life. If you refuse . . ." He paused to let out a regretful sigh. "In that case, I fear there is little hope for you."

Jaren's words echoed in her mind. *Save yourself, Athaya. No matter what you have to do.*

Athaya shifted her weight uneasily. Rhodri had made two disturbing omissions.

"What about Tyler and Jaren?"

"I can make no promises for the wizard's fate. The king is most adamant about his punishment. As for Captain Graylen, your brother seems undecided at the moment. It's true that he openly lied to Durek, but he was also extremely loyal to your father for many years and, stubborn as he is at times, Durek realizes that should count for something. But if you are cooperative, your Highness, then I can speak to your brother again and try to persuade him to be lenient.''

She clasped her hands together, trying to keep them from shaking. ''Well? What is this 'offer'?''

In most respects, Rhodri seemed quite calm, conscious that he had complete control over her fate. But Athaya noticed that his breathing had quickened, and he tapped his fingertips together anxiously. He was swollen with anticipation and that did not bode well for her.

''Obviously Hedric has told you about the ritual through which your father received his power.''

''Yes, he did. He also told me that it's been forbidden for two centuries and that you violated the laws of the Circle by performing it.''

''What I want you to do is simple, Athaya,'' he continued, brushing over her remark as if she'd never spoken. He leaned closer, and his gaze grew more intense. ''Give away your magic.''

At that moment, time seemed to stop. Athaya could not move. The muscles in her body refused to obey her, and she felt as if her blood had turned to ice. For an instant, she forgot to breathe. *Give away my power.* A few weeks ago she would have taken the offer gratefully. But not anymore. Her magic was a part of her now, however reluctantly she had accepted it at first. She could no more imagine living without it than she could without her hearing or her sight.

Save yourself, Athaya. Do whatever you have to do.

But how would Jaren have known that the only thing she could do to save herself would defeat the very purpose of her escape?

Rhodri smiled as he watched her, knowing full well the train of her thoughts. He reclined against the back of his chair, tapping his fingertips together as he waited for her to speak.

''And just who am I supposed to give my magic to?'' she said. ''Someone of your own choosing, I suppose. Someone you can manipulate into doing whatever you want.''

Then it all slipped into place, and Athaya felt her heart skip a beat. He was going to try it again! He'd already had one king under his tutelage . . . why not another?

"I won't give it to Durek," she said, shaking her head firmly. "God knows how tempting that would be, but I'm not going to doom him the same way you doomed my father. If I gave him my power, he'd only go mad in twenty years. I won't be responsible for that."

Rhodri laughed softly. "Durek is not the one I had in mind. Frankly, I think he'd sooner die than stain himself with magic. He's not too fond of the Lorngeld, you know, and I don't think even the temptations of having the power himself would make him change his mind." He rubbed his chin, casually mulling the idea over in his mind. "Although I must admit, it would be quite a challenge."

Athaya's mind raced, her thoughts tumbling over themselves in confusion. If not Durek, then who?

Then she noticed Rhodri running his fingers over the silver brooch he wore. The symbol of wizardry. And suddenly the answer was clear. Slowly, she drew in her breath. It was so simple, so very simple.

"You want it for yourself, don't you?" she asked, her voice barely above a whisper. "You want me to give my power to you so you can have double the strength you do now."

Rhodri inclined his head, as if to compliment her reasoning.

Filled with outrage, Athaya slammed her fist down on the table, ignoring the tiny shards of wood that bit into her skin. "This is another one of your damned experiments, isn't it? First my father, and now me!"

"It's exciting, Athaya," he said, his eyes glistening like polished sapphires. "Just think—such a thing has never been tried before! What a triumph it would be if it succeeded!"

"Just the kind of triumph you need to win yourself a place on the Circle of Masters, isn't it?" she asked bitterly.

Rhodri merely smiled. "That thought had crossed my mind." He touched his fingertips to his brooch, as if he needed to assure himself that it was still there. "You ruined my last experiment, your Highness. But quite conveniently, you gave me the idea for an even greater one."

"You can't possibly believe this will work, Rhodri. The Circle won't have you no matter how many new spells you discover."

"And what would you know about the Circle?" he said haughtily. "Only what Hedric told you—a bitter old man who can't accept the fact that one of his students is much more highly skilled than he is.''

''It isn't your skills that upset him. It's how you choose to apply them.''

Rhodri arched a brow. ''What's this?'' he said, his voice laced with sarcasm. ''Lessons in ethics from someone who's just murdered her own father?''

His words—true words—cut through her like a knife. Choking back angry tears, she glared at him with a look of pure hatred. But he only laughed, delighted by her disgust.

''You think I'm mad, don't you?''

''No. You're sane enough,'' she told him. ''Coldly, horribly sane.''

She ran her fingers distractedly through the masses of tangled hair spilling over her shoulders, desperately wondering what to do. Then she realized that there was one thing he hadn't thought of. It went against everything she was taught, but if Rhodri could take her power, then couldn't she do the same? Surely someone in Caithe would be willing to sacrifice their birthright for her cause and avoid the specter of absolution. But Rhodri must have gleaned the train of her thoughts and quickly dashed her hopes before she could draw strength from them.

''And if you think you can regain your power later on, then I'm afraid I have to disappoint you.'' Rhodri shook his head in mock pity. ''Without your magic, it won't take long before your paths will start to crumble and decay. Once that happens, you won't be able to take magic from anyone. Ever. That is why Durek allowed me to make you this offer. I've assured him that once your paths are destroyed, you can never again wield magic.''

She had no idea whether this was true, but Rhodri's confidence convinced her that it probably was. Defeated, Athaya lowered her eyes. To give away her power was to give away her sense of self, and if she did so, she would be left with a void in her soul. But it was more than just her own loss that dismayed her—it was the matter of Rhodri's gain.

At first she had not seen it, but now the full implications of Rhodri's plan were gradually becoming clear. Once he possessed her magic in addition to his own, he could conceivably begin stealing the magic from all of the Lorngeld throughout Caithe who did not want it. They would be eager for the chance at ridding themselves of a power they thought to be cursed. Rhodri could increase his strength a thousandfold, becoming the most dangerously powerful wizard who ever existed—one who could easily force his way onto the Circle of Masters to which he aspired and inevitably take it over. He could control the practice of magic throughout Caithe, Reyka, and perhaps beyond, bending all wizards to his will. And what sort of experiments might he attempt then?

"I won't do it, Rhodri," she said quietly. "You can't handle the power you have now. I won't be the one who gives you more of it."

Rhodri was unruffled by her refusal. "I cannot take your powers from you by force. An essential element of the ritual is that the giver must be willing. But if you refuse, then your situation remains unchanged. On one hand, the king might force you to go through with the absolution ceremony. I'm sure you're aware how useful looca-smoke can be in making you pliable enough for that," he pointed out. "Or he could save himself the inconvenience, ignore the archbishop's concerns about your immortal soul, and simply sign the order for your execution. But whatever he chooses, he'll very likely be just as harsh with Captain Graylen and the wizard. And I make no guarantees about the manner of death, your Highness. You might be fortunate enough to avoid the stake, but then again, you might not."

He paused for a moment, to allow his words to take their proper effect. "But if you give away your power, then you are free to go. Of course, I fully expect that you will be permanently exiled from Caithe, but at least you'd be alive."

"That sounds too easy, Rhodri. How do I know you simply won't kill me later, once you've got what you want?"

"You don't," he said simply. "But you don't have much of an alternative, do you?"

He got to his feet and turned to leave her. "I'll give you the rest of the day to consider your answer, Athaya. When I return this evening, I hope you've made the right choice."

He closed the door softly behind him, and Athaya heard the sentry posted outside the door turn the key in the lock. Athaya stepped tentatively toward the door, but as she expected, Rhodri's binding spell was still strong. When she came within an arm's length of it, she jumped back sharply as the hot needles of pain shot through her skull, forcing her away.

She sank down on her bed and rested her head against the cold stone wall to mull over Rhodri's offer. Later in the morning, one of the guards—not the same young man she had teased the day before—brought her a bowl of thick, grayish broth and a few slices of rye bread, but she was too sick with worry to do much more than pick at it. For as long as she could remember, she had always flinched at taking orders—at having other people tell her what to do. And now she couldn't think of anything she'd like more. This decision was too critical. How could she possibly make it alone?

Jaren. He'll know what to do . . .

Athaya sat cross-legged on her bed and held up her arms, poising them a handspan's width apart. *"Volo videre,"* she said, hastily commanding her vision sphere to appear. Channeling all of her concentration onto Jaren, the mist from her fingertips formed itself into an orb and quickly provided her with a clear, unclouded view of his squalid little cell.

After only one day, Athaya was shocked at the change in him. The corbal around his neck still glittered by the light of Rhodri's ball of fire and the gem had definitely taken its toll. His clothes were damp with sweat, and he was deathly pale. Except for the times his body convulsed with chills, he did not move at all. Only if she tried could she see the soft rise and fall of his chest, and each time he drew a breath he winced, as if the air itself was poison.

"Jaren? Are you awake?"

He opened his eyes with effort.

"It's me again," she said. "How are you?" She realized only after she'd spoken what a spectacularly stupid thing it was to ask.

"I'm . . . still alive, if that's what you mean." His voice was dry and forced, like the sound of a steel blade being scraped against a stone. "What's happened?"

"Rhodri was here. He . . . had an offer for me." She felt drops of perspiration beading on her forehead, but with the sphere in her hand she could not wipe them off. "He says that Durek's willing to let me go if I do something that he wants."

"Then do it, Athaya," Jaren said, without hesitation. "Whatever it takes for you to escape . . ."

"But I can't. Jaren, you don't understand. He wants me to give away my magic. He wants me to give it to *him*."

Jaren was silent for a long time. He stared blankly ahead, not moving a muscle except to breathe. *"What?"*

"He thinks he can add my power to his. Is that true?" she asked, fervently wishing she would hear that it was all a grand lie. "Can he do that?"

"I have no idea," Jaren said, clearly stunned by the implications of such a spell. "As far as I know, nobody's ever tried that before."

"Rhodri said that if I gave away my power, Durek would let me go. And he might be more lenient with Tyler . . ." She paused, not knowing how to go on. How could she tell him that there was no hope of his own freedom? But when she saw him close his eyes in resignation, she realized that he already knew.

"Jaren, I'm sorry. I don't think Durek's going to let you go. I can ask Rhodri to speak with him again and see if he'll reconsider—"

"But he won't. I know that, Athaya. And there's nothing to be sorry about. I knew I was risking a lot when I decided to come back to Caithe with you." His face tightened as he tried to keep from crying out. "I don't think I can take much more of this. I think I'll be glad when Durek puts an end to it. At least then the pain will be over."

"Jaren, don't talk that way . . . please." But much as she tried to deny it, Athaya knew that he was right. If he was going to die, then better for it to be a quick and painless blow from the executioner's ax than suffering through endless days of lingering torment. Surely Durek could see his way to be that merciful. Athaya wished she could think of something to say to him, but he had already accepted his fate even if she could not. Perhaps trying to infuse him with false hope would only make things worse.

"Can you hear me?" His voice was nearly gone, and Athaya had to strain to hear him.

She blinked a tear from her eye. "Yes."

"Don't do it, Athaya," he said, fighting to force out the words. "Don't give in to him."

"But what choice do I have? There's no hope for any of us if I refuse."

"You can't. You can't give away your gift."

"But if Durek lets me go, then maybe I can find someone who doesn't want his magic and get my power back. That won't be hard to do in Caithe, you know," she said, her words tumbling out in desperation. "Rhodri tried to tell me I couldn't do that, but he was lying to me, wasn't he? It was all a lie to frighten me . . ."

But to her dismay, Jaren slowly shook his head.

"He wasn't lying, Athaya. If you give away your power, it will only be a matter of days—maybe even hours—before your paths will start to decay. And don't think Rhodri will let you out of his sight until he makes sure you're completely incapable of regaining your magic. You'd be crippled for the rest of your life, Athaya. You'd never be able to use the incredible gift that you were born with."

Jaren stopped, and Athaya watched nervously as he labored for his next breath. Speaking to her was draining all of his strength, but he was determined to go on. "Whatever you do, don't give in to him. Maybe . . . just maybe there will be a chance for you to escape later, even if you have to wait until you're standing right over the executioner's block to do it. It's worth the risk."

Choking down another mouthful of air, Jaren rested his head back against the cold stone wall. "I . . . I'm sorry," he whispered. "I just can't . . . talk anymore . . ."

Athaya bit her lip. Seeing him suffer this way pained her more than she ever thought possible. If only she could be there with him. If only she could wear the crystal herself and give him a few hours of peace.

"I'll try to reach you later," she said softly, and willed the sphere to dissolve. Like frost burned off by the sun, Jaren's image faded from her hands, and the tendrils of fog swirled back into her fingertips. Once again she was alone, no more sure of what to do than she had been before. Athaya paced in tight circles around her cell, too upset to sit still for any length of time. She took a piece of dry bread from her breakfast tray, absently tearing it apart with her fingers while she watched the crumbs fall lazily to the floor like snow.

I can't let Rhodri be another Faltil, she thought. *I can't let him hoard all that power for himself.*

But if she refused him, he could simply find another Lorngeld to assist him with this newest experiment, and she, Tyler, and Jaren would be dead. It was not the thought of her own death that plagued her the most. She was willing to sacrifice herself if need be.

But how can I ask Tyler and Jaren to die with me?

Save yourself, Athaya. No matter what you have to do.

She spent the remainder of the day in black despair. Every few hours the pressure would mount too high, and she would pound the walls in anger without a thought to the ugly purple bruises forming on her hands. No guards came to bring her a midday meal, but she did not care. She couldn't have swallowed a bite of it even if they had.

Counting the hours as best she could, Athaya watched the candle on her bedstand slowly burn down to its socket. Rhodri would be returning soon to hear her answer, and from that moment on, no matter what she did, her life would never be the same. But when the candle burned down, finally sputtering out to die, she felt at peace for the first time that day.

And she had made her decision.

CHAPTER 21

ATHAYA DID NOT HAVE LONG TO WAIT. AS SHE RECLINED on the hard straw pallet, absently molding a warm piece of wax between her fingers, she heard the faint sound of approaching footsteps followed by the low murmur of Rhodri speaking to the guards outside her cell. Shortly thereafter, two sets of footsteps retreated down the corridor, and Rhodri entered the room.

She had never seen him dressed so grandly. A snowy white surplice, intricately embroidered at the edges with gold thread, was elegantly draped over a robe of blood-red silk, rimmed at the hem with black. His head was encased by a three-cornered cap and neckpiece so that only the round oval of his face was left uncovered, and the silver wizard's brooch was pinned to the upturned brim of the cap, centered directly between his eyes. If she did not know otherwise, Athaya would suppose he was a priest clad in his best vestments, preparing to conduct high service.

But he is no priest, Athaya thought bitterly. *And what he wants of me is most unholy.*

"I have dismissed the guards so that we will not be interrupted," he stated. He did not sit, but stood before her with his hands calmly folded into sleeves of his robe like a monk. "Have you made your choice?"

Athaya nodded. "I have."

She got to her feet and wavered slightly, dizzy from what she knew she had to do. Keeping her eyes fixed on him, she tilted her chin up and drew her shoulders back in the best show of strength she could manage.

"I won't do it."

There. She had said it. And it was, without exception, the most difficult thing she'd ever done. But after hours of tortured deliberation, she realized that Jaren had been right. Her magic was too precious a gift to throw away. Without it, she was completely under Rhodri's control. But with it, there was a chance—however small—of escape. And while she could not say the same for Jaren, she was also willing to wager that Durek would not be as harsh with Tyler as he'd threatened. Her oldest brother was often stubborn and narrow-minded, but she had never known him to be pointlessly cruel. Despite her often tempestuous relationship with him, Athaya could not believe that he would destroy one of Kelwyn's most faithful servants simply because she refused to capitulate to his demands. A dangerous bit of bluffing on his part, but one that she was forced to challenge.

And perhaps more than anything else, she knew that to give away her power would break the promise she had made to her father at his funeral, when she vowed to finish the work he'd begun. Her mission would be doomed to failure before it ever began, for how could she possibly be able to persuade anyone that the Lorngeld's gift was a blessing instead of a curse, if she herself was all too willing to give it away?

Rhodri stood motionless for several minutes, as still as the demonic gargoyles carved into the stone above the doors of Saint Adriel's Cathedral. He tried to hide it, but Athaya could see that he was surprised at her response. He had not expected her refusal.

But his disappointment was short-lived. A moment later, he shrugged his shoulders with seeming carelessness. "Well, then," he said, reaching into the folds of his robe. He drew out a large scroll of parchment tied with a red silk ribbon. "I suppose I shall have to deliver this after all."

Athaya felt cold fingers of dread wrap around her heart.

"What is it?"

"Captain Graylen's death warrant," he said, rhythmically

tapping the scroll on the tips of his fingers. "The king has already signed it."

The wizard's face blurred before her eyes. The floor tipped, and she steadied herself against the back of a chair, gripping onto the weathered oak with white fingers. Only seconds ago she was convinced that Durek would never be so severe. *But that was the Durek that I used to know,* she realized with cold finality. *He is acting as a king now and not merely as a king's son. And that makes all the difference.*

"In the event of your refusal, I'm to hand this to the sentries guarding his cell and let them carry out their orders." Rhodri took a step closer and waved the damning scroll in front of her. "Are you sure you wouldn't like to reconsider?"

A host of conflicting emotions brutally battled each other in her mind. Giving away her power would not change the fact that she would be a virtual outcast in Caithe in light of what she'd done to Kelwyn. An order of exile from Durek would see to that. And without her magic, the only other destiny she could follow—her wizardry—would be lost to her forever. *You'd be crippled for the rest of your life,* Jaren had said. *You'd never be able to use the incredible gift you were born with.*

The inherent selfishness of that thought shamed her. Was it fair to sacrifice Tyler's life on the off chance that she might escape from this place and learn to master her power someday? Hedric's words returned with full force, the words she had only recently tried to explain to Archbishop Ventan. *Great magic commands a great price.*

But why must someone else pay? she cried inwardly. *The price . . . it's much too high.*

Expressionless, Rhodri turned to go. "Then I bid you good night," he said, and without hesitation, slipped quietly out of the room.

It wasn't until he was gone that the brutal reality of what she had done struck her with full force. Alone in her cell that afternoon, mulling over Jaren's words, she had convinced herself that she was doing the right thing by not giving in to Rhodri's demands. But the threat was not present at that time, so it was much too easy to ignore the severity of it—like a man who never regrets living beyond his means until the day the merchants come pounding on his door demanding payment. In an instant, all of her reasons for refusing Rhodri's offer seemed meaningless. Wasn't a life more important than her own ability to see visions in a sphere or conjure balls of fire with her hands? Would Kelwyn have wanted her to go to such lengths to secure her own power? She thought not. That would only serve as evidence against her own people, for who else but a Devil's Child would allow people to die so that magic could be saved?

She had been wrong. Just as Tyler had risked his life for her, so should she be willing to give away her most precious possession for him. Knowing he was safe, she could live with the loss of her power. But with his death on her conscience, she knew she could not. Athaya saw nothing noble about her choice now. She saw only the cold face of death. A death that she could prevent with a single word . . .

"Stop! Rhodri, *stop*!"

Athaya bolted for the door, ready to beat it down if she had to, but she was instantly blinded by pain as the binding spells closed in on her, burning like a thousand red-hot irons pressed against the inside of her skull. She gasped and staggered back, clutching her head as if it would burst. Her vision blurred and grew dim, and she balanced precariously on the very edge of consciousness.

"No! No, please, come back!" she cried. "I'll do anything . . ."

Her heart beat wildly inside of her, as if trying to escape from her body just as she had tried to escape from the cell. Her eyes were dry—she was too terrified to cry—and she sank to her knees on the floor, utterly lost.

"Come back," she whispered, rocking back and forth with her face buried in her hands. "Tyler, I'm sorry. Oh God, I'm so sorry."

She never heard the footsteps. The next thing she knew, the door slowly swung open, and Rhodri returned with a glitter of triumph in his eyes. *He never left,* she realized, overwhelmed with hatred. He knew all along what she would do and had waited outside the door to listen to her pleas, probably much amused by them.

"I see you've reconsidered," he said, tucking the condemning piece of parchment back inside his robe. The faint trace of a smile still lingered on his face. "Well then, shall we begin?"

Athaya got up and brushed the dust from her skirts. Her shoulders sagged heavily, and she focused her eyes on the floor, unable to bear the swollen expression of victory on Rhodri's face.

"What do I do?" she asked softly.

With leisurely confidence, Rhodri took the two chairs from the table and set them in the center of the room, facing each other. Before he sat down, he tilted his head to one side and froze for an instant, as if trying to identify a distant sound. He promptly nodded in satisfaction.

"Good. The wards are still active," he said, speaking as much to himself as to Athaya. "I set them around the castle earlier today, just in case Hedric decides to try spying on me again."

He motioned her into one of the chairs, and they sat across from each other with their knees almost touching.

"Clear your mind of thoughts and try to relax. And focus your eyes on this." He motioned to the wizard's brooch pinned to his cap. "The ritual is simple and not at all dangerous. The only difficult part lies in constructing paths for the receiver of magic, as I had to do for your father. But since I already have paths, we can dispense with that element of the ritual." As he spoke, his voice gradually became lyrical and hypnotic, lulling her into complacency.

"I want you to imagine that you are floating, Athaya. Drifting on a cloud. You feel weightless, as if you are under a cloaking spell. Your body no longer has substance. It is fleshless, like a spirit of mist and air . . ."

His words were soothing and seductive, and despite her best efforts, Athaya found herself succumbing to them. Whether it was his magic, or simply the cadence of his voice, she began to feel drowsy, as if she'd just drunk a glass of heady wine.

"Now," he said, "command your sphere to come."

Athaya dropped her gaze from the brooch and raised her hands. *"Volo videre,"* she whispered. In seconds, the thin tendrils of white fog streamed from her fingertips, gently forming themselves into a misty orb. The sphere was clouded and showed no images.

"What should I look for?" she said, conscious that her words carried a flat, dead tone. Although she was careful to keep her eyes on the sphere, she could see the motion of Rhodri's hands as they anxiously wrung together in rapt anticipation.

"Your paths, Athaya. Look for your paths. Don't envision

them with your mind, the way you usually do, but project them into the sphere.''

Athaya did as she was told, and soon the familiar corridors—the ones she had previously seen only in her mind—came into view. She could go wherever she wished in the labyrinth of passageways and wondered for a moment whether it would be possible to work a spell by entering the paths this way. But she decided against it. She was not really in the corridors of magic at all, but only looking at them from a different viewpoint.

''I see them.''

''Now find the one that leads to the light,'' he urged her. ''Follow the paths to your power source. Your inner being.''

Obediently, Athaya searched for a corridor with a glow at the end, like an underground tunnel that leads out onto a sunny plain. While all of the corridors were brighter than before—the natural result of her intense training—only one channeled the direct light of her source, instead of merely reflecting it. She followed the brightest corridor to its end, paused for a moment to take a deep breath, then stepped inside the light.

All of a sudden she was flooded with a thousand different sensations at once. Every emotion she'd ever felt and every thought she'd ever had coursed through her mind in a dazzling panorama. Everything she was and everything she had always wanted to be filled her heart and mind with wrenching emotion. She saw herself as a little girl, wrestling in the dirt with Nicolas; she saw herself as she was now, full of conflict and indecision; and she saw a cloudier vision of herself as an old woman, looking back on a life full of discovery and finally ready to die. The past, the present, and the future were all blended into one, and she felt as if she were living her entire life in a single, intense instant in time.

And then she saw another image taking shape in the sphere. It was the image of a face, hazy at first, but slowly clearing . . .

She widened her eyes in surprise. The face was her own.

It was not a simple mirror image. It was more like the image in the locket Felgin had give her—full of dimension and life. It had the same blue eyes, the same frame of perpetually tangled black hair, the same heavy brows. But the face did not mimic her expressions like a mere reflection, but changed of its own accord. And it gazed out of the sphere with confusion and fear, as if suddenly conscious of an unexpected attack and being without defenses.

"What do you see?" Rhodri asked softly.

"I see my face." Athaya wrinkled her brow. "Only it's not quite mine. It doesn't do what I do . . ."

"Excellent. You're doing well. Now don't take your eyes off the sphere. Keep concentrating."

From the corner of her eyes, Athaya saw him run his tongue hungrily along his lips. Then, curling his fingers inward, Rhodri reached out and set his hands upon the sphere—her sphere. His touch was cold and it chilled her to the very marrow of her bones. As his hands wrapped around the delicate orb, she felt his icy presence all around her and through her, as if his essence had penetrated her skin and blood.

The face in the sphere was suddenly altered. The eyes in the image gazed directly into her own eyes, filled with surprise and pain, like a rejected child. Although she could hear nothing, Athaya saw the lips of the image speaking to her, rapidly pleading with her to stop.

"Say the words, Athaya," Rhodri prompted her, his voice trembling with excitement. "Repeat them after me. *Arcanum arcanorum.*"

Ignoring the image, Athaya obeyed. *"Arcanum arcanorum."*

"Vultus est index animi."

"Vultus est index animi."

The moment she spoke that last word, Athaya saw the image in the sphere flinch in sudden pain. The eyes—her eyes—were filled with profound sadness and loss, a black hopelessness that Athaya wished never to see in another pair of eyes again. Then, as if overcome with sleepiness, they closed in quiet resignation. Slowly, the image in the sphere died away, and her face dissolved before her eyes.

Distantly, she heard Rhodri commanding the sphere to disperse. As the sphere faded, Athaya felt a sharp, tugging sensation, as if something deep inside of her was being forcefully wrenched out. She let out a low moan, but the pain was over quickly. She watched with morbid fascination as the tendrils of fog from the sphere, instead of returning to her own hands, retreated into Rhodri's fingertips. The sphere was now his. And so was her magic.

And so is my soul.

Athaya slumped forward, cradling her head in her arms. She was drained of strength and felt dizzy and ill. But worst of all, she felt empty. Completely, horribly empty, like a skeleton with no flesh. A hollow shell of what she had been.

Tentatively, she raised her eyes and saw that Rhodri had changed as well. But where she had given away her strength, he had gained it. He hugged himself, as if warming his body over a fire. Throwing back his head, he laughed aloud, exulting in his newfound power. His breathing quickened, as if he were poised on the verge of release, and then he laughed again—a wild, uncontrolled laugh—giddy with excitement like a young knight at his first tournament. His eyes were glazed, like sapphires dipped in milk, and he stared straight ahead with a madman's fanatical intensity.

"Now I must test it," he said. His words were slightly slurred, as if he were rousing himself from a drunken stupor. He got to his feet, wavering slightly on unsteady legs.

"Volo habere lux!" he commanded, snapping his fingers to summon a witchlight. With a blinding flash of light, a fireball appeared between his fingers, crackling softly as it burned. Athaya cupped her palm over her mouth in amazement. The witchlight was nearly the size of a man's head and it lit up the dingy little cell like a hundred candles, bathing both of them in harsh, reddish light.

"Such strength. Such power," he mused, commanding the witchlight to hover above them. He was entranced by his creation and pressed his palms together as if about to offer prayers to it.

Disgusted, Athaya looked away. She could not bear to see him gloat over his power—her power—that way. Didn't she have a small trace of it left? Concentrating intensely, Athaya found she could still visualize the corridors of her paths in her mind's eye. They were not as brightly lit as before and were gradually growing darker. Finding the simple spell for witchlights, she tentatively extended her hand. Nervously, she snapped her fingers, waiting to see if the familiar ball of light would come at her command.

But her hand remained empty. Her power was gone.

After another few minutes of gazing at the witchlight with worshipful adoration, Rhodri's initial rush of excitement receded. Sobered, he relaxed into a darkly calm acceptance of his own strength. He turned away from his creation and fixed his eyes dangerously on her. The red glow from the magic fire caused tiny licks of fire to dance in the piercing blue orbs.

"And now, your Highness, there is the matter of what shall be done with you."

Athaya felt her stomach drop. "Me? But I thought . . ."

"Did you really think I'd let you simply walk away?" he said, laughing with delight. "You surprise me. I didn't think you were quite so naive."

"But Durek said . . . he promised . . ."

Rhodri clamped one hand around her wrist and pulled her to her feet. His physical strength seemed to have doubled, as had his magic. "Promises can be broken, Athaya. Even by kings. Your brother never intended to let you leave this place alive. How could he, after what you've done? And fortunately, I took the precaution of telling him how dangerous this ritual was." The wizard's lips curled up in a slow, deliberate smile. "After all, who's to tell him otherwise? I told him that the power transfer might be fatal, but he told me to go ahead. Putting it bluntly, he'd much rather see your blood on my hands than his."

All traces of amusement vanished from Rhodri's face as he tightened his grip on her. "I'm not going to let you go on being a thorn in my side, Athaya. You'd run straight to Hedric with this tale, and he could make trouble for me with the Circle. I won't have that. And once I've dealt with you, I'll need to permanently silence your friend Jaren. Perhaps he can be persuaded to part with his magic as well," he added, narrowing his eyes. "Before I kill him, of course."

Athaya clenched her teeth so hard she thought they would shatter. "You never planned to let any of us go, did you? Not me, not Jaren—and I'll wager that the moment you left this room you were going to deliver that warrant for Tyler as well."

Rhodri smiled knowingly, but just as he was about to speak, Athaya felt something snap inside of her. It was too much. Nothing mattered now—she could take no more of this. Blinded with outrage, she threw herself against him and tried to struggle out of his grasp, kicking him furiously and showering him with curses. She knew it was a useless fight—she had been a weak enough opponent with her little-trained power, much less without it—and Rhodri surpassed her in physical strength. Then, before she knew what was happening, she felt her feet leave the floor as Rhodri swung her around by the arms. Her eyes widened with fear as she realized what he was about to do. In one fluid motion, he forced her back against the door to the cell, pushing her into the realm of his binding spells with all his might.

The hot blades of pain bit into her skull with agonizing intensity. Even with her eyes tightly closed she could see the fire from inside, slowly tearing her apart from within and turning her flesh to black. Her ears rang with the echoes of a high-pitched scream, and only later did she realize it had been her own. She opened her eyes so as not to see the fire, but Rhodri's face loomed before her, filling her entire field of vision. Unaffected by his own spell, he calmly watched her writhing in his grasp as he rigidly held her shoulders back against the door, observing her every movement with cool, detached interest.

Too weak to struggle against him any more, she felt herself slipping away into dark unconsciousness. Rhodri's face swam before her eyes, but the image grew dimmer and dimmer, as if someone were slowly extinguishing the light in the cell. Unable to withstand the stabbing pain of the binding spell any longer, her head spun with sickening dizziness and her knees buckled under her. Only Rhodri's viselike grip held her upright, keeping her from tumbling to the floor at his feet.

I'm sorry, Tyler, her mind cried out. *I'm sorry, Jaren. I tried. I tried but I failed . . .*

But just as the blackness closed in, Rhodri let out a sharp gasp of surprise and suddenly released her. Athaya plummeted forward on her knees at his feet as he staggered back, his face contorted into an expression of confused terror.

"No! No, this can't be!" he said, shaking his head wildly. "It has to work. It has to . . . I was sure . . ." He pointed an accusing finger at her. "Your power is cursed! You did this! You knew . . ."

He tried to go on, but no words came. He could only make half-formed choking sounds, like a drowning man. Doubling over in pain, he clutched at his heart, afraid it was about to stop. Athaya saw the skin bubble on his hands as if something inside of him was trying to escape, and his whole body was racked with violent spasms, like a puppet controlled by some cruel, invisible master.

"Take it back" he choked out as he forced himself upright. You must . . ."

Holding his trembling hands out, he desperately commanded his sphere to come. When at first it failed to appear, he spoke the words again, pleading with his power—and hers—to obey him.

Athaya stared at him in mute horror. Tiny red lines coursed across his hands, as if the body within was rapidly expanding, breaking the skin apart. And then she saw the sphere begin to come, as delicate strands of white mist weaved their way from his fingertips. Rhodri's breathing grew more frantic as he waited for the unwilling orb to form, and it did so with agonizing slowness, fighting against him. But the sphere gradually obeyed and soon rested precariously in his grasp.

"Quickly," he urged her, using all his strength to sustain the sphere. "Take it!"

Moving a step closer, she extended her hands toward the magic orb. But just as her fingers were about to touch it, the white sphere suddenly flushed red, like flesh that had been pierced and gushed blood from the wound. Athaya drew back in shock at the bloody globe, afraid to put her hands upon it. And Rhodri stared at the thing in his hands with unholy fear, his eyes round with terror.

And then he threw his head back and let out a piercing scream. Athaya covered her ears, futilely trying to block out the tortured cry that resounded to the very center of her brain. But before she could look away, the forces within him erupted and the wizard's body shattered, showering the room in an explosion of torn flesh and splintered bones.

Clapping her palm over her mouth, Athaya jerked her face away, trying desperately not to retch. But it was no use. While a hot river of blood flowed across the floor, staining her skirts and shoes bright red, she doubled over and convulsed, emptying her stomach of what little it contained.

It took several minutes before Athaya found the strength to move. Although she knelt in a pool of congealing blood, she did not yet have the power to get to her feet. As she gasped for breath, the stench of flesh and waste overwhelmed her, making her retch again, but her stomach was empty and spilled out nothing but sour-smelling air. Knowing she had to gain control of herself, she willed herself to relax and forced herself to choke down the stifling air.

Only then, when her head began to clear, did she realize that the room was cloaked in shadows. The brilliant witchlight Rhodri had so adored was gone, and the room was illuminated only by the glow of torches quietly burning from their sockets near the door.

It was dark, but not dark enough to block out the grisly sight surrounding her. She tried not to look but no matter where she focused her eyes she could not avoid it. All four walls were stained bright red, and unrecognizable fragments of bone and tissue were scattered across the floor. Athaya's hair and clothes were likewise drenched with blood, and bits of drying flesh stubbornly clung to her gown like thistles. Only once did her gaze wander to the center of the room and fall upon the mass of formless flesh that had been Rhodri. But when she saw the fragments of his skull peppering the floor like broken pieces of pottery and the single eye that peered lifelessly out from under the silver wizard's brooch, she let out a cry of horror and swiftly turned away.

And then, next to her feet, she saw a battered scroll. The once-white parchment was now deep red, matching the color of the ribbon which bound it. With fierce determination, Athaya picked up the warrant and methodically crushed it between her fingers until it dissolved into nothingness.

Feeling closer to fainting than she ever had in her life, she crawled across the floor and rested her weight against the door to her cell. Her limbs felt heavy and obeyed her grudgingly, as if her blood had begun to harden in her veins, like cooling wax.

Athaya knew that when the guards came back and saw what had happened, no one would have any doubts as to whether her power was dangerous. They would assume she had brutally killed Rhodri, and Durek would dispatch her without hesitation. The only question was whether he would kill her first, or wait until after he'd ridded himself of Tyler and Jaren.

There was precious little time. She had no idea when Rhodri had instructed the guards to return. And when they came back and opened the door . . .

The door . . .

Wheeling around sharply, Athaya realized that the iron-studded door no longer gave her pain. She ran her fingers across the rough wood in amazement. The binding spells were gone— broken the instant their creator was dead. That was why the witchlight had gone out . . .

Suddenly she was infused with hope. If Rhodri's magic dissolved upon his death, then perhaps her power had returned to her!

With unexpected energy, she scrambled to her feet and held her palm over the iron lock. Just as Jaren had taught her during her intense days of training, she sought out the spell in her paths. The corridors were even darker now, and she found it difficult to see where she was going. It took longer than it should have, but she eventually found the proper path and concentrated as hard as she could on visualizing the lock mechanism in her mind. With a forceful command, she willed it to open.

She listened with rapt attention, waiting to hear the smooth sound of the iron bolt sliding back. She waited, but heard nothing. Trying to fight off the panic rising within her, she gave the command again, this time more angrily. But the bolt remained solidly in place. Biting her lip in desperation, she gripped the doorlatch and tugged on it, but it would not budge.

Rhodri was gone and he had taken her power with him.

Closing her eyes in despair, Athaya sank to her knees in a puddle of blood and pressed her face against the door, her hand still hovering futilely over the lock.

"Oh God, if you're really there, then help me," she choked out through her tears. "Please, *please* help me."

CHAPTER 22

✖✖

ATHAYA DREW BACK WITH A START WHEN SHE HEARD the iron bolt snap to one side. For one ecstatic moment, she thought she had tripped the lock herself—the power given to her in answer to her prayers. But she did not entertain that notion for long. A more ominous and likely explanation quickly presented itself.

The guards, she thought, fending off a rush of panic. *They've come back.*

She jumped to one side, quickly scanning the room for something—anything—that she could use as a weapon. Perhaps if there was only one soldier, she could take him by surprise and wrest his dagger away. And she would tell him to look at what she'd done to Rhodri and warn him that the same fate would be his if he didn't obey her. Choking back the bile in her throat, she snatched up a slender piece of bone with a pointed tip that looked as if it had once been part of Rhodri's leg. She flattened herself against the wall, clutching the sticky bone in her hand, and listened to her heart pounding wildly as the heavy oak door slowly swung open.

A solitary, shadowed figure stepped tentatively into the room. Athaya raised the bone, prepared to strike. But a closer look revealed that the man was not one of the guards at all. He wore no crimson uniform, and a bracelet of ugly red welts surrounded both his wrists.

"Jaren!" she cried. The weapon slipped from her fingers as she rushed to him, throwing her arms around his neck. Tears of relief trickled down her cheeks. "Thank God you're here. Are you all right?"

She felt his muscles stiffen as he held her, and she drew back a step. His face went white as he took in the scene before him, quickly averting his eyes from the gobbets of flesh spattered throughout the room.

"My God, Athaya," he said, shrinking away from her. "What have you *done*?" His eyes were filled with disbelieving horror as he stared at her own bloodied appearance and at the scrap of bone resting at her feet.

"*I* didn't do this," she answered quickly, desperate to convince him. "Please believe me. It just . . . happened." Nervously, she tried to work the dried blood from her hands. "Rhodri did this to himself."

Jaren braced himself against the wall, trying not to be ill. He set one hand on her shoulder and nodded weakly. "I believe you."

It was only then that Athaya realized Jaren looked almost as bad as she did. His hair was matted and tangled like dirty straw, and his eyes were ringed by black circles of exhaustion. And every time he moved she saw him wince from the strain, as if every muscle in his body was weak from disuse. The corbal had definitely taken its toll.

"How did you get here? I thought the crystal—"

"I suspected that Rhodri was dead when the witchlight he left in my cell suddenly went out. Without the light, the corbal lost most if its power. It hurt like the Devil to use it, but I had enough magic left to snap open my manacles and trip the lock on the cell door. And I stamped that damned crystal into powder before I left," he added with vengeful finality.

Athaya breathed a sigh of relief. At least that was one less thing to worry about.

"I jumped the guard outside my cell and made him tell me where you were," Jaren continued. "Needless to say, he was surprised to see me. But there's no need to worry about him. He's taking a little nap at the moment. In my cell."

Athaya rested her head on his shoulder. "I'm glad you're safe."

"Only temporarily, I'm afraid." He glanced down the corridor to make sure it was still empty. "The guards could be back any minute. Quick—put us under a cloaking spell so we can get out of here."

A blaze of white-hot fear shot through her. "But I can't—"

"We don't have time to argue about this, Athaya. I used up what little strength I had putting that guard to sleep. I don't have enough power left to cloak myself, much less both of us."

"No, I mean I really can't," she said, her voice fading away. "You don't understand. I gave it to him. That's what killed him." She lowered her eyes, unable to meet Jaren's questioning gaze. "I gave away my power."

Jaren fell back against the wall for support, stunned into silence. He stared blankly ahead for a long time, deep in thought, as if hoping that if he only waited long enough, an answer would come to him.

"Jaren, I'm sorry. But he had a warrant for Tyler's execution. I just couldn't . . ." Her words trailed off. It was too late for excuses. It was done, and nothing she could say or do would change that.

Shadows from the torchlight danced on Jaren's face, but he didn't bother to blink. His forehead was lined with concentration as he tried to think of what to do next and came up with nothing. After a time he looked up in silent petition, half hoping a voice from above would offer some advice, but then he sighed and dropped his eyes. He was not angry with her—only profoundly frustrated that he could not help. When at last he spoke, his voice was so low that Athaya barely heard him.

"If I had any power left, I'd give it to you. Your gift . . . it's just too great to waste."

The declaration startled her, and her eyes went wide. How could he even think such a thing? Moments later, however, she reminded herself that he was too battered and tired to be completely rational. At this point, it did seem as if only something unthinkable would get them safely away from the dungeons. But once the shock of his words had faded, she felt deeply touched; the offer alone showed how much he was willing to give up for her. Unfortunately, even had his magic been at full strength, it was an offer she never could have accepted.

She brushed a greasy lock of hair from her face. "Don't say that, Jaren. More than anything, what happened here proves that the rite is nothing to meddle with. You taught me well enough to be certain of that."

Athaya held her hands out, palms up, gazing at them like a physician suddenly left helpless to heal. "I just can't believe it's gone. It's funny, but I don't feel the same emptiness I did right after the ritual was over."

"Tell me about the ritual," Jaren said with a faint spark of hope. "Maybe there's something about it we're missing. There's got to be," he added, rubbing his eyes exhaustedly. "It's the only chance we've got."

Athaya went over every detail, from the positions she and Rhodri had been sitting in, to the exact words they had spoken. She felt her skin crawl as she reached the end of her tale, explaining how Rhodri had died, but Jaren drank in every word with quiet intensity, like a schoolboy desperately trying to memorize his lessons an hour before the test.

"Once it was over, I felt hollow and dead," she concluded, remembering how her own image had vanished in the sphere. "I felt as if my soul had been torn out of me."

"You can never give that away," he assured her. But still he frowned and rubbed at his chin. Something about her story was nagging at him—something obvious that he just couldn't pin down. "Wait, go over that last part again. You saw your paths in the sphere, but then you touched your source? The light?"

"Yes. Right before I saw my own image."

Jaren rubbed his chin a while longer, but then drew in a sharp gasp. Suddenly he wheeled around and gripped her shoulders. "Go back," he said urgently. "Quickly, while there's still time."

"But I can't conjure a sphere—"

"No, not in your sphere. In your mind. Touch the source directly this time. It might give us a clue."

"A clue to what?" Athaya asked, shaking her head in bewilderment.

"Hedric says that power can be transferred but never created. That could also mean that power can never truly be lost. Not as long as you're alive. Maybe you just need to find out where it is."

Athaya had to grant that Jaren knew far more of Hedric's teachings that she did, but didn't want to fuel her hopes too much. His solution sounded far too simple. But time was short, and instead of asking questions or arguing, she sat down on one of the crude chairs and took a few deep breaths before entering her paths.

The labyrinth of corridors was darker now, like a hall where the candles were slowly going out one by one. Had she waited much longer, she doubted she would have been able to make her way through the caverns at all. But the source glowed as brightly as before, and in the contrasting darkness, it was easier to find the path leading to it. As she approached the source, she felt her limbs begin to tingle, but she didn't know if it was from anticipation or dread. She was drawing close to something powerful, but to what, she did not know.

Bracing herself, she stepped into the light.

The onslaught of raw power struck like a blow. Gripped by a rush of pleasure, she suddenly felt alive and full of strength. Energy flowed through her veins, pulsating with wondrousness. Now she knew why Rhodri had exulted when he first absorbed her power—the feelings overwhelmed her, and she could not imagine what they would be like doubled in intensity. In an instant, she was renewed, like a river of pure spring water flowing over parched earth. She threw her head back and drank in the magic like sweet wine, letting its power permeate every fiber of her being as it gave her a second birth.

Momentarily stunned, she couldn't speak right away, but the look of amazed triumph in her eyes told Jaren all he needed to know.

"It was there all the time," he whispered, no less surprised than Athaya to learn that her power had returned. "You only had to look deep enough inside yourself to find it."

Yes, the solution had been a simple one, but one Athaya found quietly awesome. She had the power to regain her magic all along, but might never have found the key. When her attempt to unlock her cell had failed, she did not try another spell and probably would not have thought to enter her paths again. She had been on the right trail, but simply didn't go far enough. In a way, that did not surprise her. As long as she could remember, she had been afraid of looking too deep inside herself; afraid of finding out something she didn't want to know. But her center— her soul—was where the real answers were, with all their mix of pain and reward, and if she only lived on the surface, never probing her own mind and thoughts, then she was not really living at all.

She got up slowly, feeling giddy and unbalanced. When she took a step, she stumbled, as if she'd stood up too fast after drinking too much wine.

"I'm not going to have to carry you out of here, am I?" Jaren asked, forcing a smile.

"No, I'm fine. I just wasn't expecting it to hit me that hard."

Once Jaren saw that she could walk without help, he turned his attention to their next problem. "Do you know where they're holding Tyler?"

Athaya nodded briskly. "I was spying on Durek with my sphere yesterday when he told the guards to lock him in the cell next to yours. He must still be there."

"I don't think so," Jaren replied with a worried frown. "Whoever was in that cell was taken out early this morning."

"Durek must have moved him. But where?" Athaya's mind raced as she tried to piece together the puzzle as quickly as she could. An instant later, her eyes lit up. "The gatehouse tower," she said, snapping her fingers. "Since a death warrant was already signed for him, he'd be in the tower's holding cell awaiting execution."

"Then let's go. And don't forget the cloaking spell."

With all the power at her disposal, Athaya closed her eyes and fixed her mind on the desire for invisibility. Her paths were well lit now, not cloaked in shadows as before, and she was able to locate the spell without difficulty. And as she passed through the caverns, she was filled with happiness at knowing her magic had been restored to her. Until she had suffered its loss, she never realized how much it meant to her.

"*Occulta nos,*" she said, commanding a cloak to shield them from sight. The familiar sensation of weightlessness came over her, and her feet seemed to hover just above the floor. In moments, they both shimmered out of sight, dissolving into nothingness like a vision sphere.

"Just don't go running off on me," Jaren cautioned her. "I need to keep in physical contact with you to stay covered by the spell."

Keeping a tight hold on his hand, Athaya led the way down the twisting maze of underground passages. The low-ceilinged corridors were dark and blackened with soot, and only the dim

glow from the scattered rushlights allowed them to see where
they were going. Every so often they would pass a cell flanked
by bored-looking guardsmen and would take extra care to make
no sound as they crept by, unseen. The main entrance to the
dungeon was one level above them and led down to the cata-
comb of cells by means of a narrow, spiral staircase.

"Let's just hope nobody's on the way down," Jaren whispered dryly, peering up at the series of steep limestone steps
that wound their way upward, out of sight.

"Bite your tongue," Athaya muttered under her breath.

Moving quickly, they reached the top of the staircase without
incident, pausing only once when a pebble slid out of place and
clattered to the base of the steps. After a few anxious moments,
Athaya realized that the echo had not drawn any attention and,
with a sigh of relief, clambered up the rest of the steps. They
soon found themselves in a wider passageway leading to the
main entrance. The gateway leading out to the castle's courtyard
was nearby, and the hall was drafty and cold. Turning a sharp
corner, Athaya saw the locked iron gates that led out to the
courtyard, and beside them, a pair of burgundy-clad soldiers in
gold-rimmed helmets spoke in low tones as they leaned casually
against the wall. The older of the two held a circular key ring
and twirled it absently around his gloved finger as he laughed at
whatever amusing story his younger companion had just finished
telling him.

Athaya stepped quietly behind the younger man and reached
out to him with her mind. His thoughts were not on his work at
all. He was completely preoccupied with what time his round
of duty was over and of the voluptuous kitchen maid he would
be meeting later that night behind the barracks. Athaya felt her
cheeks grow warm, self-conscious of eavesdropping on what the
man assumed were private thoughts.

Just as Jaren had done to her on the night of her father's death,
Athaya whispered in the man's mind, telling him how very tired
he was and compelling him to sleep. The effect was almost
instantaneous. In seconds, his eyelids began to grow heavy, and
his shoulders drooped with exhaustion.

"Yeah, I'm tired myself," the second man said casually, stifling a yawn.

Overcome with drowsiness, the first man sat down on a carved
stone bench near the gates and rubbed his eyes. Drawing closer,

Athaya touched her fingertip to his forehead and willed him into unconsciousness. He went limp immediately, and she and Jaren propped him up against the wall. But as they shifted his weight so that he wouldn't slide off onto the ground, Jaren lost contact with her for a moment and suddenly shimmered into view in front of the other guard.

"Where in the—"

Astonished, the man fumbled for his sword, his eyes round with shock. Athaya leaped over and clapped a hand over his mouth while Jaren pinned his arms behind him and wrested the blade from his hand.

"Quick, Athaya," Jaren urged her, narrowly averting a blow to his stomach from his captive's elbow. "This one's strong as hell."

Without taking time to be subtle, she forced her way into the man's mind and willed him to sleep. It took longer to subdue him than it had the first man, he being already alerted to her presence, and she prayed the sounds of their scuffling feet would not summon any curious reinforcements. But her spell was too powerful for him, and with one final burst of resistance, his eyelids fluttered and closed, and Jaren lowered him to the ground, quickly relieving him of his key ring.

Jaren had the gates open in a flash and hustled Athaya through before anyone who might happen to be in the courtyard at this late hour suddenly saw the door open and close entirely of its own accord.

"Sleep well," Jaren whispered, dropping the keys softly in the older man's lap. Then, as an afterthought he quickly unclasped the cloaks around the two men's shoulders and handed one of them to her. "We'll need these," he said, shivering from the chill.

Athaya threw the heavy wool cloak around her shoulders, and the moment it touched her, it vanished into invisibility under her spell. Jaren winked into view only for a second as he donned his own cloak, then quietly disappeared again the moment he clasped her hand.

She pointed across the courtyard toward the south. "Come on. The gatehouse is this way."

Closing the gate noiselessly behind them, Athaya led the way toward the massive gatehouse built around the main entrance to Delfar on the opposite side from the dungeon keep. Without having to worry about being seen, she and Jaren walked directly across the open courtyard, taking the fastest route rather than taking the time to skirt around the curtain walls.

Athaya was grateful for the woolen cloak. The night was cold, and a brisk wind blew in from the western sea. Withered, vagrant leaves skidded across the gravel, making dry, crackling sounds as the wind propelled them into darkened corners. Above them, a dazzling full moon occasionally peeked out from the clouds scudding across the sky, one moment pouring silver light over the limestone towers, and the next, bathing them in shadows. The battlements were fairly deserted, and only once did Athaya see a pair of soldiers walk lazily along the parapet, their halberds resting against their shoulders.

"Once we're out of here, we'll need provisions and horses," she whispered, wondering exactly how they would go about getting either one without any money. Her hand went reluctantly to the silver locket still tucked inside her homespun gown, and she slowly drew it out into view. "I suppose I could sell this," she said wistfully, knowing that it was probably the only thing of value they possessed between them.

Jaren patted her arm reassuringly. "We'll worry about that when the time comes. Who knows? Maybe Tyler will have something we can sell instead."

Athaya nodded, hoping he was right. Felgin's gift was dear to her, but she might have no choice other than to part with it. But then she thought of something that cheered her. How could she even think of selling a locket with a magic spell inside? Certainly that would be impossible—not to mention dangerous—in Caithe. The existence of such an object, especially one with Tyler's own image inside, would inevitably alert Durek to the direction in which she had fled. With a smile, she ran her fingers over the side of the locket and snapped it open.

Athaya's blood turned to ice. The image was gone.

"What's the matter?" Jaren said, giving her arm a tug. "Why are you stopping?"

Stunned, she held up the locket. "It's gone, Jaren," she said, her voice breaking. "Tyler's image . . ."

Filled with bitter dread, Athaya slowly raised her eyes toward the gatehouse looming before them, gazing at the two towers that flanked the portcullis on either side. The wind pushed the clouds to the east, and a white blanket of moonlight coated the courtyard. First the left tower was bathed in silver, and then, as the clouds sailed across the sky to illuminate the other, the moonlight struck against the base of the slender iron pike atop the tower. And on the top of the pike, still cloaked in shadow, was a circular orb . . .

And as the silver light crept upward, the orb impaled on the pike was revealed, and its lifeless eyes stared out across the city of Delfarham, forever blinded.

"TYLER!"

Athaya's heart stopped and everything went black before her eyes. Jaren's hand quickly clamped down over her mouth, forcing her into silence, and turned her away from the grisly sight.

"Oh God, oh God, oh God . . . " she moaned, sinking to her knees at Jaren's feet. Her breath was choking her, and she felt dizzy and sick. She buried her face in her palms as she rocked back and forth, the gravel cutting into her knees, flooded with loss and emptiness more awful, more desolate than she had ever experienced in her life. Not even when she saw her father take his last breath did she ever feel such despair. And nothing . . . nothing would ever make it go away.

Suddenly Jaren's voice cut into her consciousness, edged with fright. "Athaya, your cloaking spell—it's not working!"

Taking her firmly by the arm, he yanked her to her feet and hustled her across the open courtyard into the dark shadows at the base of the tower. Skirting the walls, he pulled her into the deserted blacksmith's shop at the end of the barracks, stumbling over the discarded tongs and broken blades scattered on the packed earth floor. There, in the empty darkness, surrounded by the smell of burnt wood, he let her release her muffled sobs, while above them he heard the heavy footsteps of the guards on the battlements, alerted by Athaya's cry, but unable to detect from where it had come.

Folding her inside his arms, Jaren stroked her hair, futilely trying to comfort her. "I'm sorry, Athaya. I'm so sorry . . ."

"The order had already been carried out," she said, shaking her head. "Rhodri knew it all along. Even before he made me the offer. I did it all for nothing . . ."

He let her choke out a few more sobs before he stepped back and brushed the tears from her cheeks. In the distance, he could hear the low murmur of voices from the puzzled guards on the battlements, and wondered how long it would take before they searched the deserted shop. "Athaya, I know this sounds cruel, but you don't have time to grieve for him now. You can fall apart later, but please—right now you've got to get us out of here."

"I don't care," she moaned. She leaned her weight against him, unable to stand on her own. "I don't care what happens to me anymore."

"Athaya, you can't come this far only to give up now—"

"Why not?" she lashed back in furious despair. "What's the point? What's the point of anything?"

He gripped her by the shoulders and gazed piercingly into her eyes. "You have to save yourself. *That* is the whole point—I've told you that all along. If you won't do it for yourself, and if you won't do it for everyone else in Caithe who needs you, then do it for me. I've gone through hell to make sure you got back to Reyka safely and I'm not giving up on you now."

"But—"

"How many more people's lives have to be torn apart this way, Athaya?" he went on, fueled with intensity. "How many more untrained wizards are going to lash out and kill by mistake or see the ones they love die trying to protect them? I know it hurts, Athaya, and I wish I didn't have to be telling you this now, but there's simply no other way. It's not just your personal tragedy. This happens to someone in Caithe every day. You have to go on. You have to make this lunacy *stop*!"

She pushed him away roughly. "Don't give me any more of your noble speeches, Jaren, I'm *sick* of them!"

"If you abandon yourself, then you're abandoning every single one of the Lorngeld in your country. How can you walk away from their cause now? Tyler's already died for it. How can you forsake his memory that way?"

"That's not fair, Jaren," she said, glaring at him with contempt.

"Maybe not. But it's true. He never would have wanted you to give up like this. He'd want you to go on and fight and use the gift you were given."

Tyler's words haunted her. *I want you to be everything you were born to be, Athaya. If you have magic, it can't possibly be evil.* He had believed in her. And Tyler always risked his life for what he believed in. And she had repaid him with death.

"And your father died for the Lorngeld, too. He wanted to prove that magic wasn't evil and he tried to do it. It wasn't his fault that Rhodri didn't warn him about the dangers of taking on such power. He believed in the divinity of magic. And he was right—only he never got a chance to prove it. But you have that chance, Athaya. You can prove it to all of them."

Athaya wanted to protest—she wanted to cry out that it was simply too much, that she could never succeed in such a hopeless task. She wanted to run away from Jaren and his speeches and let the guards arrest her and put an end to her pain with one swift stroke of a blade. She wanted to, but she could not. Something in the very center of her soul told her that Jaren was right. And with this realization, and without knowing from whence it came, she was infused with strength—an inhuman strength born out of the depths of agony.

Slowly, as her breathing calmed, the despair in her heart was transformed to fiery resolve. Jaren was telling her what she should have already known. Tyler would never want her to give up. And neither, she realized, would her father. They would want her to carry on and bring the wonders of magic to the Lorngeld who were born to it, but who were denied their gift by a Church that feared it. And if that cause had already claimed both of their lives, then it was vital enough for her to dedicate herself to, body and soul. To do anything else would be to let their deaths be in vain—shallow and meaningless, and soon to be forgotten in the unending passage of time.

She met Jaren's gaze with fierce determination. "Come on. Let's go."

Relieved and grateful, he embraced her, and she could feel the gladness in his gentle touch. Then he drew back and tentatively poked his head out of the doorway to scan to courtyard.

"We've got to find a way out of this place before anyone finds out we've escaped. And the portcullis is down on the main gate. Any ideas?"

Athaya was just about to speak, but her words were abruptly cut off by the shrill sound of a warning horn splitting the chill night air. Alerted to danger, the soldiers patrolling the battlements snapped into action and clattered down the stone steps leading into the courtyard, responding to the call.

Athaya and Jaren exchanged a look of pure terror.

"Rhodri," she whispered urgently. "They found him."

CHAPTER 23

WITH ONE SWEEPING GESTURE, ATHAYA SUMMONED her cloaking spell, and she and Jaren quickly vanished from sight. They crept forward with apprehension, watching the red-liveried guardsmen cluster around the entrance to the dungeons like wasps around their nest. A chorus of angry voices and sharply delivered commands sounded clearly in the quiet of the night, and seconds later, the men dispersed with weapons drawn to begin their search. Although she knew they could not be seen, Athaya instinctively shrank back from the open doorway to the shadows of the blacksmith's shop.

"Some of the men have mirrors with them," she said worriedly. "They're looking for us, all right."

She heard Jaren's urgent voice next to her. "Then how are we going to—"

"Shh—listen."

Just outside the door, skimming the walls nearby, Athaya heard the faint shuffle of footsteps on the gravel. They came cautiously, as if aware of the crunching sound they made against the stones. Their rhythm slowed as they approached the door to the shop, and with a slow intake of breath, Athaya grasped Jaren's hand more tightly in hers, conscious of the slick moisture on both their palms.

Someone's coming, she told him with her thoughts, never

stopping to wonder whether he'd be able to hear her with his power virtually drained away. *Don't move. Don't even breathe if you don't have to.*

The moonlight spilling into the shop was abruptly blocked off as a cloaked figure crossed the doorway, his slender body bathed in shadows. On his belt, still sheathed, was a silver-hilted dagger. But Athaya had no time to worry about the dangers of the blade. In his other hand he carried a round hand mirror with a delicately sculpted handle—a mirror that Athaya thought looked strangely familiar. And she quickly realized why. It was Cecile's.

Durek . . .

Athaya's limbs went still as stone. She knew that to make the slightest sound would alert him to her presence, but to stay would mean risking discovery. Then, before Athaya knew what was happening, he tilted the mirror on an angle, and she saw a glaring flash as it reflected moonlight in her face. With lightning speed, he bolted into the shop and snatched her by the arm before she had a chance to flee.

"Let go of her!" Jaren whispered, throwing his weight against her attacker.

Unprepared for the invisible blow, the man was immediately brought down, landing with a thump on the packed earth floor. The mirror in his hand broke into shards as it fell from his grasp, and the sharp-edged pieces of glass scattered across the ground like diamonds against black velvet. Jaren flickered into view the moment he broke the physical contact with her, and straddled the intruder, pinning him down. He grabbed the dagger from the man's belt and pressed it firmly to his throat.

"Ouch—stop it!" the man pleaded, squirming under Jaren's weight. He did not try to fight back. "Listen! For God's sake, Athaya, it's *me*!"

Athaya gasped with a warm rush of relief. The voice was not Durek's.

"Nicolas!" she cried softly. "Jaren, quick—let him go."

Jaren hastily scrambled to his feet, muttering an apology to the prince as he offered the dagger back to its owner. Unnerved at having been attacked so unexpectedly, Nicolas accepted the blade with hesitation, as if afraid it might be hot to the touch. He sheathed it securely and proceeded to brush the dirt and soot from the front of his doublet.

"Athaya?" he said with a puzzled frown. "Where are you?"

"I'm right next to you."

He swallowed nervously. "Could you . . . reappear or something? I can hear your voice but . . . it's eerie."

"All right—but if I hear anyone coming, don't be surprised if I disappear again." She shimmered into sight as her brother watched with wide-eyed fascination. "Oh, Nicolas, you don't know how glad I am to see you. How did you find us?"

"The same way everyone else is trying to find you," he replied, motioning to the broken mirror. Despite the cold night, beads of sweat dotted his forehead, and he wiped them away with the back of his hand. "I've been going crazy all night long trying to figure out a way to get you out of that dungeon, especially after I found out that Rhodri had gone to see you. He and Durek have been damned secretive about something all day, but I didn't know what they were up to until about an hour ago when I overheard Durek telling Archbishop Ventan about some sort of dangerous ritual that would take away your power. That's when I started getting desperate. I made up my mind to break you out of there tonight, even if I had to kill the guards to do it." Nicolas smiled wryly. "Imagine my surprise when I got there and found the two of them sleeping like babies."

"It's one of my more useful talents," she said.

"Too bad you can't teach it to me," he remarked, seeming to forget that such a sentiment would label him a heretic. "Anyway, I knew Rhodri sure as hell hadn't put them out like that, so I realized you'd escaped before the others found out and sounded the alarm. But with all the portcullises down, I didn't see how you'd be able to get away. I figured you'd have to be hiding somewhere and I've been combing every inch of this place trying to find you before anyone else did. I was on the other side of the courtyard when I thought I heard a scream and came this way looking for you."

"Rhodri's dead," Athaya told him bluntly, trying to push the reason for that scream out of her mind. "His ritual didn't work out quite the way he thought it would."

Nicolas looked surprised, but not at all disappointed. Then he smiled, tucking his thumbs into his belt. "That's a relief. I was getting to like having a wizard for a sister."

"I'm glad at least one of my brothers feels that way," she

said dryly. Her face clouded over. "You're taking an awful risk being here, Nicolas. If Durek finds out . . ."

"Damn Durek to hell!" he burst out, his eyes gleaming with potent outrage. "I don't care if he finds out or not. I wasn't going to stand by while he did the same thing to you as he did to Tyler."

Nicolas must have seen the expression of knowing pain on her face and he put his arm around her shoulder and drew her close to him. "I'm sorry, Athaya. You shouldn't have had to find out that way. I wish I could have warned you, but they wouldn't let me talk to you . . ."

Athaya nodded, trying to remain in control. If she started crying now, she doubted that she would be able to stop and so she dug her nails into her palms and drove her grief away, at least for the time being. Later, when she and Jaren were safe—then it would be the time for mourning.

"How did it happen?" she asked quietly. "I want to know."

Nicolas averted his eyes. He and Tyler had been close for many years, and Athaya knew that her brother was grieving just as much as she. "They took him out of the dungeon just after dawn. It was quick, Athaya—a single stroke. He wouldn't have felt any pain."

Jaren drew in his breath with sudden recollection. "I heard them," he said absently. "I heard them come for him this morning. I had no idea . . ."

"You couldn't have stopped them," Athaya said, offering what little words of comfort that she could. "Neither of us could have."

"Athaya, listen carefully," Nicolas said, taking her by the shoulders. "Some of Tyler's men are outraged at what Durek's done. A few of them are almost ready to desert. I did a little investigating to find out who they were and whether they could be trusted and arranged for them to be stationed at the postern gate tonight. They'll let you pass. I've also made sure that there's a small boat in the cove and two men to take you out of the bay and around the point to Feckham. You can get horses there and head for . . ." He paused briefly. "For wherever it is you're going."

Athaya leaned against him, overwhelmed with gratitude. "Thank you, Nicolas."

"Come on, follow me."

With a whisper, Athaya cast the cloaking spell over Jaren and herself. "Care to join us?" she asked.

Nicolas gazed at the emptiness beside him with intrigue. "I'd better not. The men at the postern gate might be startled if I just popped into existence under their noses. And I've already been pounced on once tonight," he added, offering a smile at the patch of empty space where Jaren had last been seen.

Her arm entwined in Jaren's, Athaya followed Nicolas out into the courtyard. He listened to the pattern of their footsteps beside him, occasionally casting a curious glance to the side as if unable to believe they were really there. But after his initial skepticism was gone, he beamed with a broad smile, as if he'd been let in on a wonderful secret that he had no intention of sharing.

When they had gone halfway across the courtyard, one of the trio of guardsmen that had been inspecting the area behind the kitchens broke away and began to approach him, carrying a mirror at an angle to his body. In a few swift strides, Nicolas stepped into the shadows of the towers, and Athaya and Jaren huddled behind him so that the man's mirror would not pick up their image. Nicolas motioned for the guardsman to stop.

"I've searched this corner of the yard and no one's here," he bellowed out, lowering his voice to disguise it. He pointed toward the southern wall opposite the postern gate. "Try that way."

The man obeyed him and scurried away, waving for his companions to follow him, while Nicolas headed for the postern gate on the north side of the castle. There were no tall towers surrounding this secondary entrance, only an iron gate with a heavy oak door to one side. As Nicolas approached, he made a subtle hand signal to the pair of uniformed men standing near the door, and one of them quickly plucked the key ring from his belt and unlocked the door.

"Thanks, Paul," Nicolas whispered. "Wait right here. I'll be back in a minute."

Nicolas held the door open until he heard Athaya and Jaren pass by, and Athaya couldn't help smiling as the guardsman darted his eyes back and forth trying desperately to see who was producing the additional pairs of footsteps. He might have been told that he was getting involved with wizardry, but the man clearly expected to see visible signs of it.

"God guide you, your Highness," the guard ventured quietly,

staring out into space as if not quite sure anyone would hear him.

"Thank you," Athaya said. The man jumped with surprise upon hearing her disembodied voice, but then he relaxed into an accepting smile and haltingly bowed in the direction from which the voice had come.

Once they were through the postern door, Nicolas led them down the series of flat, slippery steps that were cut into the side of the cliff, urging them to be cautious as they slowly worked their way down the rocky incline toward the bay. The wind whipped against the limestone cliffs, stinging their faces with salt spray. Athaya's cloak billowed out behind her, and she had to hold it tightly around her shoulders to gain any warmth from it at all.

On the shore below was a squat little rowboat, barely large enough for two passengers, much less four. Two men clad in oiled leathers, their faces obscured by thick woolen hoods, manned the oars.

After Athaya stepped off the slick, rocky steps and onto the soft sand, she let her cloaking spell disperse.

"Kale and Robert will take you as far as Feckham," Nicolas said, pointing to the two men in the boat. "And here," he said, dropping a heavy purse of coins into her palms. "This should help take you the rest of your way."

Her eyes widened at the weight of the purse. "Nicky, you don't have to—"

"Oh, don't worry. Your escape isn't going to be at *my* expense." His eyes twinkled mischievously. "You can thank Cecile for that. She rifled it out of Durek's accounts this afternoon."

Athaya laughed softly. "Durek's going to have his hands full with her."

"He hasn't reckoned with me yet either," Nicolas said, his eyes blazing. Releasing some of his pent-up fury, he picked up a flat, black stone from the shore and flung it into the sea. "That bastard. I ought to—"

"Don't despise him, Nicolas," Athaya said, surprised at her own lack of bitterness. She expected to feel the same way—and knew she had every right to—but for some reason she could not understand, she felt no vengefulness toward her brother, only vague sadness and pity that he should be so misdirected and wrong. "He doesn't know what he's doing."

After a moment's pause, she reached out and hugged Nicolas as hard as she could, holding back the tears. "I'm going to miss you so much . . ."

"Good-bye, little sister," he said, trying to force a smile as he returned the embrace. Then his smile faded, and he looked at her with questioning eyes. "I hope I see you again someday."

Athaya drew back slowly, gazing up the sheer cliff face toward the gatehouse tower—the tower where Tyler's lifeless head was silhouetted against the moonlit clouds. "You will, Nicolas," she said, more sure of that than she'd been of anything else in her life. "I'm not finished with Caithe yet. I haven't even started."

I'll make you proud of me, Father. I'll finish what you began. I swear it.

"Take care of her, Jaren," Nicolas said, giving him a paternal pat on the shoulder. And although he did not voice them, Athaya knew the thoughts in Jaren's heart. *I know, Nicolas. I love her, too.*

Stepping over scraps of driftwood and broken shells, Athaya and Jaren climbed into the shallow boat and huddled together for warmth under their cloaks. Nicolas waved them a final farewell, and as the two hooded men pushed the tiny craft out into the black sea waters, Athaya saw her brother retreat up the steps toward the postern gate and slip back inside the curtain wall and out of sight.

Despite the cold, Athaya reached out and took a handful of icy water and splashed it on her arms, washing away the dried stains from Rhodri's blood. The men at the oars were silent as they pushed the small vessel out into the bay, and Athaya watched the moonlight make silver patterns in the water as she let herself be calmed by the rhythmic rocking of the boat against the waves.

"Good-bye, Tyler," she whispered, with one final look back.

Great magic commands a great price, Hedric had told her.

And I have paid. God, how I've paid.

She did not know how she would do it, or when, but of one thing she was sure. She would return to this place. She would show the unbelievers that the powers of magic need not be feared and despised, and she would tell those who shared her gift that they were not the Devil's Children, but beloved and blessed by God.

My people have need of me. And I have a duty to them.

The shoreline grew more distant with every stroke of the oars, and she gazed at the silvery towers of Delfar Castle slowly receding into the distance, finally disappearing from sight as the little boat slipped out of the bay under cover of darkness.

· Athaya Trelane was leaving Caithe, and now, as in ages past, there truly were no wizards in the land anymore.

But not for long, she thought, filled with resolve. *But not for long . . .*

ABOUT THE AUTHOR

JULIE DEAN SMITH was born in 1960, and has been writing since the age of five. Her first published work was a single sentence included in *Bride of Dark and Stormy*—a compilation of entries from the Bulwer-Lytton Fiction Contest.

She studied Economics and English at the University of Michigan, during which time she became an avid football fan. She played the trumpet in the marching band, and on New Year's Day of 1981, was fortunate enough to witness Bo's boys actually win a Rose Bowl.

In 1984, she earned her M.A. in English at Western Michigan University, and her interest in computers developed while she was painfully handwriting the rough draft of her research thesis on Charles Dickens. Ms. Smith currently works as a technical writer for a software company in Ann Arbor, Michigan, producing reference manuals and user guides (another form of fiction entirely).

Her other interests include Celtic music, medieval history, and computer games. Repeated viewings of *The Adventures of Robin Hood* and *Star Wars* have also given her a weakness for old-fashioned escapist entertainment, and she hopes one day to fulfill a lifelong dream of being swung by a rope over a gaping chasm, clasped in the arms of an attractive hero wearing a billowing white shirt.